SHADOWRUN:
IMPOSTER

MALIK TOMS

This is a work of fiction. Names, characters, places and incidents either are the products of the author's imagination or are used fictitiously, and any resemblance to actual persons, living or dead, business establishments, events or locales is entirely coincidental. The publisher does not have any control over and does not assume any responsibility for author or third-party Web sites or their content.

If you purchased this book without a cover you should be aware that this book is stolen property. It was reported as "unsold and destroyed" to the publisher and neither the author nor the publisher has received any payment for this "stripped book."

The scanning, uploading and distribution of this book via the Internet or via any other means without the permission of the publisher is illegal and punishable by law. Please purchase only authorized electronic editions, and do not participate in or encourage electronic piracy of copyrighted materials. Your support of the authors' rights is appreciated.

SHADOWRUN: IMPOSTER
By Malik Toms
Cover art by Tyler Clark
Design by Matt Heerdt and David Kerber

©2021 The Topps Company, Inc. All Rights Reserved. Shadowrun & Matrix are registered trademarks and/or trademarks of The Topps Company, Inc., in the United States and/or other countries. Catalyst Game Labs and the Catalyst Game Labs logo are trademarks of InMediaRes Productions LLC. No part of this work may be reproduced, stored in a retrieval system, or transmitted in any form or by any means, without the prior permission in writing of the Copyright Owner, nor be otherwise circulated in any form other than that in which it is published.

Published by Catalyst Game Labs,
an imprint of InMediaRes Productions, LLC
7108 S. Pheasant Ridge Drive • Spokane, WA 99224

ENJEE

11-12-2081
12:13 A.M. Local Time

Just beyond the evening glow of Lille, France, where the sprawl gave way to vast tracts of automated farmland and corporate-owned chateaus, two SUVs, one new and one very old, rolled to a stop in the darkness formed between towering rows of wheat.

Grim Fox squeezed out of the new vehicle first. He was small for a troll, barely cresting 2.5 meters of caramel skin and dense, ropey muscle. His one remaining horn was a curled ivory extension etched with tribal markings that, even after working together for two years, EnJee had never taken the time to decode. EnJee watched him scratch absently at the space on his head where the other horn lay sheared to a stub like a forgotten tree stump. The troll yawned, stretched, and immediately dug in the jacket pocket of his suit for a candy bar.

Shen, climbed out after him. She wore a black tactical jumpsuit with a gear harness suspending a holster under each armpit. She pulled her long black hair into a ponytail, showing elven ears studded with earrings, and a long neck marked with a snaking curve of tattoos meant to resemble lines of computer circuitry. The emotichrome ink glowed orange as her pale skin prickled against the cold night air.

EnJee watched all of this, lazily stepping out of the second car, a Toyota Gopher that had seen better days. Despite the age and the dents, EnJee proudly recognized he still managed to look worse for wear than his car. His long, pointed ears were battered and puffed like a boxer. He had a large gold hoop through his lower lip and brown skin so dark it was almost black. He was bald save for a sprout of green hair that shot straight up from the top of his head, giving him the look of a vintage troll doll.

EnJee stretched, loosening his thin frame after a drive that felt days long. He ducked his head back into the vehicle and said, "You plan to sit in there all night?"

Their fourth member, Nero, was not a metahuman. He was olive-skinned and slight of build. He liked to remind them he was Italian, wearing the nationalistic distinction like a meta-race unto itself. His face betrayed boyish features and hair that stretched past his chin to tickle the base of his neck. Nero didn't look relaxed like the others. In fact, he looked terrified.

Grim Fox cleared his throat the way he always did when he wanted the floor. "Can we go over it one more time to make sure everyone knows their part?"

After a round of nods, he said, "Okay. Our target is a female human—blond, one-point-six meters tall. She should be in room 219. At this hour, I expect she'll be asleep. The four of us will enter the compound using our decoy vehicle. Nero will provide spell cover to match our identities to the guests the facility is expecting."

"Easy peasy. So long as our boy here can do the fancy spellwork he promised, *neh*?" EnJee said.

"I told you I could." Nero sounded serious, but the way he rubbed the cross hanging from his neck told Enjee he wasn't so sure as he sounded.

Grim Fox cleared his throat again. When all eyes were on him, the troll continued, "Once we're inside, EnJee will lock down the matrix and cameras while Nero and I handle interior security and retrieve the target. Shen, you've got anything that comes at us from outside the building. We get her out and then get back here to switch cars for the ride home."

EnJee shrugged, folded his arms, and turned to study the lead car, a jet-black 2080 Rover they'd acquired for the job. His particular Londoner accent crackled through the night air. "Seems like such a waste, don't it?"

Shen's reply was a melodic sound. "Sure, you've always struck me as the type to travel in luxury cars and eat oysters. Oh, and dodge police when someone figures out their car is missing."

"No, he's more the type to glitch the Johnson's car right after a run, because he thought we got shorted on the deal and watch from a safe distance as it plows into a parked cop cruiser." Grim Fox said, his grin showing teeth.

EnJee shrugged and grinned back. "That's what I love about these long-haul jobs. The banter."

He reached into the backseat of the Toyota Gopher and retrieved an aluminum briefcase. He popped it open, revealing a drone roughly the size of a golf ball, which he tossed high into the air. It buzzed to life, hovering momentarily before it sped away over the hill and toward the only chateau in the distance.

EnJee said, "Nero, while our digital eye is opening, why don't you take a look at the astral, see if there are any surprises over there dear old Mr. Johnson forgot to tell us about."

Nero grunted and settled back and closed his eyes. He sucked in a deep breath, exhaled, and then slumped in the seat. When he opened his eyes a few moments later he said, "Everything matches the intel we got. There's a mage on-site, but she's sleeping. From the looks of things, she's probably the on-shift doctor. Definitely not a threat."

Even after being out of work for so long, everything was still playing out as expected. Runs of this sort didn't offer up the nasty surprises until it was much too late to do anything about it. That's why EnJee always did his homework. However, to hear it from his crew, he'd get lost in the plot, checking not only the job and the Johnson, but every nuance of the run that felt off.

Now he cleared his throat and said, "You three ought to know I looked at this dust-up a little closer."

Shen rolled her eyes and the other two fought to suppress groans.

EnJee said, "No, hear me out on this. The villa is owned by a corporation called Biologic Technologies."

Grim Fox said, "That supposed to mean something to us?"

EnJee shrugged. "That's the tricky part. All I found was it was one of the casualties of the Dragon War. Biologic was completely dissolved when the big boys went head-on at each other. All of its holdings dispersed among other corporate entities. No living trace of the corporate name, except for a klick up that road."

Grim Fox asked again, "I mean, what's that change about our job?"

EnJee paused. "Nothing on the surface, but—"

Shen cut in, "Then let's just get it done, EnJee."

The four of them wore that look of dreadful excitement that always came before the action. Their fixer, Vash, called the job a liberation. Every time he used language like that, EnJee knew they were running for some slotting corporation. It also told him the person they were coming to "liberate" might not be expecting their midnight call. However, that was the business. Import, export. Extractions and relocations. Only, over the past few months, business for their crew had dried up entirely. A win here could mean more work.

EnJee's face curled up into a sneer that might have been resignation and said, "All right, then. Nothing left to do but the doing."

He started to walk back toward the Toyota, but Shen interrupted. "Wait. I think there is something Nero needs to hear before we go any further."

All three of them turned to her. She looked gravely at Nero and said, "EnJee's got 30 nuyen on you screwing up the plan."

Even in the dark, Nero's blush was obvious. He looked nervously between the group and said, "Seriously?"

EnJee shrugged. "It's a new spell. You have a...particular history with new spells."

Grim Fox added, "By 'history,' he means you screw them up first time."

Nero grimaced. "So you bet against me as well, Grim Fox?"

"No. I took his action." Grim Fox paused thoughtfully, then added, "And hers."

Nero flashed a look of anger at Shen, who only shrugged in return. Then he said, "I've explained this before. You're asking me to keep multiple spells working for an extended time, in addition to the one I only recently learned."

EnJee shrugged. "Meaning?"

"Meaning weaving together that many strings of mana is difficult to achieve. Sustaining them in a combat situation is unpredictable, to say the least."

A smile worked its way around the edges of EnJee's lips "Meaning?"

Nero sighed and said, "Meaning, what happens if I do screw this up?"

EnJee said, "Depends on whether or not Grimmy here covers the bet."

Three kilometers up the road, the vine-covered walls of Chateau Bergerie hid a network of security sensors that crisscrossed the open fields leading to the main house. EnJee saw all of it through a small viewscreen display visible in the corner of his cybernetic eyes, below which a data feed scrolled all of the Horizon-built Flying Eye drone's pertinent information.

From its vantage point above the site, their Flying Eye showed all three buildings associated with the chateau. EnJee knew from both his research and common sense that the guests stayed in the main house. A second smaller building near the first held cybertechnology suites—fully outfitted surgical suites where the wealthy patients were treated to the best delta-grade cyberware available. A twinge of jealously fired through him. Most of his ware was a decade old. Even back then it hadn't been bleeding edge. A load of new 'ware running hot in his veins could prolong his career another few decades. Except slots like him couldn't afford the best. It went to corp hack jobs like tonight's target.

EnJee readjusted the drones view to zoom in on the last building: the pool house, which also held associated therapy rooms for patients in recovery. The space was large, perhaps a dozen acres in total. Yet the biological presence in the outdoor spaces was minimal.

"Alright, Shen," he said. "Ready to see your end in all of this?" He keyed her into the drone's feed so she could follow along through her own cybernetically enhanced eyes.

In the woods, small four-legged creatures loped through the forest, looking like animals at play from this distance. The Flying Eye zoomed in tight on a pair of the creatures, revealing what they truly were: drones, Ares cheetah drones, to be specific. Their small heads were littered with sensor portals that mimicked the appearance of eyes from a child's nightmare. The legs bent and stretched in an unnatural mimicry of their namesake. Each shift revealed the dangerous ring of small-caliber gun ports poking from their shoulders.

Shen muttered, "The rules of engagement are bullshit, EnJee. I cannot believe you couldn't get us a better deal on this."

"The real problem is that this is the only job he could get us at all," Grim Fox chimed in.

EnJee said, "Easy. The client said we couldn't kill anyone. That doesn't mean we can't send a few rounds in their direction if things don't go as planned. Besides, the guards are decorative. The real threat is those drones out there. You'll need to pick them off if the time comes."

"You're goddamn right I will." Shen walked over to the Toyota and retrieved her Crockett EBR Sniper from the trunk where it sat in a hardcase. They left that truck on the side of the road and all four of them piled into the Rover for the last stretch of the journey. Grim Fox drove the rest of the way, with Nero beside him while EnJee and Shen prepared in the back.

When they could see the gate from the road, EnJee jacked into his deck, making the quick handshakes with the system he'd worked out days ago. Security professionals insisted the weakest part of any network is the human element, but good hackers knew better. Network designers always took costly shortcuts.

In the case of Chateau Bergerie, the shortcut existed in a largely forgotten automation node where the recycling dumpsters interfaced with the waste management scheduling system for the local service. When the dumpster contacted the company to schedule a pick-up last week, EnJee was waiting to piggyback off that interaction and ride the interface directly into the heart of the Bergerie node. From there it was easy to create a back door that offered a glimpse into the other scheduling systems.

He was back nearly instantly. "Scheduling records still show one Gordon Gemmell scheduled to arrive tomorrow morning. I slid a note into the file that says he may arrive overnight. All right, Nero. Time to make us beautiful."

Nero closed a fist around the small wood and metal cross that hung from his neck and whispered an incantation. Then he reached out and placed one hand on Grim Fox's cheek. When the spell was complete, Grim Fox wore an entirely different face. Then Nero turned his body to place a hand on EnJee's cheek, repeating the process. The elf morphed into a red-haired white man. Finally, he set a hand on Shen's lap. He breathed in a long rattling breath, and on the exhale, Nero and Shen appeared to blip entirely out of existence.

When the car approached the front gate, all the sensors and cameras saw were two men in the car. One, a handsome ork who had the look of a driver and likely personal bodyguard. EnJee, the single visible passenger in the back seat, was now a white man, red haired and freckled, with a smile that looked like it belonged to a trideo star. EnJee waved to the camera while the driver announced him as Gordon Gemmell. The wrought iron gate trundled open, and the car drove slowly into the compound.

"Nice on you, mate," said EnJee. "Cleared the first hurdle. Just hang in there."

An invisible Nero grunted in response.

From what little EnJee understood of magic and the explanation Nero had fumbled through twice already, the strain of maintaining a single physical mask spell that could fool both organic and inorganic detection measures was not a high burden. However, combined with the second physical mask and the invisibility spells the mage extended to himself and Shen, the strain challenged the limits of what he could bear.

The luxury electric vehicle moved almost silently down the long, poplar-lined road leading to the villa. In the spaces between the trees, digital eyes of the cheetah defensive drones stared back at them. Biologic or whoever was in charge here had spared no expense of perimeter security. EnJee heard Shen clear the safety on her Crockett. If Nero's spells failed now, there would be no payday, just a hopeful escape.

Before long, the trees ended, revealing a picturesque villa. The main house was three stories tall and with over a dozen windows on each level looking out towards the road.

EnJee tapped back into his own drone's optical feed and called out the situation up ahead. "We have a welcome party. Two security guards at the bottom of the stairs."

One of the two guards was smoking, hanging back behind the other to hide his unprofessionalism. The Rover rolled to a stop in front of the guards at the base of the wide staircase leading up to the Chateau's main entrance. Grim Fox held to his character. He climbed out of the vehicle, purposefully ignoring the pair of guards as he walked around the car to let his passenger out of the back seat.

One guard approached the car while the smoker turned away, finishing his cigarette. EnJee stood up, stretching like a

man who'd spent too long in the back of an automobile, and said, "I'm here to check in."
The lead guard studied his false face for a moment and then looked down at his datapad, where he found the matching image. Finally, he said, "Apologies, Mr. Gemmell, you are quite early."
"Yeah, I wanted to settle in before all the cutting started."
Neither guard took to his joke. They shared another glance between them before the second guard called into the main desk. "We're bringing Mr. Gemmell up to his room."
EnJee thanked the men and told his driver to bring the bags up. The lead guard held up a hand and said, "I'm sorry, Mr. Gemmell, but we cannot let personal security into the building. We can take your bags up for you."
"Mr. Gemmell" tried to look impatient. They'd expected this part, but he had to stay in character. He marched up the stairs leading to the entrance and called back, "Well, get on with it then."
Grim Fox turned to the officers and shrugged. He said, "I can show you where the bags are. He brought a lot of them."
The two men followed Grim Fox around to the back of the car, where he knew the angle of the vehicle created an artificial blind spot in the camera network. The trunk opened with a *whoosh*, which was quickly followed by the *thwop-thwop* of subsonic DMSO rounds slamming into the flesh of each man's neck. Grim Fox moved quicker than anyone that size had any right to, and caught each man before he fell. He settled them against the trunk, careful not to expose them to the cameras.
Then EnJee was inside the building. He strode up to the check-in desk that doubled as a security station at night. Smiling at the guard seated there, he pulled out his own Ares SIII and fired two shots into the man, who slumped into his seat.
EnJee leaped over the counter and jacked into the security hardlink. In seconds he had control of the cameras and slaved the drones to a patrol pattern that took them away from the entrance. He left himself a back door into the wireless feed so he could continue to access the security while they were on the move. Into his commlink he said, "Right, we've got the cameras. Get those two sleeping beauties up here in case anyone happens to look out the window."

Moments later Grim Fox pushed through the front door, an unconscious guard over each shoulder. The air behind him shimmered slightly. EnJee raised an eyebrow and said, "That you, Nero?"

Nero, sweating heavily and clutching the cross at his neck, blipped into existence behind Grim Fox. Grim Fox dumped the two guards behind the security station.

"Shen still on point outside, then?" asked EnJee.

Nero nodded with some effort.

"Right, then let's change it up, shall we? How's about you turn me into one of these guards here if it isn't too much trouble."

Nero put his hand to EnJee's face again. He felt a tingle, the uncomfortable sheen of magic washing over him, as Nero shifted EnJee's appearance from the budding trideo star to the guard who normally manned this station.

He checked himself out in the reflective screen of his commlink while Nero slid on a pair of AR glasses and rolled over one of the other fallen guards for a look. The mage took a long, rattling breath, and then his face and clothing transformed to match the features of the guard. He finished the look by snatching the commlink off the guard's belt and clipping it to his own.

EnJee said, "Good on you, mate. You might win this bet after all. I'll stay in the system and keep you updated on the location of the physical security. I'm pushing directions to target to your hardware. Follow the yellow brick road."

Nero grunted in response.

EnJee continued, "Remember the situation. They're running Mitsuhama's Beta Seven security system. That means if an officer independently triggers a security alert—"

Grim Fox finished the thought, "—The physical security elements are all locked down and the drones placed on high alert until every officer gives the all-clear over their comm."

"Glad to see you studied the plan," said EnJee.

Grim Fox's smile didn't look at all friendly. "Maybe you forgot it was my plan to begin with."

When they'd planned this out, Nero had explained the mask spell only worked if the person being mimicked was roughly the same shape and size as the runner. None of the guards they encountered were even close to Grim Fox's size, so they needed to come up with another way to allow him to move freely through the building. They settled on invisibility. Nero insisted he could juggle that many spells at once, and so far he'd been right.

Grim Fox's security driver appearance fell away, and a moment later, the troll blipped out of existence.

Nero headed for the staircase. Though he couldn't see Grim Fox, through the security feed, EnJee noticed the stairwell door stay open a little longer than it needed to after Nero went through it.

"*Good luck, mate.*" He only mouthed the words so that none of the runners would hear him. Then EnJee turned his attention to the guard slumped in the seat beside him. He grabbed the guard's commlink, studied it, and then pocketed the device.

Chateau Bergerie's primary interior security camera system was not the least bit invasive, limited to a few sweeping hallway feeds, stairwells, all entrances. Outside, overlapping outdoor coverage was delivered by a score of roaming drones. The secondary security feed, the one likely known only to a handful of managers and higher-ups, gave access to each of the rooms. The cameras watched you while you slept, while you went to the bathroom, and everywhere else in between. EnJee tapped into both feeds, watching the vehicle outside where Shen was keeping watch on the perimeter, then turning his focus on Nero as he moved up the north stairwell.

Ahead, a guard was moving past the stairwell door and further down the intersection. EnJee said, "Hold just a second."

Nero waited for the all-clear, and then continued out of the door and through a T-shaped intersection toward the room where their target was sleeping.

EnJee switched to the room's interior feed, watching as the door handle turned and the their target sat up in bed, surprised and staring at the small figure clouding her doorway.

The woman, barely a wisp in a pile of sheets, started to say something when the air shimmered around her. She stiffened and then went limp, still upright but supported by something EnJee couldn't see on the camera. A moment later, the woman blipped out of existence.

"Well done," said EnJee. "All I can see now is you."

Nero didn't respond. He took a step, staggered a moment, and steadied himself in the doorway. EnJee switched back to the hall cameras, tracing the camera path back to the staircase and checking for the guard he'd seen earlier. He found him and another one coming out of a door, only a few meters away from Nero.

"Move gently, mates," he said. "Two guards coming. They'll see you cross—"

But it was too late. Distracted by concentrating on his spells, Nero walked right into the intersection. The pair of guards were engaged in a conversation, and at first, only one noticed him. Then the other turned and his jaw dropped.

EnJee barely had the time to mutter, "Bollocks," before the entire run went to hell.

One guard frantically jabbed at a device on his left wrist and then fumbled for the holster at his side. The other guard continued to look confused while the first one screamed something that sounded like *"Merde, merde!"*

Three things happened at once. The guard raised a pistol and got off a single shot that seemed to disappear into the empty space between Nero and the guards. Then both guards flew back as if struck by an invisible explosion. Grim Fox blipped into existence, his back to the guards and down on one knee, cradling the woman they'd been hired to retrieve. Then everything in the Matrix went red.

EnJee said, "Bloody hell. Alarms are running hot in the system. I can't hold them off unless I'm jacked into the hardline. The system is moving to yellow. Next step is to seal the exits and reset the drones. It's time to leave."

He jacked out of the system. He heard muffled gunshots coming from somewhere upstairs, along with booming shots from outside. He paused and felt for the stolen commlink, his backdoor access into the security network. With a few keystrokes, he linked the commlink personal area network. He heard more gunshots, this time from outside. These were clearer and a much higher caliber of weapon. Then he was on his feet running toward the exit. He burst through, DMSO loaded pistol in hand.

All EnJee saw was an empty car and a clear night sky. He ran to the car, stopping just outside the car door as Shen suddenly materialized in the front seat, her knuckles white against the steering wheel, her Crockett propped up between the seats beside her. He glanced down at himself and discovered Nero's spell was no longer disguising him either.

"Bollocks."

Shen said, "I clocked seven drones headed right for us. Dropped the closest two, but that's far from enough."

He climbed into the front seat beside her, looking back up toward the building where Nero was stumbling down the steps. Grim Fox followed, now holding the target the way a groom might carry his bride over the threshold. The samurai was less gentle about the way he shoved her into the back seat and slid in behind her. Shen didn't wait for the order to drive, kicking up dirt and gravel as the car spun back around toward the entrance.

The long, tree-line road felt like it was narrowing, closing in to a fine point like the light at the end of a too-long tunnel. EnJee could see the red glowing eyes of the cheetah drones deep in the forest growing closer with each passing second. A moment later, gunfire plinked like hail against the side of the car.

Nero dove over their target, covering her with his body. He shouted, "Why would they shoot at us with their patient in the car?!"

Shen stared at something flashing on the SUV's dashboard. EnJee felt the car drift left and Shen quickly turned the steering wheel to correct it. "They're shooting at the tires."

"Runflat tires, mates. It'll take more than small caliber weapons to bring us down."

"I think they know that," Grim Fox growled and pointed.

Two cheetah drones raced up behind the car, mechanical legs pumping like jackhammers to close the distance. The lead one leaped, snapping its teeth at the rear bumper of the SUV. It missed and tumbled away. Six more swiveled in along and behind the car slamming into the sides.

"More coming from the woods!" Nero said. He was still covering the target with his body.

Shen barked, "How many? EnJee, can you do anything?"

He didn't waste words on a response. He tried accessing his backdoor into the security network. No—locked out.

"EnJee?!" Shen's voice had an edge of fear that wasn't there before. He looked over in time to see a cheetah drone hurl itself against the rear passenger side window. The glass cracked from the weight of the impact. That drone tumbled to the ground unable to maintain its balance and momentum.

Another leaped and the glass gave, showering down across the backseat. Shen swerved before the drone could latch on to the edge of the door and the mechanical creature fell away. A third one leaped onto the hood, its titanium claws punching through the hood.

Grim Fox's lowered his window and leaned out, drawing his sward in a single swift motion as the drone turned toward him. Before it could lock on and fire, he slashed out with his blade, hitting first and slicing off its head. The drone's body spasmed and short-circuited, gun barrels spinning and firing uselessly into the sky. Using the point of his katana, Grim Fox levered the drone off the hood, and it fell away.

Two more drones bolted out of the tree cover and joined the chase.

Enjee felt around in his Personal Area Network, reading the stolen commlink's datastream for bits of information from the security feed and matching that info with what he read from his own spy drone to create a multi-dimensional view of the situation. Except he couldn't get the network to show him the locations of all of the security elements. Security was on high alert. According to the system, they'd exceeded the threshold of allowable response delays. Out loud he said, "System's locked. Too many officers didn't check back in after the alarm popped."

"Gate's closed," Shen said, pointing.

Grim Fox grimaced as he replied, "Ram it."

"That's reinforced steel. And this car is mostly plastic!" Shen protested.

Grim Fox said, "EnJee, we need something *now*!"

Then EnJee was in the network, the battered, dark-skinned elf of the meat world replaced in what he called "real space" by a glistening black suit of armor with a plume of black smoke where a head should be and a massive double bladed battle axe. He slid down through the connection of the commlink he'd stolen moments before, riding the all-clear code into the heart of the security node.

He landed in a crouch in the center of a virtual representation of a traditional *minka* home. An upturned arc of emptiness parted the black smoke of his head where a mouth should be. The tatami flooring beneath his feet felt real. There were sliding doors on all four walls. They'd kept the default immersion architecture, so finding the gate was only a matter of finding his way out of this house.

EnJee turned to his left, raised his axe and hurled it through the thin wall, racing through the newly formed hole after it. Two more doors disappeared in this fashion before he found himself outside the house. Around him, a thousand stars of this virtual nightscape blazed down like searchlights. He saw the gate just ahead, and in front of it, a silver Basilisk flicked its tongue silently in his direction. He hurled the axe a final time, racing in behind the throw with a pair of daggers drawn. The Basilisk dodged the axe, its head jerking mechanically to one side, then slamming down towards Enjee. But he was ready. He thrust his digital dagger up toward the base of the code creature's jaw. The blade extended, blossoming into a sword that plunged through the Basilisk's underjaw and on upward until it exited through the top of its silver skull. The IC dissolved instantly.

EnJee's eyes popped open and slewed to the side, jittering for a moment before regaining focus. The gate seemed to move in that same instant, slowly shuddering open. Their SUV scraped the edge of the gate as it surged through. EnJee slammed a button on his commlink and the gate rattled shut behind them.

EnJee breathed a low, rasping breath, turned to a half-conscious Nero in the backseat and said, "See, you aren't the only person who can work magic."

NERO

11-12-2081
12:47 A.M. Local Time

The shadowrunners switched cars in the fields outside of the chateau. Nero slumped against the back door of the Toyota, still groggy enough that he needed to hold on to the handle to keep himself from sliding to the ground entirely. He watched the others roll the second car into the dirt on the side of the road and set off phosphorous grenades inside to burn away any trace of them being there. One of Grim Fox's tricks.

Through fatigue-slitted eyes, Nero watched Grim Fox cram himself painfully into the driver's seat of the Toyota. A shudder of guilt passed through the mage. It was his failure that had caused Grim Fox to take several rounds at nearly point-blank range back at the chateau. His dermal deposits and armored vest must have soaked up much of the impact, but still, Nero could tell he was favoring his right side.

EnJee quickly slid into the passenger's seat. That left Shen and Nero bracketing the target in the backseat. The target was hooded and still fast asleep from the effects of the neurotoxin Grim Fox had dosed her with when they grabbed her.

Nero checked her pulse, measured it against a readout in the corner of his AR glasses, and said, "She's stable, and should sleep the whole way."

Before long, he was unconscious beside her, head resting gently against the window.

Nero clawed his way back to consciousness somewhere along the way, staring into yellow wake of a Maersk heavy transport truck. He yawned and stretched, partially refreshed, but far from feeling strong enough to work up any decent magic.

"How long was I out?" he asked one in particular.

"Hour and a half. Maybe longer," EnJee called back. The drive From Lille to Amsterdam was over three hours using the E17 and A2.

"You good?" Shen said. She reached across the captive woman and put a hand against his arm.

He nodded, forced a smile, and then fumbled through a few breathing exercises, too wracked with fatigue to keep focus on any particular one. The sum result was labored breathing and a feeling in his chest like his heart was trying to migrate to his throat.

Shen squeezed his arm affectionately. "You did really well back there."

"Says the woman who bet against me."

Shen pulled her hand back. "I already apologized for that. Besides, I was going to spend the yen on you anyway."

She wasn't lying. Her ink didn't light up. It always lit up when she was lying, as if she had to force herself to feel something in order to break from the truth.

"I hear a lover's spat back there?" EnJee's voice crackled from the front seat.

"What you hear isn't your business, *omae*," Shen shot back.

EnJee laughed, but Nero was focused on Shen. Grim Fox didn't react at all. Their driver kept his eyes on the road as he drafted the Maersk truck, staying so close their headlights didn't illuminate beyond the yellow taillights of that massive vehicle.

Nero fought the urge to ask him how he was feeling. Instead, he turned to Shen. "How long have we been in the Gorge?"

"Almost through. We rode alongside an independent cargo caravan until we found this," Shen said. Going E17 meant passing through *Le Gorge*, a precarious stretch of highway constantly fought over by seven different go-gangs. You didn't drive the stretch if you could avoid it, or unless you had a caravan of corporate vehicles you could attach yourself to.

Nero grimaced. That he slept right through told him how much strain the spell load put on him, and how vulnerable that left his team. He knew from experience that not every corporation was so agreeable with the tagalongs. Nero had been on the road once when an Evo caravan took on the barnacle weight of a three-car convoy of minivans. They'd later found out the caravan was a family trying to get to Amsterdam where they'd decided to settle down. He'd heard that bit of detail later that evening on a Horizon newsfeed, and it floored him. According to the feed, the Evo drivers had put up a fight, trying to save them from the go-gangers. But he'd been there, just a car length ahead of the Evo trucks. He'd seen what actually happened.

When a dozen go-gangers started to blaze their rearview mirror, the Evo trucks had opened fire on the minivans, shredding the tires of all three. That left them to the go-gangers, who decided to leave the Evo trucks alone. Nero wanted to turn back, but the others refused. It wasn't worth the risk to them, and he couldn't make them understand why it was worth the risk to him. After that, he'd swore on his faith that he would never again stand idle to the shedding of what might be innocent blood.

Shen must've read the look on his face because she said, "We would've woken you if there was trouble."

Grim Fox spun the wheel suddenly, breaking away from the protection of the Maersk truck unto the vast openness of the highway. He kept right, sliding into the exit lane as it spiraled away from the E17 and into the A2.

Nero looked out the window at the vast stretch of the Amsterdam sprawl in the distance, thinking about what to say to Grim Fox that would express how he felt. Grim Fox and Nero had joined EnJee's crew around the same time. That shared sense of feeling like outsiders had made the two men close, until Shen and Nero got together, and the relationship dynamics shifted again. They still had a strong friendship, strong enough that Grim told him about the side bet in the first place and even covered the action. He thought about the bet and how the others—even his girlfriend—hadn't had enough faith in him to think he could hold up his end. Grim Fox did. In fact, he'd made Nero's magic central to their plan. Nero knew the street samurai was proud enough that he would either act like he wasn't hurt, or make an excuse as to why Nero wasn't responsible.

Grim Fox had the stereo tuned low to a classic punk feed, pumping out a sound that, to Nero, was nearly indistinguishable from machine noise. EnJee nodded his head to the metallic ring of dueling electric guitars, as if the two men were commuters on the way back from work and not kidnappers with a victim unconscious and hooded in the back seat.

Shen said, "You're still thinking about the magic." It wasn't a question. She was staring at him from the other end of the bench just beyond the sleeping prisoner, her smile warm and her tattoos a flat black.

Nero met her eyes and said, "I wasn't prepared the way I needed to be. If I'd practiced maintaining that much active mana, nobody would've gotten hurt. This can't happen again."

"Null sweat, love. It got done, and we all got out intact."

He stole a glance at Grim Fox, but their driver didn't seem to notice the conversation at all.

A few minutes later, they passed into the United Netherlands. The place he'd come to call home had only been a country for around forty years, since Flanders and the Netherlands had formed a political alliance that morphed into a protectorate. Amsterdam had become the shared capital and base of operations for all forms of political interplay as the newly formed nation attempted to avoid being subsumed by Lowfyr's Saeder-Krupp and the Allied German States.

Their cargo started to come around just as the Toyota pulled off the main highway. Nero shifted in his seat, making sure he was prepared in case she woke up in a fighting way. From this angle he could stop any punch she threw.

The Toyota meandered through local traffic toward Amsterdam's docklands until finally coming to a stop along a dense stretch of warehouses and shipping containers stacked half a dozen high under the open night sky.

No one spoke as they all exited the vehicle. Nero went last, pulling the cargo out with him. Shen held her in place while he uncuffed her. As he worked, he said, "I apologize for any shock or mistreatment we may have caused you. Unfortunately, this was a necessity of the transaction."

The woman responded with a sleep-garbled sound that wasn't quite a word.

EnJee stepped forward and pulled the hood off her head. She blinked in the sudden transition from pure darkness to evening light. To her credit, she didn't scream. A lot of them screamed. Instead, she blinked several times before her eyes focused on EnJee. Nero wondered what she must have thought in that moment, to be roused from bed by kidnappers and your next moment of consciousness was standing in the middle of a foreign city facing a man who, in the right light, looked to have more piercings and cyber than skin.

In spite of all that, EnJee was soft-spoken and friendly. He fixed her with a grin and said, "How are you feeling, Ms. Novak?"

She blinked again, taking in the rest of the team. Only Grim Fox hung back. Nero took note that he was wincing as he surveyed the area. Their captive said, "Where am I?"

"A fair question," EnJee replied. "You're at a dock in Amsterdam. This is where we were told to deliver you."

Grim Fox subvocalized, *"We got three approaching. Same direction."*

EnJee nodded and continued, "My friends here are going to put you in a shipping container now. They'll stay with you until I tell them it's safe for you to come out. If you scream or do anything to draw attention, they will do what is necessary to keep you quiet. Do you understand?"

She nodded, and went with them willingly. Nero and Shen ushered her into the shelter of the nearest row of shipping containers. Nero counted out the row, stopping at the seventh. The latch unclasped easily, and the door swung open with a rusty squeal. Inside, it was completely dark. The light from the warehouses didn't reach this far down into the stacks. Shen flicked on a small flashlight and led Ms. Novak into the container.

Nero stayed outside, as per the plan. He gently closed the door behind them and stood beside the container as the headlights of three cars blazed up from the south, blocking one end of the container row. The rear two vehicles flicked off their headlights and eased to a stop several car lengths behind the lead vehicle. The last in the line of three had the looks of a security escort vehicle—an off the lot model, likely a Hyundai or a Ford. The second car, long and silver, was a limousine, and probably held the Johnson.

He subvocalized to the team, "We weren't expecting three, were we?"

EnJee replied, "*Stay frosty, Nero. Grimmy and I have this all under control.*"

Nero nervously looked on. The first car in the queue was a 2070 Westwind with white racing stripes flared down the left side. Nero felt a little of the tension drain from him then. The driver stepped out, leaving his lights on to illuminate the row of containers. The man called from beyond the headlights. "I see you out there, Grim! You can put your guns away, it's just me and the clients."

Then he stepped in front of the headlights, hands raised and open. The pudgy form of the man looked distended and alien against the backdrop of light. However, the voice belonged to their fixer, Vash. The second car shut off its lights and idled in the near distance, leaving Vash's car as the sole light source for the exchange. Nero tried to reach for the astral, but the mental exertion of reaching for that trigger wobbled him a little. Instead, he was forced to rely on his physical senses.

Vash approached them. He was smiling and kept his hands open and visible. EnJee stepped out of the shadow of Grim Fox and went to greet him. The two shook hands at the forearm. Then he and Vash walked toward the second car in this impromptu caravan.

The limo pulled forward, unloading a man in a crisp black suit. Vash and the man spoke for a moment before exchanging a handful of credsticks. EnJee raised his left hand and waved, the agreed upon signal to bring Novak out. Nero did as he was asked, banging once on the container door with his closed fist, pausing, and then banging twice more.

The container squealed open beside him and Ms. Novak walked out alone. She paused briefly, staring at Nero, and a look of what might have been embarrassment spread across her face. She turned away from him, heading directly for the cluster of three men like a sailboat mindful of the wind at her back. As she drew close to the group, EnJee reached out to stop her by laying a hand on her shoulder.

Nero wasn't close enough to hear the exchange. He trusted EnJee to handle that part, and EnJee trusted them to handle theirs in case it went wrong. The voices stayed low and polite. Vash and the suited man—Mr. Johnson, or maybe Mr. Johnson's security chief —shook hands, and then the man escorted Ms. Novak to the back of the car. She stared back at Nero the entire time, her face still wearing an expression he didn't understand. The Johnson shut the door and climbed back into the passenger seat. Then the limo and its escort car backed up, turned around, and disappeared into the night.

"What was that about?" He hadn't heard Shen come up beside him.

"I don't have any idea," he said. With the cars and cargo gone, Nero visibly relaxed. They'd done jobs where the Johnson had treated them like loose ends, and what should've been a fair exchange of money for service turned into a shootout. It was a relief to know this wasn't one of those.

"Well, let's go see this son of a bitch." Shen said, and strode forward to join the others. Nero followed behind her. Since joining the crew, they'd worked for a handful of fixers, but none more than the skinny Israeli man in the tracksuit and newsboy hat.

Nero didn't like him. More specifically he didn't trust him, perhaps because Shen didn't trust him. As Shen and Nero approached, he watched the man's eyes darting around nervously. The man's face was drawn tight, save for the dark bags of skin under his eyes. However, what drew Nero's attention every time was the ear. Vash had one cybernetic ear replacement, noticeable by the obvious difference in skin tone on and around the ear. It was the kind of thing that could be done right for the money he had to be making arranging these runs, but Vash never fixed it, and Nero found that unsettling.

Vash also had a gambler's smile, easy and fleeting. "Good pay for an easy night's work, eh?"

EnJee said, "Not too easy. Grim Fox took some lead. He might need to see your doc to clean it up."

Nero met eyes with Grim Fox, who was trying not to wince.

"Easy enough," Vash said. He handed each of the runners a credstick, keeping the fifth for himself.

Shen said, "Do I have to ask if your stick has the same balance as ours, Vash?"

The fixer shrugged. "You do every time, Shen. It's always the same answer. I get the finder's fee. That's all."

She stared at him a while longer and he held that smile, showing white teeth. "Enjoy the downtime," he said. "I'll drop EnJee a line when I have more work for you." With a wave, he turned and walked back to his Westwind.

"I don't trust that guy," Shen said, watching Vash drive away.

Grim Fox said, "Neither do I, but his creds are good and he keeps feeding us jobs when nobody else seems interested."

EnJee shrugged and added. "You gotta admit, he's the best fixer we've had in a while."

Shen said, "He does seem to like working with you, EnJee. I cannot for the life of me figure out why."

Nero said, "Probably because he and EnJee have the same aversion to getting their ears fixed."

EnJee stared at Nero, frowning. "Says the man who just lost a bet."

A flicker of green moved through Shen's tattoos like a current through a circuit and she broke into a laugh. Grim Fox laughed too as he unbuckled his armored vest and pulled it off with some effort. Blood soaked the back of the troll's gray shirt underneath.

Nero said, "Shit. That looks bad."

Grim Fox shrugged, still grinning. "No worries, *omae*. I'm built tough."

A part of Nero wanted to believe that and dismiss the wounds as the cost of doing business, but it was his fault and that didn't sit right with him. He shook his head. "No. I screwed up. Take the medical out of my cut."

Nero hesitated in the fresh silence, watching the faces staring back at him, and then added, "And the first round of drinks are on me as well."

EnJee shook his head somberly. "You know that's not how it works with us. Besides, Shen's buying the drinks. She won the bet."

Looking at the blood stains, Nero thought Grim Fox was the real loser here. He'd put his faith in Nero, and once again, Nero hadn't been up to the challenge. Had this been an exception, it would've put his mind at ease. Unfortunately, it was starting to become the rule.

NERO

11-12-2081
3:25 A.M. Local Time

The front tire on Shen's gray Honda Spirit needed air. It didn't show on the analytics cycling across the dash readout, but Nero felt it in the way the car clunked over the asphalt as he sped away from automated corporate constraints of West Amsterdam into Spaarnwoude where the graffiti started to take hold and the city felt like a city again. Shen hummed along to the Corp-driven folk sounds of Green River Burning, snapping her fingers in time with the banjo loops. Nero grinned and shook his head.

Shen turned to him and hummed louder. "Get into it, Nero! This is what winning sounds like!"

He loved the sound of her singing, the way she got into it, moving with the music and letting her lungs empty with the sound of joy, even if he didn't think the music sounded like winning, or even sounded good.

Nero listened a bit longer before he slid his Matrix interface glasses over his face and eye clicked to a familiar link, The Church of Saint Conus. He allowed the feed to fill his glasses, letting the Honda Spirit glide unpiloted along the Gridlink data stream toward the nightclub they'd all decided to meet up at to celebrate the successful run. In the cameras, he could see church wasn't in session, but nearly a dozen parishioners still moved throughout the space. Some lit candles, some prayed. Others sat in pews, staring up at the art and carvings.

A young girl, perhaps seven years old, skipped up the steps toward where her mother was bent in prayer at the front of the space. She set her hands on her mother's shoulders, shaking her gently. He zoomed in on the interaction, working to read the girl's lips.

Shen leaned over and tapped on his glasses, interrupting his reverie. "Anything on there worth telling me about?"

"No, just checking in before we get to the club."

She shrugged. The music played on. "I know. It's your thing. I'm just curious about it. Do you expect to see someone in particular there? Why do you check in so often?"

Nero sighed. "That church was my family for a long time. Probably too long. When you're a part of something, you feel like you can't be yourself without it. On the other side of that, you feel like it can't or at least should not be a thing without you. But I'm gone, and it still rolls on."

"So you miss it?"

"No. I'm happy to be here and to have all of you."

"But you can't say goodbye."

"I'm...not too good at those, no."

"Good thing you haven't had to say too many, then."

Nero thought about the way he'd come to the team. It was just Shen and EnJee back then. The pair had worked with other runners before, but none had stuck—or maybe they just hadn't survived. EnJee never told the whole story. Nero had worked alone before that, turned on to clients by the few people in the church who knew what he could do.

"The church is why I'm here. They convinced me of what I had begun to doubt. They reminded me that my magic was a gift—perhaps even a gift from God, though I was never so true to the faith the believe that."

Shen's tattoos pulsed red when she looked at him, a color he'd come to associate with her feeling amorous. She said, "You ever think they were just recruiting you? Gassing you up so you'd become part of their order?"

"Isn't that what all churches do?"

Shen rolled her eyes, tattoos warming to an uncomfortable and angry pink.

He sighed, disappointed at how he'd extinguished her desire, "At times. Before I left, I was introduced to a priest from the south. He told me of a group of gifted individuals like myself that he led. He said they were part of an order called the *Vigilia Angelica*, and if I was willing to follow the faith, I could unlock many more of the gifts God had in store for me."

"Shit, Nero, even I've heard about them on the boards. They're a magical order, right? 'God's Spies' or something like that?"

He said, "Watchful Angels, but I did do the research. When I decided against it, my life at the church became...difficult. It led me away from the people I'd come to call family and toward the shadows."

"Where you found us."

"Where I found you."

She winked, colors shifting back to red. He placed a hand on her leg. The car slowed, stalled by the stagnant flow of traffic closer to the nightlife. In the distance they could see Policy Eleven, a local dive supposedly from before the nation came to be known as the United Netherlands. Nero liked it because it was dark and served well drinks with good alcohol, not the synth stuff most places mixed into their wells. Shen liked it because the club was an afterparty locale—the place people went after hitting the more popular spots in the Spaarnwoude club scene, and even at this late hour a crowd would be working its way into fruition.

The tradition was, after a run, one of them burned a hundred creds buying the first few rounds of celebratory drinks. Once, Shen confided in him that she believed the tradition had started when EnJee got in deep with a bookie and couldn't afford to spring for drinks after a particularly low-paying run. Yet it still went around like clockwork, and tonight was Shen's turn.

The Honda Spirit auto-parked on a side street four blocks from the Policy Eleven, close enough to walk, but far enough that no one would be able to tag them leaving in the vehicle. Before joining this crew Nero only thought about operational security issues during the run. EnJee taught him that security was a full-time affair. Most of it was probably bluster from the old elf, but some of what he said about staying safe made sense. Most of what EnJee did was entirely bluster, and it often pissed Nero off.

"Why does he do that us all the time?" Nero said, feeling the anger in his voice. He and Shen were holding hands, walking close as they turned the corner leading to Policy Eleven.

She slowed and turned towards him, smiling "By *he* I'm guessing you mean EnJee, and by *that* I'm going to assume you're still wondering why he makes side bets on us during a job."

Nero nodded, chastened by her calm and how quickly she understood what he was thinking.

"He's done it since I've known him. I'd love to say it's his way of dealing with the stress of what we do, but it feels like he turns everything into a game or a conspiracy."

"Doesn't it ever get to you?"

She shrugged and leaned into him as they neared the club entrance, a set of wooden doors set into the side of a squat stone building with a queue of clubgoers forming along the street. "EnJee gets to me all the time, but he's the closest thing I've got to family. Has been for as long as I can remember. Take that away, and what am I left with?"

Nero wanted to say, "*you're left with me,*" but he let the moment fall away as they slid past the bouncer with a nod and on into the club. Policy Eleven was lit by long strips of blacklight that pulsed gently with the heavy bass beat thrumming from floor and ceiling mounted speakers set throughout the dark space.

Tonight, the club was hosting more than its normal share of corporate ex-pats looking for a chance to escape their enclaves and mingle with so-called real people. He could read it in their clothing and the way they clumped together aligning by brand like players contrasted on a soccer pitch.

Shen tended to enjoy that contrast, but Nero had little patience for how corporate citizens carried on. When they came out of their walled-up enclaves and skyscrapers and mixed in with the locals at places like this, he felt like they treated everyone who lived here like the animals in zoo. It became a problem from time to time, especially given that corporate citizens had protections people like him didn't have. A corporate citizen being assaulted in the middle of the city made bad headlines. Anything that made bad headlines tended to put the underpaid and overworked local police on edge. He didn't need that sort of trouble.

They staked out a wide booth close enough to the bar that getting a refill was as easy as standing up and turning around. Shen took advantage of that proximity, ignoring Nero's fears and returning to the bar again and again as the club started to fill with evening partygoers. By the time the other half of their small team arrived, Shen was five drinks in, sitting in Nero's lap and singing more hits from Horizon's Top 20. Her tattoos blazed a carefree green beneath her long black hair.

Despite the crowd filling the dance floor, it was hard to miss Grim Fox ducking low through the doorway to enter Policy Eleven. The blacklight caught the carvings in his tusk, highlighting them briefly. EnJee trailed a few steps behind him, chatting up the bouncer as he entered. Nero kept his focus on Grim Fox. In the low light, he couldn't make out a grimace of pain or see bandages beneath the troll's long coat.

A bubble of anxiety built in Nero's belly as he watched him. "How'd it go with the doc?"

Grim Fox clapped him on the shoulder. "All good. Bullets hardly nicked me."

Shen grabbed Nero by the face and turned him toward her uncomfortably. "Stop bein' sush a pansy..." she slurred, "Gettin' shot's all part of th'job."

Nero shrugged her aside. She swayed a little, partially from the drinks and partially from the rhythm of the music thumping through the club. Nero reached out a hand to steady her, and then he pulled out his credstick and offered it to Grim Fox. "No, this one's on me. Tell me how much, and I'll pay out of my cut."

Grim Fox raised his hand in a stop gesture, but Nero said, "I lost the bet. I ought to cover it."

Grim Fox grinned broadly. "Like EnJee said, it's Shen's night to pay. The rest of it we forget, okay?"

"Okay." Nero slumped back in his seat.

"Perfect time for another round," Shen said. She leaned over Nero and playfully tugged at the cross around his neck. He managed a weak smile in return and watched her head for the bar. The church had taught him it was wrong to engage in drunkenness. He refused to impose his beliefs on others, but that didn't make it easier for him to be witness.

EnJee slid into the booth beside him. He said, "You don't look quite as relaxed as she does, mate. More of your post-run religious guilt rearing its head?"

Nero frowned, "No one died, so what would I have to feel guilty about?"

"Exactly my question."

Nero turned to check on Shen. She looked completely happy, dancing and spinning in time with the music as she waited for a space to open up at the bar. A woman and three men were huddled at the, faces hanging so low they almost scraped the frothy surface of their mugs. Their just-left-the-office dress and attitude were so different than everyone around them that it made them stick out of the crowd the way a pimple sticks out on your skin. One of the four even looked young enough to still have to worry about pimples.

EnJee followed his gaze. He said, "You are a right prude, aren't you?"

"It isn't prude to believe in behaving a certain way. We all have a code we follow."

"That's just you and Grimmy over there isn't it? Never found the need to tie myself in knots, personally. Neither does she, mate."

Shen shuffled up beside the group crowding the bar, waved the bartender over, and ordered more drinks. Then she turned to the closest, a fresh-faced kid who couldn't be more than eighteen. He wore a black blazer with khaki pants and a tie. Nero would've thought him a grey-suited church missionary if not for where they were. The kid looked like he'd been crying. Nero watched Shen frown and shout, "What's the matter with you?!"

The bar was crowded and the music loud. Shen made a point to make herself heard, not just to the four, but anyone who cared to listen. The kid's response was lost in the sound of the bar. Shen leaned in, trying to listen and called, "Who?!"

Louder now, the kid replied, "I said we work for Spinrad Global!" He nodded solemnly, as if his corporate affiliation somehow made everything clear.

Then suddenly it did, and Shen started to laugh. "Old man's dead, right? You a relative or something? If so, it will be raining money on you soon!"

The kid's sadness vanished in a flash of anger. He puffed out his chest and said, "I was born and raised in Spinrad Global. Johnny Spinrad was a god among men!"

Shen looked confused for a moment, and then that look dissolved into laughter. She grabbed the four fresh bottles off the counter and turned to walk away.

Nero shook his head. Shen liked to stir up trouble. It was one of the few things that put them at odds. He was glad this hadn't escalated.

Then the kid called, "Don't walk away when I'm talking to you!"

Shen stopped and turned around, checking to see if there was anyone else the kid could be talking to. There wasn't. Nero tensed. The crowd of SpinGlobal employees were looking at her now. The kid's face was red, and the woman standing next to him was holding on to him, perhaps even trying to hold him back.

Shen took one slow step toward the bar and then another, the beers jostling loosely in her hands. She said, "Spinrad wasn't a god. None of them are. Yet you all sit here pretending he is, for what? The four of you certainly didn't lose your jobs when he died, did you? In fact, I bet it was good for business!"

Nero couldn't help but chuckle at that. Unfortunately, the kid didn't find it funny. He stood up and took a step toward her. Nero's grin froze on his face like a bug caught when the lights come on. He cursed under his breath and started to stand up, hand on his cross, mind already reaching for the magic. EnJee grabbed him by the shoulder and held him to the seat. If the hacker was smiling, it was lost among the scars and blisters of his weathered face.

"Hang back, mate. Let her have her fun."

Nero tried to pull away, but the old elf was stronger than he looked. He turned back toward Shen and saw her ink still radiant in green and visibly relaxed. Shen leaned in close enough to the kid to whisper something in his ear. His flicked toward Nero and the others and then back to her for a long moment before sat back down on his barstool. Then she smiled and walked back to their table.

EnJee chuckled. "Good for business?"

She shrugged, her lips curled into a smirk. "Our business, if not theirs."

EnJee said, "That's my girl. We make a hell of a team."

Nero said, "What did you whisper to him?"

She shrugged and smiled. That irritated Nero. For as much as he loved Shen, there was a part of her that was all too much like EnJee. He supposed it was a result of the years they'd spent together before he and Grim Fox came along. He wished more of Grim Fox's nature would rub off on her the way EnJee's clearly had.

EnJee raised his cup. "Twentieth job in the books, mates. I'm not too big on sentiment, but we've been rolling together like this for over three years now. I just thought I'd point that out."

Shen said. "Cheers to that, then."

Grim Fox sipped the beer he was nursing. "It was a clean run, too. Maybe it gets us back on the right side of the local fixers."

"Sounds, like you're suggesting our not getting work in our fault, Grimmy."

"I think he's saying it's your fault, and he's right," Nero said. Shen laughed loudly. Work wasn't hard to come by in Amsterdam, but you had to look for it. Vash was a good fixer; he'd found them plenty of opportunities over the years. He'd even played a role in bringing Nero and Grim Fox into the team. However, he was one of the few fixers willing to work with EnJee anymore.

EnJee frowned momentarily, but then his expression brightened into a grin. "I admit not every bloke is a particular fan of my way of seeing the world, but the ones who do get top quality work, and that's because of the lot of you."

EnJee's commlink flashed. He held up his hand, tapped into the call and said a few words. Shen didn't seem to notice. She was taken by the music, moving along with the beat and sipping at her drink. Nero and Grim Fox watched Enjee's face scrunch up into a puzzled expression. Then the hacker said, "I suppose." and hung up.

"That was Vash," said EnJee. "He said the Johnson wants to meet us and talk about doing more business."

"When?" Nero said.

"Today."

Grim Fox and Nero shared a glance, and then the samurai said, "That was quick. Not sure that's a good sign."

"The warehouse?" Nero asked.

"No. Vash says the Johnson wants a face-to-face this time. No intermediaries."

Shen groaned. Grim Fox whistled low and said, "We better set the terms on this one if we agree. Use one of our shared spots for the meet?"

"The Mall?" EnJee offered. Shen nodded quickly.

"No, not that one." Nero said, "I think we should use the loft. We'll be able to better control the entry points in case this turns dangerous." He turned to Grim Fox, who nodded in approval.

Shen slurred, "When'd you get so paranoid?"

Nero said, "When did you stop?"

ENJEE

11-12-2081
4:30 P.M. Local Time

When the call came down from Vash, EnJee's first instinct was to say no. EnJee had found himself in situations before where a corporate Johnson wanted to put him on retainer. He'd refused. He always refused. He'd rather be a gutter punk than anything that resembled being a corporate dog. But here and now with a crew to look out for and no other fixers taking his calls, he wasn't left with much choice. The one choice he did have was how safe to play the situation.

For as much as the trids portrayed shadowrunners as wild spirits who cared more for the action than the business behind it, EnJee found the people in his line of work were generally a smart lot. His crew understood that if a corporate Johnson wanted you back in the room this soon, precautions needed to be taken. To that end, he and his team had invested in a number of quiet partnerships with places they frequented—safehouses, but they were often more than that. They understood the value of space they could rely on. Tonight, the group would choose a location best suited for their own personal security. One they controlled—and one they were willing to burn if things went badly.

The choice came down to an abandoned office in a strip mall rented out by a hacker collective Grim Fox did security work for on the side, and a loft space Shen rented above a dive bar called Spotters near the Westwijk scum village.

They chose the loft space. It wasn't larger than a bolthole, but it suited their purposes. Shen had excellent sight lines to the street from a hole in the boarded-up window. Not counting the roof, there were two points of egress—one down the back stairs and through the bar, and a catwalk exit to an alley behind the building where they kept a car powered up and pointed at the street.

Grim Fox's plan called for them to meet downstairs in the bar. EnJee would take the meeting, just the way he liked. He'd keep a comm channel open to broadcast it all to the team. Nero would second him, making sure to sort out any magical support the Johnson might be using. Grim Fox would lurk elsewhere in the small bar, blending in with the patrons as much as someone his size could, keeping a watch in case of trouble. Shen would stay upstairs with the long gun. She'd spot for the team in case any other trouble came their way.

It was a good plan. It'd worked in the past.

That did nothing to keep EnJee's nerves from jittering like he was about to stare down Black IC. He couldn't shake the feeling that something about this meetup was off. He was sipping the suds off a traditionally warm pint when Shen's voice came in low over the shared comm channel. "Grey sedan pulling up. Three suits getting out—all armed."

"Any sign of the Johnson from last night?"

"Well," she said, "it's *someone* from last night: Katerina Novak."

"Surprise, surprise." EnJee said. "Stay sharp for a backup vehicle. I can't see how all of this is good news."

Ms. Novak entered the bar with one of the guards. She was fresh-faced, bio-scrubbed and cheeky like a trideo real-estate sales sim. The newly cut and dyed blond hair and conservative pantsuit did little to shake the image of the dark-haired woman who'd woken startled in their backseat. Her off-the-rack bodyguard scanned the room looking calm and professional.

EnJee didn't bother waiting for them to spot him. This was his turf. He stood up, smiled, and waved her over.

She nodded and walked quickly over to their table. The guard remained by the door.

Ms. Novak said, "EnJee, Nero. It's a pleasure seeing you both again."

EnJee said, "We were told we were meeting the Johnson who set up that last job. Not the target of that job. You can imagine our concern."

Ms. Novak actually blushed. EnJee and Nero shared a look. Either she was offering genuine emotion or she was running charisma-ware dialed up enough to sell it pretty well. She said "Actually, *I* am the Johnson who set up the last job."

EnJee drummed his fingers on the table, waiting for her to continue.

"You deserve an explanation, of course," she said. "I arranged for the job as a test of your group's abilities, and to see if you were capable of following very specific orders, especially under difficult circumstances."

EnJee snorted, unable to hold back his amusement. He continued drumming his fingers on the table. "So was you getting shot at in the hallway part of your test as well?"

"No, and while I was not awake to witness that part, I am told you handled yourselves professionally. Thank you for the excellent work."

Nero looked like he was going to punch her. The mage started to speak, but EnJee put a hand out to stop him and said, "Your test put my friends and I at great personal risk. I don't know why you thought coming down here and explaining it to us was a good idea, but it wasn't. It's time for you to leave."

"I'm afraid I can't leave until you've heard my offer."

Nero found his voice. "We are not interested in anything you have to offer."

She frowned, her cheeks reddening to a darker shade than they had before. Quietly, she said, "It has to be you. I need *you* to do this job. I am willing to offer you twice what I just paid, plus a healthy retainer to ensure that it gets done."

Again Nero started to speak, and again EnJee cut in first: "What makes you think we'd take a job from you after you've already deceived us and put us at risk?"

"As I explained, I needed to know firsthand how your crew operated. This job is important, and I cannot afford to have it screwed up. I need you to kidnap a man named Enzo Moretti." She stared directly at Nero as she spoke.

Nero's eyes widened with surprise. He clenched his fists reflexively. EnJee eyed the gesture and then turned toward Novak, saying, "Not good enough, lady, we're out."

The flares of nervous blush fled her face like a light being snapped off. Her eyes looked cold and serious now. Motioning for her security guard she said, "Fine. I don't need all of you anyway."

Her security officer took a few steps closer. Novak leveled a finger at Nero and said, "I just need him."

Over the comm, Shen said, *"Who is she talking about?"*

EnJee felt more than saw Grim Fox rising to his feet in the back of the club. It was in the shift of the security guards gait from confident to unsure.

Novak continued, undaunted. "I wanted your team to kidnap Enzo, but Nero, I need you to *become* Enzo Moretti. I need you to pretend to be him, just for a few days—long enough to vote on some very important business for me."

The security officer stopped, showing his palms. He slowly reached inside his jacket with one hand and pulled out a datastick. He handed it to Novak. She immediately passed it to EnJee while Nero watched in stunned silence.

She said, "This is a file from the Senise Social Records Office circa 2059. It is a small city in Italy, not extremely noteworthy these days, unless you're a mobster or a cultural scholar. The records here detail the birth of twin boys, Enzo and Emiliano Moretti. Later records show the death of Emiliano Moretti." She waved her hand dismissively. "For some reason, Enzo had his personal records doctored to indicate he never had a brother, but the Matrix never forgets. I wouldn't even have known about this, but Enzo talks a lot when he's drunk. Most of it is nonsense, but every so often a golden nugget slips from his lips."

Novak's security officer moved back toward the door. She continued as if she didn't notice. "Emiliano, I'm offering you an opportunity to get even. I'm offering all of you an opportunity to get rich."

Shen said, *"What is she talking about?"*

Nero didn't speak. His tongue darted nervously out of his mouth licking at his upper lip. He rubbed nervously at the old wooden cross hanging from a chain around his neck. EnJee looked between Nero and Novak his own expression morphing from distant amusement to a sharper-edged confusion.

Ms. Novak folded her hands together and said, "Please, take the day to think about it, but this is a time-sensitive matter. I'll be on the road, but my personal number is on that datastick. When you have your answer, reach out."

She stood and left, but EnJee didn't watch her go. He'd already slotted the datastick. His jaw worked slowly in rage. He was staring at Nero.

NERO

11-12-2081
4:40 P.M. Local Time

Nero was aware of a headache echoing throughout his brain like the comedown from a massive casting. He turned to the old ways of dealing with the pain he'd learned in the church. He tried to focus on the details around him. He focused on how the well worn back stair rail to Shen's loft felt smooth beneath his fingers; how the stairs groaned in protest as each of them tromped upward, EnJee and Grim Fox trailing behind Nero like gallows guardsman.

The old ways weren't working. Underneath his focus on the details, memories sparked like dry kindling trying to become flames. The more he sought to turn away from them, the more they flickered. *A boy standing in an open doorway, mimicking every movement he makes. When Nero raises his hand, the boy raised his hand. The boy is his mirror image in every way.* The pain of the long-buried memory seared through him, watering his eyes. They were supposed to stay buried—the ones that remained. But just the another memory wound its way into his consciousness.

Nero huddling between the pews, a gibbering mess. His head feels like it is on fire. He is bleeding from his nose and crying out in a broken version of the Italian he's spoken since he could speak at all.

"*Figurati auguri,*" Nero mumbled under his breath. He hadn't spoken those words in that sequence for a half-decade. They were triggering words, the way he used verbal incantations to trigger spells, but it wasn't magic. It was psychological training. The words were repurposed to trigger other memories. Months were spent looping those words around specific thoughts until they burned out anything presently running free through his mind. The memories still lived, however, buried so deep in a corner of his brain that he hardly remembered they were there. *Nero standing in front of the altar. His hands are extending to grasp a small, round wafer and a thimble cup of red wine. These are the elements of the Eucharist. He feels warm inside. He feels loved. He belongs here.*

"What are you on about, Nero?!" EnJee barked and then added, "It better be a blimey explanation about who she thinks you are."

Nero slowly walked up the back stairway to Shen's rented loft with EnJee trailing silently behind him. He hadn't felt this much anger directed at him in well over a decade, not since the last time he saw Enzo, and now that momentary flash of rage came back full in his vision like a still frame.

Nero rocking gently on a rowboat, staring out at the far shore. A loud pop and the sensation of being shoved into nothingness.

Nero blinked the image away before it could settle fully. With great effort he forced it into the far corner of his mind where it always waited; where it could not find him. There was nowhere to hide from the coming conversation, however. There were only these four walls, partly covered in beige paint, a forgotten DIY project.

The door to the loft creaked shut behind him and locked. EnJee fixed the bolt in place. Nero felt the problem working itself through his mind, the anger and fear still building in him. His hand unconsciously found the cross at his neck. He concentrated on his breathing the way *Padre* Carlo taught him all those years ago when he was just a nervous boy whose abilities terrified people. His mouth felt dry. He closed his eyes and licked his lips.

Slowly, his breathing steadied, and he opened his eyes. The space was mostly empty. A board was set up over two workhorses to make a table. Old empty kegs served as chairs. Shen sat at the window, staring down the sight of her rifle, watching the street. Grim Fox posted up against an unfinished support beam and cracked open can of his favorite X-X-X-BierZille-Export he'd brought up from below, the can all but disappearing in his fist. Nero took in all of this in one wide sweeping look and then walked, head down, toward one of the kegs. Neither of the two men sat beside him.

EnJee moved to the table silently, sitting on the spent keg across from him. The hacker was staring off into the middle distance, a datajack trailing from his commlink, memory chip cresting out the base of the machine like a shark fin.

Shen finally pulled her eyes away from her scope. She looked from EnJee to Grim Fox and finally to Nero. He turned away from her stare. With a huff she said, "I'm not sure I heard it all correctly. You want to run me through what happened, Nero?"

Again that jagged flash of memory, *A loud pop*, mixing with another, *Monsignor Giuseppe holding him down while Nero tore violently at his own scalp, trying to get at what hummed beneath. Trying to rip that part of his brain out.* He forced down the broken memory, wincing against the accompanying flare of pain.

He watched the others talking and moving around him as if it were happening to someone else and he was far away. Grim Fox's voice was deep and filled with gravel. He said, "Lady wants us to do another corp job. Says Nero has a twin brother on the inside. But better that we wait until EnJee jacks out with the facts."

Shen didn't wait. "Can't be. That would mean that you have a family and a System Identification Number we've never heard about, Nero. Can't be."

Nero turned toward Shen and stared at her neck. Her tattoos were radiant, deepening from dark blue to a blistering purple. *I can see you are angry right now and I'm angry too*, he thought. *This is all* tempi antichi, *long before I found this life. Novak had no right to dig it up.*

He said, "That's all in the past."

EnJee coughed twice, covering his mouth with a fist. His eyes were wild, the way he looked when he cut a hard exit after tangling with something in the Matrix that he shouldn't have. Nero wondered momentarily where it was the hacker had just been, but then EnJee's eyes refocused as he said, "What the bloody hell, Nero?"

Nero shrugged. He folded his hands in his lap. "I didn't know we had to share everything that happened in our lives before we hooked up."

EnJee growled, "No, but you should be sharing that you have a fucking SIN. You understand how a SIN works, *neh*?"

Nero opened his mouth to speak, but EnJee cut him off, making it clear the question was rhetorical. The hacker growled, "It is the very thing that separates people from being part of the system and being outside of it. We can do what we do because we exist outside of that system. Not having a SIN was a huge part of that, mate."

"I don't see the problem. My having a SIN changes nothing," he lied. The number was the individual datapoint provided to infants born within federal or corporate jurisdiction—a digital record of a person's life stored in an NEEC database, linking your name, DNA records, and all other record tags together. It allowed a government or corporate entity to track you across national and extraterritorial lines and keep a record of your actions.

EnJee's eyes narrowed. His mouth flattened into a line.

Nero realized the hacker was about to hit him. He could see EnJee's measuring the space; considering what it would take to leap across the table and bury a fist in his face. Nero's hand went to his cross, reflexively reaching for the magic.

Then he felt Grim Fox leaning over his shoulder. The big man said, "We all need to take it down a notch. It's not like he's been lying to us the past few years."

EnJee barked, "That's *exactly* he's been doing!"

Nero winced, his mind unconsciously shifting back to memories he fought so hard to suppress.

"We all have a past, EnJee," said GrimFox, "and we never ask each other about it. I didn't ask you why you left London. You didn't ask me why I left the UCAS. Nobody but you seems to know where Shen came from, and nobody asked Nero who he was before all this."

"Emiliano Moretti, apparently," Shen said, opening a copy of digital file EnJee had just scanned to all of them. She walked over from the window and sat atop a keg. "Son of Marco and Anna Moretti. Born in Senise, and died at the ripe old age of 13. Survived by his father and his brother."

EnJee said, "This is serious business. This little slag has been withholding information on us, and now we got a Johnson trying to capitalize on it."

Shen pulled his hands into her own. He watched her fingers softly pressing against his skin. He watched her throat, the ink fading to a light blue as she worked to control her anger. She said, "We need to understand the situation we are in right now. We need to know exactly what this Johnson is talking about."

"I erased it."

"What the fuck does that mean?" EnJee snapped.

Nero looked between each member of the team. He said, "I discovered a way to use magic to remove memories. I tried it on myself."

Shen gasped. Even EnJee couldn't stop a low whistle from escaping from his lips. Only Grim Fox was stoic. He said, "You need to explain it all. Right now, *omae*."

He took a deep breath, exhaled, and said, "I don't know all of it anymore, but you deserve to know what I remember."

ENJEE

The Plex music filtering up ~~~~~~~~~~~ floors sounded to EnJee like the soundtrack to a bad day. He couldn't make out the lyrics, but every so often, a beat hit so hard that it jostled the old piece of plasticrete that Shen or someone before her repurposed as a table. He guessed from the uptick in energy below that the evening crowd was rolling in, swapping out with the day drinkers.

Grim Fox had asked to take a break before hearing the story. He said he felt like they needed more alcohol for this one. However, EnJee figured he was giving Nero more time to get his bearings and figure out what to say. EnJee didn't like it, but the looks Shen kept flashing him when he scowled at EnJee told him he needed to mind his manners here—at least until he heard Nero out.

Now the troll tromped up the stairs with another round of that X-X-X swill he called beer. He handed one out to each of the crew sitting around their makeshift table, slamming EnJee's down purposefully beside the flat black datachip that had darkened their day. He dragged an empty keg over and squatted down on it. He angled his head down, which had the effect of pointing a horn at Nero and said, "All right we're ready. Tell it."

Nero took a deep breath and said, "I was twelve when my parents first noticed my magical aptitude. There was a school test, sponsored by a corporation that did business in the area. I passed. Enzo did not. I don't think you can appreciate the attention a boy gets when something like this happens.

ery close up until then, but my
ng between us. He became jealous
 my abilities brought. I didn't want it,
 rdless."
 ppreciate what he was talking about. He'd
 lf to human parents not long after the birth of
 There were expectations that he could do magic,
 Nero did or as the more recent physical adepts
 eled mana through themselves. However, he was not
 t kind of elf. The letdown was palpable. EnJee blinked
away the memory. There had been a question from Shen, her
voice gentle. Realizing Nero was still talking, EnJee forced
himself to listen.

"No, we weren't what you would properly call a corporate
family. My father was an operations manager for a small, local
corporation sold to another one of the megas. I didn't follow it
that closely; it didn't affect our lives in any real way. No part of
our lives extended beyond our Senise prior to that test."

Nero stopped to take a swig of beer, winced at the taste,
and continued. "After that, corporate schools offered to get
me training for my talents and putting me in line to work for
one of the larger corporations. My father loved the idea. You
see, If I got in, they would have to hire him as well. He told me
this was the way these sorts of corporate transactions worked.
He would make sure it was a promotion from the pay and
station he presently held. We would all benefit."

EnJee was talking before he could stop himself, the words
coming out in a wave of anger and disappointment: "So there
you are, ripe old age of twelve, and all you wanted was to get
caught up in the corporate machine, because why? Your dad
wants to move up another rung on the corporate ladder?"

Nero didn't respond, not right away. EnJee watched him
take a long breath. He reached for his cross the way he always
did when he was uncomfortable. Then he did the other thing
he did when he was uncomfortable: he turned to Shen and
tried to find her eyes. EnJee didn't have the patience for that
right now. He said, "Answer the blimey question!"

"My mother was sick," said Nero. "She'd been sick since
giving birth to Enzo and I. For our entire first year, she would
not hold us. That responsibility fell to my father. Later she
would only become symptomatic when father was away, and
it was just the three of us around."

EnJee didn't understand what any of this had to do with what he asked, and opened his mouth to say so, when Shen shot him a steely-eyed look that meant he'd already gone too far. He shut his mouth and continued to listen.

"None of the doctors could figure out what was wrong with her. In fact, none of them believed that anything *was* wrong with her. When I objected to my father's plan for corporate glory, he reminded me that leaving Senise meant a chance to get mother proper care. I believed him. It didn't matter that I knew that she didn't want to leave Senise. Father knew what was best for all of us, so I followed along."

Grim Fox asked, "Who ended up recruiting you?"

"Shiawase. They wanted to move us to their enclave outside of Florence. When we sat down as a family to discuss it, mother refused to go. My brother didn't want to go either. Still, my father insisted that we take advantage of the opportunity. In fact, he'd already put in the paperwork."

EnJee ran the calculations through his head briefly. It meant Nero was recorded as a corporate citizen with Shiawase, one of the ten largest megacorporations in existence. How hadn't that caught up to him by now? How hadn't it painted a big bright arrow toward him? EnJee did a lot of work against Shiawase over the years, enough that he was certain to be on a detain or kill list somewhere. He said, "Isn't how that works, mate. Even if you're a kid, you have to agree to do what they ask."

Nero replied, "I suppose I did not understand that it was ultimately my decision. I was young and scared. In my mind, the only solution was to run away. If I was gone, then mother would be able to stay, Enzo would not need to live in my shadow. Father would be fine, though he would be forced to stay in the same job. Before he believed he had the opportunity for more, he'd never complained."

Shen asked, "So you ran away?"

"No. I don't think I would've ever followed through with that idea. I even talked about it with Enzo, but I was afraid. He knew before I did that I lacked the courage to run." Nero's accent seemed to thicken with each word. "My father had a boat. Just a skiff. He always told us he would make it big in the corporation and buy us a real one someday. Anyway, Enzo asked me if he and I could take the boat out one day. When we really wanted to talk, we always would take out the boat and ride out to the middle of the lake to talk where nobody else could hear us. It was peaceful. Safe. We called it the place where the digital world died."

Nero stole a glance at EnJee and then looked away. "I remember looking off at the shore when I felt the first bullet. It felt like Enzo had thrown a sinker at my back as hard as he could. I don't think I even heard the gunshot at first. I remember the pain and the panic. I jumped up in shock. Then I just stumbled into the water."

Shen said, "The scars on your back. You said they were from a run that went bad. Was that a lie, too?"

EnJee watched a frown wriggle across Nero's face, his emotions mirrored in the pink circuit lines of Shen's tattoos. Then, Nero reached up with his left hand and touched his right shoulder blade. "This one here was from a run. But the others are from Enzo. They never healed right. Nothing in that part of my body ever heals right anymore."

EnJee looked between the other three members of the group. Shen took Nero's hands in her own. Even Grim Fox looked swayed by the tale. The samurai cleared his throat, breaking the silence. Then he said, "Why didn't you go back?"

Nero said, "My brother shot me to keep me from uprooting our lives. What did I have to go back to?"

EnJee had to admit it was a good story. A real gut-tearer. He could practically see the sympathy radiating from the others. He felt a smile spread across his face, the curve of his cheeks tightening with anger. He said, "You spin a good tale, mate. None of it explains why you lied to us."

Nero threw up his hands plaintively. "I never lied to you."

That was too much for EnJee. He dashed over the table, full of rage and purpose. Nero was a blur of motion, pushing back away from the chair and out of range. Then a second blur of motion, this one larger, and Grim Fox was between them pushing him back.

EnJee panted from the sudden exertion. He said, "You didn't tell us everything. That is the same thing as a proper lie."

Nero threw up his hands. "How is that fair? What do I know about you before we met, about Shen? Even you, Grim Fox? You never told us what went down in Denver to make you come all the way out here."

EnJee struggled to get free, but Grim Fox held him firmly in one gnarled hand. When EnJee tried to struggle again, Grim Fox lifted him off the ground and let him dangle in the air. EnJee imagined this was what meat felt like after being slid unto the hook. The one thing he could say for the samurai was that he was quite strong. Ignoring him, Grim Fox turned back to Nero and snarled, "You don't need to know my history."

"And you need to know mine?"

"If it means you have a SIN, frag yes! They can track you, Nero. Novak *did* track you, right to us!"

Shen said, "We have a bigger problem right now. We need to decide what to do about Novak and this job."

Grim Fox said, "I think that's up to Nero."

EnJee said, "Bollocks." He spat on the ground, still dangling a half-meter above it. "We decide together how we do things. If *we* decide to do the job, then we do the job."

Grim Fox lowered him to the ground and then slowly released him, clearly watching to see if he'd go after the mage again. When he didn't, Shen said, "Nero, do you think you can pull it off, being under as a suit?"

Nero shook his head. "I don't know the corporate world or their language."

EnJee said, "Don't you worry about that part. It's in your blood, isn't it?"

Nero flipped him the finger. EnJee shot two back and kicked at a spilled beer can for emphasis.

Grim Fox rejoined the conversation. "I don't like the way we were set up, but we need the work. I'm not sure how long we can get by on the money from this last job. I'm less sure when we'll see another."

"There'll be other jobs," Nero said. "It's like you said, Shen. With Spinrad dead, there's certain to be more work out there."

EnJee replied, "How do you know this isn't that already? Up 'til yesterday we hadn't worked in a month."

Shen said, "Well, there is another part to this. We haven't talked about what the Johnson will do if we don't take the job. You think she tells us all this, about Nero's brother and the kind of danger he's in, and thinks to herself, *It's okay to let them walk away before I get what I need?*"

Nero's face scrunched up in anger for the first time since they'd come upstairs. "You think she'll come after us?"

"If she believes she can't do the job without you," said Shen, "then yes. But I think that also means we have leverage."

Grim Fox added, "It's worth finding out how much more she's willing to offer to get this job done."

They were speaking EnJee's language now. He said, "The credits could set us up nicely for a bit. We wouldn't have to worry about finding other work right away."

Shen looked directly at Nero and said, "I want to meet him. If this is the way that needs to happen, then I'm in."

EnJee didn't think face-to-face was a particularly good idea. Nero didn't either. He folded his arms and made a face and said, "I'm not comfortable with this job."

EnJee finally felt his anger being replaced by something entirely different and muttered, "Doesn't much matter anymore, Nero. It's looking like the vote comes in three to one. Let's see how much this work is worth to Novak."

Enjee linked to his commlink and dialed.

Novak answered on the first ring. "Have my credits convinced you?"

EnJee said, "Double them."

She replied, "I offered a rather large fee to begin with. How about I raise it 15 percent and double the retainer?"

EnJee watched the others standing around, anxious. They could only hear his side of the conversation. He said, "No, double your original offer and we'll do it." He looked to Nero. "*He'll* do it."

She sighed. "Let's meet and go over specifics. I'll send the location."

EnJee nodded to no one in particular and ended the call. Looking down at his screen, he saw she'd tagged a location. He raised his eyebrows, then turned to his crew and said, "We meet her tomorrow night in Brussels."

NERO

11-13-2081
8:16 P.M. Local Time

As far as Nero understood it, no one in his makeshift family was fond of independent city-states. The laws, when they did exist, were often subject to whatever corporation had the most holdings in that town. In rare places like New York City, a consortium of corporations worked together to provide a unified set of laws that benefited those corps more than anyone else, but still left the residents with the sense that they were standing on level ground. The entire city wouldn't fall to chaos if a stock trade upended the market or a CEO got killed.

As Grim Fox navigated them through the narrow streets of lower Brussels, Nero thought about how the world around him was becoming increasingly volatile and independent. In what still remained of the UCAS, Seattle had just declared independence. That news shared the daily headline space with the massive upheavals in Spinrad Global caused by its iconic leader's death.

Brussels EC—or as Aetherpedia described it, Brussels European City—was a sore spot for all of them but for EnJee in particular. The government had been among the first to pass regulations making testing and registration of technomancers mandatory. They'd made Brussels the centerpiece of their witch hunt. Moreover, determining who was a hacker versus someone with those higher order abilities meant instituting a series of grid-wide monitoring mandates that gave Grid Overwatch Division so much control over the workings of the local matrix that the nickname GOD was no longer a slick joke. EnJee's reaction to the Brussels accord had been like watching a nuclear missile explode at close range. It was the first time Nero had been scared of the hacker, though not the last.

The team had only had the crossed into Brussels once since. Now back in the city all of them were on edge. They'd acquired a nondescript American for the transit. EnJee wiped and recoded the vehicle records to match ownership to a local resident profile he'd bought off the matrix. Nero rode shotgun in the front seat while EnJee and Shen sat in the rear.

"Uniforce cruiser on our left," Nero said.

"See it." Grim Fox nodded tightly. Uniforce represented what passed as law enforcement in Brussels, the city was thick with them like flies on a new corpse. Their heavily mechanized security units roamed the city streets, moving in well-defined patterns between the places the government and the corporations wanted to keep most safe. Grim Fox weaved expertly around a pair of slower moving local vehicles, staying just under the speed limit as not to arouse suspicions.

EnJee said, "Our tags will hold up so long as we keep our distance from the Government sector."

The city's continuing success relied on people moving freely through the city, making deals in private corners and never being seen coming or going. Ms. Novak apparently understood this, as the location she selected gave her the cover of being out for a business dinner at Fin de Siècle without having to worry about the team getting to the harder-to-reach parts of the city. EnJee's hunt through the Helix earlier that day revealed the restaurant was a relatively unknown mid-tier place promising classic French cuisine.

Fin de Siècle sat close enough to the Rue des Chartreux that they could still feel the glow of the corporate towers that lit the night sky. The crew left their car in a parking structure a block east of the restaurant. Novak had told them to dress professionally. Shen wore a black skirt with a pink and black V-neck pullover that showed off the line of tattoo ink that swirled down the side and around the back of her neck. As she fidgeted with her purse, Nero could see she'd brought a pistol, though none of them expected trouble at this stage. The early trouble had already passed, and the real problems were over the horizon.

Given Grim Fox's tremendous size, anything he wore made him look like security. He didn't help matters much by choosing an all-black ensemble consisting of slacks, t-shirt, and sport coat. In contrast, EnJee looked like what *Padre* Carlo would call a *teppista*—a hooligan. His green plume of hair was split into two braids that flopped to either side of his head. He wore combat boots, a leather jacket, and a gray shirt promoting Johnny Banger's 2073 tour. Nero rounded out the entourage looking dressed like a miniaturized version of Grim Fox, though he'd gone for a black dress shirt instead of a tee. Once they realized EnJee was in no mood for playing nice, they'd decided to dress in a way that could cover his behavior.

Seeing Fin de Siècle now was more impressive than the flat images EnJee shared with them on the drive over. A massive circular bar held the center of the room, and towering above it was a curved fish tank containing more species of fish than Nero had ever seen in one place. More interestingly, Its gothic-styled architecture was marked by small booths that could be made private by the drawing of a what he presumed to be noise-dampening curtain. This evening, piano music whispered from concealed speakers, offering a selection EnJee informed them was Claude Debussy's greatest hits with a little Chopin thrown in for color.

"Still isn't posh enough to order up a real pianist," EnJee added.

"I never knew you were into classical music," Shen said as she followed him through the main entrance. The restaurant was structured so that the people at and near the bar could be seen. The edges and alcoves of the space were less obvious. You could only find someone if you stared long enough or if you knew exactly what you were looking for. It gave the space a duality. You came here when you didn't want to be seen, or you came here when you wanted to be seen by people who didn't want to be seen themselves.

EnJee shrugged. "I have an autoscript that retrieves song information on anything my cyberears pick up. My script kitty isn't responding as fast as usual, which means they must be jamming Matrix traffic. Makes sense why Novak decided to meet here."

Nero paused at that. He settled his breathing, blinked and opened his vision to see what the astral space around him contained. The aquarium at the very center of the space was alight with the auras of all the fish present. It served as a sort of natural barrier to his awakened vision. Likewise, the smaller aquariums around the room created a kind of background noise, like trying to hear a specific instrument in an orchestra. He said, "No astral security here, but a handful of the customers are Awakened."

"Any of that Awakened energy coming from over there?" Grim Fox dipped his one horn toward a spot at the opposite end of the room. In astral space, Nero saw nothing but the lifeless gray. When he shifted his eyes back to the normal spectrum, he could see exactly what Grim Fox was pointing to. Across the crowded room, Novak sat alone in a booth large enough to accommodate a party of friends. She wore a long blue dress with a pearl neckline accenting the low cut. She looked beautiful.

Shen must have noticed Nero staring; she looked hard at him, then slid her arm into his, redirecting his gaze toward the bar, where she politely waved at the security detail who'd accompanied Novak to the meet earlier in the day.

EnJee ignored all of this. He strolled directly up to Novak's private booth and bellowed, "Katerina Novak. Fancy us all meeting in a place like this!"

Novak smiled, flushed a bit for effect, rose, and extended her hand to each of the group as they headed over. Only Nero refused to shake. The expression on her face didn't change. Nero found himself glancing at her neck the way he did with Shen, but there was no telltale ink to let him know how she really felt. Like Shen, Novak's bioware responses were designed to obscure her true feelings under difficult social situations, offering a mask of expectation.

She invited the group to sit with her. "I am so glad the four of you decided to join me for this opportunity."

"It seemed like a bright choice, it did." EnJee slid into the booth and the rest followed. A waiter appeared to take drink orders. With the orders collected, he slid the privacy curtain closed and left. EnJee started in with a question: "Why is it you corporate types always want to meet at a restaurant or a bar? Writing this bit off, are you?"

Novak laughed. "Indeed. It is one of the few times I can get in a full meal. I'm certain you'll enjoy what they have to offer. Just as I am certain this work can be quick and extremely profitable for all of us."

Nero said, "You understand we expect to get half of our payment upfront, for the added risk."

She cocked her head to one side in a mockery of confusion.

Shen pointed to Nero and took up the conversation, "You're putting our boy here in the cat's mouth and dangling him there. That's added risk. Something bad happens, we have to go in and get him."

Up until now, Nero had been able to avoid thinking about Enzo—at least, as a mark. He was a distant target, a box further down the checklist. Now all the old memories bubbled up yet again, and he had to look away, gripping his cross in an effort to force the memories back down. He did not want to do this job. He said, "Why do it this way?"

Novak touched her fingers to the nape of her neck. It felt more staged response to his own gesture rather than reflexive. "I'm not sure what you mean."

"Why use me? I don't come from the corporate world. Don't know it. You could hire someone with more knowledge than I have, and use prosthetics or even magic to mimic his appearance."

"I considered each of those options, but prosthetics can slip. Illusion magic is difficult to sustain for a prolonged period of time. You are identical to him, Emiliano, even now. With a little bit of hacking from EnJee here, you could change his passwords and biometrics to your own. You could become him, and no one would be able to prove the difference."

"That's not good enough. I knew him half a lifetime ago. He grew up, went to school, made friends, relationships—he became a man, all without knowing I continued to exist."

Novak gently and deliberately set her hands on the table, palms down. As if speaking to a child, she said, "Enzo tried to end your life a dozen years ago. I'm offering to pay you today." She reached into her purse to retrieve a credstick and slid it across the table toward Nero.

EnJee snatched it away and scanned the balance. He tapped his little finger on the table as he thought. Finally he nodded. "I suppose it will do."

Grim Fox folded his hands on the table and leaned in. "Not quite. This can't be like it was in France. You're telling us we need to grab Enzo and switch him for Nero. For this to work we need to have complete control of how the extraction and the insertion happen. No guidelines on violence or anything else that could put us at unnecessary risk."

"I recognize that. However, you need to recognize that this needs to go smoothly. There will be parameters regarding what you all, and more specifically, what *Nero* does, beyond the initial snatch-and-grab operation. If there is any indication that Enzo is behaving abnormally, they could pull him off my deal. This entire thing is about my deal."

Shen folded her arms and said, "So, you want to tell us about that deal?"

"One step at a time."

The light at the center of the table flashed twice. The five of them fell silent, and a moment later the curtain slid back and the waiter set drinks in front of each of them. When he was gone, and the curtain reset Nero cleared his throat. He spoke softly and slowly, controlling the tone of every word the way she'd done earlier, "With all due respect, you are asking my friends and I to agree to a job without knowing anything about your ultimate goal. If any of this is going to work, I need to know what is expected of me, and I need to know it right now."

Her smile wavered slightly. She said, "Your brother's company, Lewis-Klein, is divesting itself of a particular product—a specific bespoke CDO. It's a Junior Debt portfolio, nothing major on the surface." She waved her hands in the air as if to dispel the cloud of corporate speak.

Nero asked, "What does it do?"

She stared at him, a question on her face.

"This product they make, what does it do?"

She chuckled. "No, darling. A CDO is collateralized debt. The product in question is debt owed by the specific companies tied up in the transaction."

He nodded slowly. What little he remembered about the world of finance centered on the concept of investment. This was the kind of work his father did, and the kind of work he'd been expecting to do before he woke one day with the ability to gaze into astral space. It made sense Enzo would fall into the same line of work.

Shen cut in, "So you want to buy someone's debt."

Novak nodded. As she spoke, Nero steadily tapped his little finger on the table, a habit he'd acquired the longer he spent time around EnJee. "It was intended to be a small, private sale, pre-arranged. And then, magically, word spread about our intent to buy. Others got involved and reached out privately to your brother. Once that happened, it became competitive." Her gaze flicked down to Nero's hand, then back up to his face.

"I don't like competition. We need to close this deal, quickly, and your brother is unwilling to close. He's kicking the tires on this purchase and he shouldn't be. He's involving more people than there needs to be."

"Leverage?" he asked.

She said, "I need you to make that sale, Nero. The longer this sits, the more eyes the sale draws. This is an inconvenience. Money is at stake."

Grim Fox leaned over the table again and said, "Tell us about his security."

"He doesn't have any, but he keeps to semi-public spaces. The itinerary shows clubs, restaurants. He likes to be seen."

Shen cast a glance at EnJee before she said, "I know the type. He thinks the notoriety keeps him safe."

"Good. I'll leave the extraction details to you. I can offer a fairly precise itinerary for the target for the next three days. My people worked this up and we believe he will stick to this routine."

Grim Fox nodded. "We'll run through it all."

"It needs to happen before the markets open Monday. I need Nero in place to work the deal by then." Novak pushed a memory stick across the table. "In addition to my research on Enzo, this contains instructions on how to break up the CDO. Once you do, you'll be able to give me what I want, and the vultures can tear at all the rest."

Nero stopped tapping. He said, "What happens to him after?"

Her smile flared automatically for just an instant, bioware kicking in to adjust for her obvious discomfort at a question she'd clearly been hoping to avoid. She got it under control and said, "If he comes back making a lot of noise about what happened, it could raise flags. However, Once the deal is settled, there is nothing he can do to change the outcome. Officially, he's irrelevant to me at that point."

"And unofficially?" Shen said.

Novak said, "I leave what happens to him to your discretion."

EnJee said, "We'll get it done."

Ms. Novak replied, "I expect nothing less."

ENJEE

11-14-2081
5:49 A.M. Local Time

Enzo Moretti was not presently in the NEEC, a detail Ms. Novak chose to leave out during the negotiations. It wasn't until after the handshake and the deeper data trawl that EnJee and the others learned where Enzo presently was: Azania. By then, the clock was running and they needed to choose between backing out entirely and following through on the agreement to do the work. Understandably, Nero remained opposed to the job. However, despite the risks, Shen and Grim Fox recognized it for the big payout that it was. Nuyen made the final decision, the way it usually did.

Before dawn Friday morning, the team found themselves at Eindhoven Airport, slated for an 8 a.m. flight to Cape Town. Their cover was that they were a security detail employed by Risk Minimizers PLC.

The fact Novak had been able to get this kind of clearance this quickly told EnJee a little more about his employer's connections. The security guards from her fake extraction test came from a company called Midlands Guards. With a few minutes of Matrix research, EnJee discovered that both security companies routed back to Hildebrandt-Kleinfort-Bernal, or HKB, one of the largest megacorps not in the Big 10. She didn't work for HKB, but she knew someone high up enough to make moves.

Of course, that could also be a smokescreen. The banking corporation was big enough that it wouldn't be hard to spoof your action through their subsidiaries if you were willing to throw around enough nuyen. That made EnJee want to ask more questions, the kind you only find answers to in places like the Helix or Dumpshock forums. He'd stayed up all night, digging into Enzo Moretti, Katerina Novak, and every data trail that was remotely attached to either of them. There was more to this job than Novak was letting on. There always was.

However, what limited connections he found between Moretti and Novak didn't constitute a smoking gun, or entirely even make sense yet. Novak was hiring Nero to stand in for his brother on a complex financial deal she knew Enzo wouldn't make on his own. Why she was so certain Enzo wouldn't cooperate wasn't clear. What EnJee could tell was that thing being sold was linked to Enzo specifically, and he wasn't about to let it go. He hadn't brought it to the attention of the team. They'd just chalk it up as another of his crazy conspiracy theories. He'd already setup a meeting with a contact down in Africa who specialized in corporate finance. He also planned to talk to Moretti himself. Until EnJee had more hard data he wanted to sit on his theories a bit longer, weighing it over in his mind.

Passage by High Speed Civilian Transport meant having a SIN and having that identification thoroughly examined to ensure you weren't a criminal or eco-terrorist bent on resetting the planet's carbon balance. People like EnJee didn't even try to fly via these supersonic commercial aircraft. His travel was limited to ground transport or whatever he could manage through the network of smugglers he kept in contact with from the old days, when Laesa still flowed freely between the continents, and work meant riding digital shotgun on a T-Bird shipment headed toward London proper.

EnJee saw the world as a fat Pippin apple. The corporate world represented the outer layer, all polished and pretty. These people who dealt in smiles and handshakes. They lied to each other openly and felt disrespected if a bloke dared to share an uncomfortable truth.Now he was standing in line with these shiny people, waiting to be checked in through airport security using the SIN profiles Novak provided. He didn't know how she'd come by the passes so quickly, and that unknown buzzed around in his head like a wasp threatening to sting him. A few nervous moments passed as each of them slipped through security. EnJee was the only one at ease, his boisterous nature well served under these circumstances.

The others had forced him into a suit, demanding he look the part for once. He let it happen, amusing himself by dying his hair chili red and putting it up in a top knot that adopted the look of a modern samurai, a move that made Grim Fox grimace.

That in of itself made it worth the trip for EnJee. Honor was a thing the street warrior took extremely seriously. Grim Fox was their action man, but he fancied himself a bit of a samurai, honoring the Bushido code—and EnJee liked walking all over his that code. Grim Fox wasn't Japanese; in truth, he was an undersized troll from some Native American Nations tribe who came across the pond for a fresh start. He liked Grim Fox. He was a smart bloke when it came to figuring out how to best snatch someone without getting killed in the process. He had questions about the kind of drek Grim Fox ascribed to, though. Acting like a Japanese samurai? EnJee often wondered if the big man truly understood how repulsive the Japanese found him. They'd been calling his kind *oni* long before the Awakening. It wasn't a term of endearment.

When they reached the front of the line, the transport security agent eyed EnJee's data, looking back and forth between him and the image Novak provided. Finally he said, "Nice hair."

"You're damn right it is," EnJee said back, smiling a toothy grin.

The group had barely boarded the 4-hour flight before Grim Fox grumbled about the seating. Even in a place as liberal as Amsterdam, there were few accommodations made for metahumans. The restrictions in seat size meant that their Johnson had been responsible for buying two seats for the troll—except she didn't, and Grim Fox wound up crammed into an aisle seat next to EnJee, because the elf was the smallest of the group.

The window seat belonged to an old woman that none of them knew. Shen traded seats with the woman after one of EnJee's tirades got so loud and bloviated that the stewardess needed to come to see what was the matter. What was wrong was that the troll didn't fit in the seat, of course, and as a result, EnJee couldn't entirely fit in *his* seat. Shen graciously gave hers up and wedged herself into the window seat, where she abruptly closed her eyes and slept through the remainder of the flight.

Shen was good like that. EnJee, not so much.

He insisted on going over the file with Nero. They kept the conversation subdermal, using a mixture of cyberware and AR support devices on a short-range mesh network that EnJee maintained for operations such as these. After several failed attempts at trying to get comfortable in the too-small seats, Grim Fox joined the chat. The trio studied a shared file, trying to make sense of the man Nero was being paid to become.

Enzo Moretti wore glasses. It was part affectation, and partially a way to stay connected to the everpresent corporate datastream. He didn't have cybereyes like so many corporate drones. He barely had any cyberware.

Grim Fox said what they all were thinking: "He must've been holding out hope that he got the touch of magic."

EnJee said. "Ahh, but it doesn't work like that. Think he would've known, neh? Yet he's wired up as much as you are, Nero. Should make things easy."

EnJee looked at the file, studying the image on the viewscreen. It was Nero. And yet it wasn't Nero. The differences were so razor-thin that you'd have to study the two for a while to notice.

"She expects me to behave like Enzo," Nero complained, "but I don't even know him."

Grim Fox said, "He has the same accent and mannerisms as you do. But he's quite a bit less pious and humble to be sure."

"I've studied all the footage Novak gave us of him," said EnJee, "especially that clip from the bar. I don't think you'll have much trouble with the behaving-like-him part. He keeps to himself in the office and outside of it. When he's with clients, he's usually on his own."

"The longer I'm forced to be him, the more chances I get it wrong."

"So we do as she says. We keep you off the grid as much as we can. You go in for the meeting, call out sick after, and then we get paid."

Nero said, "I can pull off the visuals, but there is a long way to go to figure out how this corporate thing works, and more importantly how to behave like Enzo."

Nero was making a point to not talk about what Enjee and the rest of the crew would be doing with Enzo while he was walking in his brother's shoes. EnJee had his own thoughts about what they ought to do with Enzo Moretti. He decided not to stir up that conversation. Navigating that social minefield made the trip feel longer than it already was.

The nation of Azania encompassed the southern tip of the African continent, so the six- and-a-half-hour long flight gave EnJee far too much time to worry about what would happen if Novak's SINs didn't hold up when they landed.

Azania participated in the Global SIN registry, which made them part of the system and part of what EnJee referred to as *the grand problem*. That unique number, if you're unlucky enough to have one assigned to at birth, follows you around for your entire existence. Like early blockchain, it was immutable, each block representing a year of your life, and that data divided into tranches including work, legal affiliations, family connections, and finances. He'd peeked under the hood more than once, and he knew from those looks that corporate citizens had additional tranches often including voting history, specific debt categories such as alcohol purchases, and more. Any interactions with the law existed there. Your entire debt history existed there. Each bit of happenstance in your life was recorded and stored in the system, irrevocably defining you by the things you did, were done to you, or were done in your name.

In EnJee's experience, most people either didn't know or didn't care about their rights and how a System Identification Number was impacted by those rights. Chip truth was, they didn't know how much they already gave up just by existing in the daily world.

Someone else knowing your SIN, knowing exactly how to use it, was a lot like having root access to your life. A few authorized keystrokes, and a dataslave could jander through your history and pluck out any individual action tied to you. If you believed the one-percenters who designed all these drek-driven laws, the system was meant to keep people honest, but instead it de facto criminalized any action that corporations might find distasteful.

What EnJee did and how he lived was completely foreign to a SINner's existence. He kept a dozen SINs, each a spoofed chain and history about as useful and real as the people he pushed it toward. Fake SINs were easy to come by. Any hacker worth his deck could generate a fake. How good it was depended largely on skill and how deep your access into the global registry went. You had to broadcast your SIN on your personal area network in order to do simple things such as shopping at a local Stuffer Shack.

However, creating a SIN useful enough to be able to buy a beer and not get red flagged was an order of magnitude easier than creating one that could pass the background check needed to sign an apartment lease.

And creating a SIN that got you through international security checkpoints was an entirely different set of rules.

EnJee found himself staring at Nero. The mage was pretending to be asleep, but EnJee could see him tapping his finger against the armrest the way he did when he was nervous or confused. It still bothered him that Nero had a real SIN, the kind that traced all the way back. The kind you couldn't simply delete when it got too hot. What's more, he couldn't understand why it didn't bother anyone else.

He thought back to that moment in the loft when he'd tried to attack Nero. He should've been able to explain it better then. In the heat of the moment, EnJee could never find the words to explain himself. It took long reflection on the situation to actually decide what was best to say, but by then it was always too late.

What was it Grim Fox called him? A "Monday-morning quarterback." Damn if EnJee didn't hate sports.

What he'd needed to say when Nero told them about his SIN was what that *meant*. A SIN was linked to your DNA—and they'd left DNA records at multiple jobs. It was unavoidable. If the cops ever caught up to him they wouldn't just come for him. They'd come for everyone associated with him.

EnJee closed his eyes for a minute, trying to rest but kept awake by the sheer volume of unanswered questions ringing in his head. So instead of sleep he leaned toward Grim Fox and whispered, "I still don't know why you felt we had to fly halfway across the world to get this done."

Grim Fox sighed, obviously irritated at the question. "Too many variables, *omae*. For one, there are less prying eyes in Cape Town—corporate allies and spies flooding the streets of the city, digital eyes. You know what London is like."

London was among the most wired cities in the world. Cameras existed on nearly every street in the 'plex, making a snatch-and-grab an extremely difficult thing to do unnoticed.

EnJee said, "That bit's right, but Enzo is due back in London Sunday evening in time for a night's rest. We could've taken him at his home. No eyes there—digital or otherwise—that we can't handle."

Grim Fox shrugged, the slight movement jostling EnJee. Grim Fox said, "You're not thinking about the second problem. We're supposed to turn Nero into some kind of corporate salesman. *Nero*. The man who actually prays at night and tunes in to a church feed just to hear what the *padre* comes up with that day. A couple of days sinking into the role might give us a fighting chance that he pulls it off."

Grim Fox was right. When it came down to bullets and spells, Nero was worth his weight. Unfortunately, he was a bit daft in the finer points. He knew bollocks about how to deal with dishonest people—in other words, corporations and those who worked for them. He wanted to trust right up to the point he got betrayed, and then he wanted to bark about it. By that time, it was always too late. That's why EnJee did the negotiating himself, or Grim Fox, if the situation called for it. Shen was good in a pinch, but would go all pink around the collar and start shooting if you pushed her too far.

EnJee leaned back and sighed. Grim Fox turned to one side and tried to go to sleep.

After a moment Shen tapped EnJee on the head. She sounded concerned when she said, "You're not sleeping, and you're not jacked in. What's up?"

"Just wool-gathering again, love. Nothing to be worried about."

The ghost of a smile flitted across her lips. "What's the conspiracy this time? I bet you're just dying to tell me."

He was. But he wouldn't. Not until he was sure of how to say it. Instead he leaned back again and closed his eyes. He was learning. With effort, he pushed away those difficult thoughts and closed his eyes. Eventually, sleep found him. The next sounds he heard were the gentle beeps notifying passengers it was time to buckle up for landing.

The landing was on the smoother side of what he'd dealt with. He wondered if it had anything to do with flying in a plane that offered business-class seating. He stood up with the others and grabbed for his bags.

EnJee kept reaching for his collar. Being in a suit made him feel like a cat on a leash. It wasn't in his nature. He was street, punk rock. Sighing, he said to no one in particular, "You know what I hate about Africa? Everyone accuses me of being a Zulu."

Nero's forehead creased into a stack of frown lines. "How's that an accusation? You ought to see it as a complement."

"How many Black elves have you met outside of me? At least when I was a kid, it was always, *"Don't you belong in Tir na nÓg?"* Now I get, *"Aren't you a Zulu?"* Makes it hard to be a proper Brit and not want to slag someone for saying otherwise."

They exited the plane and joined a long queue of people headed for the exits. Security here came in the usual flavor: tall people in crisp white shirts and blue gloves primed for inspection. Each of the dozen or so officers had a firearm strapped to their hips. It occurred to EnJee that there was a lot more security coming into a country than leaving one.

Shen moved to the front of the group. She flashed her credentials marking her as the executive liaison for their little security detail. The passes provided a precheck loophole that granted them only a cursory inspection. Bags and person. No screening for 'ware.

Novak's assistance ended at the airport. The Johnson had no strings to pull down here. It wasn't their first time in this position. The K&R industry, or "corporate reclamation," as Vash called it, was a travel-based industry. You went where the client was and figured out the situation on the ground.

The sun was almost gone from the sky when they finally made it out of Capetown International Airport. Crowding into the back of a taxi van, the four watched the lights of the city thrum to life.

Nero whistled low, pointing out the flat brown expanse of Table Mountain. "Does it give anyone else shivers to know that one of the Great Dragons is up there looking down on us?"

Shen's laughter was infectious. She poked Nero and said, "This remind anyone of that time in Barcelona?"

Nero sighed, "Barcelona was the worst time of my life."

EnJee laughed, too. "Of course you'd say that. You got caught up with all those bible-thumpers that thought they could turn you into their priest."

Grim Fox chimed in, "Remember the nuns at the Basilica de Sant Miquel? When we came to pull him out, they splashed holy water on him and told us we couldn't have him. He 'belonged to the Lord now.'"

EnJee clapped Nero on the shoulder. "You ought to stay out of churches, *omae*."

"Old habits."

EnJee looked around at the three of them as their cab sped deeper into a city that was all but alien to them. Unlike Barcelona, there would be little time for sight-seeing on this trip. The clock was running and there was plenty to get done. The smile remained on his face in spite of pre-run jitters beginning to fill his veins. He said, "Down to business, then. I'll work up a place for us to crash and then head down to test our connections with the people at the docks. Shen, you and Nero need to get us a proper set of wheels for the job. Two, right? We'll need something proper for Grimmy's plan and a second for what comes after. Grim, that leaves it to you to put eyes on the target and keep them there this time, *neh*?"

Something that resembled anger flashed briefly in Grim Fox's eyes. That only made EnJee smile wider. He started to relax a bit then. Putting others on edge always mellowed out his pre-run jitters. He said, "Shen want to lead us through the extraction plan?"

"I run point on the inside. I lure him away from whomever he's with and convince him to take me to a different location. Grim Fox, you pose as his driver. Once he's inside the vehicle I'll incapacitate him. EnJee and Nero will wait in the second vehicle as backup. We take the target back to the safehouse for interrogation before we load him on a boat for immediate transport back up the coast. Easy peasy." She looked at each man in turn as she spoke.

EnJee watched Nero watching everyone else and nodding in all the right spots, but he could tell Nero wasn't really there. So, EnJee said, "Nero, care to make a wager on how this one plays out?"

Shen poked EnJee in the side—hard enough for him to grunt. He met her stare and said, "Well, perhaps we best take gambling off the table this once."

ENZO

11-14-2081
10:00 P.M. Local Time

Enzo Moretti was bored.

The three Russians sitting in the booth beside him weren't what he expected. Each man commanded enough resources to pay for Enzo's lifestyle ten times over. That type of wealth should've led to more engaged and interesting people. At the very least it should have led to people who knew how to enjoy themselves on a Friday night. Instead, they sat glumly as beautiful people danced around them and the music of Club Silver thundered on.

When Enzo was a boy, he'd learned how to memorize names very quickly. His mother kept a large datastore of baby names and she always thumbed through it with him, searching for a name for the baby she would never have. He studied those names alongside her, memorizing their etymology as a sort of game they would play each time she asked him what he should name his soon to be little sister or brother. When the etymology method didn't work, he fell back on the tried-and-true method of mentally linking a name to a physical feature of that person, or an item he could associate with the name. Over the years the memorization game served him well—especially in situations like tonight when the people he was forced to be friendly with, and even entertain, were about as dull as a lunar drone feed.

The names of the three men who sat with him were easy to remember as a group. Sacha Drozdov was the key. He was a barrel-chested man with a bushy black mustache and straight cut bangs across his forehead that made him look just as

Russian as the name indicated. The other two were thin men, more suited to the look of corporate bankers they probably hoped to achieve. Timur Kalashnik was a slight man with wireframed glasses that, judging by his obviously cybernetic hand, were largely an affectation. More than once tonight he had to stop himself from rolling his eyes at the banker.

Enzo had no cyberware himself. He rejected the datajack his father tried to force on him at the age of fourteen. He'd heard stories of magic blooming late, and had reason to believe his magic would come, so long as he kept his body pure and fit.

That regimen had the side effect of attracting people to him. Across the room, a woman in a revealing electric blue dress continued glancing at him. He kept looking back, hoping she'd approach but she didn't. He flashed her another compelling smile and then turned back to his associates and offered them another round of drinks.

He said, "I dedicate this round to Dimitri. You've done an incredible job setting up the initial data trail for our new venture. Even my company's auditors would be hard-pressed to find anything out of line."

The third man, Dimitri Molchalin was as grim of a dwarf as Enzo had ever met. Molchalin frowned as he sipped his 100-nuyen glass of vodka. He frowned through being praised. If Enzo didn't know better, he'd think Molchain didn't like making money, or the wonders money bought.

Timur Kalashnik and Dimitri Molchalin had last names that formed a mnemonic only when you factored in Sacha Drozdov. Together it was Kalashnikov and Molotov. Enzo didn't think anyone else would understand that one, but it brought a smile to his face. He said a second cheers and tipped back another 100 nuyen glass of vodka.

Out of the corner of his eye he saw the woman looking at him again. Azania was known for strange magic and beautiful women—his two favorite pursuits. It was why he'd chosen to meet here, using his official company audit as a cover while he got to know these men a little better. If everything went as planned, he'd soon be working closely with at least one of the three Russians, and maybe all of them.

His commlink buzzed. Enzo slid on his AR glasses and fed the call data to his visual feed. Yeun again. The kid kept reaching out. Enzo hoped he'd try to find a different mentor, but it wasn't happening, at least not fast enough. Enzo checked the timestamp. London was only an hour behind them. So, he was calling to chat and not for professional reasons. He'd get back to him tomorrow. Or never.

He had an earlier missed call from Selina. He didn't want to deal with the office now. Besides, the call probably meant everything was in place to close the Dorada Genetech deal he'd negotiated early that day, or it could be a proxy call— Arturo Olgin being needy again. If things worked out with these Russians, he wouldn't have to deal with the nonsensical hierarchy of Lewis- Klein anymore. That had to be worth being bored on a Friday night.

His eyes fell on the woman again. She had a line of tattoos snaking across her body in a pattern that resembled circuitry. He liked those tattoos. He'd seen something similar to them before. Was it that time in Seoul? He couldn't remember, and didn't think it mattered. Still, he had to know if this situation was on the up and up. He tuned into the club's AR feed. The space came to life with a secondary light show filled with strange virtual projections and data tags lighting up most of the people in the room. Several of the people here offered tags suggesting they were pay to play. She wasn't.

That was good. Enzo didn't pay for sex. He didn't need to. This woman was interesting, and perhaps even a challenge. At least for a little while, she could be an occasion to rise to.

And now she was heading toward him. She seemed to be focused on the server pouring them a new round of drinks. Stopping a few meters away, she said a few words to woman, who looked down at the bottle and said something back. He couldn't hear their exchange over the music and the sound of the crowd gathered just beyond their private VIP space.

Enzo took a risk. He made eye contact with the woman, and waved her over. When she was close enough to hear him, he said, "My apologies, but I do not think I will be able to stop staring at you."

She giggled, a sound like tiny bells ringing.

He said, "Please, tell me your name."

She smiled, still enjoying the flirtation, and said, "My name is Miyoko."

His AR glasses processed the name, and shot back the relevant data. He took off the glasses, pocketed them, and said, "Miyoko is lovely Japanese name."

She raised her eyebrows, "You speak Japanese?"

"No. I am just very good with names. It means 'beautiful child,' does it not? I imagine, your parents couldn't have found a more fitting title for someone such as yourself."

Her tattoos began to flare to life with color, the porcelain white of the space between the lines of circuitry blushing toward a pink color.

"My name is Enzo, which means ruler of the manor."

He watched this lovely woman, Miyoko, deliberately bat her eyelashes at him. He said, "I am also very good with colors. Am I right in saying that pink is the color of passion?"

She only smiled and leaned in close, pressing her lips against his neck gently. When she pulled away, she was smiling, and he had no more interest in staying here schmoozing these men.

Azania was better to him than he could have hoped for.

With a sense of daring, Enzo leaned in and kissed Miyoko on the neck. Her skin was warm and smelled luxurious. He glanced at the Russian trio. Then he leaned back close to Miyoko and said, "I'm growing bored with this place. Have you ever seen the Kirstenbosch Botanical Gardens at night?"

"I thought they were closed at this hour." A frown played at the edges of her perfect lips.

"Not to me." Enzo cracked a smile. He scooped his commlink out of his pocket and made a quick call, explaining to the service that he was ready for pickup. He turned to the others and said, "Gentlemen, I've had a wonderful time this evening. I encourage you to stay and enjoy drinks and music courtesy of Lewis-Klein."

He extended his hand and shook with each of the three men. The big man, Drozdov, held his grip. "Mr. Moretti, we are not quite done discussing business matters with you."

Enzo smiled, fighting the urge to wince. He said, "For tonight, I believe we are. Once your boss agrees to terms, we can continue setting up the operation."

Drozdov released his grip, but continued to study Miyoko as they stood and moved toward the door.

Outside, a black BMW X89 slid to a stop and the back door opened automatically. Enzo paused, watching the driver, a troll, stare directly ahead. Enzo said, "Excuse me, I rode with Franco on the way here. Who are you?"

"I'm Sam." The troll sounded like his voice was strained through gravel. He affected a smile that only made Enzo take a half-step back.

Miyoko leaned into Enzo and walked her fingers up his shoulder. She whispered, "Are we going?"

That jolted him out of his stupor. He led her to the rear door and escorted her inside. He threw one last curious glance at the driver before ducking and entering the car.

The car began to move down the road and Miyoko continued walking her fingers up and down his arm. In spite of this, he couldn't get away from himself. He pulled out his commlink. When Miyoko asked what he was doing he said, "I'm calling the service. This change is very unusual."

She leaned into him, climbing atop him as if she planned to share herself with him then and there. He leaned back, accepting her weight, arms open and wanting more.

But her hand shot upward, cracking him square in the jaw.

He saw a flash of white, and then all was darkness.

ENZO

11-15-2081
11:00 P.M. Local Time

Enzo Moretti woke to a tap on his shoulder. His head felt woozy. His eyes couldn't focus. His mouth felt like it was stuffed with cotton. It felt like the worst hangover in his life—even worse than New Year's Eve 2078, when he had been on the yacht with the crew from Hildebrandt-Kleinfort-Bernal and—

"Wake-up time, Enzo." The voice was unfamiliar to him, a punchy British accent that could've been from Westway, or worse, the Squeeze. He looked up, struggling to focus on the face wavering before him. The man was thin and Black, with a crooked sprout of red hair rising from the top of an otherwise bald and tattooed head. His ears were elven, though battered and pierced to the point where they hardly looked like ears at all.

The elf spoke again. "Welcome back to the world, mate. You can call me EnJee."

Enzo tried to move, but quickly discovered he was tied to a chair. He was in a hotel bathroom. Not his. A cheaper version—smaller—cramped, even—with cream-colored walls and tacky faux brass fittings on wall the directly in front of him.

It came to him that he was in the walk-in shower. Then, to his horror, he realized he was no longer dressed, a thin film of sweat covering his body. They'd spared his dignity by leaving him his underwear and socks, but the rest of his clothing was gone. He thought, *This is a kidnapping.* Then he sucked in a breath to scream.

EnJee leaned in quickly and grabbed Enzo by the sides of his head. Enzo's scream died in his throat as a desperate croak.

Pain followed, shooting out like fireworks when EnJee jerked his head quickly to the right. He said. "Right here is Grim Fox. You've met my girl, Shen."

Standing outside of the shower stall were two people. The girl from the club, Miyoko, was there. She looked different now, dressed in black fatigues with her hair up in a bun. The tattoos still radiated pink. *What is this?* Enzo recognized the person standing beside her as the one-horned troll who'd be driving the car before...*what?*

He managed a stunted, "What do you want?"

EnJee said, "Wait for it. Here's the real prize now. Come in here, Nero."

There was a shuffling of feet and a man came into view. Enzo felt his body go cold and still. The man stopped, framed by the bathroom doorway. His hands were in his pockets and he slouched a little. A frown played at the edges of his mouth.

There was no mistaking this man's face. Enzo saw it every time he looked in the mirror. Seeing him standing there was like staring into the water and seeing that alien version of yourself peering back.

"Much like my own family reunion," EnJee said, chuckling.

The one-horned troll, Grim Fox, said, "Why don't we give these two the room."

They filed out of the bathroom one at a time, leaving Enzo alone with the man who looked like him. The man closed the door and leaned back against the edge of the sink, staring at Enzo.

Nervously Enzo said, "You can't be real."

"I am real, *paperetto*."

"*Paperetto*," Enzo repeated, his voice thin with fear and confusion. "My brother used to call me that a lifetime ago. He is dead."

The ghost standing before Enzo started to respond, but lapsed into silence.

"What are you?" Enzo asked again. He understood magic. He'd researched and studied the craft for years, waiting for the day his own powers would emerge. He knew of such things as this. "Illusionist? Doppelgänger? Revenant?"

The man crossed his arms and shook his head. "Still looking in corners for ghosts, I see."

"Then what sort of trick is this? What do you want from me?" Enzo felt the fear split his voice as though he were a teenager.

The man's frown deepened. He reached under his collar and pulled out a cross. He wrapped one hand around it, squeezing it as he spoke. "I did not intend to ever see you again. After what you did, after you left me in the water to die, I knew that if I came back, it would be to kill you."

Enzo shivered. This was no doppelgänger. No illusion. He could see the subtle differences now in the harsh bathroom light. This man—this other version of himself—had harder features. It was in the unflinching way he stared back; the set of his jaw. Once, a long time ago, Enzo had a twin named Emiliano. Had that twin somehow survived what was done to him, this man could be him.

Enzo imagined for a moment what path that other version of himself would have taken. What he would've been forced to do to survive and end up in this very spot. Fear worked its way up his throat, leaving behind it the first prickles of nausea.

When the truth of the moment finally landed, Enzo was too far gone to stop what happened next. He tipped his head forward and vomited.

The one they called Nero—*Emiliano*—sighed. He walked over and patted Enzo on the shoulder. "No ghost. No doppelgänger. No dream. The others thought I needed to say things to you, to listen to you explain why you tried to murder me. Only, I know all of it already. Who you were is no different than who you are today."

Enzo could not bring himself to look at his twin. Still, he asked, "Are you here to kill me, then, Emiliano? Is this my dream, and you're the ghost of my past haunting me for my success?"

Emiliano stared down at the vomit on the floor with a frown, then shook his head. "That would make me the same as you."

"I don't understand," Enzo said, "If you are not here to kill me, then why are you here?"

"You made enemies, *paperetto*. You refused to do what they asked, and now I am here to do it for you."

Years of tight-lipped corporate negotiation could not stop confusion from playing across Enzo's face. The bathroom door opened. EnJee walked in, followed by Miyoko. No, not

Miyoko. They'd called her Shen. She spoke now, her voice almost cheerful. "Everything good here?"

Emiliano nodded. "My brother does not understand why he is here."

"Besides generally being an arsehole, that is?" EnJee said, and laughed at his joke. "You are here because our friend Nero is going to take over your life. He's going to drive over to your home this evening, sleep in your bed, step into your suit in the morning, and go to your job. Meanwhile, you will stay here with us and make sure he knows the right things to say and the right people to say it to. Afterward, if you're a good little rakkie, we're going to let you go. Otherwise, my friends and I get to box you up real nice."

Enzo breathed through a shiver, locking eyes with EnJee. No. None of this was real after all. The Emiliano thing was a trick. An illusionist's sick game, but a game nonetheless.

They wanted leverage. That's all this was about.

He understood this kind of game. This was just another high-stakes negotiation. He'd been in boardrooms a lot scarier than this. He just needed to find the right angle to play in order to work his way out of the situation.

He said, "I'm not sure you needed to go to all this trouble. I'm sure I can do whatever it is your client needs from me on my own."

"Right," huffed EnJee, "I'm sure our client believes that as well. That's why you're tied up here with the lot of us."

"Just tell me what you want—"

EnJee sighed loudly, cutting him off. "I'm getting knackered over all of this. See, we aren't negotiating. This is what's happening. Shen, why don't you go help Grimmy get Nero all dressed up for his big acting role while I get Enzo here to tell us what we need to know about how to get into his home, and what passwords we might need for anything else."

The ghost of Emiliano looked sad when he said, "Goodbye, *paperetto*."

The door closed behind him, leaving Enzo alone with the elf. Enzo felt relieved by this. The other one, the illusion, knocked him off his axis. He knew how to deal with men like this EnJee. He was a shadowrunner. They wanted for money and power, and Enzo had plenty of both. He said, "I see you are in charge. Now, tell me how much you are being paid, and I will tell you how much more I can offer you to let me go."

EnJee's grin reminded Enzo of a jackal. He walked behind Enzo and slowly turned a knob. Enzo heard the water come on before he felt the warm drops hit his skin. He felt a brief moment of relief as the water cleansed him, washing away the vomit. He closed his eyes, trying to gather his energy.

Behind him, the elf said, "There were a lot of hotels to choose from. Places that don't ask too many questions. Places that don't natter when things get loud. You know why I chose this place? Great showers. It's in the review."

The water grew hotter, and Enzo found himself wincing. "Please, stop. It's too hot."

The elf's voice had a hard edge to it when he said, "I thought I'd made it clear we weren't negotiating."

NERO

11-16-2081
12:15 A.M. Local Time

The hotel elevator *ding*ed, letting Nero out on the nineteenth floor of Enzo's hotel. A few steps later, he pressed a stolen passkey against the door of suite 1980. The room at Trots Waller Hotel stared out from the bowl of Cape Town into the black waters of False Bay. He'd hoped to find Enzo's room facing the city and the flat plateau of Table Mountain beyond it. The distant lights of boats on the water only served to remind him of what was out there, and what he'd left behind.

Outside, it was the kind of dark that only midnight on the ocean can bring, and the sounds of Cape Town pushed through his closed windows and wafted up toward the ceiling. Inside his head, clips of his forgotten life played in his head like memes, jittering and repeating.

He, Enzo, and their father on the boat.

Mother at the dining table, helping them with math problems.

He and Enzo in their shared bedroom under a sheet, pretending to be spirits and dragons battling for control of the world.

It didn't merely feel like another life. It felt like a shadow reality, a show he'd watched about another person.

Nero softly closed the door behind him. He could barely remember a time on the road when he didn't need to share a bathroom and there was more than enough space to sleep. Now here he was, in a suite on the southernmost tip of the world. Pursuit of this kind of luxury was the basis of the SINner's life. He hadn't thought of that life in over a decade.

While the shadowrunners' world was constructed of coffin motels, hostels, even roadside motels, SINners chased these majestic views, and treated a hotel with a breakfast buffet like they were settling for something lesser.

There was an unmistakable allure to this lifestyle. Not for the first time, he wished he could've brought Shen with him, offered her a taste. Offered more than evenings sitting on used kegs and playing cards, or cuddling in a bedroom with walls and floors so thin they could hear what the neighbors were whispering about each other—and about them.

Instead, here was a king-sized bed with a bed skirt and a white bedspread so wide that it nearly scraped the ground on both sides and the front. He supposed this type of luxury was part of the attraction that defined corporate life. The thousand-nuyen-a-night Lewis-Klein paid for him to stay here equaled Nero's cut on some runs.

On the wet bar, there were shooter-sized bottles of liquor ranging from Monongahela Rye to Jabifu synthol, in case you wanted to slum. Nero opened the small fridge below it and laughed out loud. Inside sat three cans of X-X-X Zille Export. He made a note to tell Grim Fox.

Enzo's carry-on was still packed. A suit hung from the rack in the closet. It was covered in a thin film of plastic with a dry cleaner's receipt affixed to the hanger. It appeared nearly identical to the one he already wore—the one he'd taken off his brother when they'd extracted him. Both were Vashon Island. Both felt like the sort of thing you were expected to wear in Enzo's line of work.

Nero was no stranger to suits. He wore them when the occasion called for it, but his suits generally came off the rack with aftermarket Kevlar weave add-ons that suited his situation. In suits like these, it was easy to tell that his brother's body and his had changed in different ways over the years. The differences weren't terribly noticeable in the face, but in the particular cut of a bespoke suit the changes stood out. Enzo's muscles were sculpted in a gym where the focus was on the parts of him people would most want to touch or stare at; the parts that stood out. Nero was slimmer, his body shaped with lean muscle, hardened by everyday use.

He sat down on the bed and fished out his brother's commlink. The image that flared on the screen was Enzo and their father at some type of corporate event. Nero hadn't thought of his parents in years. He hadn't framed his thoughts in a way that allowed anything prior to his time with the church to creep in.

His brother used AR glasses just as he did. Nero slid them on as he unlocked the commlink. Enzo's personal area network only contained a small number of linked devices—presently, only earbuds, the commlink, and a Cyberette-brand digital cigarette. He accessed the commlink, lazily scrolling through the list of contacts. He didn't know who he was looking for, but his eyes came to rest on a familiar name.

Vittoria Greco.

So, Enzo did still keep up with old acquaintances. A smile twitched the corners of Nero's mouth as he thought about Vittoria. She'd been a great friend at an age where kids were beginning to see each other as more than friends and experimentation became the priority. Unlike others they knew, she still wanted to hang out and have fun. What was her life like now?

It would be a simple matter to find out. Nero quickly typed her name into a search window. His hand hovered over the search button, but he couldn't bring himself to press it—to slide down deeper into that rabbit hole. Instead, Nero sighed and dropped the commlink on the table beside the bed.

Unconsciously, he reached for his cross, only realizing the motion once he found his cross was no longer there. That emptiness weighed on him. He'd tried to convince the others he could pass it off as a souvenir, but they'd balked at the idea. Enzo wasn't a religious man. Moreover, the cross was more than a cross. It was imbued with magical energies that allowed him to focus a portion of his spellcasting through it, taking some of the stress of sustaining spells away from him. He argued that this was specifically the reason he needed it, but he knew it wasn't. The cross was his talisman. When they'd parted ways, he handed it to Shen and said, "It's a way to keep a part of me close to you through all of this."

As he thought of Shen, he fished in his pocket for his own commlink, remembering to pull out the battery. He shoved both the commlink and battery under his pillow. EnJee gave him clear instructions on what to do, and more specifically, what *not* to do with the electronics. It infuriated him to have to listen to EnJee walk him through it. Nero wasn't Matrix-illiterate. He understood having a second PAN, especially in hidden mode, would draw attention. The smarter play was to keep his personal commlink turned off and the power supply disconnected. Just as it was too risky to bring his cross, a commlink operating on a separate PAN with an entirely separate list of contacts would raise flags he couldn't afford. He needed to sink into the role. He needed to be Enzo.

Except he wasn't Enzo. In some ways he didn't even know who Enzo was.

He'd read his brother's file ten times on the flight over, scrolling through the same pages, spiraling through Enzo's contacts and relationships as though he was reading a script. Enzo was famous for entertaining his clients. He was quiet and confident. He tossed money around as if each nuyen he spent would bring him four more. Nero thought he could do that. He'd seen Shen play the role of their face enough times to understand how the act worked. However, acting like a person wasn't the same as knowing them or even understanding them, and there was so much about Enzo he did not understand.

He dug into his brother's pants pocket and found the Cyberette. He didn't stop to read what it was loaded with, and didn't care. He sucked in recklessly. The tip lit with a red LED glow. He let the smoke filter out slowly through his nostrils. Almost without thinking, he linked the AR glasses to the local Matrix node and then navigated to a site he knew by heart.

The church stayed open around the clock. On cold nights, homeless people would find shelter in the pews. *Padre* Carlos used to walk the pews at night, gently tapping the homeless to wake them and lead them downstairs to the basement, where there were a dozen beds they could use overnight. Enzo had slept in those beds for a long time before his relationship with the church became more than a place to keep warm at night and perhaps scrounge a meal.

The camera showed an empty church this evening. Whoever was in charge of shepherding the flock had done their job well this evening, or perhaps conditions were not so bad that there was need—though he doubted that.

He wished he could talk to one of the *padres*. He wanted to give confession. He wanted to speak of what filled his heart when he saw Enzo. He wanted to speak about the deep anger he felt. He wanted to talk about the peculiar twinge of fear that wriggled through him the moment he stepped into that bathroom, as if Enzo could still hurt him after all these years.

He wanted to share with someone the guilt he felt standing in this hotel room wearing his brother's clothes and his brother's life. He'd fought for years to forgive Enzo and never could. He'd long since resigned himself to the fact that it could not happen, and vowed to never see his brother or family again.

Nero set the glasses and Cyberette down. He glanced appreciatively at the opulent bathroom. He couldn't remember the last time he'd taken a bath. So, he undressed and started the water. The hot water was unfamiliar to his skin, but felt luxurious nevertheless. Nero sighed deeply, and in a matter of moments, he was asleep.

He awakened to the angry jangle of the commlink. He scuttled out of the now-tepid water, slipping several times before he gained his footing and reached for the commlink. He answered, working the earpiece into his still-wet ear. "Hello?"

"When I call you, I don't expect to wait for you to pick up." The voice on the other end was angry and carried an air of expectation, like a boss talking to a petulant employee.

"Um, yes." He looked down at the commlink. The caller ID read **Arturo Olgin**. Nero recognized the name as Enzo's immediate superior at Lewis-Klein. Nero perked up and said, "Yes, yes sir."

"How was the meet with the Dorada Genetech people?"

"Fine," he lied. In spite of his best efforts, the slightest hint of a question still lingered in his voice. Enzo had been entertaining a group of Russians when the team snatched him. The schedule Novak provided listed the late-night session as a potential investor meeting. From what Nero had heard over the comms, they were just that—representatives of a wealthy Russian oligarch looking to invest capital. But that's where his information ran out. If Nero had to report back about a meeting with Dorada Genetech, this run might be in trouble long before it ever got underway.

Enzo's boss seemed distracted. "Good. Well, there has been a change of plans. I need you on a meet-and-greet in Dubai. Selina already rearranged your flight. You leave at 6:10."

"In—" There was a time readout on the upper left-hand corner of the screen that read 5:18 AM. He didn't realize he'd been asleep that long. "—an hour?"

Olgin continued undaunted. "I expect you on-site in the morning. This could be our line into more of a foothold in the area. Chalmers and Cole is pushing for control of this piece of the Atilla fund, but Olive Investments is willing to sit down with us before they deal with them. I need to know if this fund they're warehousing is a star or another one of these bullshit piles of derivatives Atilla was holding onto for the sake of God-knows-what. You look under the hood before I get there. Understand?"

Sweat prickled Nero's forehead. This wasn't the plan. The plan was to get to London and be ready to make the deal Monday morning. He'd prepared for that. He understood how to do that. He said, "No can do, sir. I'm on my way to London for that CDO auction. Soon as it's done, I'll be on a plane for Dubai."

The phone was silent for a beat and then that cold mix of anger and expectation washed back over him. "What did I just say about bullshit derivatives? That tranche sale of yours is meaningless. It's just window dressing to keep the upper executives from feeling like this dissolution is stalling. I'll have Selina push it until Wednesday. This matters more to Lewis-Klein than anything else you have going on, Enzo. We get this right, and we'll be in the front running for a good chunk of the reinvestment capital from the dissolution of Atilla's accounts. Do you understand what that means?"

He had no idea. What he did know from the mission briefing was that Arturo Olgin was high enough up the ladder to kill the deal Novak wanted so badly, and thus the run. Nero said, "Yes, of course I do. I'm on it."

"Good. I'm sending you the info."

Nero held Enzo's commlink in his hand. He rocked the device back and forth between both hands. Finally, he set it down on the bed and retrieved his own commlink from under his pillow. He slid the battery into the case, closing it with a loud *snap*. Then he dialed EnJee's number.

When the hacker didn't respond, he put in a call to Shen. By the time he dialed Grim Fox, the reality already settled in. They'd reached their boat and were off the grid. He couldn't reach them. He pulled on his clothes quickly and figured out how to check out of the room.

Downstairs, he quickly called for a cab. Once underway, he pulled out his own commlink again, careful not to let it link to his active PAN, where traces of that connection would show should anyone who bothered to look close enough.

He dialed a number. He took the call live—ear to device. She didn't answer the first time he called. The second time, she did—and she sounded groggy and confused. Anger showed through her tone. And he presumed she hadn't turned on her charisma softs.

Novak said, "What are you doing?"

"I'm getting on a plane."

"Fine. We will meet in London tomorrow."

"I'm not going to London."

Her tone changed. "What?"

"Arturo Olgin called me and told me to get on a plane to Dubai. He wants me to look at a piece of Atilla's asset fund—whatever the hell that is." The auto-cab stopped and he climbed out, dragging his travel bag behind him.

"What about the deal?"

"He said this was more important. Then he told me he pushed it back. He said Wednesday."

He heard the muffled cursing and the sound of ruffling sheets. When she came back to the line, it was clear she'd turned on her charisma softs. The strain in her voice felt genuine, if not desperate. "When do you land?"

"I don't know, it's a High Speed Civil Transport, so two hours in the air. Eleven a.m. maybe? I haven't looked into the time zones. I'm supposed to be picked up at the airport. Look, this wasn't the deal. I was supposed to go in on Monday, do the meeting, and get out. I can't do that now. We need to call it off."

"No, that cannot happen. You're going to have to pretend to be Enzo for a bit longer." Her voice had a hard edge now, and it made him nervous.

"I don't know how to do that. Your file showed me how to work with the specific people I would come into contact with, not some random suit from Dubai."

"Calm down. I'll get down to Dubai and walk you through it. There's a tea house called Shai Al Hatab, in the Jumeirah commercial district. Find a chance to get away. Meet me there after your business."

"What am I supposed to do with the Olive Holdings people?" He looked toward the airport check-in nervously.

"Pretend to be who you're supposed to be. Try to act like someone who knows how to have a good time and other people want to be around."

The soft *click* in his ear let him know the call was over. He stuffed the phone back into his pocket, tried for a cleansing breath that escalated into a shiver, and stared at the airport before him.

Seventeen hours ago, he'd landed here with the handful of people he'd come to know as family, with a mission to kidnap and replace the person who deserved that name more than any other. Now he was supposed to fly back across the world and into a life he never wanted and could not understand.

Nero sighed, shouldered his bag, and walked into the airport.

ENJEE

11-16-2081
4:15 A.M. Local Time

The first time EnJee ran the shadows was with a crew calling themselves the Uhuru Commandos. They were a street gang, so he forgave the name. It was a one-off job, supposed to be a simple smash-and-grab. They'd nicked a minivan and drove to the spot where they meant to crack a safe and steal whatever they thought was inside. The crew brought him along in case there was a security system they couldn't shut off. Back then, everything was hardwired, so if you needed to jack into a system, you had to get your hacker inside the front door. Nowadays, that only applied to sites with isolated systems.

It was after hours, so no one was supposed to be at the site. Turns out there was a worker there, maybe cleaning staff or someone trying to put in extra hours angling for a raise. She called them in, and security came screaming down the block in a matter of minutes.

Things got dodgy right then. The six of them piled into the minivan and made a run for it, but the minivan wasn't built for speed. It wasn't built for handling, neither. EnJee never came to realize what it was built for, because the security caught up to them and tried to run them off the road.

Their leader told everyone to open up on that car so they could get away. EnJee was new and didn't know much about drawing down on a person or drawing a gun at all. He tried to pull the gun out his trousers, but it got caught on the lip of the pocket and went off. He was lucky the shot just scraped his ankle and not buried itself in his thigh. At the time, all he could think was *This bloody hurts* and *I hate minivans*. He was lucky they didn't get nicked, but he didn't make money either. All of this because of that blimey minivan.

That was all to say that EnJee *hated* minivans. Grim Fox knew enough about that history that the choice of the gray Northstar Passenger Wagon felt *personal* to EnJee. As they cruised down the N1 past Century City, he griped, "All the options for a vehicle, and the best you could come up with is a minivan? I'm really starting to doubt your ability to make the proper choice."

The minivan came with three rows standard. Grim Fox drove with EnJee in the front passenger seat, playing co-pilot. The middle row was filled with industrial cases stacked three high. Grim Fox said, "You didn't give me a lot of space to plan how we do things from this point, so don't complain about what I come up with on short notice."

"You could've kept the blimey BMW. Isn't that right, Shen?"

Shen didn't respond. She sat in the far back row, rubbing absently at Nero's cross that now hung around her neck and staring at a gagged and handcuffed Enzo Moretti. The prisoner's face was still red in spots from where the water had scalded his skin.

Enzo had come around to EnJee's way of thinking after ten minutes under a pulsating shower. At first, EnJee just let the water rinse away the grime and sick. Then he pulled Enzo's hair back, let the water smash him full in the face. Enzo held his breath at first but after a while he couldn't do that anymore, and it led to him choking briefly. All the while EnJee was there, softly cooing in his ear about how easy it would be for all of this to simply go away.

"BMW didn't have room for the air purifiers. In case you forgot, it was your bright idea to trade air purifiers for a boat ride up the coast," Grim Fox said, bringing EnJee back to the problem at hand. He turned off the main road and maneuvered through the thick knot of traffic leading to the docks.

EnJee sighed, "We can't all be as lucky as Nero and fly back first class. I've been running goods up and down the coast for a long time, mate. Azania's borders are locked down tight everywhere but the water. We can take a boat to Lagos. It's null sweat to get a T-bird up north from there."

Grim Fox grumbled, but nodded. He slowed the minivan as they neared a checkpoint. Cape Town's docks were loaded with checkpoints, many of them baring corporate labels. They pulled up to one emblazoned with the Evo corporate logo. EnJee offered the gate attendant the password he'd been given. The woman nodded and waved them through.

They continued along the docks toward the warren of shipping containers stacked eight high in places. There was so much cargo here it seemed as if there weren't enough berths to load it all. As they drove further down the strip, past the megacorporate berths, the common corporate symbols they all knew became sparser, replaced by symbols they didn't recognize.

"The big corps get their own docks, but the tramp shippers rely on protection from pirates, if not outright service from them, to move goods in and out of the region." EnJee said.

"Tramp shipper?" Grim Fox asked.

Shen said, "It's a type of transport that doesn't rely on a fixed schedule. They'll go wherever, whenever."

"Exactly the type of transit we need," EnJee added.

There were over a hundred berths just in this particular section of the docks. It was loud with the sounds of machinery and the *boom* of cargo landing heavily on decks or in a ship's hold. The low growl of diesel engines, the bird-like call of horns as ships moved in and out of the docks, flowing to destinations around the globe, spoke of an environment alien to what they were used to. Despite the near vertical trajectory of technological improvements, the world's commerce still moved in the bellies of ships.

Break just one shipping lane and the world would stop. EnJee thought the same might happen if one of those too-big-to-fail megas actually broke. But he hadn't seen that—not in his lifetime. They just changed names and got fatter eating the corpses of the parts that failed.

They came to a section of the docks that looked even more run down than the rest. Ahead was a checkpoint of a different sort. Several rough-looking trolls stood around, watching the minivan come toward them. EnJee thought, *If things go bad now, I'll be worse off then I was with the Uhuru Commandos–and I'll still be in a blimey minivan.*

"Stop the car," EnJee said.

A massive dark-skinned troll lurched toward their vehicle. His horns could've been antlers. EnJee pointed at him and said, "Now Jafari over there, well that's a bloody troll. You ought to stay here, Grimmy. I'll go take care of this."

Grim Fox clenched his fists and then unclenched them slowly, mouthing curses at EnJee as he left the vehicle. EnJee kept his hands in his pockets as he approached the three men. Keeping his eyes on the largest of the three, the one in the center, he said, "We good, Jafari?"

EnJee felt the troll's deep bass voice as much as he heard it. He spoke in a pidgin dialect that sounded Fanti, but the Humbers—Jafari and his people—were no pirates. "I talked with Black Mamba. She says you are safe. She also says you are an asshole."

"No laws against that down here, *neh*?" EnJee said with a quick grin. He stepped forward, extending his right hand to shake, a credstick palmed in his grip.

The troll met the gesture, enveloping EnJee's hand to the wrist in his meaty grip. He turned and handed the stick to one of his men behind him. EnJee watched the smaller troll (a subjective measurement at this point), hand it to another foot soldier behind him, who ran the credstick through a scanner. Finally, the scanner said, "We good here."

Jafari broke out into a grin. He said, "I got you a spot on a ship. They leaving in a little bit from here. We will see that you get to the boat safely."

EnJee raised his eyebrows. "Expecting trouble down here?"

"Humbers make the trouble." Jafari cocked his head to one side. "Who you taking so far up coast?"

"Just a guy."

"Anyone we might know?"

"He's not from here."

The other Humbers began to look bored with the exchange, gun barrels slipping low as they gazed around the dock. EnJee took it as a cue. He turned toward the minivan and gave the whirly bird signal.

Grim Fox climbed out of the car and went to the back to retrieve Enzo Moretti. The foot soldiers walked over to the minivan and started pulling out crates, lifting them onto their shoulders like they were carrying empty boxes.

He, Grim Fox, and Shen walked together behind them as they pushed Moretti down the dock. The corp man tried to make a sound through his gag but Shen smacked him in the back of the head, a blank expression on her face. He was quiet after that. Grim Fox also stayed quiet. He kept one hand near his weapon, the other resting on Moretti's shoulder, nudging him forward. They passed boat after boat this way, each smaller than the last until EnJee finally said, "Which one of these is ours, mate?"

"Just keep walking," said Jafari.

It occurred EnJee then how much of this business was built on trust. Trust came hard to people like Grim Fox. He had to trust EnJee's word on this. He had to trust that Jafari's men would accept payment and help him get to where he wanted to go. At any point along that chain of trust, things could break down, and the only repercussion was reputation. And sometimes, retaliation.

All along the dock, a half-dozen Maersk-Jorgenson Class fast freighters were being loaded by people dressed in street clothes, signaling these were perhaps all pirate vessels. EnJee looked closer, and saw some had Fanti graffiti stitched on the side.

The Fanti ruled the waters in this area, though the term *Fanti* collected a lot of different types under its umbrella. Fanti crews were clans or families ranging from as large as a thousand to as small as just two.

EnJee said, "Which one of these is our ride?"

Jafari laughed and said, "You ride special this time."

He pointed further down the dock where these larger boats gave way to smaller ones, and beyond those were perhaps a dozen trollers—fishing boats. Some flew flags of various African nations. The largest of these boats would fit a dozen people, half that if trolls or even orcs were aboard. Among this grouping of boats was the long red silhouette of an Evo Waterking. The boat was marked with Fanti graffiti and the front was painted to cover up corporate markings denoting the original owners. It was a shit paint job. As he looked closer, he could make out angular white sun rays of the horizon logo beneath the peeling red. Then again, maybe that was the point.

Jafari said, "This here is the *Scuttlebutt*."

The boat had to be 18 meters, if not more. EnJee could see three of the crew on deck, all Black women who looked enough like one another to be family. What caught EnJee's eye were their jumpsuits that bore Horizon corporate logos graffitied over with Fanti markings. He whistled low. "My kind of people."

The oldest of the three called down below to a fourth crew member, a boy with long dreadlocks. By the looks of him, he was barely into his teens. He shuffled to the gangplank, wiping his hands on a dirty rag. He stared up at Jafari and said, "This our cargo?"

Jafari nodded, chuckled, and then turned to walk away.

The boy addressed the crowd of runners standing at the edge of the dock and said, "This our ship. When we on the water, you follow our rules, and the first rule is you pay before you come onboard."

As he spoke, the three women looked on almost as though they were grading his performance. The one who looked to be the oldest called out to him in a dialect. EnJee couldn't understand. He grimaced and waved her off, like he was swatting at a fly. Then he said, "So you understand, nuyen ain't no good here."

EnJee pointed to the crates and said, "Ought to be worth something to you."

After examining the crates, the boy turned back toward the women and shot them a thumbs up. It felt to EnJee like handling the transaction was akin to a rite of passage for the boy.

"Say whatever goodbyes you need to right now," the boy continued. "Matrix coverage doesn't extend along the route we follow at sea. You'll be out of communication range a few days. You won't be talking to your loved ones until we make it to shore."

EnJee noted the pirate spoke in the same unusual pidgin Jafari did, and wondered how deep the relationship went between the Humbers and Fanti. He also wondered again how safe they was in this situation. He said, "We're good. I talked to Black Mamba before I left. I told her I'd reach out once we touched shore with our cargo."

The young pirate's grin was a mixture of false and gold teeth. He said, "That's very good. Smart too."

The three runners passed a look between them. Grim Fox's dark stare lingered on EnJee long after the moment was over.

NERO

11-15-2081
8:35 A.M. Local Time

Once upon a time, Nero dreamed of flying. He thought he'd leave Italy on a shiny jetliner and travel all over the world. Then life had stepped in and kicked him in the jaw.

But over the past few days, that dream quietly became his reality. First class might have well been a summer vacation in the Alps, as far from his reality as it once felt. Now he eased his chair back and swirled a curious concoction of crushed mint leaves, sugar cane, and a blood orange syrup with a champagne base.

Relaxing in his oversized seat, he slid on his AR glasses and tapped a few commands into his commlink. Dozens of links populated in his field of vision, results of the research EnJee had compiled before they split ways. Nero's hand hovered over a link, a connection to datastore containing Enzo's family history—*his* history. There would be pictures of his parents there, last known location, state of health, all the things he could have reached for in cyberspace and perhaps even in meatspace, had he been willing.

Now all of it flooded back into him along with the drunken buzz of fine alcohol, and he swiped angrily at the link, knocking out of his view. He pressed on another link and stumbled down the rabbit hole of Enzo's professional history.

Enzo Moretti's official designation read: *Portfolio Manager*. Nero knew enough to understand that the title was a catch-all, like *executive*. In this case, it meant Enzo was responsible for managing a large sum of money. He held a personal International Swaps and Derivatives Association agreement through Hildebrandt-Kleinfort-Bernal, which, if what Nero was reading was right, served as a kind of voucher that said Enzo could be trusted to make and to pay on investment deals in the billion-dollar range. That type of trust wasn't handed to every trader. In fact, it meant his brother must be very good at what he did. However, Nero still wasn't entirely clear on what exactly that *was*.

He understood that, like his father, Enzo bought and sold things. According to EnJee's research, Enzo had bought and sold enough things to be noticed and entrusted with multiple high-level sales and exchanges in addition to the massive fund he managed.

In short, Enzo was doing quite well for himself.

He kept a flat in London close enough to the office that he could take the Underground, but he owned two cars and a motorcycle. That brought a grimace to Nero's face. As kids, they'd always talked about owning motorcycles, but their mother was quick to set them straight whenever she heard such talk.

And there it was again, that painful twinge of familiarity and memory. Once upon a time Nero had been a boy named Emiliano. He had a mother, a father, a twin brother, and a sister on the way. Then he turned twelve. He took a test. And everything changed.

Nero shivered. The ever-attentive stewardess came over and offered to adjust the temperature. He turned down the offer and smiled politely. The way his skin prickled now had nothing to do with the cold.

He looked more closely at the data. It seemed that businesses borrowed money from banks to buy materials to make and move the products they sold, and to pay their employees—all the things necessary to stay afloat. Then, when consumers purchased and paid for goods, that profit would be sent to the banks first, with whatever remained going to company ownership as corporate or often personal gains.

Nero thought Enzo was the bank in this scenario. His job was to schmooze the corporations and convince them they should borrow money from Enzo's bank. So, twelve years later, his older brother by under ten minutes was still schmoozing people the way he had in primary school. This much Nero understood. Enzo had been a boisterous soul ever since he'd figured out how to speak. However, that couldn't be all of

Enzo's job. That middle-of-the-night call had nothing to do with lending money.

Nero needed more information. For once, he wanted to reach out to EnJee and have the man walk him through this, even through all the paranoid delusions that were sure to come with EnJee's thoughts about what it meant to be a corporate operator. But EnJee wasn't in range of the Matrix. Nero imagined EnJee must feel naked and helpless, much like how he would feel if he couldn't use his magic.

It struck him that there was some truth in that. Nero himself couldn't use magic right now, at least not in any meaningful or visible way, or he'd risk showing he wasn't Enzo. That made him feel alone in a way he hadn't felt since he found Shen and the others.

Shaking off the thought, Nero dove back into his research, but there was nothing that gave him a clear sense of what he was expected to do once he landed. This entire situation was off-script. He even tried searching available business info databases for "look under the hood," the term Arturo Olgin used, but found nothing beyond information about buying used cars.

An Aetherpedia search into Atilla Finance gave him a little more to work with. Over the past month, hundreds of investors had tried to pull their money out of the fund. Meanwhile, parts of Atilla were being chopped up and sold like a prize cow. Nero supposed "look under the hood" effectively meant take a closer look to figure out if they were selling a good product. He didn't know what a "good product" looked like, however. He suspected Novak would, so he'd get what data he could when he met with the Olive people, and share it with Novak so she could prep him on what to say when Enzo's boss arrived.

He pulled off his glasses, putting the research aside. He needed to get some sleep. After a second heady cocktail and ten more minutes of glancing around the near-empty plane, Nero gave up on sleep. The feeling of being in first class was still incredibly jarring; the idea of a life where this was the norm felt alien to him. Yet this alien world also comforted him somehow. It drew him in. It scared him that he could get used to this life. It made him feel dirty, and more than a little desperate for anything familiar. So he slipped his glasses back over his head and navigated to a familiar site.

The Church of Saint Conus was in session early this morning. The warmth of comfort filled his belly at the sight of *Padre* Luca. He wasn't Nero's favorite priest, but he always seemed to have timely sermons. *Padre* Luca was midway through his talk. His voice chimed melodically through the scripture.

"'*We are brought down to the dust. Our bodies cling helplessly to the earth. Lord, rise up. Rise and help us, oh lord. Rescue us because of your unfailing love.*'"

Psalm 44, Nero thought. He watched and he reflected, wondering on the purpose of the sermon, of why *Padre* Luca chose those words and that theme at this time. God spoke in mysterious ways. Was it so far-fetched that here and now he was speaking to Nero through the words of *Padre* Luca's sermon? And what was his message? He was not so arrogant to believe that God spoke to him alone. God spoke to the faithful. Nero remained faithful. He followed God's law before man's law. He lived by the code set before him by both the bible and the leaders of the faith. He did not kill unless doing so was the only way to save his own life or the life of those he loved. He fought to protect the innocent people of this world, even though he struggled to recognize there were still innocent people in this world.

If God were speaking through this sermon, what was he saying? Nero found himself wondering what *Padre* Luca would think about Nero pretending to be Enzo; betraying family for the purpose of making someone rich.

He frowned at that and set his drink down, losing the will to finish it. Perhaps Nero was the one who needed rescue. Not for the first time, he wished he could give confession and, in that confession, find some guidance on what it was he must do next.

NERO

11-15-2081
12:50 P.M. Local Time

From the moment Nero touched down at Jebel Ali Airport on Saturday afternoon, Dubai felt different than other places he'd lived or been. It felt different than Italy, different than Barcelona, or Amsterdam. Even the endless streets of Rhine-Ruhr did not have the feel of this place. Dubai felt *clean*. More than that, it felt like a city built from new corporate money and renewed each time a new corporate leader entered the space. Yet the city also felt very old, as though beneath the streets there were ancient tunnels carved out by a people who existed before the Persians walked the sands.

Nero stepped off the airplane and slung his carry-on over his shoulder. In spite of the luxury, he felt tired and overwhelmed. Everything was new to him. He barely exited the security gate when a suited driver waved him over, a sign in hand that read *Enzo Moretti*.

It took him a second to realize the driver was gesturing at him—that the sign was his name. The driver was a tawny-skinned man with a hard-set jaw and bright eyes. "My name is Deron, sir. I was told to deliver you to the offices of Olive Holdings."

Nero shook the man's hand and handed over his bag when he offered to take it. Deron continued, "The office is located in the Jumeirah commercial district. This is also where tourists such as yourself go for entertainment. We have everything here you could ask for. The district was designed with this in mind. It is where we host all the international conventions."

Enzo climbed into the back seat of the big Cadillac Nocturne, his pants sliding along the cooled leather seats. He felt the automatic doors lock him in. By the time the car accelerated away from the airport, Nero had given over to near-panic. He couldn't walk into a corporation and pretend he belonged there. He didn't belong.

Moreover, he didn't even know how to do what his brother did for a living. It would only take one unanswered question or misspoken phrase before everyone else knew too. Then what? Would he be arrested? Would he need to fight his way out? He started to sweat. His breathing grew erratic to the point where he started to wonder if he was going to hyperventilate. So, he shut his eyes and focused on his breathing.

Slowly, the panicky feeling faded. After a while, Nero opened his eyes and let the sights of Jumeirah commercial district overwhelm him.

According to the signage, the International Defense exhibition had just left. The echoes of past desert wars lived here in the advertisements, the dress, all the evidence of adopted culture lining the streets as if war were another sport to be bandied about like soccer. From the AR imagery to the storefront displays, everything that spoke of violence was being replaced by imagery representing the upcoming Zu al-Hijah and accompanying pilgrimage that those of the Muslim faith made to Mecca. He respected those of the Muslim faith. In particular, he respected how steadfast they were to their practices in the face of a modern society that made such adherance difficult. It felt similar to how he tried to remain true to his faith, despite living outside the law.

As they drove, he thought he could see evidence of the true city beneath the colorful signage. He got the sense that the Jumeriah district pretended to be something it wasn't for the sake of foreigners such as himself. Now he could practically feel the district shifting away from the unnatural war footing. He imagined the city and its people put on a mask each time one of these conventions came into town. And each time afterward, it slowly pulled itself back into the shape of a holy land the way a snake having devoured something nearly larger than itself pulls itself back into its natural shape. It comforted him to know that this city could pretend to be something it wasn't and then just as quickly return to what it actually was.

"What's the district like when the war machine isn't in town?" he asked.

"Not much different. There are no Sharia laws here. I can help you can get anything you want. Women, drugs, anything." When Nero visibly blanched, he added, "They understand you are not like us."

The commercial district was neatly separated from Dubai proper by the Sheik Zayed Toll Road. Nero's car left the road and looped further into Jumeirah, toward the shore and Mercato beach. Deron was giving him the full tour. Nero couldn't tell if it was by order of his employer, or just a thing drivers did to improve their tip.

Dubai continued to amaze. The skyline was awash with narrow, twisting skyscrapers, more resembling an artist's fantasy than the practical arcologies dominating places he'd been before. When he peered up, he saw some of the spires were connected by walkways hundreds of floors above the ground. He imagined what type of security existed in those passageways, magical or otherwise. He shuddered at the thought of performing an extraction in one of these behemoths.

Despite the breathing exercise, he couldn't shake off the growing fear. He couldn't stop checking corners, or turning around, or glancing in the side and rearview mirror for cars following him. Auto pursuit was rare, so long as you had enough drone coverage to work the trick, which is why it surprised him to see a silver Honda turn the same corners he did.

After the second turn, curiosity overcame him and he asked the driver to pull to the side of the road for a moment. The driver did. The other car slipped by them and Nero chalked the incident up to paranoia. EnJee had taught him that a little paranoia was a good thing. Of course, coming from EnJee, the suggestion itself was suspect.

"Were you looking for something specific?" Deron asked.

Nero shook his head. "No. Drive on."

Not every building was a skyscraper. Some stopped well below fifty stories, and those that did featured architectural designs that seemed closer to pottery or blown glass than anything else. One building resembled a giant golden picture frame in which a massive illusion swirled, shifting between depictions of what he assumed were Islam's sacred places.

Nero could barely process how much mana it required to sustain such an illusion. It was beyond what he could do alone.

He suspected ritual sorcery at play, but to what end? Was all this just for show? Was it a way to promote the power of the corporation who funded such an extravagance?

It wasn't until the car pulled to a stop in front of the Olive Holdings building that he realized he'd been expecting it to be a skyscraper. Olive Holdings' Dubai headquarters was actually three teardrop-shaped buildings encased in frosted glass. The lead building, slightly taller than the rest, stood out in front of the other two.

Deron came around to open his door. Nero climbed out of the car and stretched, using the gesture to check out the area around him. Pedestrians flooded the sidewalks. Cars raced back and forth across the streets as the sounds of the city greeted his ears. Nero froze when he thought he saw a glimpse of the silver Honda from earlier. It was parked a block away. When he looked again, it was driving off. Hondas were common, and silver cars even more common, but that small paranoid part of him, that mental whisper from EnJee said, *"Watch out."*

Deron offered to keep his bag for him, but Nero refused. He didn't know if Enzo would give his personal belongings to a random driver or not. Like so much of this, he was making it up as he went along. He walked up the short flight of steps to the front of the white glass building. The doors slid open automatically. Inside, Olive Holdings continued the postmodern experience that started outside. The glass he thought would be see through from the inside was in fact opaque. It felt like being inside of a giant egg. The lobby was white and glowed from recessed lighting. White sofas were arranged in patterns to form multiple sitting areas in front of a long white information kiosk.

But he didn't see a single person. Although it was Saturday, he did expect someone might be here to greet him. Even the information kiosk was vacant. After a moment, he put on his AR glasses and almost jumped out of his skin when he saw a man in a gray suit standing next to him.

"Mr. Moretti? Please follow me."

He slid off his glasses and the person disappeared. When he put them back on again the person was walking away. Nero followed the persona to an elevator toward the rear of the enormous lobby. They stopped on the 9th floor, still well below the upper tier of the building. Nero exited onto a floor bustling with activity. He was in a small lobby. To the right, a long window separated him from an open bullpen filled with a maze of desks. Each was manned by a suit jacked into their respective terminal. At first he thought the glass was soundproofed, but as he continued to stare, he realized that none of their mouths were moving. Everything these workers did was in silence.

The avatar cleared its throat, the sound coming in low and persistent through the audio uplink on his AR glasses. Nero looked over and the avatar was standing against the other side of the room, where a white-walled hallway led to a series of conference rooms. He followed the avatar down that hall, finally stopping at one of the larger conference rooms.

It was separated from the hallway by a clear glass partition, but as soon as Nero stepped through, the glass flickered and went completely opaque. The first thing he noticed in the room was the conference table, a long seamless sheet of wood that looked like it was carved out of a redwood tree, lacquered and artificially replanted in the center of this room. Behind the table, another expanse of glass showed the city below them. Three people sat at the conference table.

Nero found himself unconsciously pulling off his glasses to make sure they were really there. They were. He shakily announced himself as Enzo Moretti, and reached out to shake hands.

The first of the three to respond was a clean-shaven man in a suit that struggled to hide his middle-aged belly. "My name is Steven Adelson. My associates are Jennifer Chan and Matthew Frieling."

Chan was a slight woman with short-cropped black hair and dressed in a light gray pantsuit. She stood, shook his hand, and sat down again beside her boss. The other one, Frieling, couldn't have been older than sixteen. He didn't stand or shake Nero's hand, and it was only after Nero sat down that he realized Frieling shared an uncanny resemblance with the avatar who'd escorted him in.

Adelson said, "I know it's been a long flight, and an early one. We appreciate you coming in to see us ahead of the formal meeting."

"Yes, well, Mr. Olgin likes to make sure I peek under the hood with these things. You know, make sure everything is as it seems." Nero tried to paste a smile on his face. He could feel sweat prickling his hairline.

"I worked with Arturo about a dozen years ago on a merger," Adelson said. "He's always been the type who wants to get things done before the market opens, as if he can magically stretch the margin by having fresh news at the start of the week." He leaned back and clasped his hands together, relaxing into the comments as if he and Olgin were old friends. Perhaps they were. "Worse than that, he's a terrible golfer."

"Well, that explains why he keeps me around," Nero said, too quickly.

Adelson raised his eyebrows. "You play? What's your handicap?"

Nero could feel a thrill of nervous energy rush through him. "I dabble. Off the record? I let him win. A lot."

Adelson laughed. Chan smiled politely. Frieling didn't move. Adelson said, "Dubai has some of the finest courses I've seen anywhere. The rooftop experience at the Spinrad Global Arcology is unforgettable. What do you say to putting in a round after you look over the information on Atilla?"

Nero felt his throat go dry. He hoped the three people staring at him couldn't see the panic spreading across his face. He'd never even seen golf on the trideo. Finally he said, "You know, my boss might be a little upset if we left him out of the fun."

Adelson pointed at him. "You're right! As a matter of fact, Chan here has a decent game—better than Arturo's, at least. How about we shoot a greensome after settling up in the morning?"

Nero relaxed a little. "It would be a pleasure to check out the greens here. I warn you, though, I'm only contractually obligated to let Mr. Olgin win."

"I wouldn't expect anything less. Frieling will set it up."

Chan spoke next, "In terms of exploring the portfolio, Mr. Adelson tasked me with walking you through the files. Would you like to begin, or do you need a few minutes to get settled first?

Panic rose like acid in his throat and he coughed once, hard, fighting down the fear. He said, "Excuse me!" Then, sensing an opportunity, Nero pressed, "If you don't mind too much, I would prefer to examine the data in the privacy of my own hotel room. As you say, it was a long flight and followed a night out with clients."

Adelson's answering smile felt genuine. "Of course. Frieling here will put together everything you need and beam it to your PAN."

The Cadillac was waiting for him out front with instructions to take him to his hotel. By the time he got in, his armpits were damp with sweat. At the hotel, Nero fired up his commlink and tried to check in with his team, to no avail. He fired off messages to each of them about where he was and what he was doing.

Nero briefly considered traversing the astral plane. He could theoretically leave his physical shell behind here on this bed and soar across the planet toward Africa until he found his team. He knew he could find them, even out in the middle of the ocean. Shen was holding on to his spell focus. He was connected to it. The focus was bonded to him, and that offered him a way to reach out to the team beyond the physical.

The question, however, was time. He'd never reached out more than a few miles away from his body in astral form. He had no idea how long a traversal to Africa would take. He wasn't even sure it was possible to travel that far afield from his physical form, not to mention the things that existed in astral space along the way. He knew from experience that not all of them were friendly. No, he needed to stay focused on maintaining his cover. That meant linking up with Novak. He desperately needed to her help to make sense of the data Enzo was supposed to be perfectly capable of figuring out.

After a quick shower, he dressed and headed downstairs. Deron was still waiting for him, and drove him to his next meeting. Nero briefly considered getting out of the hired car a few blocks down the road and then catching a local cab to the tea shop where he was supposed to meet Novak. It would make for better spycraft, but he wasn't trying to be Nero. He was trying to be Enzo, and the Enzo he read about in the file would take advantage of having a personal driver.

Shai Al Hatab wasn't very far from his hotel. It sat just beyond the high-end side of the district in the space where the locals gathered. Nero knew this by the change in scenery, an invisible line marked by tourists in haute couture on one side and a growing mix of locals on the other. Even so, this wasn't the slums of Dubai. Far from it, in fact. This section of town felt like where tourists went to feel like they were mixing with the locals. It was what De Wallen in Amsterdam and the Reeperbahn in Rhine-Ruhr used to be. The matte-black Cadillac slowed as it moved through the evenly spaced blocks of prefab tenements and the parlors and malls that sprouted up between them.

Deron said, "This is a fine tea house, but this part of town is not known solely for traditional beverages. Are you sure tea is all you want?"

He began to wonder if Deron didn't have a second job putting his passengers in contact with less-than-legal services. A sort of fixer. Nero smiled at the thought and wondered what the driver must think of him. To everyone here, he was nothing more than another wage slave, a piece of the machine that fueled the public economy. He said, "I'll be fine here on my own. I won't need a ride back to the hotel." Then he thanked him, making sure to transfer a large tip from Enzo's credstick.

Katerina Novak was sitting near the back of the tea shop. She wore a bright yellow sundress that showed off her long legs. She smiled and waved. She'd chosen a spot with good sight lines to the front door and to both sides of the street, thanks to the large window separating the patio in the front of the shop from the darker interior space.

Shai Al Hatab was busy enough that there was only one other open table. He'd done a cursory Matrix search on the way over, and found it on the list of places to visit while in the district. It struck him as odd that she'd choose such a public venue.

Nero looked around the space before settling into a seat across from her. As soon as he did, a server arrived. The server wore wide-saddled pants that looked like a well-designed costume. The look was completed by round hat with a black tassel hanging over one side. He held a tray with two glass cups of tea. He smiled and set a cup before each of them. "This is *maramia*, a local mixture unlike anything else in the world."

Novak gestured toward Nero's cup as she lifted her own to her lips. She sipped slowly, drinking in the ambiance of the place as much as the tea.

He said, "I don't think you're taking this situation nearly as seriously as you should be."

Novak sipped slowly, then softly replied, "I flew all the way from London to meet you. Is that not serious enough?"

"I need your help analyzing this data and figuring out what I'm supposed to say about it," Nero said, and slid a datastick toward her.

"How was your meeting?"

"Fine," he lied.

"I expected it would be. You're a natural at this. You know, you and I are quite similar, Emiliano. In truth, your abilities would've provided you an edge most of us in the financial industry only dream of."

Nero said, "Don't call me that."

"Of course. We should remain in character. So many watching eyes. I'll call you Enzo."

"Nero."

She sighed, but otherwise remained silent.

He sipped the tea. It tasted of mint and flowers. He sipped again. Finally, he said, "How am I supposed to go back into that company tomorrow and pretend to know how to talk about all of this financial information?"

She sipped her tea again before responding. "I know you read the files, but do you actually understand what it is your brother does? What I do?"

He shook his head.

"He—*you*." She paused, correcting herself. "*You're* a financial consultant—a banker. You deal in algorithms. You read the data, and buy and sell things at the right time in order to make money."

"Right. It's the same thing my father did."

"Did you ever watch him work? Go into the office and do his own particular form of magic?"

"A few times."

"What did you see?"

He wasn't enjoying the way this conversation was going. "I don't see the point in any of this. I'm not interested in reliving old memories—especially not with you."

She sighed. "I'm here to help you. I'm trying to explain how it all works."

"Then tell me what I'm supposed to tell my boss about the Atilla thing tomorrow."

When she smiled this time, it felt smug.

"What?" he pressed, frustrated.

She said, "You called him your boss. That's good. You're falling into it."

Nero opened his mouth to respond, but found he had nothing to say.

"Don't worry," Novak added. "I won't tell your friends you're enjoying this."

He started to stand, but she placed a hand over his and said, "I'm just having a little fun. Please sit down. Don't make a scene."

When he lowered himself back into his chair, she continued, "Okay. The business we do is largely about making things look pretty when they aren't. You talk up selling one stock, you talk up buying in on another to make that market look good. All of this comes together like a complex dance, or an algorithm. Most of the time we are not actually buying or selling anything. We are creating the conditions for things to be bought or sold at a price that's most beneficial to us. It is our version of magic to make money out of all of it."

Nero shook his head. "That doesn't tell me what I'm actually doing tomorrow. It doesn't tell me how to be him in there or to be him in London to close whatever deal you expect me to do then, does it?"

"When you get to London, your job is to make sure I close exactly the way I scripted. That's it." She wiped her hands together in a figurative gesture of cleaning.

"I get it," said Nero. "I don't get paid to be nosy. I also don't get paid to get caught, so I need to know how to get through this day in your world. I need you to tell me exactly what to say and do tomorrow."

So she did. For the next hour, they sipped cups of tea as she ran the data through a series of computer programs on her commlink and explained the ins and outs of corporate deals such as these. It was a crash course, nothing that would fetch him a degree or even work outside the parameters of what Enzo specifically was required to do in this particular instance. There were times during the conversation when her UCAS accent fell away—a failing of software perhaps? It revealed another piece of the person underneath.

From time to time he looked away, casually glancing around the shop or out the window the way EnJee taught him. It wasn't long before he recognized the surveillance team watching him. The men were discreet and professional, but he read the tells. Through the plexiglass windows of the tea shop he spotted one across the road, posted in the silver Honda from earlier. That is how Nero knew it was a surveillance detail and not her security team. The Honda had been following him before he met up with her. A third member of the detail sat alone in the busy shop, close enough to them that he could provide security support if needed as he sipped at cup after cup of tea and pretended to play in the augmented reality all around them.

If Novak noticed him spot her surveillance detail, she pretended not to. She kept her focus on the task. She told Nero exactly how much to tell Olgin the deal was worth. Then she explained that Nero's role in the room was largely to be quiet and, when asked, to refer to a series a datapoints that she highlighted and keyworded on his datastick. When her instruction was done, Nero felt it might be enough to get him through the meeting without being hauled away by the police.

He finished his tea, and then brought up a final point. "You say Enzo does the math. He does work, the algorithms to figure out when to buy and sell, but that's all stuff that a computer can do, and *is* doing in this instance. That doesn't explain why he's important or what I'm supposed to do if a question comes up that you haven't keyworded for me."

"What Enzo does, and ultimately what your father did, is to convince people to trust him with their money. Not a thousand nuyen or even ten thousand. We are talking about millions here. Billions. They *need* to trust you. They need to see you are capable of taking their money and turning it into more money instead of losing any of it. They need to know that you're willing to do anything to make that happen and that whatever you do, it won't touch them. Ever."

She set her hand on top of his again and smiled.

He pulled his hand away. He met her eyes, and she looked away demurely, all part of her game. In that moment, she didn't notice him glance at each of the three men still watching them.

"Let me try to explain this in another way," said Novak. "Do you know what a short is?"

"I've heard the term. Something about buying and selling objects and manipulating the price, right?"

"To an extent. It's about knowing value. You see, you sell your position, your investment, knowing the price of the object will drop. Then, when it does drop, you buy it back. So, you still own the thing, but you made money on it, or you own more of it than you did before because you took what you sold it for and bought even more at that lower price. The good ones, the gamblers, wait until the price falls low enough that the property—company, commodity, et cetera—makes you the most money without ultimately destroying the value of it."

"Tricky."

"That is why trust is important."

"So, I'm supposed to get the Olive people to trust me?"

She laid her hand back over his and said, "You're supposed to get them to trust *him*."

He understood then that Katerina Novak did not trust him, and she'd come here with the intention of protecting both her anonymity and her investment—and if necessary, terminating that investment, and him along with it.

He rose without shaking her hand. "In that case, I better get back to it."

She smiled flatly. "We'll do this again in London, as planned."

Nero left then, making his way to the curb where he stopped, considering his next move. He suspected Novak's people were there to make sure he did what he was supposed to in Dubai, and wouldn't do anything that could blow his cover and ruin the job. He'd already dismissed Deron, so he should catch a cab and head back to his hotel; let Novak's surveillance detail see him playing the role she paid him to play. On the other hand, he could blow off the run entirely. He could head off the grid, take a cab to the edge of the city and seek out the Bedouins. Perhaps through that ancient network of smugglers, he could find a way out of the city, out of this nightmare of a run, and back home.

He hailed a taxi. Moments after he loaded into the cab, the surveillance detail got into the silver Honda and followed after him. He told the driver to head to the hotel. When he stopped and got out at the hotel, they discretely slowed and pulled off the road, just at the edge of his vision where they thought he couldn't see him.

Where they could wait to see where Nero would go next.

NERO

11-16-2081
7:50 A.M. Local Time

Sunday morning brought with it the perks and fears of another day of pretending to be Enzo Moretti. Nero ordered room service on the company tab. When it came, he opened the door in his robe. He let them wheel in the cart, pausing ever so briefly to consider his own hedonism. He'd ordered one of everything, and even some things from the lunch menu. Now his eyes fell upon fresh-squeezed orange juice, which he hadn't had since he was a kid. He lifted the glass to his lips and sipped.

Still sweet.

Some of the things the wealthy and the SINned enjoyed were made special only by their ability to have it. Caviar was not by any means useful or tasteful, but it was special. It tasted buttery and somewhat salty, with a texture that reminded him of the synth-boba they made at Luvie's in Lower Amsterdam. He hadn't ordered it because he thought it would be good. The having it is what made it special. The having it when others could not. This is what being born into the system was: having access where others did not.

He missed Shen. She was on a boat speeding across the Atlantic Ocean on her way to Lagos where EnJee had arranged for a no-questions-asked flight to take them and Enzo the rest of the way to London.

For the first time since this all began, Nero wished he could talk to Enzo. He'd spent half his life burying the anger he held for his brother, and now he stood in his brother's shoes, forced to make the choices his brother would make, and it reminded him that his brother still existed.

He wanted to believe Enzo was in this for more than profit. The files showed a brash and carefree soul not terribly different from the boys they'd once been. Only where they used to skip stones and trade barbs over video games, Enzo traded the lives of people and fates of corporations in multi-billion-dollar deals. He ran in the light, following the schema of the corporate system, using algorithms like *telesma* to conjure wealth. This is what wealth bought. But was this all Enzo had become?

Nero could not shake a strange feeling from his meeting with Novak. Before he'd gone to sleep, he'd checked the windows, searching for the silver Honda that had tailed him all day. It was gone, but the feeling remained. He went to sleep thinking about that sense of wrongness, chalking it up to the fact that he was being watched. When he woke, he found that feeling was still there but the reason behind it had shifted subtly, like ice in a tumbler.

It wasn't being followed that disturbed him. That sort of behavior felt familiar, even served as a comforting reminder that the world he came from and the world he presently occupied weren't too far apart. No, it was something Novak said in their meeting yesterday that bugged him.

Nero made it a point to always consider the cost to ordinary lives in what he did. He could not run the shadows as a man of faith without being mindful of the consequences of his actions. In church the *padres* instructed him in the doctrine of double effect. They taught him to understand that causing harm can be permissible in the eyes of God, so long as it was a side effect of bringing forth a greater good to the world. This was different than directly causing harm to bring about good. The difference was intention.

If Nero encountered a security guard in the course of a run, he made every effort to harmlessly incapacitate the officer. If violence escalated to a lethal response, it was the result of the choice that guard made. As the *padres* explained it, killing is only justified in self-defense, and only then as a last resort. On the rare occasion that Nero took a life, he would mourn the loss and take confession for his actions. However, he'd always been able to live with the lives he'd taken and the terrible things he'd done because of intention.

When Novak explained what Enzo did for a living, and what Nero would be expected to do in the office today, she spoke about it in terms of killing a corporation. The keyworded information on his datastick explained how much the company in question, Atilla Finance, was worth. She said that Enzo's company wanted to buy Atilla in order to break the company apart and sell it off in bits and pieces in order to make more money for themselves.

What he was doing in Enzo's name was helping to tear apart a corporation. Atilla Finance still impacted thousands of people. If what Nero understood was right, how he brokered this deal had lasting repercussions on the wealth and retirement of all of those people. Not one of them had a choice in what happened to their money. If he did what he was supposed to, most of them would lose their savings, and Lewis-Klein would get that much larger. This wasn't physical harm so much as moral harm, but the same rules of faith must apply.

Nero never considered himself a hooder—the type of runner who does work because it contributes to the greater good and perhaps even the greater freedom of the world. He understood the self-serving nature of his work, and of the work of corporations. Even the corps like Shiawase, who prided themselves on doing good, were ultimately about profit first. What harm they caused was not a side effect. In truth, the good they brought about was the side effect.

To pretend to be Enzo meant willfully engaging in a transaction that would negatively impact thousands of lives. That went against everything he stood for. He wanted to believe that the Enzo he once knew would not let it happen— that he would find a way to turn a profit that wasn't zero-sum.

He shook off the thought, swallowing the caviar down with the last of the sweet orange juice. Pulp remained in the glass, a reminder of the thing it had once been.

He unzipped his brother's carry-on bag. He hesitated, knowing once he unraveled the neatly folded suits, he would not be able to fit any of them back in the bag. He hadn't even tried with the one he'd worn after they grabbed Enzo. He'd left it there, replacing it with the freshly pressed one his brother left in the closet. They'd need to be pressed when he reached London.

Unwrapping the first suit felt like unfolding origami. The pants were folded around the jacket, which was shaped into a weirdly compressed design. Beneath it were two more suits in the same style, and beneath that, several shirts sat on a bed of neckties.

He wished for Grim Fox, then. He'd have more of a sense of proper fashion than Nero did. Nero never took to fashion, preferring layers of black or grey. Here he faced the daunting task of matching a brown suit with a shirt and a tie.

He picked out one he thought might work, a white shirt with thin gray vertical stripes. He found a solid gray tie and added it to the ensemble. At least he knew how to tie it. There'd been a few jobs, security work mostly, where they'd needed to put on better threads than he was used to. That experience served him well now.

When he was finally dressed, he stood in the mirror and sighed. Enzo and Nero had been born identical twins. The years had pushed them further and further apart, but it was nothing a haircut and shave couldn't fix on the surface. The eyes, however. He wondered if the people who knew him, people like the man he was going to see today, would know the difference. He took another deep breath and let it out slowly.

When he was done, he felt ready to take on the day. He called down for a car and by the time he exited the elevator, Deron was waiting for him at the front entrance. Nero, now Enzo once again, settled back into the seat and waited to be delivered to the Olive Holdings complex.

The Cadillac rolled quietly through the streets of Dubai, its insulated compartment shielding Nero from the noise of the thriving city. Deron was quieter today, probably understanding how to be tipped after yesterday.

For his part, Nero tried not to be nervous. He tried to remind himself this was no different than any other run, but on any other run, he'd have support. He'd tried to talk Novak into linking to the meeting through an earpiece, but she'd told him Olive Holdings constantly monitored all communication in and out of the office. They'd know he was talking with her and that would blow his cover.

When he pulled up to the entrance, he saw an identical Cadillac parked in front of him. As soon as he climbed out his car, the passenger in the other car did the same. He didn't need to review his files to know who it was. Arturo Olgin carried himself with a majesty reserved for royalty or upper management. He was a form of the latter.

"You're early for once." Again, that petulant voice that sounded like the class bully whom nobody ever stood up to, so he grew up believing no one ever would.

Nero offered a nervous smile. He reflexively reached for his cross, but it wasn't there. His heart beat a little faster.

"Give me the quick rundown before we go in," Olgin said.

Nero did. "This sale is a wet dream. At the asking price, we're in position to profit on almost every area of the Atilla portfolio." He continued, repeating the financial specifics Novak had given him yesterday. While he spoke, he tried to maintain eye contact, but he kept looking toward the teardrop-shaped buildings and back toward the street, wondering how safe it was to hold this conversation while they were so exposed. As he looked toward the street for a third time, he thought he spotted a silver Honda rounding the corner.

"Something on your mind, Moretti?"

Nero snapped out of his reverie, fumbling for an answer. He said, "No!" Then added, "Actually, yes. Yes, sir. Given our profit position, I was just wondering, in light of circumstance, don't we have a moral responsibility to figure out a way to help save the people associated with the company?"

Olgin raised an eyebrow and Nero swore he saw the man's cybereyes focus and unfocus in a way that made him shudder. He said, "What is going on with you today? Our first responsibility is a fiduciary one—to our leadership and our shareholders. Now get your head out of your ass and let's get this done."

"Y-yes, sir," Nero stammered, and followed him into the building. Frieling's strangely alien avatar didn't lead them to the same conference room as before, or even to the same floor. The elevator stopped on twenty-three this time, much closer to the curving pointed top of the teardrop.

The dozen or so people who were present moved about in a distracted fashion. There was a strangeness about the people of Olive Holdings Nero couldn't quite place. He thought to reach out into the astral and check his other sight, but he was afraid he'd be noticed spacing off. It was a rabid and foolish fear. They couldn't see him use his astral perception. But he'd heard stories that some corps placed spies in a room to detect the use of magic in meetings such as these, and that made it risky. Enzo Moretti could not use magic, so neither could Nero.

They arrived at a conference room larger than before. It was still white. It still felt cold and alien. The center of the space was dominated by a long and narrow table. Steven Adelson sat at the head of it. The only piece of artwork in the room, a depiction of a meadowed landscape, green and idyllic, hung above his head. On the side of the table closest to the window, a man stood and made his way toward Nero and Olgin. A smile beamed from his face.

Adelson said, "Arturo Olgin, Enzo Moretti, this is Bill Shipley from Chalmers and Cole."

"Oh no need for that, Steve. Enzo and I met a few years back. Madrid, wasn't it? The Stratyx buyout?"

Nero's heart stopped beating as he stared at the man, then he smiled and stammered, "Oh-oh, yes! Bill, of course—I didn't recognize you for a minute there!"

Bill laughed and clapped him on the back twice, but his smile stopped well short of his eyes.

Olgin spoke up. "So, this is an open bid after all, then?"

Adelson replied, "No, not at all. Mr. Shipley is just here to be part of the conversation."

"How's this for a conversation starter?" Olgin's voice had a poisonous edge to it. "Chalmers and Cole is far too busy cleaning up the mess Spinrad left behind to entangle themselves in yet another corporate dissolution."

"Hey, we're all friends here, Mr. Olgin." Shipley frowned and spread his arms. "I'm just trying to track the progress of some key funds we've earmarked for investment."

Olgin glanced at Nero, but Nero didn't know what to say. This wasn't in Novak's notes. After a moment Olgin said, "Am I here to do business with Shipley, or am I here to do business with Olive Holdings?"

"You and I are doing business, Mr. Olgin. And afterward, we're still on for that round of golf, aren't we, Mr. Moretti? Unfortunately, Ms. Chan had a family matter come up. Since Mr. Shipley was nearby, I asked him if he could join our match."

Olgin didn't have the charismasofts Novak employed, so when he smiled, it was clearly coming from a place of surprise and confusion. He looked again to Nero, who said, "Business first. We can talk about golf later."

The meeting went quickly after that. Nero only offered his voice in the few instances that aligned with Novak's briefing. Even then, he only served to echo his boss's sentiments. With

Shipley in the room, Arturo Olgin appeared to want to take control of the situation. Nero was more than willing to let him. It felt almost lucky, but Bill Shipley was a red flag. He didn't know what sort of history these two men shared or what had gone on the last time they'd met. He would need to deal with that later, especially if they were meant to play golf.

Finally Adelson rose to his feet and said, "Gentlemen, I think we have a deal."

Olgin stood and shook each man's hand in turn. Nero did the same. He couldn't be sure, but it felt like Shipley's presence had raised the asking price of the deal. He wanted to ask Olgin about it, but he couldn't be sure whether the answer was something Enzo should already know, so instead he said nothing.

In the hallway, Arturo Olgin turned to him and whispered, "You set up a game of golf?"

He nodded, unsure how much to say in the space. Olgin said nothing further on the matter. They both rode the elevator in silence. Outside, their respective cars waited on the street. Nero started toward his, trying casually to search out Novak's detail in the silver Honda. Olgin stopped him by putting a hand on his shoulder. "You ride with me."

He followed. Deron came around the car to open the door for them. Their driver started to say something, but snapped his mouth shut when he caught the expression on Olgin's face. Olgin slid in first and Nero followed.

The door had barely shut when Olgin snapped, "Your handicap is *seventeen*! Are you trying to make us look bad?"

Nero blinked at the sudden rage. "No...I just—thought it might create some goodwill."

Olgin glared at him. "You're off today. Way fragging off. I don't know what you did down in Africa, and frankly I don't want to know. Just get your drek together. Get it together fast, before you really frag something up."

Olgin's driver climbed behind the wheel and started driving. He didn't ask where they were going, just drove off down the road.

"Shipley had no business being in that meeting," Olgin grumbled. "When I spoke to Adelson about this, he told me we had first crack at that deal. Was Shipley there when you came in yesterday morning?"

"No."

"And him adding that man to our golf game? There's more going on here, to be sure."

"I agree, sir." Nero stole a glance at the street. He didn't see the Honda anywhere.

But as they moved through an intersection, he saw a white truck in the cross-street speeding past other cars and through the red light—straight at them.

Nero shouted, "*Look out!*" as he curled himself into ball between the seats.

The truck slammed into them; the Cadillac lurched violently. Tires squealed as the wheels briefly lost contact with the road and then found it again. The car spun and then stopped with a hard jolt that slammed his head against the door again. The impact crushed Nero into the side door, his head crashing against the window with a sound like a gunshot. Something gave in his shoulder and his arm went numb.

His mind went blank.

He lifted his head, pulling his hands away from the protective crouch he'd fallen into. Everything around him felt hazy. He tried to focus, but his head rang and his vision splintered through his broken AR glasses. Nero found his voice before he found his vision, and quickly said, "Mr. Olgin?"

His boss hadn't been strapped in, either. Now he was splayed out over the seat divider. One arm flopped back toward Nero while the other seemed to reach toward the dashboard. That arm jerked and spasmed. So he was alive at least.

The driver hadn't been as fortunate. The door was collapsed in on his body. His head flopped lifelessly over the wheel where the airbag had first deployed, and then deflated.

The white truck peeled itself free of their Cadillac before Nero heard its massive engine roar. For a moment he thought the truck might ram them a second time. He heard doors opening and the sound of footsteps. Nero tried to make himself smaller, using the seats and bodies as cover. The first man he saw wore a balaclava. He said something in a language Nero couldn't understand and pointed around the side of the car. That was when Nero saw the second man, who moved where the first had pointed, out of Nero's line of sight. He couldn't let them get behind him. He had to keep them in view if he had was going to survive.

He pushed at his door, finding it locked. In the distance he heard sirens, and Nero knew these men would be moving faster now. He jabbed at the autolock mechanism and pushed again, and then a third time before the door finally creaked open.

His head was pounding now. He staggered out of the vehicle, trying to find his legs as if he'd been at sea too long. He put his hands on the Cadillac's crumpled hood to steady himself.

Around him, the street was chaos. The truck idled in the middle of the road. Traffic around it backed away or attempted to race by. People were running down the sidewalks, trying to get away. Others stood on the fringe, watching. In the middle of it all, two more men were approaching him in matching balaclavas. They all carried submachine guns and moved with the practiced efficiency of a paramilitary team. One shouted to the others in what sounded like Russian and pointed at Nero.

All four raised their weapons.

Still dazed, Nero reached out with his magic, struggling to draw on his connection with the manasphere, forming a mental image of a bubble, a divide between the manasphere and physical reality. The four men drawing down on him did not see what was happening. They might have felt a tingle at first, or a shimmer in the air, but mana did not manifest naturally or visibly on the physical plane. They continued to shout at him, coming around the car. One tried to open the door to get to Olgin.

He concentrated, growing that sphere until it was large enough to encompass all four of the armed men around him. He let his strength, his mana, pour into that bubble.

Nero popped the bubble, his manablast unleashed. All of the pent-up energy flowed into the meatspace where they stood. All four men seized and crumpled to the ground, puppets with their strings cut.

The police were close enough now that Nero could see the flashing lights. He wanted to run, but he was too dizzy. He felt his legs give out beneath him and he slumped to the ground. He thought of Shen, still at sea with the others. He wouldn't make it back to her now. He would break that promise.

NERO

11-16-2081
9:28 A.M. Local Time

The paramedic hovering over Nero pressed a small brick of a device against the inside of Nero's wrist and a second against the side of his head. Nero fought the urge to squirm away from him.

They were in the back of an ambulance, hurtling toward the nearest medical facility. From the snatches of conversation taking place around him, he understood he had a police escort and that a second ambulance was ahead of him, holding his—Enzo's—boss, Arturo Olgin.

Nero tried to tell them he was okay, but it was clear the medical technician trusted his equipment more than he did the near-coherent babbles of a corporate suit who must obviously be in shock. Except he wasn't in shock. He was groggy from casting a spell with what had to be a concussion. Nero settled back on the gurney and tried to look around the too-bright interior of the ambulance. The medic pressed a hand against his chest and said, "Don't move your neck. You could have sustained an injury."

"I'm fine." Nero mumbled.

The medic said, "What's your blood type?"

Nero told him and then immediately regretted it. He thought he and Enzo had the same blood type, but he didn't really know for sure. There were differences between them. A medical doctor could look though the records and know immediately. That couldn't be allowed to happen.

Nero tried to sit up. "I'm fine. Seriously."

The medic shook his head and eased him back down unto the gurney. "We won't know for sure until we get a full work-up on you, sir."

"No. That isn't going to happen!" He slapped the medic's hands away and sat up again, trying desperately to think of a reason why he shouldn't be checked out.

"Sir, you are likely in shock and may damage yourself further. Please lay back down."

He fought the impulse to fire off a stunbolt. From there, he might be able to subdue the driver or at least jump from the back of the ambulance when it slowed to round a corner. But what then? He needed to stop thinking like a shadowrunner. A career business operator thought differently than a career shadow operator, so he tried, "What you are going to do is get me to my boss so I can make sure he is okay. If you can't do that, then you can tell the judge why not when we sue your ass and your entire corporation."

That did the trick. The medic threw his hands up. "Look, if you want to sign off that you refused treatment en route, that's your business. We will deliver you to the hospital as-is."

Nero nodded, calming as he did. Then he verbally assented to the refusal of treatment. There were forms the medic wanted him to fill out, but he claimed distress over the uncertain condition of his employer and agreed to fill out the forms later.

There would not be a later. He planned to slip away the moment the CrashCart wagon slid into the hospital bay. A few moments later, the wagon arrived—but a small group of police officers were waiting to escort Nero from the vehicle. Quickly, he shut down Enzo's commlink and slipped the battery into a different pocket. He didn't want to risk police hackers digging through the files and raising any questions about his search history, or going back through the logs to see if they could reconstruct any part of the attack from his commlink.

Nero tensed, stepping down from the CrashCart wagon into the waiting arms of the officers. He was a wreck in his torn suit, and sweating heavily now, but kept his mouth shut.

One of the officers was dressed in plainclothes. The other three wore their uniforms and fell quietly behind the first. The plainclothes officer said, "Mr. Moretti, I am Detective Bilal, Sphinx Security. We hold jurisdiction here in Jumeirah. My apologies for what has transpired here under our watch."

Detective Bilal was a squat, light-skinned man. He had a graying beard and sharp eyes so black they had to be cameras. Nero met those eyes with a mixture of suspicion and confusion, struggling to think of corporate security as anything other than the enemy. Sphinx Security in particular survived in the margin between corporate and Sharia practice, just Muslim enough to be accepted by the caliphate but commercial enough to operate in intercorporate zones such as these without triggering suspicions of corporate or religious fealty.

The detective said, "With apologies, we need you to answer some questions for us about the incident."

Nero stuck to his script. "Tell me where my employer is first, and then I will answer your questions."

"He's being moved to a surgery. His injuries are extensive. It will be some time before you will be able to see him."

Nero's mind filled in the unspoken *If you see him at all again*. Had this happened in the shadows, there was no way Olgin would've survived.

Detective Bilal was still speaking. "Would you be willing to come down to the station to answer our questions?"

Nero's heart skipped a beat. "No. I want to stay here with him."

The detective nodded. "Very well. We can arrange a more private space here where you and I can cover the details of the incident. I would appreciate your cooperation in this matter. We would like to resolve this and locate any additional persons responsible as soon as possible."

Nero translated the corpspeak for what it was: they wanted to clean this up, sweep it under the rug before word got out that a high-level extraction attempt had taken place on their streets, and they couldn't do a thing about it.

They had turned a private lounge into a staging area for the investigation. By the time they led Nero in, all the chairs and tables had been pushed to the walls to make a clear space in the center. A dozen security officers milled about that space now. A trio of officers were seated in one corner of the room, jacked into terminals and waving their hands in the air, interacting with AR objects. A few others stood by the coffee machine on the side wall. Nero walked toward the far wall, where space had been made for seating.

His shoulder hurt so bad he worried he'd broken his collarbone. He wanted to reach for his magic, but casting was dangerous here; there could be a mage in the security detail, and that would mess everything up. He quickly peeked into the astral, examining the people in the room so he'd know if he needed to mask his aura—a trick he learned from the church.

He found no mages, so he felt a little more comfortable trying the spell. Now it was doing the hard work of knitting his broken body back together. He only wished that when he'd learned this spell, there'd been a way to do it without the accompanying pain. Sweat prickled his skin and he felt himself blanching.

It unnerved him to be around this much security. People were staring at him now. He walked faster. The urge to run was overwhelming. He forced himself to move deeper into the room, the way he thought a suit might, the way he thought Enzo might try to seize control of the situation. Desperate, Nero raised his voice, playing into the role. "How could you people let this happen?!"

Everyone fell silent.

Detective Bilal caught up to him and said, "Sir, we have reason to believe the incident was planned well in advance of your meeting this morning. By all accounts, this was an attempted extraction of your principal—Mr. Olgin, I mean."

When Nero slumped in the closest chair, he was not acting. He was exhausted. It felt good to hear his suspicions confirmed. Their initial research on Enzo hadn't come up with any known enemies. On the other hand, extractions happened all the time. It could be a simple coincidence that he had wound up in the middle of a play for Olgin. Bilal nodded to him then moved away to take a call.

Nero struggled to find his calm, glancing backward at the three police hackers as he waited for the detective to resume his questioning. He desperately wanted to reach for his magic. He fought his hand down and away from his neck. He wanted to run, to find his way out of this space and into the desert where he would seize upon those Bedouin traders, work his way back toward the NEEC on the trade routes. It could work. He could ask to use the bathroom and then trigger his invisibility spell. No one would ever see him leave.

When the detective finished his call, he walked over to Nero and pulled up a chair. He said, "Mr. Moretti, do you remember anything else about the people who attacked you?"

Nero blinked twice, sighed, trying to fall back into the uncomfortable skin of a corporate operator. "All I remember are gunshots and people in masks reaching for me. It all happened so fast."

"Yes, of course." The detective tried to affect an expression of sympathy, but he was anything but sympathetic. "What I meant was, can you walk us through what happened to the four suspects?"

"Did they get away?"

"No. All four were found dead at the scene."

It wasn't hard to feign surprise in his state. The emotion was close enough to the genuine panic he felt that when he spoke, even he felt it was genuine. "How?"

"We are not sure. It's far too early to speculate. There is a forensics team on sight, so we'll know more in time." He scratched his head and added, "Did you see anyone else at the scene or notice anyone doing anything unusual? Making unfamiliar gestures with their hands or muttering perhaps?"

"No. I don't remember anything like that."

"What can you tell us about your driver?"

"Nothing, I didn't know Mr. Olgin's driver."

Detective Bilal nodded. "What about today? Where were you and Mr. Olgin headed when you were intercepted?"

"We were going to play golf."

"Was that the route you had planned to take, or did you have to take any detours?"

Nero frowned and said, "This is a lot at process. May I use the bathroom?"

"Sure. I think I'm done with my questions for now anyway. I'll make sure one of these officers stays at your side. You'll be safe here, sir." Detective Bilal stood, then stopped. He touched his chin thoughtfully and said, "Officers at the scene said they found you outside of the car on your knees. What were you doing there?"

Hurriedly, Nero said, "I need to contact my office to let them know what's happened."

"Your office has already been contacted. They are sending an official liaison along with a security team to bring you home safely."

"Thank you," Nero said. As that sheen of sweat prickled his skin again, he felt anything but thankful.

NERO

11-16-2081
1:11 P.M. Local Time

Nero sat in the sectioned-off lounge the local authorities had converted into a staging area, pretending to sleep off the excitement. Once the adrenaline high wore off, the pain had peaked above the level of tolerable as the healing spell did its work, and he had to bury himself in the blankets they'd given him so nobody else would notice how much pain he was in and demand he be checked out by a doctor.

Whenever one of the officers approached him, he'd groan and turn away or curse at them, demanding they only talk to him if they had answers about who was responsible for the extraction attempt. Now they mostly ignored him as he slouched between two chairs, shifting and pulling the blanket up around his shoulders. He tried to sleep. He tried to close his eyes and bury his fears in the warm memories of Shen, but the pain overwhelmed him. His right shoulder ached down to the bone. He felt it every time he tried to move.

Healing was the first spell Nero had learned. He'd done so largely by accident. He'd been playing near an abandoned house with Enzo. All the older kids were afraid of it. They believed a ghost lived there. Once Nero had discovered his abilities, he and Enzo became enamored with the place. The first books he read on the subject of magic talked about astral perception. Most mages could see into other planes of existence. They could see the ghosts that existed just beyond the realm of normal understanding. Enzo believed that if Nero could see the ghost, then maybe he could see it too.

One day, they decided to go inside. They slowly crawled through a broken window, careful not to cut themselves. Once inside, they could tell that someone had been there. Open cans of beer littered the floor. When they heard voices coming from further in the house, they knew it was time to go. The boys ran back to the window and crawled through as carefully as they could, but Nero's jacket got caught on the edge. When he tried to pull it free, he ripped a long red gash down the side of his arm.

Enzo kept running all the way back to the safety of their own home, but Nero slowed on one of the side streets and stared at his wound. The bleeding had stopped, and the wound was slowly stitching itself back together. He wasn't entirely sure how he healed himself that first time. He'd done it unconsciously. It was the only reason he had survived after his brother shot him in the back.

After he healed himself that time, he cut himself and healed himself over and over again. It was a painful experience, as he discovered that healing isn't instant and didn't numb the pain of the wound. He studied what happened to his body when he cast that first spell, learning how to read and shape the mana around him. He visualized the mana surrounding him flowing into the wound and sealing it. Each time learning the best way to manipulate the mana to stitch the wound back together. His entire framework for how he cast spells was born in that moment.

The magic worked on him as he tossed and turned uncomfortably in his makeshift nest between two seats. Not long into Nero's self-imposed corner isolation, the mood in the room shifted. There was a rumbling of low voices as two new suits arrived. Both were black women with close-cropped military haircuts. They moved nearly in unison, scanning the room with the professional aplomb of high-end security.

Nero sat up straighter.

Behind the new suits, two more security men flanked a tall, bulky man in a flashy electrochromic suit that had to be Vashon Island or some equally elegant-sounding brand. Nero had read the files on Enzo enough to know this man at first sight.

"Enzo!" Everett Yeun said. He threw his arms open and gathered Nero into an awkward hug that made him grunt loudly in pain.

Yeun's was one of the first co-worker files Nero read, and even then, Nero did not like him. From what Nero understood, he was a corporate climber, the type of employee who believed that the trappings of success meant that you'd achieved success, no matter how good, or in this case, bad at your job you were.

In spite of this, Nero managed to work up a smile. He said, "Easy on the hugs, man. It's good to see you."

When Yeun spoke, he wiggled his shoulders like he was dancing. He said, "That's all you have to say after all this went down? Seriously? I want details."

He kept on talking, treating Nero's silence like a green light. "We've brought a team in to protect Mr. Olgin. Centurion Security, top-notch guys. They're all kitted up out there in the lobby like it's the fragging Desert Wars. I got scans of me walking in with them behind me. Really wiz stuff. I put it on my feed."

Nero glanced nervously toward the entrance. He wasn't in any condition to take on a full security team. If they somehow figured out he wasn't Enzo, there wouldn't be a thing he could do to escape.

Yeun continued, "We tried to contact you about it, but you turned your commlink off."

"Yeah, I kept getting calls from the office and I wasn't ready to deal with it."

"We figured. Well, Lewis-Klein brought a mobile detail for you as well, full escort to the airport, and then straight to London."

"What about my stuff?"

"Don't worry about it. I stopped at the hotel on the way. I got your bag and everything else." Everett paused, holding his stare longer than he needed to, as if to say *We'll talk about it later*. "Let's get you out of here."

The Centurion team was all business. They bracketed Nero and Yeun as they walked down the hall. By the time they reached the entrance, the second heavy response team assigned to Olgin was nowhere to be seen, likely taking positions closer to their principal.

Nero was familiar with Centurion. In order to be good in his line of work, you had to know the ins and outs of the different security services you were likely to encounter. Their units weren't likely to be supported by magic, but they more than made up for it with firepower and cyber. How much cyberware were his four escorts packing under those expensive Kevlar-lined suits?

Nero said, "I don't understand. Who sent you down here?"

"The upper management called me up and put me on a plane to come get you the moment they heard what happened to Olgin. You're a big deal now, bro. This shit is all over the feed. The bigwigs are saying you get Olgin's desk until they figure out their next move."

It made sense, but he hadn't given it any thought until now. Enzo's particular office dealt in millions, if not billions of nuyen each day, and Olgin was the man responsible for coordinating that. He hadn't realized that with Olgin out of commission, that responsibility fell directly to Enzo—to him. He shuddered.

This is some crazy drek, right?" Yeun said, but he didn't look like he thought it was crazy. The man looked like he was living on the wild side, glad for the opportunity to be part of anything that separated him from the mundanity of his life. He likely only watched this sort of thing happen on scripted trid shows. Maybe they even felt it was exciting because it only ever happened to someone else. It was headline news on the feed; it could never happen to them.

Nero wondered at that. He didn't think Yeun realized how comforting a life of normalcy was. Privilege often worked that way. You didn't recognize the freedom inherent in your life until a situation arose where those freedoms no longer existed. It was like realizing air existed only after you were choking and couldn't breathe. Autonomic response. That's how it felt to Nero as security ushered him into the back of a black car.

What Yeun treated as everyday freedom had the ring of a gilded cage to Nero. This world of paid drivers and personal security kept Yeun locked into responsibilities and fealty he would never escape. He was a salaryman, and the only reward for his life's work would be a higher salary and more perks.

Yeun pointed toward the airport and said, "Upper management got us a jet. A G4."

When the car stopped to unload them, security retrieved Nero's carry-on bag from the trunk and handed it to him. Nero checked it quickly, finding his personal commlink inside one of the pockets, the battery nestled beside it. He slung the bag over his shoulder, trying to act casual, but he couldn't avoid noticing Yeun watching him and smirking.

They traversed airport security without the international scrutiny Nero had come to define as commonplace over the last few days. The security detail handled all of the paperwork, and then lead Nero and Yeun onto the tarmac, then into the cabin of the private jetliner.

First class already impressed Nero, but this was entirely different. There were only eight seats in the executive cabin. Four of those seats were positioned near the front of the aircraft, facing each other, one on each side of what passed for an aisle in the private space. The other four were grouped together near the rear of the aircraft and all faced a table. Beside it was a wet bar with a mix of drinks and snacks locked away for takeoff.

"Don't tell anyone," Yeun said, "but this trip is my first time flying in one of these. I know it's old hat to high-risers like you, but I'm still getting there. My membership to Beaufort South just came through, so I'm getting there faster than you thought, *neh*?"

Nero just nodded in response. He was tired, but also on edge. Everyone around him treated him like he was Enzo. He felt like every one of them actually knew Enzo better than he did—especially Yeun. They knew his quirks and habits. They knew how he laughed, what he laughed at.

Novak had put together a file that explained many of these things so Nero would be able to mimic them. She even provided footage of Enzo at a bar and additional footage of Enzo in the office. It was all iris-cam stuff, close and detailed enough that Nero felt uncomfortable watching it. Now they were watching him as he tried to remember to sit the way Enzo sat, smile the way Enzo smiled. It was all too much when what he really wanted to do was go to sleep.

They strapped into their seats for takeoff.

"So," said Yeun, "I made sure I grabbed that burner commlink of yours. What's the deal there?"

Nero feigned a smile to mask the fact that he didn't really know what to say, and turned to look out the window. He hoped Yeun would get the message, but the executive was wired up on excitement and dying to talk. He said, "I have one, too. I use it to make sure my main girl doesn't ever figure out about my side girl. That would be nuclear."

Nero continued to ignore him. This time he closed his eyes like he had in the hospital. A little more time passed, enough that he could think about what he would do when he landed. He would have to call the team and check in. If the Centurion people escorted him back to Enzo's flat, he'd need to wait until then to make that call.

Shen would go ballistic. She'd probably demand they call off the run. She didn't do very well with deviations to the plan. She did even worse when someone she cared about was in the crosshairs as a result. He wasn't sure if he wanted to reach out to Novak again. Odds were she already knew what went down. She clearly had eyes watching him.

"So, an extraction," Yeun said suddenly. He was grinning and nodding like a kid who finally got to meet a professional Urban Brawler. "What was that like?"

Nero just shrugged. "It all happened to fast to think."

"The cops said there were four people standing out there in the middle of the street waving guns at you, and then they just *died*. I mean they didn't really say it like that, but I pieced it together."

"I didn't actually see any of it," Nero lied.

"Sounds like heavy magic stuff, right?" Yeun leaned closer to him, whispering so security wouldn't overhear. "Was it you?"

Nero felt the panic crawling across his skin. Suddenly he was hyperaware of his situation. He was 40,000 feet in the air and surrounded by an executive security team. There was nowhere to run. Instinctively he reached for his cross, hand closing around the empty space there.

"Come on, you can tell me. We all gossip about the no-cyberware thing. Carlisle swears he saw you do a spell once. I bet Selina's tired of people asking her all the time."

"No. I don't know what happened." Nero said each word slowly and with more malice than he'd intended.

"Okay." Yeun put his hands up in the international gesture of *Fine, I'll drop it*.

So that was it, then. Enzo was pretending to be magically active.

If not directly, he made no effort to dispel the rumors. It struck Nero as sad that even with all the trappings of wealth and success, his brother could not let go of this one small thing. Magic was not known to appear beyond the puberty phase, yet Enzo refused cyberware as if continuing to wait could change the cosmic trick the universe played on him. Nero thought they both had something the other did not.

Yeun's attention drifted when the stewardess made her appearance; he started chatting her up. She was polite, even playful in her responses. Nero took his turn in the conversation, asking for one of the mint concoctions he'd had on the previous flight.

He held it uneasily and sipped it, trying to ignore Yeun as best he could. After a while, he allowed himself to relax.

The plane touched down at Gatwick Airport late that evening. Despite the elegance, he thought if he never got on a plane again, that would be okay. Every flight he'd taken had gotten him into progressively worse situations. Now he was trapped in the hands of a security detail that, it seemed, had no intention of letting him out of their sight.

Centurion Security did not, in fact, let him out of their sight. They had a car waiting. Once he deplaned and parted ways with Everett Yeun, the two women in the detail joined him and escorted him home.

He thanked them for their service, but they insisted they see him to the door. They offered to check inside the house, but he refused, reminding them he wasn't the one targeted for extraction in the first place. He waited until they left, standing on the stoop the way his mother used to when she sent him and Enzo off to school.

There it was again. The weight of fatigue and memory crashing down on him.

Nero didn't want to go inside, but some distant part of him needed to know what lay beyond that door. He'd seen Enzo's work life, but none of that felt like the real Enzo.

When Nero thought about it, he recognized he hadn't objected to the job more because he *wanted* to know more. He wanted to know Enzo. What was the real life Enzo had made for himself? What was it he'd created that was worth murdering his own brother for?

He fished his brother's e-key out of his pocket, deactivated the security system, and stepped inside.

ENJEE

11-16-2081
6:11 P.M. Local Time

The *Scuttlebutt* pulled into the crowded docklands just as the Sunday sun ducked beneath the horizon, signaling night in Lagos. It hadn't been the fastest route to get up the coast from Azania, but the open waters under the protection of Fanti pirates was the only reliably safe way out of Azania with live cargo.

EnJee climbed up the stair from below decks. He stretched his arms and back and watched Grim Fox laugh and joke with two of the Fanti women. The three shared war stories as they unlimbered the ropes to tie the ship to the dock. Dozens of locals moved around the docks, some helping bring the boat in, others standing around and shouting useless instructions or joking with the Grim Fox and the others.

Grim Fox melted into cultures in a way EnJee never could. EnJee found himself grateful for his friend's ability, if not a bit jealous of the easy way the samurai fit in with people. Shen had hints of that ability herself, but she hadn't been above decks since the first sunrise. She'd offered to take extra shifts with the prisoner. He'd objected at first, but he could tell by her expression she was going to keep her eyes on Enzo Moretti regardless of what he said.

EnJee understood it was her way of dealing with things. He'd known Shen longer than anyone else in the crew, since she was a kid. He knew her when she'd still been a *kiseang*, owned by the Triads and trained to be a courtesan. He knew how rarely and how greedily she offered her trust and love. But he'd seen her when they'd lost members of their crew before;

seen how the absence of people who truly mattered to her ate at her soul. An admirable trait he'd spent years trying to train that out of her, to no avail. He understood her love for those close to her made her who she was, but it also made her weak. In this life, loss was a real possibility on every run, and this one especially indicated that Nero might not come back. She openly blamed EnJee for accepting the job, and would blame him more if Nero didn't survive it.

EnJee allowed himself to wonder how it must feel to her to stare into the face of their hostage and know he wasn't Nero. And know what he'd done to her friend and lover.

Then EnJee didn't allow himself to wonder any longer, or to reach for that tether of understanding that made her life so very different from his own. He packed away those feelings with a sigh. They still had a job to do, and Lagos was no place to have your guard down.

He called out to Grim Fox, "We planning to stand around making faces at each other, or we going to get this done?"

Grim Fox sneered at EnJee before turning to hug each of the three women. The troll clasped elbows with the one male of the crew and bent his forehead toward the boy until the tip of his good horn touched the boys inked skin. He whispered something EnJee could not hear, and then moved to help Shen unload the passenger. Enzo Moretti walked down the gangplank, arms still handcuffed behind his back, shoved along by Shen.

They'd dressed Enzo in some of Nero's clothes. He was wearing jeans and a black shirt. He had a jacket over his shoulders that partly hid the fact that his hands were bound behind his back. There was no hiding the gag stuffed in his mouth. Enzo was looking around the busy dock but kept focusing on one group of locals in particular. They were five or so blokes, ordinary by Lagos standards, but the gang paint lining their arms and faces must've seemed alien to Enzo. They stood around laughing and talking and watching dock workers moving items on and off the ships.

"That's how the other half lives, Enzo. Not so much like your catered dinners and white-collar office work, is it?" EnJee called down after him. EnJee read the look on Enzo's face as a guy who finally recognized how far out of his depth he really was. Enzo was used to being in a certain kind of world. This was certainly not it.

The Fanti boy turned to EnJee. He said, "The air purifiers will sell good here. Your crew done good for the Fanti. We will remember you."

EnJee thanked him, avoiding the courtesies Grim Fox had shared. Instead, he jumped from the ship, his boots hitting steady land for the first time in days. Relief flooded him like a hit from a stim patch. More relief took hold as he reached out toward the local network, his scripts connecting passively. He shuddered slightly, feeling the information of the Matrix flood through his cyberware. No matter where he was, the Matrix was his true home, and he'd been away too long.

There were dozens of messages on his personal feed. He clicked on the one from Nero. He'd sent it to the group the night he left. As he read, he could see Grim Fox and Shen doing the same.

"Bollocks. Plan's gone to pot, per usual." EnJee said, cursing under his breath. He fought down a shiver of fear. He didn't like that Nero was operating on his own halfway across the globe. It put the mage in a spot where he wouldn't be able to defend himself without breaking cover. It put the entire run in jeopardy if it came down to that.

Shen was already on her commlink, trying to get through to no avail. Grim Fox studied Enzo, who still stood wide-eyed and making no move to run away. The troll said, "We prepped him pretty good. If he gets in over his head, he'll reach out and we'll get what we need from Enzo."

"He already did reach out, Grim. And now I can't get a hold of him."

"Doesn't mean he's in trouble. We'll keep trying to make contact," Grim Fox said.

EnJee nodded. "In the meantime, we still need to make our end work."

EnJee reached back out through the Matrix, firing up old pathways. He confirmed a meet with his primary contact in the area and then reached further, restarting conversations with people he hadn't known in years. He located several shadowrunners and fixers he'd worked with long ago. The few who were still around couldn't help him at present. That was the way of the shadows. He reached back out to his primary contact, who put him in touch with a fixer who agreed to meet and exchange credits for a T-Bird flight out of Africa that evening.

They'd come to Lagos because of what it was and also what it was not. Lagos was one of a handful of Nigerian cities that held sway on the global stage. EnJee liked it here. He liked that the city and the dozen or so nations that surrounded it did not participate in the Global SIN Registry. He liked that the preferred coin was naira, and the digital trails of nuyen were nowhere to be seen. His anonymity was a certainty here.

There was no standard Lagosian language. To get by, you needed to speak a pidgin cobbled together from any number of languages, often with a pan-European or major indigenous dialect serving as the base. You could tell a newcomer by the confused looks as the slew of languages overwhelmed them, and their linguasofts, even the fancy new Horizon models, seemed unable to find a database that could keep up. EnJee was the team's point man here because knew the right people to contact to move live cargo out of the city and across the many borders that stood between them and London proper. This was not his first time running the shadows here, nor would it be his last.

"What are you talking about, EnJee?" Shen said. "We need to get on a T-bird right now and get to Nero."

EnJee said, "Let's settle this elsewhere, shall we?" The group of locals eyeing Enzo kept staring. That wasn't a good sign. People in this part of town learned not to notice things. Call it a defensive mechanism or effective socialization. They knew better than to point out the bound man standing on the dock. Still, there were too many eyes watching, maybe deciding if it was worth the risk to steal the prisoner for themselves.

Now the small group of locals started down the dock toward EnJee and his crew. EnJee muttered, "Trouble coming."

The lead man shouted in a language EnJee couldn't understand and pointed at Enzo. Enzo's eyes went wider and he screamed at them, the words lost in the thickness of his gag.

EnJee clapped a hand on Enzo's shoulder and said, "Is there a problem here, gentlemen?"

The lead man spoke again, this time in a broken English. "Pay tax or we make trouble for you, smuggler."

In answer, Shen flashed a pistol. She leveled it even with the lead man's head. Then she lowered her aim to his knee and squeezed off one shot.

The *crack* of gunfire was enough to draw the attention of everyone in the area. The man screamed and fell to the ground, clutching his bloody leg. His friends quickly backed away, hands raised. Shen kept the gun pointed at the others, shifting her aim from man to man as she said loudly, "Any other tax collectors here?!"

"I think we've outlasted our welcome." EnJee looked at the crowd nervously. There wasn't a police presence at these docks, but like in so many slums and free cities, the local gangs kept order. EnJee knew staying here would lead to more trouble than they'd signed on for.

EnJee watched the injured man groan and curse at Shen. She ignored him, glaring at Enzo and dragging him forward by the collar. EnJee heard her mutter, "Keep your mouth shut and eyes on the damned ground next time."

Enzo tried screaming once more, but Shen showed him the end of a knife blade, close enough to his face that the serrated edges must have looked like the teeth of a hungry animal. He was silent after that.

Grim Fox found a small cab willing to convey them to the airfield. Most transports here were the small motor bikes called *okadas*, since the narrow and crowded streets meant that cars were a liability, but they couldn't move a prisoner on a bike.

"You two head for the airfield," EnJee said. "Shen, you know our contact down there." He pointed at the bound and gagged Enzo Moretti. "Let's get this bloke tucked away on a Banshee and out of sight of prying eyes. In the meanwhile, I need to take another meeting."

Grim Fox gave him a stare that betrayed confusion and curiosity.

Shen fought a grimace when she said, "Ekon Abioye? You're going to meet with that slitch while Nero is in trouble half a world away?"

EnJee nodded. "Any chance you want to come? Soften the ask?"

Her face gave the answer.

"Plane doesn't take off for another hour plus. I'll meet you at the airfield before it does."

EnJee caught a ride on the back of an *okada* taxi bike, the dirty air playing through the loose puff of hair on the top of his head. He wound up in Festac Town, where the tallest buildings weren't much taller than the shanties that stood alongside them and the streets were crowded with black faces like his own. It was a small comfort to move through cities such as this, to be lost in a crowd of sameness.

As much as EnJee craved anonymity, he also craved the expression of his self and his style. He didn't want to stand out, but when he was noticed, he did not want to at once be overlooked or underestimated. This careful balance defined him and his work. It was why, in the Matrix, he was known as a "code reaper," a person whose mark, when seen, never meant anything pleasant.

EnJee exchanged *naira* with the driver and walked the last three blocks, taking in the city. Among other things, Lagos was known for *bukas*, restaurants built from shanties or shipping containers with only three walls. The food in such places was amazing. They usually served *ifokore*, a yam-based soup that could be customized to match your specific taste preferences—much like the *pho* he enjoyed back home. The majority of customers sat at outdoor tables that spilled into the narrow streets. Only the toughest or most foolish customers sat inside the *buka* itself, as doing so meant their backs faced open air. It was a dangerous show of strength.

When EnJee arrived at a one called Nandi's, the man he was looking for was already there. Synthetic drums and the unearthly rhythms of the Last Dawayu thundered from nearby speakers. EnJee's contact stood out as one of a small handful of suits mixed in among the shadowtypes, locals, and streetwalkers gathered in the shared space. Unlike the others, he sat inside at the serving counter, facing the kitchen. In spite of the obvious plastic surgery and the cybereyes, his long skinny arms and legs gave away what he truly was.

"*Sasabonsam,*" someone in the busy street whispered and pointed as they passed by. They picked up speed, hurrying away. It was Nigerian word for "ghoul," and here, ghouls carried power, both spiritually and financially.

EnJee walked up to his contact, hands in pockets, and said, "So, this is where they hide you these days?"

Ekon Abioye didn't look up from his bowl of *ifokore*, but he did chuckle and point to the seat beside him.

EnJee took the seat, plopping down on the stool like a much older man. He heard the fatigue in his voice when he said, "When you took the cushy office job, I suppose you weren't expecting a homecoming."

Abioye said, "Quite the opposite, Nigel. Festac was a pit growing up. I had to learn how to fight just to make it to the store to bring milk home. Feels right to be able to bring a bit of corporate clarity to the scene."

EnJee clamped a hand on Abioye's slender shoulder. "How is it that we are friends?"

"Is that what we are?" Abioye nudged a second bowl toward EnJee and said, "Eat first."

EnJee glanced at his *ifokore*, watching the yams bob on the surface. It looked delicious. Then he looked at Abioye's bowl, considering what must be lurking beneath the surface to make it palatable to a ghoul. The thought made EnJee's mouth dry. He pushed those dark thoughts out of his mind, as he always did with Abioye.

"How is Shen?" asked Abioye.

"She told me to tell you to bugger right off."

Abioye grinned. "So the same, then."

"It might have something to do with you buying people and eating their flesh." He tried hard not to glance at Abioye's bowl again.

"Everything everywhere is for sale, my friend. She must grow to understand that if she truly wishes to be a citizen of the world."

EnJee settled. He closed off his mind long enough to take a bite of soup, enjoying the spices. It was hot and tasted of roots and honey. Thoughtfully, he said, "The world is too much. I'd bet Shen would settle for a one-bedroom flat with a porch and an ocean view, if she could afford it."

Abioye laughed, a rich sound that belied his narrow frame. "Then you should remind her my offer still stands. I can arrange for what she wants."

"Best you tell her yourself if you ever see her again. In fact, probably best you never see her again."

Abioye laughed again, a sound that came so easy to him that EnJee could almost forget a hostile city waited behind them, just out of view. "So, enough of this small talk. Tell me what you are planning to do with the information you asked me to gather."

EnJee said, "How about you scan me the data first, and then I'll decide if I want to share my end?"

"Should I ask how you came to know about such an intricate financial transaction?"

"I'm involved."

Aboiye picked a sliver of pink meat out of his teeth and said, "Tell me what you think your client's play is, so I can understand yours."

EnJee set down his spoon. He put his hands together and pressed them against his mouth as if praying. He sat like that for a long moment and finally said, "I think she's running a dead cat bounce—she feels that once the smoke clears from this Spinrad Global thing, her slice of the action will double, triple, what have you in value. She'll make a killing on our action."

"So, you want to find a way to roll your money into the sale, maybe even bring someone like me in to steal the buy, and then get even richer for the intel and your cut?"

"I'm glad we understand each other." EnJee grinned broadly and dug into his soup again. He licked his lips to clear away the spices and said, "Does this mean you're interested?"

By way of an answer, Abioye clasped his hands together. He stretched out his way-too-long arms and flipped them around, making his knuckles crack. Then he turned to EnJee and said, "There was a man a few years ago. He was well placed in the Monobe corporate hierarchy. He made his place by leveraging smaller companies, buying them out and selling them for parts."

"A corporate raider."

"Yes, though we in the industry no longer use that term. We call them investment strategists now. His strategy encouraged him to buy bigger and bigger corporations, until finally his actions were noticed by those in other multi-nationals."

"That's the game, isn't it?"

"Indeed. However, when the game is more about the player than the company, things can end badly for everyone."

Abioye was a storyteller. He was also a man who needed you to ask him to tell the story. He was a grandpa by the fireplace, spewing knowledge from the end of his pipe. EnJee hated the dance, but he still followed the steps. "So, what happened?"

"He fell into a bidding war over a company called Ginseng Health. Yakashima insisted on purchasing the company, and raised his bid at every turn. Operations were carried out on both sides to damage the other's position."

"I'm guessing he lost out in the end."

"On the contrary, Nigel, he won. He gained full control of Ginseng Health, except when it sold, it was weighed down by the expectations of the bidding war. It was not worth near the purchase price. In the end, his company lost millions on the exchange, and he lost his position."

"I think I get it. Zeik Weisz is our Ginseng Health in this story."

Abioye didn't answer. Instead he chomped down on his *ifokore*, the sound juicy.

EnJee could feel his face growing hot, and it was not entirely from the spices. "What are you really telling me, here?"

Abioye shrugged. "Zeik Weisz is a junk bond. The more you look, the less you see. They own a nothing security firm, some real estate holdings, a few flower shops, and what looks like a small marketing firm. This isn't anything worth investing in."

"Then why does my client want it so badly?"

"That is the real question you should be asking."

EnJee drummed his fingers on the table. After a moment, he asked, "Do you have the answer?"

I believe your client is playing a game." He swept his hand around him in a wide gesture. "Imagine this place here, Nandi's, needs a loan. They borrow money from a lender, that is called a 'debt obligation.' The lender will only lend it to Nandi if she has an underlying asset to serve as collateral for that loan. What does Nandi have?"

EnJee replied, "She's got these three walls."

"Indeed she does. So, these three walls, her business, becomes that collateral for the loan. If she fails to pay for the loan, then the bank will own her business. Now—what if Nandi's business did not ever exist?"

Before EnJee answered the question, he stopped the woman behind the counter and requested a beer, using the time to consider what to say. Then he turned back to Abioye and said, "Then how is she repaying the loan?"

"Exactly right. Perhaps her business was a front for, say, a criminal syndicate that could not effectively get their nuyen usable, because the way they earned it was, in fact, a crime?"

"They would need a way to launder their money."

Abioye nodded. "So now Nandi's pretend business becomes their way to legally put their money into the system."

"That doesn't explain why they need my fund manager."

When the ghoul grinned, it looked absolutely feral. "The hedge fund serves as the bank. The money your man provides is given to the criminal organization up front. The organization then pays the investors of the fund he manages with the ill-gotten gains they refer to as profits. Now, who do you think the investors of this hedge fund are?"

EnJee shook his head in confusion. "You're saying the people investing in the fund are the same people who own the business and take out the loan? So when they pay the loan back, they're actually paying themselves?"

"Yes. However, this is not without risk. If someone else—say, Shen—buys that debt obligation from the original lender, what do you think happens?"

EnJee thought for a moment, then said, "If the debt obligation now belongs to Shen, then Nandi now owes Shen that money. If Nandi does not pay, the collateral becomes Shen's property."

Aboiye smiled and clapped EnJee on the back. "Correct. They need to pay that money back to whomever owns the debt. You see, it all falls apart if someone *other* than the syndicate takes ownership of the loans these false companies are taking out. I believe that is what your Johnson is attempting to make happen."

EnJee was smart enough to follow along, but he felt like Aboiye was leaving out a lot of the complexities. He said, "So, what you're saying is, if my fund manager sells that Zeik Weisz debt to my client, then they will effectively own the syndicate's laundering operation."

Instead of answering directly, Aboiye said, "This is not the only strategy being used. I suspect the engagement with the syndicate began by making stock in this false business public, and arranging for another fund or firm to buy the stock. He then shorted the stock, and through the magic of financial wizardry, the price of the stock tumbled, and they were able to buy back the entire value of the company post IPO for pennies on the dollar. It would take a very smart and specialized fund manager to be able to conduct business from multiple angles like this."

EnJee said, "You could do it."

"Our firm *has* done it, which is why it was so easy to spot. It is also incredibly dangerous to do without the backing of a major financial player."

"Major like Lewis-Klein."

"No, major like a megacorp."

EnJee eyed his bottle of Horizon Bottled Sunshine. *Even here, the best I can get is a conscripted corporate ale.* He wanted to drink what the locals drank—the homebrews mixed in oil drums and bottled in people's houses. But he wasn't a local, a thing he was wise to remember. Outside of Africa, people might assume he was African, but here, the truth was evident.

If Novak and Enzo were involved in something so incredibly complex, then people on the inside would quickly see through the ruse. Nero was not Enzo, and if that truth became evident, it could mean real trouble for him.

Abioye took another bite of his *ifokore*. Finally, he said, "Where's your boy now?"

"Dubai. He left word when we were out of contact, and told us he had to go get the rights to sell something called Atilla Finance."

Abioye chuckled, "Can your man get me that?"

"I don't believe he's the one making that sale."

Abioye sighed. "Remember how we started, Nigel?"

"There's no way of forgetting that. Smuggling Tamanous shipments up and down the coast lost me a lot of friends."

"Ah, but you still have Shen. I've never quite understood your need for so many friends who are faint of heart."

EnJee shrugged. "So what's your point?"

"I used the money from those Tamanous shipments to create a considerable amount of leverage both in the shadows and in the light. Enough that it won me the job I have now. That is to say, I may be able to find out who the syndicate behind all this truly is."

"Are you offering?"

Abioye nodded. "Call it a favor. I'm sure you'll repay it down the road."

EnJee thought hard on that. He wasn't fond of owing people. However, he was less fond of lacking enough information to know what the right moves were. Finally he nodded and stuck out a hand to shake on the deal.

Aboiye shook his hand and said, "Are you staying for the night? Perhaps visiting the dog races?"

Now it was EnJee's turn to laugh. "No such luck. There's a crew making the run to London in a few hours. We plan to be on board."

"Safe journey, then. I will contact you when I have your information."

EnJee left Festac Town the same way he arrived, on the back of an *okada*, shifting through the busy streets. As his driver pushed further away from town, the streets widened, the texture of the road shifting from nanocrete to asphalt and finally to dirt. They wound up on the edge of town on an airstrip bustling with activity.

The security here was cursory, young people in ripped jeans and T-shirts carrying whatever weapons they could afford. What kept the airstrip safe was the need for it to exist. A dozen VSTOLs in various states of disrepair waited in hangars that bore a close resemblance to the shanties of Festac Town. He found Grim Fox in one of them, helping to load small cases into the storage locker of a VSTOL. It was no Banshee. On this trip, his money only bought them passage on a dented Ares Venture whose markings suggested it'd once been a military light transport.

Grim Fox closed up the last of the storage bins, and with that done, the aircraft looked ready to take off. EnJee nodded to the pilot, a dark-skinned dwarf with a spiky afro, dressed in a too-large flight suit with rolled-up sleeves and pant legs.

Shen was behind the aircraft, pacing angrily. Grim Fox jogged over to meet EnJee. He said, "Enzo's in the plane. We're good to takeoff as soon as the three of us get on board."

"What's her deal?" asked EnJee.

"Our boy Nero found himself in the middle of a failed extraction."

"Bollocks. He okay?"

"Yeah, he handled himself. He doesn't think he blew his cover. Enzo's boss was the target and caught a few rounds."

"Sloppy."

"Don't I know it," agreed Grim Fox. "Think this is going to affect the deal?"

EnJee said, "Hard to say. Not likely a company that big lets a little extraction get in the way of doing business."

Grim Fox looked over his shoulder and said, "Shen told me about your guy from Lombadier & Zienz. Still chasing the bigger plot, *neh*?"

EnJee said, "I told you, the more we know about what's really going on, the better our chances of still standing when it is all over."

Grim Fox sighed and said, "Might as well hear it, then. What'd you find out about this Zeik Weisz deal?"

"As it turns out, Zeik Weisz is actually a shell company."

Grim Fox looked surprised. "Why would Novak go through all that trouble to buy up a shell company?"

"Yes, well that's the thing about shells. Sometimes they hide pearls."

ENJEE

11-17-2081
12:58 A.M. Local Time

After hours in a cramped VSTOL, it was good to feel real earth beneath his feet. EnJee stopped himself from kissing the cracked surface of the tarmac, but he smiled and clapped all the same.

"Back in the Smoke," he sighed. Rain fell in sheets so slow as to resemble a fog descending from the sky. No alarms chimed or warnings flittered through the AR space, so the crew knew this wasn't the acidic variety, just the daily rain show in one of the oldest sprawls in the world.

Once upon a time, this had been EnJee's territory. His list of contacts in the city were impressive back then, but he hadn't been under the Smoke in years. It was like in Lagos. Some faces disappeared; others got out of the business. He hated how people in the data havens talked about Rhine-Ruhr or Seattle like the end all of running. It was an easy thing, running in a place like that. Each were large enough that you made plenty of contacts. Even when you burned one or seven, there were more out there. You found a network of people you trusted and you worked your gigs over and again. It was the auto-racing equivalent of shadowrunning—you just turned left.

By the time they landed, he'd already tapped into his ganger acquaintances to arrange for transport as far as the M25. That circular loop of freeway represented a line of demarcation of sorts. Cars even used different gridlink codes and plate tags in order to get inside of the loop. Those same fellows brought EnJee a car that worked inside the city, proper plates and all.

It was nothing that drew an eye, and made all the important gridlink interfaces it needed to.

They stayed at a motel just beyond the bright ring of the M25 highway. Money was short after acquiring a car, so they settled on a single room. They wired two cameras outside the motel door, offering different angles of the hallway.

Shen took off the moment they settled in, racing off to check on Nero. He understood her motivations. It was the first time since the plan had gone to pot that she'd have a chance to see her boy.

Not long after she left, EnJee got to work on setting them up with weapons and a place to stay long term in the city.

EnJee's chosen gig, what he preferred to think of as "import-export," meant making contacts in a lot of different cities, and taking the time to nurture those relationships to the point where he could go a few years without seeing a bloke, and they'd still pick up the comm when he called. The bloke who picked up tonight was a big brute of a West-Ender named Blackjack. Strictly speaking, the relationship wasn't what Enjoy would call friendly.

Blackjack fancied himself a ronin. EnJee found his interpretation of the term more deplorable than Grim Fox's own bastardization of the Bushido code. Blackjack wasn't honorable in any sense. EnJee could trust him to follow through on a handshake and make a deal that benefited him first. On the other hand, he'd work for anyone. Worse than that, he measured himself by who he took down. That kind of "tougher than you" hierarchy often just got a target on your back.

A few minutes after Shen left, he was waiting outside their motel room, smoking and leaning against the wall in his leather duster, flicking ashes into the mist. Blackjack smoked actual tobacco. EnJee didn't know where the man found the papers or the leaves. He imagined a good deal of his profits went to supporting the expensive, outmoded habit.

He said, "You running the Smoke again, *neh*?"

"I go where the nuyen is, mate."

"Added some muscle, I see." Blackjack flicked ash toward Grim Fox.

"Not here for that today, *omae*. Let's just get the business done."

"Right, you'll wanna talk to Koury, then. He can set you up proper." His eyes never left the troll. Grim Fox returned the favor, staring Blackjack down the entire time.

They got down to business, arranging for the weapons they would need to handle anything that might come up during this end of the job. He put an order in for sniper rifle and rappelling gear, so Shen could get in and out of any situation she needed to. Grim Fox added a pair of submachine guns and a shotgun to the order. Then, after consideration he called for a pistol on top of all that.

Blackjack said, "Guns are inelegant weapons, don't you think? Big boy like you ought to be good with his hands, like me. You any good with yours?"

It could've been mistaken for a pass, which it wasn't. Grim Fox ignored the challenge, turning his attention to a can of soda he'd plucked out of a vending machine outside. EnJee wasn't much for firearms, but put in an order for a Remington Roomsweeper. It was a large gun, built more for show than practicality. He didn't expect to be using it. That's what Grim Fox and Shen were for.

Grim Fox said, "We aren't planning on staying here for long, so the faster you can get our gear, the better."

After Blackjack departed, Grim Fox said, "You want to tell me why every chummer of yours I meet is as big an asshole as you, or worse?"

"So you'll understand how good of a mate I actually am."

They watched Enzo Moretti in shifts. EnJee took the first shift while Grim Fox stepped out to get food. EnJee spent most of that shift spinning through the Matrix, an optical feed allowing him to treat his cybereyes like a remote camera that stared at the prisoner while he dug a little deeper into their client.

Katerina Novak had broken the cardinal rule. You never give a runner your real name. Of course, she was short on choice in this instance. The nature of the job meant Nero had to sell her a product, and that meant he had to know her name. It also meant knowing her employer's name, which was CNI. A quick review of that organization revealed it to be a finance company owned by Lusiada, who itself was part of Spinrad Global.

It all felt like a Russian nesting doll, only in reverse. Each layer you added meant adding another atop it until finally the Johnson you found yourself working for was just another proxy for one of the Big 10 megacorps.

At least it wasn't Shiawase this time.

But knowing this did nothing for EnJee's understanding of the motives and how to manipulate them. The basics remained the same from bottom to top: Katerina Novak wanted a specific product, the debt portfolio of a company called Zeik Weisz. She'd gone to extraordinary measures to plant Nero inside of a corporation in order to sell her that product. However, on the surface, Zeik Wiesz was worthless—a junk bond. Either she didn't know Zeik Weisz was junk, or there was another element to the job he hadn't uncovered.

There was a way to find out. He logged off the matrix and sat a little straighter in his chair by the bathroom door. They had Moretti in the bathtub handcuffed to a chain double wrapped around the toilet and stripped down to his boxers in case he managed to find a way out of his bindings. The bloke hadn't bothered trying. He hadn't done much more than sulk since Lagos.

"Things are looking up for you, Enzo. This business is getting closer to the end." EnJee reached out and patted his prisoner on the cheek. Moretti flinched away.

EnJee said, "Don't be such a tosser."

"If you want to help me, then let me go."

"I'm afraid that isn't part of my offer, but I can help you be a bit more comfortable. Tell me about Zeik Weisz, and I'll unstrap you from this toilet and let you move around a bit."

Moretti shrugged. "I don't know much about that company."

"You're a better liar than your brother is, I'll give you that. Except I know Zeik Weisz is linked to you, and I know our Johnson wants it, so how about you explain why."

"Zeik Weisz is a junk bond. If the person who hired you wants it, I'm happy to give it to them. Just let me go and let me get back to my life. I'll give you whatever you want." The words were polished and smooth, as if Moretti had been asked questions about the corporation before, and knew how to dodge them.

It wasn't the answer EnJee wanted to hear, but it was enough for him to know Zeik Weisz wasn't a junk bond. He pretended to be satisfied and unclipped Enzo's handcuffs from the chain attaching him to the toilet. Then he shut the bathroom door. There weren't any windows in there, so it did no harm to make him more comfortable.

After that, sleep came all too easy for EnJee. No matter the situation, home felt familiar. Even here in a motel, he was comforted by the fact that he was only miles away from where he grew up.

He woke just after dawn to find Grim Fox simmering in the corner. "Small for a troll" didn't translate to small in any other language. Despite his relatively diminutive nature, Grim Fox stood almost to the ceiling, his broad shoulders taking up the entire corner of the room, arms folded and mouth set into a sneer. He said, "We had an arrangement here."

"Not in front of the prisoner." EnJee lazily pointed his thumb over his shoulder toward the open door of bathroom, where Enzo Moretti was asleep in the tub.

"Enzo tried to run."

EnJee cracked a surprised smile. "Well, good on him. Nice to see the suit have a bit of a backbone."

"He said you unlocked him, EnJee."

"Might have been the case."

"Want to tell me why?"

EnJee shrugged. "I needed information from him. I told him I'd make him a bit more comfortable in exchange. Seems to me he took advantage of my hospitality."

"You brought me to the team because you trusted my planning and know how," Grim Fox said.

"Aye, that hasn't changed."

"Then why is it I keep finding out what's going on after it's already happened?"

Someone knocked at the door. A quick glance at the cams told EnJee it was Shen. She held a pink rectangular box in one hand and a carry-all with three coffees in the other. EnJee went to the door and opened it.

"You two playing nice?" she asked.

"I'm nothing if not a sweetheart," EnJee said.

Grim Fox grunted. Shen rolled her eyes.

"How's our boy?" EnJee asked.

Shen replied, "Stressed. He's meeting the Johnson now. How's our cargo?"

Grim Fox spoke up, "EnJee here almost let him get away."

"Just having a spot of fun with the old boy."

"Was that before or after he was about to bunny hop out the front door?" growled Grim Fox.

"Both." EnJee grinned.

EnJee and Shen left Grim Fox at the motel, watching Enzo Moretti while they went to meet with Blackjack's broker contact, Koury.

The broker was a tall fellow, thin as a rail, with dark skin. He waved to the pair as they exited the sedan. EnJee nodded and headed his way while Shen held back a few steps, checking the surroundings.

This could've been any middle-class street in Great Britain, long and winding with houses packed together tightly. Nothing was higher than six stories, with most of the buildings constructed before the Awakening. There were a few cars on the street and a family pushing a shopping cart. The sky was gray with a lump of clouds that seemed fixed in the air above them, like a cartoon of a person with bad luck.

But the clouds here brought more than bad luck. On the worse days, acid rain fell that ate away at the walls and roofs, and even the people unfortunate enough to be trapped outdoors. The handful of people EnJee saw on the streets were metas. A few orks, and a family of dwarves.

Shen followed EnJee and Koury inside. Under her breath, she muttered, "I hate London."

The building's interior was beige, chipped paint. It smelled like molasses. Shen scrunched up her nose, flashing EnJee a dissatisfied look.

EnJee said, "Koury here says we can have the place for five hundred a week."

Shen mocked surprise. "What a great price for such a place!"

Koury said "No need for theatrics. I was told you needed a place that where you and your friends could blend in. This one doesn't have too many bugs and the neighbors are quiet.

Besides all of that, it has an underground garage. 500 is a good price."

EnJee's smile showed crooked and yellowed teeth. He said, "Two-fifty is better, isn't it?"

"I'm not quite sure I can make that much of an adjustment."

"Sure you can. This is all off the books, credits up front and all." Though the AR signage had been thoughtfully removed, the trace elements it left behind told the story. The house they were looking to rent for the job was a foreclosure locked up by the bank for review a few more months. People like Koury made money renting the spots short-term and off-book.

"Perhaps I can go as low as four hundred," Koury said.

"Perhaps you can go 350, then."

Koury considered it, nodded, and quietly sent the keycode information to EnJee's commlink. EnJee sent back a week's worth of rent.

After the broker left, Shen said, "You could've gotten it for three."

"Slot off, Shen."

She laughed softly.

Off the entrance there was a living room. The house was sparsely furnished. There was a couch in the living room facing a wall that, by the looks of the dust patterns, once held a trideo. Opposite the living room was a small kitchen. A staircase led upstairs. Shen walked up and through the three bedrooms. EnJee followed. The previous tenants had tried to clear out what they could. It looked like the people had left in a hurry, leaving a handful of personal items behind.

Shen found a teddy bear on the floor of one of the rooms. He watched as she scooped it up. The name *Anna* was scrawled on the inside of a closet door in the room with the bear. EnJee came up behind Shen. He didn't need to see her tattoos to know how she was feeling.

"Want to tell me what has you upset?"

She said, "You've been pretty hard on all of us lately. What was that stuff with Grim this morning? I'm not talking about that anti-samurai shit you keep using as an excuse for why you have a problem with him."

"Grimmy's a big boy. Literally. He can take it."

Shen said, "He shouldn't have to. He's good at his job and he's one of us. Him and Nero both."

"Yeah, well, Nero's been lying to us the whole time, love. I don't see what it doesn't bother you any."

Shen held the bear gently in her hands, inspecting it. "We talked about this. Omission isn't lying."

"He didn't tell us something that is crucial to the team. Do you realize how many times we could have been nicked just because he has a SIN? You can't operate in the shadows that way, Shen. You know it."

She turned to him. "He's burned just like the rest of us are burned. The world thinks he's dead. Him popping up on the radar didn't do much more than help some nosy Johnson track him down for what she needs. It didn't mess up any of the work we've done or will do. It's fine." She paused. Then she held out the bear to EnJee and said, "Besides, it isn't like we didn't lie to him, too."

"You mean about you and me? How we met? That's practically pre-Awakening at this point, isn't it?"

When he didn't take the bear, she hugged it into herself.

It didn't sound like she was going to answer, so EnJee said, "You mean to say he's never asked? About the ink I mean."

"No. I don't think he wants to know. I don't think he needs to know either. Nero is different than we are. He has a moral compass. I don't know that his morality can come to terms with the fact that you plucked me out of a triad brothel."

"You weren't there by your own free will." EnJee frowned.

She said, "That doesn't change the fact that I was there or what I did while I was there."

"Well, if he doesn't want to know who you were then, don't make it our fault for him not asking."

Shen said, "It still makes us liars, EnJee."

"Well, a lie for a lie then."

Something in his tone caught must have caught her attention, because she said, "What are you planning?"

"Not much, really. It's just that we have all the power, don't we?"

She didn't seem to follow, so he continued. "It's like this. Nero goes into that meeting pretending to be Enzo, and Novak needs him to vote the way she wants. But what if he doesn't? What if we squeeze her once he's in, find out how much this deal is really worth?"

"I don't know. It's dangerous. We don't know what she'll do to Nero if we start changing the rules."

"I trust our boy. He can take care of himself—certainly a bit better than anyone else on that side of the shadows."

"Trust this, EnJee. If anything happens to Nero over something you did..." She didn't finish the sentiment. She didn't need to.

NERO

11-17-2081
1:51 A.M. Local Time

When Nero and Enzo were young, they played a game called "mirror." They would face each other and try to mimic the other's actions. At first, each would move very slowly, portraying simple actions like smiling or waving. As the game went on it, grew faster and more complex. They graduated to a mimicry of brushing their teeth and making goofy faces. The game itself was goofy, but it reminded them of how in sync they were. Enzo knew what Nero was going to do as soon as he moved. Nero knew what Enzo would try just by the way his brother looked at him.

The two knew each other so well that at times they would play the game with their eyes closed and their parents would clap and laugh at how remarkably close the movements still were. Enzo claimed that they would always know what the other was thinking and feeling, because twins were magical.

Nero sat in his brother's kitchen, thinking about how far he'd drifted from those early beliefs. He tipped back another beer, his fourth in the last hour. When the bottle was only suds, he set it in a row beside the others. The alcohol did little to help him forget where he was. Sitting here alone in the kitchen, he was powerless to stop remembering the years he'd spent with a mother, father, and yes, a brother; his non-magical twin with whom he shared every thought.

He stood, wobbled slightly, and took another long look around the two-story flat. Enzo Moretti's house felt staged. It looked like an executive's bachelor pad in a trid. Nero was no stranger to corporate extractions; he'd been in several homes

that bore more than a passing resemblance to his brother's flat. He could list each item as though it were off a checklist:
- Fine art from an unknown but talented artist.
- Music pumped in through hidden EvoAudio speakers, cycling between Uptown Monk and a handful of other corporate-approved artists.
- Thermador refrigerator stocked by a private service with beer and unopened platters, in case he needed to entertain.
- Biagiotti wine fridge brimming with expensive bottles.
- Berkshire sectional couch, white leather, inviting enough to want to curl into, yet large enough to seat guests.
- Medina dining room table cut from polished and reclaimed wood. Eight matching seats, enough to accommodate a small dinner party or double as a workspace for off-book corporate engagements.
- Framed picture of Mom and Dad—an actual photo, printed from film, and not a digital one-off.
- Framed Dancheckker Guide page listing Enzo's name as a top broker that year...

Wait, no, Enzo hadn't made enough money for that last one yet. He was still climbing. He wasn't top man. He didn't have the perfect corporate spouse. His house was in Old Ford, not Limehouse.

There were other outliers as well. A bag from Jabberwok's, a no-frills soup shack, sat out on the counter, its contents long since devoured. Upstairs, in Enzo's bedroom, a ring encased in glass sat on the mantel above the trideo screen. The labeling beneath it read *Ipsissimus*. Nero knew the brand. They sold high-end *telesma*. The ring was lined with enough orichalcum to make it visible in the astral spectrum. A focus of some sort, then. One Enzo purchased with the hopes of eventually using? Nero shook his head. Enzo never gave up on the idea that he could one day manifest magical abilities. It was a sad self-delusion. An expensive one as well, by the looks of the ring.

Nero wandered into the bathroom and picked up Enzo's toothbrush. It was such an ordinary thing, a reflection of life that had nothing to do with corporations or money. It was hard to remember Enzo was still a man under all that.

Behind the first toothbrush, Nero found a second, round with medium bristles. Perhaps a partner stayed here for a while, but not forever. Nero couldn't imagine his brother with a partner.

He walked out of the bathroom and flopped down onto the bed. He winced unconsciously, memories bubbling to the surface again. He took in a deep breath and forced them back down again.

Over the years, Nero tried everything to tear those memories from his mind. At one point he'd even studied the church's books on magic that could work the problem. He learned very quickly it was bad practice to try mind manipulation magic on yourself. Even as stubborn as he was, the second time one of the nuns found hum half-naked and gibbering in a bathroom stall, he'd finally recognized that he had to live with the memories.

The hardest thing he'd ever done in life was to try and move on from what had been done to him. Except he'd never expect to see his brother again. He'd used his magic to scrape as much of the memory of Emiliano from his mind as he could. It wasn't forgiveness. It wasn't coming to terms with what had been done. It was running away. At the very least, it was a way of moving on. Emiliano died in the lake all those years ago. He was Nero now. He did not play mirror. His movements were different than the man who lived here. This was business, and business meant knowing who that man was and how best to imitate him when the time came.

The doorbell rang.

Nero steeled himself and stood. He eyed the clock. It was well past midnight. He slid on Enzo's AR goggles and fumbled through the sub menus for a moment before he figured out how to work the front door camera. The woman he saw on his doorstep wore a long coat. She held her head down, shielding herself from the ever-present drizzle that never quite became rain.

He knew it was Shen before she looked up.

Nero stopped the camera feed and told it to erase itself. Then he headed downstairs to the front door, taking two steps at a time. He stopped to catch his breath before he opened the door. When he did open it, he smiled and said, "Miss me?"

Her tattoos shifted anxiously from orange to red. She stepped inside and threw her arms around Nero. They stood like that for a long while before Nero shut the door behind her.

He studied her. She looked tired, especially around the eyes. "How are you?"

"Here now." She pulled off her wet coat and hung it on a coat rack by the door. He could see now she was wearing his cross. She fabricated a weak grin and said, "Grim Fox and EnJee are fighting again."

Nero sighed. It occurred to him that they were less like a team and more like a family, with EnJee the bully big brother who poked at everyone's soft spots. He didn't do that with Shen, but he'd done it for years with Nero. Since he and Shen got together, Grim Fox had taken the full focus of Enjee's ire.

"Fancy digs," she said, moving further into the flat. She ran her hands across the surface of the couch, the table, the chairs. "Show me around."

He did, starting in the living room. She moved ahead of him as they walked around the flat. When she saw the bottles lined up in the kitchen she said, "Rough night?"

He shrugged. "Just lonely."

She stopped at the wine fridge, knelt, and studied the bottles inside. She pulled out a Riesling with a name he couldn't pronounce and uncorked it. It was a simple matter to find two glasses and fill them both. They sat on the couch and drank. They let their fingers intertwine as each sipped from their own glass. After a while, she said, "Tell me about the extraction."

"It felt strange to be on that side of it. We've done so many extractions that I've never thought about what it must feel like to be in the middle of it, confused and uncertain how to defend yourself." He paused to take a drink and added, "There was something off about it, too."

"Like what?"

"I don't completely understand what went wrong on their end. We've done a dozen extractions. Have we ever injured the principal?"

A smile flickered across her face. "There was that time when we were pulling out the Evo exec—the dwarf, not the troll from Hamburg. Remember, he took one in the hip?"

"I remember that job, but that was crossfire from his own security. We weren't the ones doing the shooting. This time, I got knocked around pretty good when they rammed us, and Olgin took the worst of it."

"You think it was a hit and not an extraction?"

"I don't know what to think, but I'm grateful to be out of it soon."

"Soon." Shen repeated the word like a mantra.

"I'll see Novak tomorrow."

She ignored that. "You aren't going to ask about your brother?"

Nero tried to imagine what it must have been like for her, staring into the face of a man who looked and perhaps in some ways felt like Nero. While he was flying across the planet playing his role, she was experiencing the other side of that mirror. He said, "How is he?"

She shrugged. "He's scared. He's trying to negotiate his freedom. He's nothing like you, Nero. I doubt he ever was."

Nero nodded, but did not meet her eyes. He focused on the wine, pouring himself a second glass and drinking it quickly.

Shen reached across and settled her hand over his before he could prepare a third glass. "Show me the bedroom."

He took her upstairs, gathering the bottle of wine and his glass. Shen went ahead of him again. When she reached the bedroom. she ran her hands across the expensive bedding and said, "Executives always have the same kind of stuff. Back when I was little, some of the older girls used to say, 'be nice as you can, and perhaps one day, they will take you away and you get to stay in a place like this forever.' I wanted that for myself at first, but then..." She trailed off with a faraway look in her eyes.

"You mean in school?" Nero asked? Then he looked to her tattoos and saw the warning shades of orange taking root there. Quickly he said, "Is there anything you've ever wanted that you couldn't have, you know, because of the life we live?

"I always wanted a dog."

He said, "We could get a dog."

"We couldn't. We move around too much. We couldn't take care of a dog."

He shrugged, taking her by the hand and leading her to the bed. "What kind of dog did you want?"

"Not anything crazy like a hypoallergenic hellhound. Or even an Akita or a purebred Golden Retriever. I've always liked mutts. They're special because they're...*not* special. They had to be tough to get by, when everyone can customize what sort of dog they want. Nobody really asks for a mutt. That's why I wanted one."

What Nero wanted was her warmth and the comfort of her. He sat on the bed and she sat beside him. He said, "You're what I want. You're special."

When they made love, their bodies moved together in frenetic conversation, saying what their minds could not. Afterward, when his mind fogged with the promise of sleep, he said, "If we lived like this, you could have a dog."

He drifted off and dreamed of a life where he and Shen could have a dog and a yard where it could run.

When Nero woke in the morning, it was to the sounds of Shen fumbling around in the kitchen. He crept out of bed and watched her finish preparing a breakfast of eggs, toast, and real orange juice. The toast was burnt. The eggs looked to have come from a powder solution, like the one his mother used to use when he was little.

He cleared his throat and she turned to him, smiling. She said, "No reason to let all this food go bad. Besides, I can't send you off to meet the boss on an empty stomach."

They ate, and she helped him pick out a suit that looked appropriate. As he left, pausing at the door to offer his partner a goodbye kiss, he considered the life they could've had if Enzo, and not Nero, had been the one born to magic. He considered the life he could still have in Enzo's skin.

"Let's take the money," he said impulsively. "Let's find a way to take the money from my brother's firm and disappear. You, me, even the guys could come along. We could live well and forget about the shadows entirely."

She held his face between her palms and said, "It's a beautiful fiction. But it isn't who we are. Eventually the beaches would get cold, the money would run dry, and where would we be then?"

"It would work for a while."

She shook her head. "We chose this life, Nero. Maybe not directly, but we chose to be here and we chose to be in this together. I know you and I are not as die-hard about the shadows as EnJee—hell, nobody is—but we know what works for us. We are smart. EnJee is smart. He takes care of us and keeps us all safe."

"And not a week ago, he was ready to kill me."

"He trusts you. That's hard for him. You can trust him too. We're a family, the four of us."

They were a family in more ways than his flesh and blood would ever be again. Nero saw that now, and he knew that he had to finish this job and close the door on these memories once and for all.

But he couldn't do that without seeing Enzo again.

It was a chore for another day. He'd already called into the office and told them he wasn't ready to come back yet. Today, he needed to see Novak. The Dubai situation pushed back the clock. It might have done even more damage that he didn't understand, because he didn't understand this world and what was expected of him in it. He needed to understand what he needed to do to put the run back on track.

Nero took the cross around Shen's neck in both hands. He kissed it and then he kissed her. Then he walked out of the door, just another exec joining the queue to start his work week.

NERO

11-17-2081
11:00 A.M. Local Time

It was common for people on different sides of a business deal to meet for drinks. The ability to tear each other's throats out during the workday and retire for drinks together afterwards was part of what made them civilized.

When his dad had talked about it, Nero always compared the act to how he imagined it must be on and off the pitch for soccer players. In a game, that player across from you was your enemy. Afterwards, you could hang out and even become teammates if the trade winds blew in that direction.

Enzo had never agreed with Nero on that last front. He'd wanted to play soccer, and knew there were teams he could never stomach playing for.

When Nero reached out to Novak, he found she'd arranged for them to meet at the Hive, a private social club located at Belgrave Square, a stone's throw from Buckingham Palace. Though he had expensive tastes, Enzo Moretti didn't make the kind of money needed to support a driver and car, so Nero parked a few blocks north and walked the short distance to the club.

The Hive sat along a row of arched entrances that fronted embassies and private corporate residences. The area was conspicuously absent of drones and cameras, but there was security and surveillance if you knew where to look. Thanks to EnJee, he did. As he crossed the near-empty street toward the club, he eyed a handful of individuals posted at corners or under terraces, shielded from the rain. He'd done a few high-end extractions before, and this type of security felt familiar to him. Somewhere, someone was scanning his face through the Matrix, making sure his SIN popped back as active. Likewise, he knew there would be magical surveillance in place nearby, so he focused in on himself, masking his aura the way he learned back at the church all those years ago.

The doorman waved him inside the club without bothering to check his credentials, further evidence of the heightened security.

Katerina Novak waited for him inside the common room. She stood as he approached, smoothing out the ruffles of her Vashon Island skirt. He fought the urge to track his eyes upward as she moved her hands from her hips up across her midsection to eventually tuck a loose strand of hair behind her ear. He felt guilty, not just for the urge to look at her but because he hadn't told Shen about the weirdness of their interaction, and the sense he'd had that Novak was coming on to him when she touched his hand. He wondered about her relationship with Enzo. Perhaps they'd extended it beyond the professional, and the way she kept touching him was a form of kink for her. Or perhaps the physical contact was just another layer of manipulation, like the charisma-softs that reddened her cheeks; another tool in her arsenal to make sure Nero did what she wanted.

Novak leaned in and kissed him on the cheek. Then she directed him to a small table. She sat down in front of a pink drink in a martini glass. He sat down opposite her.

She said, "Enzo continues to look good on you. I mean it in the best possible way. This lifestyle suits you."

"Well, the suit doesn't entirely fit."

"Are your friends listening in?"

"No." This wasn't the sort of place where you could pat a person down or sweep for bugs, so had he considered it, he could've had his team listening in. However, his personal commlink was tucked away inside a jacket pocket, battery still removed.

"A shame, that EnJee fellow has quite a lot to say. He's fun." She smiled flirtatiously. It made him feel uncomfortable.

"Why this place?" Nero asked.

"Your brother has a penchant for private clubs. Nobody would be surprised to see him come in here. Besides, I thought you might enjoy the place."

He didn't. It felt wrong. It felt like his skin was crawling just being inside the building. There was a wrongness here that he couldn't entirely place.

As if he'd spoken his discomfort aloud, she said, "It used to belong to the Universal Brotherhood, before all of that nasty business in the UCAS. They sold this location and a dozen others. Most were demolished. However, given the marquee location, this one was merely renovated and sold to the highest bidder."

The Hive. He understood the name, then, and swallowed down the urge to vomit. The Universal Brotherhood had been responsible for summoning bug spirits into the material plane. They'd been active around the world, but Chicago had been ground zero for their operation. Thousands of human-sized cockroaches and other bugs poured through the metaplanes and into the city. The same could have happened here had the Brotherhood not been stopped. The taint of what they did was felt on the astral plane everywhere they operated. Had he'd tried to use magic here, the disgust he felt now would have overpowered him.

Katerina Novak pretended not to notice his expression. "Have you been to the office yet?"

"I'm taking as much time as I can. I'm claiming to still be shaken up by the attack. I left a voice-mail with Enzo's assistant saying I wasn't coming in today, and I've been dodging calls from everyone."

"That's not much of a lie, is it?" She studied him, and then continued, "Well, maybe it is. That is the life you lead. Your boogiemen carry guns and come for you in the night. Mine have bespoke suits and talk about liquidity. They're both dangerous in their own ways."

She sipped her drink and set it back down, waiting for him to respond. When he didn't, she said, "Would you believe I found out your brother tried to screw this deal yet again? He pushed to Lothian-Vaea PLC, but they didn't show the least bit of interest. It's almost like he's trying to move Zeik Weisz to anyone but me."

Nero made a face betraying concern, but in reality, he didn't know who Lothian-Vaea PLC was or why this was a problem.

"At any rate, we ought to start thinking about moving this meeting to tomorrow, as opposed to risking waiting until Wednesday. With your boss out of the picture, it might be easy to get this done and get you out of there before people start expecting you to take on more responsibility."

"You think Enzo is poised for that?"

"I think Enzo is good at what he does and has a certain level of free rein already. I don't think he'd want that job." She saw him tapping his little finger against the table and softly set her hand over his. "You have to go back to work tomorrow. The markets are open. You'll have sales calls you need to make and business to do with your team."

Nero pulled his hand away. "And I'm supposed to know how to do all of that?"

"No. But if you screw it up, that messes things up for Enzo. I'm sure he wants to believe that once this is all over, you'll let him step right back into his life. So, talk to him. I'm sure he will be willing to help point you in the right direction to get things done."

"You don't know my brother."

"Well, neither do you. Not anymore. Get on your comm now and call Selina. I'll walk you through what to say to get the meeting moved up. This is the only way we both stay safe."

He did as she asked. He pulled out the commlink and made the connection to Enzo's secretary. He kept the call voice only, so Enzo's assistant wouldn't see where he was and ask questions he couldn't answer.

Novak whispered, "Tell her you need her to contact the buyers and push the meeting up to tomorrow, as early as possible. Tell her it's because you want to clear your deck to deal with overflow from Olgin's accounts."

Selina answered. *"Enzo, my God, I've been trying to reach you since the incident. Are you okay?"*

"I'm surviving. Look, I need you to move that CDO sale up. I have to get all my business cleared so I can focus on Mr. Olgin's overflow. Can you make it happen tomorrow?"

"I'll handle it. Anything else?"

"No, I'll call you as soon as possible." He hung up. His hands were shaking.

"That was very good." Novak said. "You sounded just like him there."

"I sounded like an imposter."

She sighed and stared down at the table, shaking her head. She swirled her drink with her cocktail stick while she talked. "That's just you being inside your own head over this. I meant what I said. Talk to Enzo. If you explain what you are doing, he will have no choice but to help you. With everything going on at Lewis-Klein and beyond that right now, it is in his best interest to make sure you get this right."

He let out a breath he hadn't realized he'd been holding. "Is this about Spinrad Global?"

She looked up. "Why would you ask me that?"

"Everything I—Enzo has been doing so far is tied up in Spinrad Global, and I just wanted to know what I'm getting involved in."

"You don't have to worry about it because you're not involved in anything. Enzo is. Once we are done, you can walk away." She snapped her fingers. "*Poof*, no more problems. You'll get paid and go back to your life."

Nero gradually became aware he was tapping the table with his fingers again. Novak watched him with an expression that floated between curiosity and boredom.

He said, "Was it you? Were you responsible for that hit on Olgin?"

She frowned. "No. I thought you said it was an extraction."

"Who did it, then?"

"I don't have the first clue who it was. Olgin is a major player. His ISDA qualifies him to move billions. It could have been any number of companies wanting that sort of capital access."

"You had people watching me. Didn't you gather info?"

"I didn't have people watching you."

"Yes, of course you didn't. And you don't have them watching me now, either."

She raised an eyebrow, but said nothing further on the matter. She finished her drink, then stood. "Consider what I said about reaching out to your brother. It is critical that you look the part, up to and through the meeting."

She gathered her purse and swept out of the room without looking back. When she was gone, Nero pulled out his commlink and inserted the battery. Seconds later, his call to EnJee went through.

"Everything good there, mate?"

"I want to see him."

EnJee shot back, "Might not be the best idea. You don't sound like—"

"Send me the address. I'm coming by."

A long silence passed between them, then Nero saw the location tag pop up on his HUD. He disconnected the call and headed for his car.

ENJEE

11-17-2081
12:45 P.M. Local Time

GOD is always looking down on the Matrix, eyeing the digital borders that divide cyberspace in the same way meatspace is carved up and dished out to the powerful. The Grid Overwatch Division doesn't know who EnJee is, and he wants to keep it that way. Except nowadays, each corp has its own cadre of watchers. DemiGods roaming their particular corner of the Matrix, looking for a fight.

For a decade now, EnJee's been running a little hotter than normal, punching up the haptic feedback that runs directly into his brain. No soft rig here. He already ran hot. For years, people thought he was a technomancer. He'd run in those circles and slammed with a few of the ultra-hot, but no technomagic. No resonance. Just a smart hacker with a datastore full of tricks.

He's using those tricks now, sleazing through Renraku Globalink. He's staying under the radar, because any movement in the system not strictly legal risks convergence. He's come close to that too many times as of late, and he knows GOD wants to find him.

He takes the long route to a public gambling node that promises winnings of over one million nuyen per day. That number doesn't reflect the amount of nuyen they rake in from all of the people who didn't win. Among the losers, he finds the one he is looking for.

In the Matrix, Ekon Abioye is a manga-idealized version of himself. He towers at nearly 3 meters tall. He has a broad chest to match the oversized arms and legs. His hair indicative of a Shōnen hero, wild and bright hanging over his near black skin.

The persona is meant to intimidate in all the ways his physical modifications are meant to put people at ease. Here he is weak, so he must project strength.

EnJee settles his persona into the seat behind Abioye. He watches the poker game unfold, pretending to wait until the next hand to join. He says, "I thought you gave up gambling for stocks."

Abioye's affectations are more pronounced in the Matrix. He does not look up. He says, "The odds are about the same, except at the tables I'm smart enough to know I'm getting screwed. Come on, let's go somewhere a bit more private."

He pockets his chips, stands, shares a destination code with EnJee, and vanishes. EnJee follows. When he rematerializes at the new location, he is not impressed.

"You could've picked somewhere more interesting," EnJee says, glancing around the default office sculpting of a node built on Horizon software. "Why here?"

"I thought since I had you, I would get you to open that door for me." He points to the entrance to the manager's office. The double doors are coded shut. A black-suited security guard with mirrored shades stands in front of it, arms folded.

"This is the favor you asked for earlier, then?"

"No, this is a small matter for someone of your considerable talents. One that will considerably speed up our current business."

EnJee groans and unlimbers his scythe, trudging toward the door like a kid called upon to do chores. The risk of convergence is high, but the risk of alienating his contact is significantly higher.

The security guard shifts, moving into a defensive posture. It never completes the gesture as the scythe flashes through the air, slicing the IC in half as if it is made from cheaply rendered basic code. EnJee shoves his scythe into the space between the double doors. Something pops and the door opens. He fights against the urge to say, "*Open sesame.*"

Abioye's persona claps slowly. Even his gestures are Shōnen. He starts to drift toward the open door, but EnJee stretches a hand in front of him in a *hold on* gesture. "What did you find out?"

Abioye's arms drop to the side. He turns to EnJee and dials up a stock expression of impatience.

EnJee fires back a custom grin. The power dynamic here is clear.

Abioye says, "Have you figured out who your Johnson works for yet?"

"CNI. They're a subdivision of Spinrad Global."

He nods. "They're Spinrad Industries. So, who else is at the table?"

EnJee thinks for a minute, noting the clarification. According to the file, there are a handful of buyers for this slate of properties. He reads off the list, "Commonwealth Enterprises, Ifrit Holdings, and Danske Bank."

Abioye folds his arms. "My friend, you are sitting in the middle of a family dinner you do not want to be at."

Family. That word keeps coming back around. It never means anything other than trouble. EnJee says, "What kind of bad are we talking here?"

"When Spinrad died, it set a lot of pieces into motion. I mean, I'd heard rumors about him being in deep with organized crime, but I always figured it was just talk, or that maybe he was connected to one mob boss or another."

"And?"

"And he wasn't locked in with just one mob. He laid off bets *everywhere.* There are no less than one hundred and seven separate unrated corporations connected to Spinrad and, because of legal loopholes, not subject to his will. Officially, he doesn't own any of them, but my company was curious about some of these. We checked into it with some difficulty. Nineteen of them don't actually exist. Each one of those is tied to a different group of investors who, also unsurprisingly, don't exist."

"We were hired to help our Johnson broker a deal for control of Zeik Weisz. Are you saying Zeik Weisz is one of these shell corps Spinrad built to pay off criminal debt?"

"Zeik Weisz is indeed on that short list. Your Johnson buys this debt, and what they are really doing is buying into a conversation with the Asociacion Vasquez. I'm betting your guy Enzo knows about this. In fact, I am guessing he is either the only one in his corporation that knows about it, or at least the only one in his company authorized to do anything with Zeik Weisz."

"What's your take on all of this?"

"My take is I ought to get what's in this datastore and be on my way. You ought to finish that job and keep your name clear of any involvement. The *Asociacion Vasquez* will want to know who messed up their sweet thing. You don't want them thinking you played any part in that."

EnJee drops his hand. As Abioye walks into the datastore, EnJee backs out of the node and then out of the system. He doesn't want to know what data he just released to Abioye. He thinks knowing is more dangerous than not.

He spends a few more minutes deleting his trail before heading deeper into the Matrix to the Helix to gather what info he can on the *Asociacion Vasquez*.

When EnJee finally jacked out, the first thing he saw was Grim Fox sitting directly across from him, waiting. The big warrior was eating a carrot. EnJee said, "You look pretty silly with that. More rabbit than samurai, *neh*? You bring it back from our trip?"

Grim Fox rolled his eyes. "You ought to learn to appreciate vegetables, *omae*. Appreciate more than that slop you buy at Stuffer Shack."

Shen was standing by the window, the shade slightly lifted in one hand. "What did you learn?"

"My guy says it's not worth the trouble. We stick to the Johnson's plan. Take the money and dump Enzo after."

Between bites, Grim Fox asked, "We really gonna just let him go?"

"That's up to Nero." EnJee stared toward the bedroom where Enzo Moretti was being held. "If it were up to me, he'd never leave that room."

"He's here," Shen said, dropping the window shade back into place.

EnJee muttered, "Isn't this just cor blimey."

Shen opened the front door before Nero had a chance to knock. He was dressed in a business suit. With his hair done in the corporate style and the AR glasses plastered to his face, he more closely resembled a Johnson than anyone on EnJee's side of the shadows.

Shen and Nero shared a hurried kiss at the front door. Nero was clearly distracted. He waved to the others. Grim

Fox chuckled and held his arms out. Nero disappeared into a bear hug.

EnJee said, "All right, Nero. You're here, then."

"Where's Enzo?"

Shen pointed toward one of the bedrooms. Nero nodded, took a deep breath, squeezed her hand and started walking toward the space. When EnJee stood and followed, Nero said, "I don't need babysitting. I can do this."

"Right, well, if its business, I'll have my eyes on it, too. Maybe we all should."

Nero considered it for a moment. Even how he moved felt different. It hadn't been a week, and the corporate already clung to Nero like a stench. It was getting hard to tell if he was acting like a suit or becoming one. The mage shrugged, as if agreeing to the audience optional.

Nero entered first, and stopped just inside the doorway, taking it all in. They'd lined the room with a sound muffling spray foam Grim Fox was fond of using in situations where the needed to hold a prisoner for an extended period of time. It made the space look less like a room than a cave with dull yellow walls, and false stalactites hanging from the ceiling.

Of the furniture, only the bed remained. Enzo Moretti sat on the bed dressed in blue shorts and a gray t-shirt that read *Take No Prisoners*. His hands and feet were bound with zip ties. When he saw the four of them enter, he gasped. "You've come to kill me, finally."

Nero barked a harsh laugh. "If my friends wanted to kill you, they would not have gone to the trouble of dragging you across all of Africa."

Enzo looked from Nero to EnJee, searching for confirmation. EnJee offered a half-hearted shrug.

Nero took another deep breath before he said, "Arturo Olgin was seriously injured in an assassination attempt. I need to go into your office tomorrow and pretend I am you. I need you to help me do whatever it is I will be expected to do now that Olgin is gone."

EnJee noted the surprise on Enzo's face. Enzo said, "What, so you can destroy all that I've worked so hard to create? Why would I do that?"

"Destroy? I am trying to make sure the people at your work believe I am you so that you can return to your life when this is over."

"So you are trying to take my life away from me!"

"Stop behaving like a child, Enzo! I don't want your life!"

EnJee's laugh made both men look at him. "Pardon me for saying it, but I think you might owe Nero here a bit of courtesy, considering how you tried to geek him in the first place."

Enzo opened his mouth to speak and then closed it again. He licked his lips and said, "Emiliano. It was not my choice to shoot you. I did what I had to be done."

Grim Fox got to Nero before EnJee could, catching the mage mid-lunge, scooping Nero up and spinning him away from the prisoner. Nero was cursing and screaming, his face red with exertion.

"Get him out of here, mate," EnJee said and moved to close the door as the melee tumbled into the hallway.

The sounds of violence faded, replaced by Enzo's wet blubbering. "It wasn't my fault."

EnJee crouched down next to him. "Bugger all that. You pull the trigger, you make the choice."

"Yes, but if I did not, she said Emiliano would've killed us all!"

Enzo raised an eyebrow. "You saying someone told you our boy was all primed up to murder his family? And you're just the poor hero who had to put him down?"

"No! I mean, yes. That's not how it happened, but there's more to the story than what he—"

The door opened and Enzo snapped his mouth shut quick as a mousetrap. EnJee glanced back. Nero stood in the doorway, red-eyed and angry. EnJee said, "Enzo here was just telling me stories about the early years, weren't you, Enzo?"

Enzo didn't speak. His eyes never left Nero.

When Nero spoke, his voice trembled, "I will not forgive you for what you did to me. However, I may excuse you, so long as you do what I ask."

He did not wait for the answer. He backed out of the room and closed the door. EnJee couldn't help but smile at that. Intimidation and manipulation were twin games EnJee played fairly well himself. By the looks of Enzo, Nero just won that confrontation.

Pressing, EnJee said, "I'm going to let you think on that a bit, mate. Then I'll come back and we'll have a chat about how everything might still work out for you in the end."

Out in the living room, Shen and Nero were parked on the couch. Nero's eyes were wet. Grim Fox posted up against a wall, munching another carrot. EnJee rolled his eyes and found a spot near the kitchen counter to sit down. After the silence filled the space long enough to grow uncomfortable, EnJee said, "We good here?"

Shen offered a weak nod. Grim Fox continued to chomp noisily on his carrot. Nero cleared his throat and said, "EnJee, do you know anything about Lothian-Vaea PLC?"

He shrugged. "SK subsidiary. Fair-sized player out our way."

"Novak seemed pretty pissed that Enzo went to them with this deal."

"That tracks with my info," said EnJee.

Nero perked up. "You found out what this is all about?"

"You know the deal. This is about power and leverage. Novak wants it, and Enzo is offering."

Nero said, "What if we made it about more than that? We have a chance to make a difference here. If we can move the sale to another organization, one that will do something better with it, shouldn't we try?"

EnJee shared a quick glance with Shen and said, "That's not the game, mate. Everything in the world is owned by one entity or another, and corps like this think their job is to put market control of space, of air, of water, of everything in the hands of their people, because they are the only ones who know how to use it."

"Yes," said Nero, "but there's more going on here. I think this whole thing has to do with Spinrad. When I was in Dubai, there were other deals happening that had to do with Spinrad as well. You're right about leverage. This entire thing feels like it's about giving leverage to someone, but who can we trust with that power?"

Shen set a hand against Nero's cheek. She said, "I'm not sure it matters, love. Everything we do in this world is a bid to maintain the edge, in order to tile the deck in someone's favor. Nobody wants a fair playing ground. Everyone wants an advantage. Moreover, they want a sword and a shield. The sword is the mechanism by which they can cut through to the consumer, the knife edge upon which they bleed you for your personal wealth. The shield is the protection, the language and precedent that obfuscates the people behind the actions. You will never see the people running any corp having the kind of moral dilemma you're having right now. The only question they ask instead is, 'Do I own this or does someone else?'"

Nero looked crestfallen. "You're telling me it doesn't matter who gets this sale."

EnJee said, "It only matters that we do our part and we get paid."

Nero sighed, then looked toward his brother's room when he said, "Then I suppose we better come up with a plan that helps us get paid."

NERO

11-18-2081
7:10 A.M. Local Time

Shen stayed the night again. She wanted to be there in the morning when he went in. She wanted to go with him, at least be on the ground floor waiting for him to exit the building, but Grim Fox warned her off that strategy. Novak wasn't about to make a scene in the middle of downtown London. The real danger, if it came, would be after the job, when they met with Novak to get paid, and the team would be ready.

They went through everything again in the morning before Nero left. This time he made the eggs and coffee. He found it hard to eat, with his nerves so frazzled by his fear of the coming task, but it helped to keep busy. They sat in the living room, sharing the couch as he ate.

She smiled and adjusted his tie, running a thin finger along the line of his freshly shaved chin. He watched her tattoos flare red, and his eyes followed the line of them down to his cross, which hung against her chest.

"I like this look on you," she said.
"Don't get used to it."

She drove him to the tube station, where they said their goodbyes a second time. According to the files, Enzo parked his car in a parking tower near the end of the tube line and took the train into the heart of the city like a mid-level corporate suit. Her research suggested he did this to look like a man of the people and thus win the support and loyalty of the lower-level employees around him. Nero figured he did it because he was too cheap and too low on the totem pole to be able to park his car in the company facility. As he descended into the Underground, he checked for signs of a tail car, but found none.

When they'd discussed getting in and out of the corporate office, EnJee told Nero about how the new tube network had replaced the older Victorian tunnels, and how some of those older tunnels were shut down. He said those had become home to all manner of baddies—and just as often, regular poor people looking for a place to stay dry. If Nero was tailed by corporate security or Novak's own people after he left the offices, the tunnels gave him the best chance of losing that tail.

Nero replied, "Sounds like you know this from experience."

Then EnJee said, "I'm not saying I do or don't. I'm not saying much of anything about the before. Not 'til you shed some real light on your time as a SINner."

"You know my history."

"Pretend I don't."

The conversation had devolved into a stonewall, with Nero saying it wasn't the time or place, and Enjee insisting it was.

Now, he caught his reflection in the train window and felt like someone else. He sat back in his seat and reached for the trigger. He felt the magic rising inside of him, separating him from this world. Heard the hum of the human world growing into a terrifying buzz around him as his head slumped gently forward.

He was in the astral space. He looked at all of the people and studied them—human sardines wrapped in a metal tube hurtling along beneath the city. He adjusted his form to keep pace with the train, though the speed of the vehicle was enormous.

He hovered there in astral space, watching it all. Then, out of the corner of his eye, he spotted a watcher spirit. It was an astral bit of nothing, a small blob with eyes. It looked like those eyes were watching him. He stared at the spirit a moment longer, and then started toward it. The thing floated backward and then blinked entirely out of existence.

He hustled back to his body, re-inhabiting the flesh. He then stood up, two stops away from where he was supposed to be. He couldn't sit anymore. He was nervous and sweating, and worried he may have blown the entire deal by going astral.

What if it had been watching him and he spotted it? Enzo couldn't do that, and if the someone watching him was from Lewis-Klein, then they'd know he was not Enzo.

The two stops went by faster than Nero would've thought, though he was so caught up in his own imaginings that he didn't move toward the doors until they sounded to close. He just made it out. He stood on the platform for a moment, staring after the train as people headed toward the exit. He gathered himself and followed after them.

Lewis-Klein existed in a monolithic structure in the heart of the city, whose offices housed a dozen major banking corporations. He rose out of the station near the massive Overmann tower and quickly discovered he was within walking distance of the Bank of England and the London stock exchange. As he turned the corner, the HKB building shifted into view. It was at that moment he realized how seriously out of his depth he was.

Nervous tension spread like warmth beneath his suit jacket. The L-K building was a towering silver needle that cut through the soup-thick cloud cover and continued on above it. He didn't think he'd ever done a job in a building this tall.

"Just going to stand there and look at it?" The voice came from behind him as he stared up at it. It belonged to a jovial-looking young man, possibly twenty years old. He spoke in an accent that, if not actually Chinese, was cultured to appear as such. Nero looked at the man, struggling to remember the face from the handful of data cards he'd studied over and over. Either he couldn't remember, or this man wasn't on the cards.

Nero faked a laugh and tapped his head for emphasis. "I keep thinking I'll have an office above those clouds one day, and it's gone to my head."

The man eyed him curiously, and said, "Well, better get it together. Big business happening up there."

Inside, Nero walked across the glass and marble lobby to the elevator. It shot up so fast, Nero barely had time to tap the forty-eighth floor button before it was slowing to stop on his floor. When the doors slid open, the noise of the space hit him like a wave. Even knowing what to expect hadn't entirely prepared him for the chaos.

The forty-eighth floor wasn't entirely one level. Where the elevator spit him out was more of a landing or a balcony. It wrapped around the entire floor, which was as open as an outdoor mall. The walls were lined with offices. Enzo Moretti had been at Lewis-Klein long enough and done well enough that he had his own office, an executive assistant, and a team of his own occupying what they referred to as "the chop shop" in the center of the space.

The chop shop was, in essence, an office bullpen. However, once Nero exited the elevator, he had to descend down into the space via a short flight of stairs that separated the landing from the pit in the center. Novak's files told Nero where his brother's office was. He stared across the space until he found it along the back wall, where seven others like his flanked the double-sized corner office belonging to Arturo Olgin.

He also knew from those files that Enzo always walked through the chop shop, another affectation that said he was just one of the guys.

Except Nero wasn't. He scanned the space for Enzo's team. He found them, matching his memory of the digital cards to each face and nodding as he walked by. He measured his steps, counting them in his head to remind himself not to run and not to walk so slowly that this too was a red flag. He walked like a man unaffected by the world around him, while all around him, this strange world was a mess of desks and cubicle walls and trid screens flashing numbers at an alarming rate. Someone was singing a tune he didn't recognize, and other people sang it back, a call and response that felt more like it belonged at a Premier League soccer match than a corporation that traded billions of dollars each day.

Nero made it to his private office. He paused to nod to his secretary, then shut the door and closed the blinds. He leaned against the door and exhaled a long breath. He wanted to reach for his magic more than anything.

But it was as Novak said: the people who ended up in corporate boardrooms like this weren't mages or shamans. They were ordinary people who found a way to grind out an existence based on the skills they did have. Nero had to pretend he was ordinary, and in that state, he was not in control of this situation at all. He was hiding behind an office door 48 stories in the sky. Everyone on the other side of that door thought he was someone else, and, with Olgin out of commission, all of them thought he was the one in charge.

By the time he caught his breath, Nero's comm had beeped six times. To make matters worse, there was a gentle knock at his door. He ignored the knocking, making the choice to slide in his earpiece and pick up the call.

EnJee said, *"You in?"*

"I'm in." Nero felt the relief in his own voice.

"Okay, I'm logging into the system with Enzo's clearance. Shouldn't ruffle any feathers. Link me up. Then you can sit at your desk and relax."

The Matrix and AR space out on the chop shop floor was a mess of signals and feeds from the dozens of workers stationed there. However, here in the private offices, executives like Enzo—like himself—had baffles installed so they could maintain a level of privacy in their dealings, and nobody would be able to listen in unless they were let in.

Nero pulled on a pair of AR glasses, tapping the side to activate them. He pushed a kernel access code from his comm to the glasses.

EnJee responded immediately. *"Now I see what you see."*

"What's next?" Nero said too quickly.

"We get to work."

"That doesn't give me a lot of clarity, EnJee. I already have people at the door and I still don't know what I am expected to do before the vote this afternoon."

"I got Enzo right here at my side, mate. He's come around to helping us through this, and Shen here is making sure he doesn't change his mind."

As EnJee explained how to pull up an AR wheel of everything Enzo was currently working on, Nero slid on a pair of AR gloves sitting on the table and clicked through the list. He saw the Atilla deal at the top of the wheel. Next to that was a red-flagged file labeled *"Chalmers and Cole."* Further along the circle, he spotted another red flag file named *Ofenya*. There were a dozen more files without flags. It took him another moment to locate the CDO sale.

"I found his files on the CDO sale."

"Has Novak contacted you?"

"No." He started to say more but the gentle knock grew more urgent.

EnJee said, "Deal with it."

He told whomever it was to come in. The door opened and the woman who stuck her head in was Selina, his executive assistant. She was tall and thin, with long black hair and a serious face. He wondered if she was the owner of the mysterious toothbrush he'd found in his brother's bathroom.

She said, "Got a minute?"

He nodded and waved her in.

"Six calls from Sacha Drozdov. I'll shoot the messages over to your PAN." She spoke softly, saying the words as if they were a question.

He nodded as if he knew what that meant and said, "Anything else?"

She went over a few more items. There were calls Olgin needed to make, and in his absence, Enzo was authorized to make them. The team was looking for some face time with him to see how Olgin was doing and let Nero—*Enzo*—know what they were doing. Upper management wanted to talk to him about next steps. Afterward, she stood there, stiff and silent.

He watched her for a long moment, wondering if he should stand up, or say something. He settled on a thumbs up sign. She looked at him, confused, and made no move to leave. He wondered again who she was to Enzo.

EnJee must've read his silence for what it was. He said, "*Enzo says they aren't together, but they are close. She knows him, Nero. Make her go away.*"

Shen came on the line then. "*Tell her you came back too soon. Tell her you're not all there.*"

Nero said, "I'm sorry I'm a bit off. I'm not really back yet. Not all the way. I have to be here for the meeting today, but—"

"I understand, Enzo. I'm so sorry you had to go through all of that."

EnJee said, "*Get rid of her, mate, before she makes it weird.*"

He said, "Thanks, that's about all I can handle for now."

An expression he couldn't quite read rippled across her face. She turned quickly and grabbed the door handle. Nero called to her as she was about to leave. She stopped and turned back, a question on her face. He said, "Do you think you can keep everyone off my back until the meeting? After that, I'll go. When I come back tomorrow, I'll be a whole new me."

She nodded. The sadness on her face was genuine enough that Nero had to consider Enzo again. In spite of what happened when they were young, his brother wasn't entirely a monster. He was enough of a person that people cared about him. This Selina apparently cared about him. Someone who had people who cared couldn't be all bad, could they?

EnJee's voice streamed into his ears. "*Well played. Might have bought yourself a few hours. Now let's go over this plan again.*"

Nero said, "I start the meeting, listen to everyone's offers, and then Novak makes a counter-offer."

EnJee picked up from there, "*Right. You nod and smile through all of those offers and when she makes her counter, that's when you pull out the offer we're supposed to execute. You both agree to it and then you get out of there. We'll meet up after to have that talk about Enzo,* neh?"

"*Si.*" Nero said. He wasn't ready to think about the after yet. He couldn't think about that. Not now. He had to find a way to get through what was next.

The boardroom at Lewis-Klein felt identical to the one in Dubai. The room itself was decorated completely differently, but the central table was the same idea. The level of intensity the space conveyed was the same. This was a different type of DMZ, one that swapped out spells and bullets for relatively bloodless transactions.

Nero felt a shiver careen through his body at the memory of the last meeting. What came after the meeting felt familiar, even comfortable, despite the obvious danger he'd been in. This space, with all of its rules and mores, held the real danger, the danger of being discovered.

This was also different than Dubai in one critical way: there nobody knew him, and his boss had done most of the talking. Now his boss was laid up in a hospital somewhere, the victim of an extraction or perhaps even an assassination gone wrong. Nero was sitting here filling his shoes—and filling Enzo's shoes as well.

He'd read somewhere once that everyone had the dream of being on stage, completely naked as everyone else in the space looked at you. For some people, the audience would point and laugh; others they would stare silently waiting for the dreamer to say something that was obviously the wrong thing.

He'd never had that dream, but it was easy to imagine. He'd read the script, practiced the words and exchanges time and again, but he didn't know what he didn't know—how to answer the unexpected. It left him feeling as naked and vulnerable as all those people on the stage.

He thought about the *padres* at the church. *Padre* Luca always knew the right thing to say to the crowd. *Padre* Josef always moved the partitioners with his voice and his spirit. Nero imagined the being at the head of a boardroom table could be the same way. It was a sermon, the path of belief veering toward the financial. Everyone had to believe in something, even if it was just bits of data scripted to be considered valuable.

Without realizing it, Nero had started to think that being in the corporation was a form of religion in and of itself. It was a way of seeing the world and interacting with it along the course of your life. Religion had helped him form the schema through which he came to fully understand his magic. He understood that magic operated on the principles designed by the user, and adherence to those principles formed the path that one set out upon. One could not change the principles once created. Corporations had been created and operated under principles created hundreds of years ago in a world that did not truly understand the power they were unleashing, and now were powerless to stop it.

In fact, this world didn't even speak the language required to stop it. This world no longer spoke in terms of malevolence. It spoke in terms of inefficiency. It did so in everyday terms and conversations. It did so through commercials that promised to make your life easier, faster, closer to your fingertips. That mindset continued to be reinforced by everyday people who wanted to believe in something and more often than not wound up believing in exactly what they should not.

That's what Nero had gotten out of his last talk with EnJee. The old hacker wasn't a hooder. He doubted any of the crew he'd grown to think of as a family believed in doing good above all else. He wasn't even sure if any of them believed good still existed, but Nero had principles of his own and they wouldn't go away. He still believed that he could make a difference, if only a small one. He believed it enough that he would find a way to keep trying.

Nero stood as the participants filed into the room. Everett Yeun escorted them in. Nero expected that. Lewis-Klein's operating philosophy was that in deals this size there be a second corporate officer in the room. The exec grinned back at him, nodding his excitement.

The next person to enter was a dark-skinned man who identified himself as Cedric Kale. He represented Ifrit Holdings. Kale was followed in by Danske Bank's representative, a broad-shouldered man with blond hair and teeth so perfect they probably cost more than Nero was set to make on this run. He hated the man a little for that, and was secretly grateful Danske wouldn't be winning this bid. He bellowed his name, Erick Masters, to the group, and seemed surprised that they didn't automatically recognize it.

Katerina Novak came in next. She was professional and courteous. She made a bit of small talk with Yeun as she entered, but treated the situation as if she didn't know Nero at all. She sat on the far side of the room with her hands clasped neatly in front of her, waiting for the negotiations to begin.

The last person to enter introduced herself as Mrs. Helena Chomsky, from Commonwealth Enterprises. She had dark blue eyes and her brown hair was tied up in a tight bun. Mrs. Chomsky felt more like the nuns at church than a corporate executive. She was polite and friendly in her introduction and she made a point to shake hands with everyone.

Nero wished he could have brought EnJee and even Enzo into the room with him, but at this stage he couldn't afford to have anyone questioning the earpiece. He could less afford one of these savvy investors hacking his signal and figuring out the entire thing a was a ruse. He would rely on old fashioned memory and, if available, good luck.

Nero cleared his throat and said, "Good afternoon, everyone. Why don't we get started?"

Across the room, Ms. Novak thanked him and started her pitch. Her offer was filled with a ton of corpspeak he couldn't understand. Nevertheless, he sat up straight in his seat and pretended like he understood. Nero thanked her once she was done and asked the others who wanted to pitch next. He listened to three more companies deliver their pitches, each laying out a different path to divide the collection of assets currently in trust with Lewis-Klein.

Erick Masters, however, thought he had this in the bag. His proposal was also filled with a lot of numbers and corpspeak. What Nero did understand boiled down to the fact that Danske was backed by Maersk, and nobody else in the room was. That information clearly mattered more to Masters than anyone else present.

The Ifrit Holdings representative, Cedric Kale, was the third person to speak. Nero felt the man had a genuine smile, and an attitude less suited for the corporate boardroom than the business side of a confessional booth. He reminded Nero of a bartender in that way. By the numbers, Ifrit had the most to offer. Kale made that fact clear several times during his presentation.

Nero read some tension between the Commonwealth rep and Ifrit. It didn't seem like they knew each other personally, but instead very much disliked each other's companies. From what EnJee had explained earlier, both ultimately served Spinrad Global, as did CNI, so he couldn't understand the tension. He couldn't understand why all three of them were in the room. The Commonwealth rep offered a deal similar to what Ifrit put on the table, but the specifics were tied up in corporate language he had no way to unravel. He wondered what Enzo would've done. From the little he could make out, Nero would've boiled his choices down to Commonwealth or Ifrit. Katerina Novak certainly would have stood no chance.

Once the last pitch ended, everyone turned toward him expectantly. Nero felt his mouth go dry. He knew what he was scripted to say here, but it didn't make him feel any less nervous. He tried on a serious expression and said, "Well, unless there is something else, I am ready to make a decision."

Novak cut in, "If you're willing to indulge me a moment longer, I have a counter-offer. While we'd like to purchase the entirety of the collateralized loan obligations within the CDO, we understand that all of you want some of the pie, too. So, we'll take these." She pulled up a file and shared it across everyone's virtual screens. The file contained a list of corporations numbering nineteen in all.

The Ifrit man spoke up first. "You're asking to take a specified chunk of investments from a variety of these tranches, which would lower the value and security of the remaining product. You added on a bunch of fluff at the end here, but you aren't leaving the rest of us a lot to secure our risk."

The Commonwealth representative, Mrs. Chomsky, laughed and added, "You want to take on all the toxic waste, that's fine by me, but I have an objection to you grabbing the Super Senior assets as a counterbalance. You're basically leaving us with just the leftovers."

Nero expected the objection; Novak had prepared him well. He turned to Katerina. "Take Sargent Supplies. It isn't much but, depending on your risk appetite, it could help to counterbalance a lot of the equity risk."

"No," she said. "I'm going to need something more to balance my cost benefit. If I'm eating all this corn paste and bull crap, I'm going to need a stiff drink to go with it."

A murmur of laughter rippled across the room. Nero felt the tension ease out of him at the sound. He showed his hands and said, "Okay, okay. I have another investment piece, not officially part of the sale, but if it helps our securitization efforts here, I could see fit to package it as part of a deal. It would mean you letting go of some of the Super Senior assets, Ms. Novak, but it is a fairly equitable mezzanine level object."

Nero pulled up the file the exact way she'd packaged it for him, mirroring the display to everyone else.

He tried to fall into the role. He tried to remember all those times he'd joined his father at work, again reopening the floodgates on a history he fought so long to suppress. He shrugged and smiled and said, "It's all just commercial paper, but when you put it together, I think you'll agree that it looks good enough to counterbalance the risk."

Novak nodded.

He went on, "With those low-grade investments off the books, it creates space for me to divide the rest of the prime cuts evenly amongst the three of you. How's that sound?"

The Danske man shrugged. Mr. Kale nodded. The other woman, Chomsky, said, "Perhaps when you're ready to deal with those Atilla assets you just picked up, you wait to work things out with Ms. Novak first? When the two of you have decided how to properly split those new assets, we will be happy to take the scraps."

For a moment, Nero and Novak shared a look. Then Novak said, "What are you insinuating?"

Nero fumbled for something to add, and found nothing. Chomsky rescued him, finally. "Kidding. Just kidding. We'll take the offer as it stands."

And then it was over.

The representatives all filed out of the room, shaking hands with Yeun and Nero as they left. Katerina Novak stopped at the door and said, "There is additional information about the offer I can share, if one of your number would like a follow up meeting?" She looked from Yeun to Nero.

Nero cleared his throat and said, "I'll take that meeting. How about now?"

He pointed her toward his office. She smiled demurely and walked in that direction.

Yeun watched the exchange and said, "Wow, man. I did not think you liked blonds."

Nero looked repulsed. He said, "I don't. I do like money, however, and I think she can make us a lot of it."

He caught up to Katerina Novak and walked her back to his office and closed the door beyond her. He leaned against the closed door, took a deep breath, and exhaled.

She extended her hand to shake his and said, "You did really good in there. You were a natural."

He shook his head. "I was an imposter."

"That's because you're new to this. Give it a little more time, and this could be a way of life for you, Emiliano."

He shook his head and sighed, settling into the chair behind Enzo's desk. "What was that thing with Chomsky at the end?"

She shrugged. "I don't know, exactly. It felt more directed at you than at me. If I had to hazard a guess, I'd bet she had an arrangement with Enzo going into this deal, and you messed that up by selling to me. You should ask Enzo about that."

Nero looked thoughtful. After a moment, he said, "I don't know what to do with Enzo."

She raised an eyebrow, "My agreement with you and your team is that I pay you this evening for the work done today and leading up to today. The rest I leave entirely to your discretion."

"So, you don't have an opinion on the matter?"

She stood and said, "I tend to avoid involving myself in family affairs."

She made it all the way to the door before he decided he couldn't let her go thinking she'd won entirely. He said, "The watcher was a nice touch, by the way."

She looked back over her shoulder. "I don't know what you mean."

"Of course not, but you do know I spotted it in the train station and again as I was heading here. If it came from Lewis-Kline, they would've already known I'm not Enzo. This deal would not have happened. It had to be you. Magical surveillance can't be cheap. Perhaps you should be paying us more than you offered."

She quickly turned to face him. "Emiliano, I didn't assign anyone to watch you."

His smile broadened into a grin. "Of course you didn't."

But her face didn't change. Her charisma softs didn't pump the fake flush into her cheeks. Her cyber eyes stayed locked on him, betraying concern.

At once, he knew she wasn't lying.

NERO

11-18-2081
1:19 P.M. Local Time

The chaos and elation of the multi-million nuyen deal faded almost immediately in the bullpen. Everyone outside of Enzo's office still smiled and offered high fives, but were quickly moving about their day, on to the next business.

Well, almost everyone.

Part of Nero wanted to fall backward into the office chair and let the energy of what he'd just done overtake him. He'd brokered a deal that moved millions of nuyen from one place to the other. There were more credits in that deal than he'd see in his lifetime, yet to the people who worked there, it was just a Tuesday, with more deals and more nuyen to be spread around throughout the week.

He thought he could adjust to this life. He thought about how comfortable Shen had looked in his brother's robe. How she'd tried to cook real eggs and burned them, not understanding how the process worked with non-synth product. He deserved this life, and it should've—*would've*—been his had things not been the way they ended.

The more he thought it over, the more he convinced himself he could slide into Enzo's life. With work, he could pick up the relationships and the habits and the job. If that didn't go as planned, he'd just live in this life as long as he could on Enzo's existing wealth and then melt back into the shadows when it was over.

Shen deserved it. They deserved it together.

But he couldn't let himself think like that.

He cycled through what Novak had said before she left. She hadn't been the one tailing him in the train station. If he believed her, which he did, that only left two other possibilities: either Lewis-Klein set a protective detail on him, or someone else was watching him. If someone else, then who? Were they watching Enzo Moretti, or were they watching Nero? He couldn't wrap his mind around why anyone would be surveilling him. Nero was a nobody, a shadowrunner with no real connections.

But there was a third possibility: he could be overreacting. The stress of the extraction and trying to pretend to be his brother could've led to him seeing ghosts where there were none. He'd seen a watcher, yes, but what proof did he have that it was watching him?

Nero pushed aside the privacy blinds and stole a glance toward the bullpen. Everett Yeun hovered at Selina's desk, peppering her with questions as he shot curious glances toward Enzo's office. He didn't want to deal with Yeun right now. He pushed a message to Selina's station that told her to ping him when Yeun was gone.

He left as soon as Selina pinged him. He walked by her desk quickly, blurting that he planned to take the rest of the day off. There was a level of concern in her eyes that unsettled him. She didn't look at him like an employer, but as a friend. She said, "Are you sure everything is okay?"

"It's fine." He kept walking until he came to the elevator. He heard Yeun call to him from across the room. Nero pretended not to notice. He chanced a look out of the corner of his eye. Yeun broke into a jog to catch up to him.

He went to press the button for the elevator, but the woman standing there pressed it for him. She had long, blond hair with a wide-brimmed hat to protect it and her from the rain. She was wearing a long coat that complemented her hair and her features. He found her look curious, since they were indoors.

The elevator door buzzed open. The woman walked inside and Nero followed. The doors started to close, but Everett Yeun managed to catch up. He stuck a hand between the doors and they stopped. Then they slid back open. He got into the elevator, straightening his tie as he did. Once the doors closed he said, "What was all that stuff about in there?"

Nero looked at Yeun and then purposefully looked at the woman with the hat. She smiled back nervously at them both, probably uncomfortable to be in this cramped space in the midst of what was clearly a private argument.

Yeun didn't seem to care. He was waiting for an answer, so Nero offered, "What do you mean?"

Yeun finally glanced at the woman and lowered his voice. "I asked you about ZW at least a dozen times, and you said you'd never move that debt. You said you figured out something and had a way to make big money off it. Don't you know the people who own it or something?"

Nero shrugged, trying to keep the panic out of his voice. "That's all in the past now. This is business."

Yeun fixed him with long and hard a stare that started sweat beading at Nero's temples. He looked away first. The woman beside them was looking down, pretending not to pay attention.

Yeun clapped a hand on Nero's shoulder. "What's with you? You've been different since Dubai. What, you find God or Allah or whatever after they shot at you? What's going on, man?"

Nero's mouth flattened. He said, "Nothing. I'm just still a little shook up by it all, okay?"

But it wasn't okay. He could see it in the man's expression. The distrust creeping into his eyes. Nero understood in that moment that stealing Enzo's life would mean making peace with people like Everett Yeun, and he didn't know if he could do that. It wasn't as if he could walk away and look for another job. That was, as Shen had said, a pleasant fiction. Contracts made you the property of the corporation. When you did leave, it was usually the result of extraction, a shift from one extraterritorial power to another with the only legal recourse being a corporate court that did not care. You couldn't just walk away—not for very long. To stay here, to be Enzo Moretti, he would need to make good with people like Everett Yeun and Selina Villarreal.

Thankfully, the elevator came to a stop and the three passengers exited into the lobby.

Nero said, "Look, I'm going to head home and rest a bit. See you tomorrow?"

"Yeah, whatever, man."

He kept walking, pausing only briefly to make sure Yeun turned back to the elevator and wasn't planning to follow him.

The lobby was full of people dressed in suits and wearing serious expressions as they moved in and out of the building. Nero kept his eyes focused on the front door and escape. He wasn't paying attention the way he normally did in runner situations, which is why it took him by surprise when the woman with the wide-brimmed hat sidled up alongside him and slipped her arm into his. He gave her a quizzical stare.

She said, "Mr. Moretti, please understand that there is a gun trained on you right now. There is also a man walking behind us who is armed, and if you try to use any magic or try to shove me to the ground or do anything other than continuing to walk where I lead you, the spike in my forearm will project backward, directly into your ribcage."

She elbowed him playfully for emphasis. With a giggle that was more shown that felt, she added, "Do you understand?"

Nero nodded. Eyes wide, he looked around. No one else in the lobby noticed the exchange. No one else seemed to care at all about a man and a woman walking out the building arm in arm. He'd been on the other side of these kinds of runs so often that he couldn't believe that he was the one being kidnapped and had never even seen it coming.

"Good," she said, "Then the rest of this shouldn't be too painful."

She led him away from the building toward a gray sedan that pulled up to the curb. The driver was human, and looked to be a regular service driver. The rear door opened. She instructed him to get in the back seat. Inside was a dwarf nestled in the space between the seat and the floor where he couldn't be seen cradling a shotgun leveled at Nero's head.

Nero could tell by the looks of them that this was a seasoned shadowrunner crew.

Which meant if he got inside that car, he may never get out again.

He reached for his magic.

Pain exploded in his ribcage. Then everything went black.

ENJEE

11-18-2081
5:30 P.M. Local Time

They decided to meet Novak at a spot EnJee knew in North Kensington, far enough from Grand Union Canal that police didn't bother. He'd given her directions to a collection of old buildings between Barlby and Oakworth that formed a U-shape, inside of which a warren of walled of yards, dividing eight different low-rent apartment complexes and three separate gangs.

EnJee knew the territory from the old days. He'd grown up there a half-decade ago. He also knew if they stayed around too long, one of Westway's many gangs might get curious and come asking questions. They'd need to do this fast.

The courtyard EnJee chose had once been considered a demilitarized zone for the gangs that fought to rule this patch of London. He didn't know what it was now.

The years hadn't been kind to the place. It was less green and more plasticrete than before, though the weeds were fighting the good fight to take the space back. Busted basketball hoops marked the high walls separating the various courtyards. Their vantage point offered a clear line of sight to Barlby road on one side and the narrow concrete path leading to Oakwood on the other.

It felt like the perfect place to settle up.

Rain fell like a steady drumbeat. EnJee couldn't keep himself from wondering when one of those drops would sizzle instead of plop. It was part of what drove him out of the Smoke the first time. It's bad enough having the opposition keeping you on your toes during a run, but to worry that the weather might kill you, too? Amsterdam was better. Hell, Rhine-Ruhr was better. But he was here now, and he was dealing with it all the best he could, especially considering he thought he was being set up.

EnJee wasn't big on trusting people in general, and Johnsons not at all. It bothered him that he hadn't heard from Nero yet. It bothered him more that Shen hadn't. It didn't surprise him that Nero missed the rendezvous. He hadn't given word on what he wanted to do with his brother post run, and was likely off somewhere sorting it out on his own.

They'd be moving Enzo. Nero's brother was in the trunk of an Americar on the other side of the lot, bound and gagged so he wouldn't cause any trouble no matter what Nero decided to do with him. EnJee was betting on a bullet.

He glanced over at Grim Fox and said, "Any word from Nero?"

Grim Fox shook his head.

In the distance, two cars peeled off the main road and stopped at the entrance to the complex. EnJee said, "Our guest is here. We good, Shen?"

Two clicks came back over the commlink. It was the closest they'd had to a conversation in hours.

EnJee made the mistake of telling her to give Nero space when he'd missed the rendezvous. Someone had to be the one to say it. The kid must be going through a lot. He'd never been the face before, and here he was walking in and out of a mega like he belonged. Moreover, he was walking into a life that could have been his, had he not been shot down and dumped off a boat. Now he had to decide what to do with the man responsible for that as well.

Shen was parked on one of the nearby rooftops with the big gun, a Crockett EBR sniper, settled into a tripod staring down into the courtyard. Grim Fox had set her up with a rappelling rig in case things went bad and she had to come down the side of the building in a hurry. EnJee was hoping it wouldn't come to that.

Several concrete tables were set up with matching benches. A few of the tabletops were painted to look like chessboards. No one was in the courtyard, thanks to the heavy rainfall. Though it wasn't toxic, but it was enough to force the normal business of these streets indoors.

Grim Fox sat on top of one of the tables, checking the building windows. He hadn't been in full agreement with the meeting spot. There were too many variables here for his liking, but once again, he didn't have a better plan. EnJee beside him on the bench itself. He watched the warrior scanning the space protectively and said, "Quite the scene we make here, *neh*? Like a father and his son sitting in the rain. Now here comes mum ready to make it a party."

Novak's entourage parked at the mouth of the lot. She brought half-a-dozen security with her this time. Grim Fox watched them and said, "Given the situations you've gotten me into already, I don't know that I would have survived very long had I been raised by you."

EnJee grinned, looking at Grim Fox from toe to head. "Consider the size of you, mate. I was thinking you'd be the father in this scenario."

Grim Fox rolled his eyes.

Katerina Novak wore a long black coat to shield herself from the rain. She walked up to the table with her hands stuffed in her pockets. None of her security walked with her; from what EnJee could tell they were settling into sight lines along the perimeter. Part of him admired her boldness. Most of him felt she was a bit too cocky.

Grim Fox didn't bother to get up. She nodded once to Grim Fox, and held her hand out to EnJee. He didn't take it. Novak said, "Still not long on trusting me I see, even after all we've been through? I can respect that."

EnJee said "Not looking for your respect so much as your nuyen." Then he paused, again gauging the distance of her security men, then said, "We did our part. Care to settle up?"

She shrugged and smiled, stepping forward to hand Grim Fox a small case, the kind of thing you'd expect to hold a pistol or a jewelry. Grim Fox opened it. Inside were four black credsticks. She said, "I split it evenly, as discussed. I have truly appreciated doing business with you all, in spite of the obstacles."

Grim Fox ran a finger over each of the sticks. He stopped at the last one, looking up. "Where's Nero?"

That gave her a momentary pause. She recovered quickly and said, "I have no idea what you mean."

EnJee said "He means Nero's not with us, and yet his share is right here. I thought maybe you settled up separate, and he was off somewhere having a pint, working out what he wanted to do with that slag of a brother of his. Except that's not what happened, is it?"

She shook her head. "I left Lewis-Klein directly after the meeting. He stayed behind. I have no idea what came next."

Grim Fox stood. His growl was laced with barely restrained anger. He said, "We've done what you asked and played it straight. No more games, lady. Where's our friend? He's been out of communication since he finished the job."

Novak took a step back. She held up her hands in a placating gesture and said, "Emiliano didn't tell me anything about where he was going. We finished the work and I moved on."

EnJee's eyes widened briefly. He was staring at a red spot over Novak's heart. He subvocalized, "Shen, no. We aren't escalating."

The red dot didn't go away. Novak followed his gaze and found the red circle of a target designator on her chest. She said, "What is this?"

"I was going to ask you the same." EnJee mouthed the words slowly. His own hands were up, patting the air in calming gesture. "My girl has a clear shot on you. Tell your security people to stand down."

"What are you doing?" Novak said again, panic edging her voice.

"I'm asking the questions. Our boy hasn't come home yet. We know you got what you wanted, and that makes the rest of us loose ends. It doesn't have to be this way. Give Nero back and everyone walks away from this."

"I'm telling you, I didn't do anything to Emiliano. Maybe he's still at the office, or he went back to Enzo's house. I don't have any clue what he's doing."

Grim Fox shook his head. "None of those things are true." He took a step forward.

"He said he was being followed. He thought it was me, but it wasn't," she said quickly. "Whatever is going on with him doesn't have anything to do with me!"

EnJee watched Novak's security detail closing in around them. There were four men all identically dressed in gray suits, blurred by the gray sky and still grayer rain falling. Grim Fox licked his lips in anticipation.

EnJee said, "That might be true and it might not be. Either way, here's what's going to happen. You're going to walk out of here with us, and then you and I are going to have a talk, all right and proper. Your security is not going to follow. Instead, they are going to go get Nero from wherever they are keeping him and bring him back."

Novak's shout caught them all by surprise. "Listen to yourself! Do you really think I'd show up here and hand you money if I snatched your friend?! Do you think I'd bring his cut?! Do you think I'd show up at all? I would send people with guns to meet you and to say goodbye."

EnJee hesitated. She'd moved past panic, sliding toward a desperation he generally ascribed to Stuffer Shack cashiers on the wrong end of a robbery and schoolteachers. He didn't believe a word she said.

She stuck a hand on her hip and said, "This is entirely unprofessional."

He considered giving the signal for Shen to slam a bullet through her and then making a dash for the courtyard exit, staying low to avoid incoming fire from her security detail. It would be satisfying enough. It would be like scratching an itch right at the small of your back that you couldn't quite reach.

He considered what would happen to Nero if Novak had him. He considered what had happened to Nero if she didn't. Finally, EnJee said, "I'm not going to put a bullet in you. I'm asking for your help."

ENJEE

11-18-2081
5:45 P.M. Local Time

When the suits stepped out of the vehicle and into the Westway rain, it set two things in motion. First, the civvies poked their heads out of windows, started putting in calls to the local gangs. The Lions of Juddah were the closest thing to an armed police force in these parts, and they weren't fans of corporate intervention. The time between them learning corporate security was nosing around their turf and them coordinating a response could be measured in minutes. It was part of the reason EnJee had chosen the meeting spot he did.

Second, he knew when the Lions started moving, that would get the rival Westway Stranglers on their feet. Since the courtyard didn't belong to either gang, it belonged to both gangs equally. No way the Westway Stranglers were going to let the Lions going to police this turf for them. No way were the Lions going to wait around until the Westway Stranglers were ready to mount a response. EnJee spotted a kid, no more than eleven, done up in Lions of Juddah black with a red bandana wrapped around his head. He darted out of a doorway and into another.

That set the clock running.

EnJee subvocalized, "Time to go, mates."

Up on the roof, Shen would be double checking the harnesses on her rappelling gear and readying herself to come down the side of the building. Down here in the courtyard, Grim Fox started back toward their car, while EnJee turned to Katerina Novak and said, "This is about to become ground zero for a gang fight, all because those four blokes of yours decided to get out of their cars."

Novak looked around. Nothing had changed on the surface. The rain still fell, the courtyard was still empty save for her people and EnJee's.

She started to shake her head in dismissal, but EnJee said, "I'm going to walk out with you. And we'll get in your car nice and proper and take a drive. Then you and I will have a discussion, and maybe that will lead to some understanding, neh?"

She started to object, and then stopped, listening to something in her own earpiece. EnJee said, "What your security is probably telling you right now is that tossers are starting to gather in doorways, and they don't look too friendly. Now, we can stay here a while and find out what that means, or we can go get in your car."

Novak was cooperative—surprising, considering she was only a few minutes removed from having a gun pointed at her chest. EnJee followed her back to her car, escorted by two of her security. They checked him for weapons before letting him into the back seat, an exercise that only served to waste more time they did not have. By the time the car was underway, a half-dozen teens dressed in red and black were moving toward the lead car. Novak's driver peeled back out on to the main street and away from the gathering trouble.

As they drove, Novak placed a call to Lewis-Klein asking after Enzo Moretti on an important business matter. EnJee listened to the call from her end, but couldn't make much sense of it. Novak laughed and made jokes and even flirted with the person on the other end. When she clicked off the call, she sat there silent and thoughtful.

EnJee pointed out past the driver and said, "Left at the next turn here."

The driver glanced in the rearview mirror but didn't turn. EnJee looked between her and the driver, a request in his expression. Finally, Novak nodded, and the driver obliged.

Novak continued, "I was able to get a hold of one of Enzo's associates. He said Enzo—Nero—left with a blond woman. He thought it was strange because he rode the elevator down with them, and they didn't seem to know each other."

"That had to be who grabbed him. Can you find out who she is?" EnJee said.

"I can ask around, but too many questions may raise red flags. Their security is already on edge after what happened in Dubai."

"Do it. Find out what you can about the woman," EnJee said, and then to the driver, "That's good right here."

Novak directed her driver to stop. She looked out at the street and said, "What makes you think I'll help you?"

"Because me losing my mate could be bad for your life expectancy." He eased out of the back seat and then offered a wave to Katerina Novak. She didn't wave back.

A few minutes later, Grim Fox and Shen pulled up in Enzo's BMW. EnJee slid into the backseat. Grim Fox was underway again before he closed the door.

Shen said, "What does she know?"

"Our boy got nicked by a blond woman on the way out the building."

"Just one runner?"

"She can't be too hard to find." EnJee said.

"If we're even assuming she's local talent," said Grim Fox. "Nobody else got a look at her companions." If the face was good, then the face was all you saw. The rest of the crew melted away into the background. Then once the job was done, the face could change from cosmetics, to cybernetics, to magic. They could be dealing with practically anyone.

Shen said, "Why did they want Nero?"

Grim Fox's answer was another question: "What if they weren't after Nero?"

EnJee and Shen both turned towards the back of the car, their thoughts leading them to unconsciously look toward the person crammed into the trunk.

Grim Fox said, "Do we really think Zeik Weisz wasn't the only front business Enzo was operating for organized crime?"

EnJee thought about it. "That's a fair question. If he did this fancy money trick once, he could've done it a dozen times for any number of organizations. We need to ask him who else he was working with."

"Enzo met with Russians in Africa," Shen pointed out.

Both men looked at her. Grim Fox said, "How do you know that?"

"Those men at the club were Russian Vory. I could practically smell it on them. Enzo promised them some kind of financial setup. He said he had a blueprint of how it worked. It sounded like more corpspeak at the time, so all I did was file it away in case he wanted to talk me up about it."

"So you think this is that?"

She said, "I don't know what this is, but if whomever grabbed him thinks he is Enzo, we need to find him before they figure out he's not."

EnJee said, "Head to Notting Hill. I got an idea of who might contract for a snatch-and-grab."

NERO

11-18-2081
7:30 P.M. Local Time

The first thing Nero realized when he woke up was that he was moving. He was on a train, a fast-moving one by the feel of the rumble beneath him. He was on his back on a mattress jammed into the corner of a what looked like a cargo container. He tried to speak but found that his mouth felt like it was filled with cotton. He smacked his lips together, trying to make moisture. He felt dizzy. Did he get knocked out?

The woman from earlier knelt beside him. She had a UCAS accent that he didn't remember hearing in that brief moment in the building. He remembered getting into a car. There was a dwarf waiting inside, hiding below the seat line then, what?

None of that mattered here. And he had to find out where *here* was. When he started to reach for that familiar well of energy, that place where his magic came from, two things happened. First, he saw a small spark of green light, an unnatural-looking light, flash in the corner of his vision. Then pain blossomed in his groin. He screamed, and for a while, he could not stop screaming.

When the pain began to fade to a roiling hotness and not the static flare of the sun, he opened his eyes again. The UCAS woman was looking at him. She held a slim black taser in one hand, waving it like a flag. She said, "I want to be polite. I don't want to continue to harm you in any way that may make our employer unhappy. However, I prefer my safety to your own."

Nero croaked, "What is this?"

She said, "You were dosed with a sedative. Nothing in your file said you were Awakened, but we did our research.

We learned about what happened in Dubai, and thought we'd be better safe than sorry."

"Did you stab me?" He reached for his ribs and found a stim patch there. He pressed on it gently, and felt the edges of a small wound beneath.

"I did what was necessary at the time," she said. She opened a canteen and held it out for him. The water tasted cold on his lips, and he sucked greedily at the bottle.

When he had drunk enough, he looked around the cramped space. Definitely a cargo container. Corrugated paneling surrounded him. Beyond the thin mattress he was strapped to, there were a few crates. Beyond the crates, a handful of people were gathered. He recognized the dwarf from the back seat. There was another man, slim and pale-faced, who must've been the driver.

"I wouldn't try anything again," said the woman. "My friend's shotgun might be filled with rubber bullets, but they hurt like a son of a bitch. And of course, there is this." She waved the taser again.

It felt like he was moving. The entire cargo container was moving, but it wasn't like being on a boat. Nero said, "Where are we? Who are you?"

"That doesn't matter much either."

"Are we on a train? This isn't the Metro." He took a second, slower look around the space and now saw there was something else: a small vial the dwarf was holding, spinning it in his hand. A tiny bit of green moss floated inside.

The man in the corner laughed a genuine long and loud laugh. "Not exactly the Metro. No."

Nero expanded his senses, reaching out to the astral to see what was around him that could be a threat. But what he saw was the vial. It burned in astral space, and at once he knew what it was.

The woman punched him in the face. He snapped back, his vision doubling for an instant, the pain jolting him back to a physical reality he did not want to accept. He grunted.

"I prefer you not do that." The vial was still glowing. She added, "The stuff in this vial is called glowmoss. Hard to find. Expensive, but extremely effective at recognizing the presence of activated magical energy. There is a theory it feeds on the stuff as though it's sunlight. Try that again, and you'll be sleeping the whole way there."

Nero spat blood and said, "The whole way where? Where are we going?"

"You're going to meet your new employer, Mr. Moretti."

"I'm not Enzo Moretti."

She actually laughed. "Like I haven't heard that one before. We've got the wrong guy, right? Except you have all his credentials and I pulled you out of his office."

He coughed again and settled his head back on the mattress. Nero said, "You're making a terrible mistake. I'm really not Enzo Moretti."

The others in her crew were chuckling as well. There was something hard and uncaring in their faces, and Nero thought just for a moment that this must be what it is like to wake up with EnJee, Grim Fox, Shen, and himself standing over you.

Then the woman said, "Look at Enzo here with the jokes! You can pretend to be whoever you want to, *omae*. It won't be long before you understand that the person who hired us to grab you has a short temper and no sense of humor I've ever seen."

ENJEE

11-18-2081
6:30 P.M. Local Time

Grim Fox parked the car along Portobello Road in front of a Biscos Grocery, where the BMW was the nicest car around it. Hondas, Espirits, and GMCs lined the gray streets. The buildings in this part of town were older than the ones that blanketed North Kensington. Most of them were still low-end apartments no higher than ten stories whose ground floors housed a collection of family-oriented and no-frills stores. AR graffiti dripped from the walls and the lampposts, assuring anyone who cared to notice that the Nightwraiths still ran the show here. If not for the ever-present threat of acid rain, it could've been any sprawl in the world.

Grim Fox locked the car. "Sure I shouldn't stay here with the cargo?"

EnJee noted how careful Grim Fox had become about not referring to Enzo as a person anymore. He considered their prisoner, cuffed and gagged in the trunk. EnJee didn't think Enzo had the guts to run. He also wasn't worried about the neighborhood. Out loud he said, "Lots of shadowrunners hang around this block. I don't think anyone would risk trying to nick a vehicle."

The samurai tensed. "If I'd known that, I'd be packing something bigger than this pistol."

EnJee shrugged and pointed down the block toward the building on the corner. It wasn't quite as tall or quite as well kept as the others. Still, it had a classic look about it that argued it would be worth your nuyen to check it out. "Look there. It's not too often you find an enclosed patio on the side of the road in a part of town like this. That's the beauty of the Elgin, mate. It doesn't care what part of town this is. It's been here longer than any of it."

Grim Fox and Shen both rolled their eyes. EnJee fished around inside his coat until he found the black case Novak had given him. He opened the case, revealing the four credsticks packaged inside. He pulled one free of the foam casing and closed the case up. Then EnJee dropped the credstick into his outer pocket and patted that pocket twice. He said, "You two fancy a drink?"

Grim Fox said, "We go to a lot of bars, EnJee. What makes this one so special?"

"Not just a bar, mate. This is one of the old places. Dodger, Kham, Argent; all the legends have come through here at one point or another. Place has seen so many runners that we're just a small part of its history."

So far as EnJee knew, they didn't build bars like this anymore. Light streaming from the first three levels of the establishment indicated they were all part of the bar. A simple sign over the front door read *ELGIN* in all caps.

Thick black curtains across the windows left the inside was dark enough that the people gathered at the booths or along the bar could feel they had a bit of privacy. The patrons were a collection of shadow-types. Some were obviously posers. EnJee could tell, because they were stationed closest to the door, trying to be seen or trying to act like they were watching whoever came in. The walls of the bar were faced with polished wooden panels. A few walls had been plastered over, and there were spots where the plaster gave way to expose the gray brick behind it.

The bar itself was a long slab of polished wood with a mirrored display behind it that doubled as a fine spirits rack. The bartender was wiping down a glass. He was old enough to have gone bald naturally, though he still had a few scraps of hair left below his chin. He peered toward the four of them with his one cybernetic eye and said "I know you, don't I? It's been donkey's years, hasn't it? You're that dosser what used to run with Union Jack. Or maybe it was Dodger?"

"No, mate," said EnJee, grinning broadly. "In fact, I used to run with your mum out in Bow Bells. The rest is all conjecture." He extended a hand to the bartender, who shook it and smiled.

"He's still got a smart mouth on him, doesn't he?" A voice called out from further down the bar. It belonged to a woman in her sixties. She had black hair done in a bob that hid the scars around her obviously cybernetic eyes. Her one flesh hand held a drink while her silver cyberarm gripped the bar top.

EnJee said, "Carol K. You got old."

She laughed. "Aren't you the one to talk. Most elves never look like they've aged a day over thirty. You look older than Lofwyr."

Carol K stood and took a few hobbling steps forward and embraced EnJee in a hug. She moved with a jerky motion common to cyberware at least twenty years out of date. He'd seen it happen before to people he knew. He couldn't stand seeing it happen to people he liked.

"Ahh, you must be Shen." Carol K took one of Shen's hands in both of hers and shook it gently. "Back when Nigel here still felt I was worth talking to, you were all he'd talk about."

An expression of confusion and embarrassment started on Shen's face and radiated down her neck in bright orange lines of circuitry. EnJee was grateful for his dark skin, because it hid his own embarrassment. Carol K laughed melodically, patted Shen's hand, and said, "He told me about those tattoos, too."

EnJee ordered a G&T for Shen and a X-X-X-Export for Grim Fox. When the two had their drinks, they drifted off, leaving EnJee to speak with his old friend.

Carol K had started running in the forties. She'd stopped running in the sixties. Twenty years later, she still found a way to make herself relevant. Shadowrunners didn't tend to get old. The ones who made it out of their twenties were exceptional or lucky. The line of work was too volatile. Once you stopped living on the bleeding edge of magic and especially technology, everything catches up to you fast.

EnJee said, "I was sorry to hear about Spider."

"No, you weren't. Spider was a tosser. You said it yourself."

"I did, but when the old gang starts getting fitted for boxes, I thought it might be right to show respect."

Carol motioned to the bartender for another glass of whatever it was she was drinking. The bartender set it down in front of EnJee. Carol K said, "To Spider."

EnJee replied in the same fashion and they both drank.

Carol replied, "You added new muscle, I see. Your friend there looks a bit uncomfortable."

Grim Fox stood close enough to filter the conversation through his cybernetic implants but far enough to seem polite. He sipped his beer while scanning the room for any potential trouble.

EnJee nodded. "He fancies himself a bit of a samurai."

She squinted, studying everything about Grim Fox, from the way he stood to the details etched into his remaining horn. "He's from the Cheyenne warrior caste," she said. "At least he was. The history is all there in his horns."

EnJee looked over, noticing the etchings again. He'd never fully appreciated them or even paid much attention. Whenever he did look at the carvings, he assumed they were like most tattoos he saw on street types—a way to make you look tougher than you actually were.

Carol K watched him watch Grim Fox. She shook her head and said, "You've always had trouble with the ones who care about anything larger than the job. You've been giving him a hard time, haven't you?"

"I'm fine with moral codes, long as they don't clash with what I'm doing. I just don't see why you need to put so many rules around what you do and how you go about it."

She laughed out loud at that, causing more than a few patrons to look their direction. She said, "You're certainly one to talk! Do any work for Aztechnology lately?"

"That's not about morality. That's just smart business."

She raised her glass. "As you say."

They both drank again. She said, "So, you're finally back in the Smoke, *neh*?"

"Not really. Just passing through, but I'm chasing after something that's gone missing."

"Your message earlier did say you came here for business. Missing items, was it? And here I thought you were still pretending to have a proper job in transportation logistics."

His smile felt more like a wince. He told Carol K about Enzo Moretti getting extracted from Lewis-Klein in what passed for broad daylight. He left out the particulars about Nero, but made sure to mention he thought the Russians might be somehow involved. "The short of it is, this fellow I need to find has gone and walked off the planet. I'm hoping you know who was responsible, and maybe even where he went."

"That's easy enough, chummer. I didn't order up the work myself, but I know a bloke who knows a bloke and so on."

EnJee nodded, anxious for the answer.

"What's it worth to you?"

EnJee frowned slightly. Although he'd expected this part, it didn't soften the blow. When you fell out of touch with people you knew and worked with, you no longer had the same arrangements. You couldn't expect them to move the way they used to. Rusty wheels needed grease.

He put his hand into his pocket and pulled out a credstick. She pulled out her commlink. He touched the stick to Carol K's commlink.

When the transaction cleared, she said, "Several Russians visited here a few days ago. These were serious men, mind you, and quite likely of the Vory variety. They needed a rush job. They were looking for a crew that could pack your missing corporate friend up and get him to Moscow quietly."

"My missing corporate friend." He scrunched up his face in distaste for just a moment, correlating between Nero and the suit Nero was walking around pretending to be. "You know who took the job?"

"Turbine Mary and her crew."

"I don't know her."

She swiveled her barstool toward EnJee. "That's for the best. She does clean work. However, she and hers aren't the friendly sort. A bit like you that way. Prickly."

"You're going to make me blush. Any chance you can get me a line to them? I have information they may want to hear."

"Like I said, she's a bit like you. There is very little chance she pops her head up while on the job. They're probably well on their way by now."

EnJee took another sip, paused thoughtfully, then said, "What if I need to find the people who hired them?"

She said, "I know that look, Nigel. You're aiming to get into the kind of trouble you can't come back from."

He shook his head. "I'm just trying to fix a thing that went the wrong way."

"I do wish you wouldn't," Carol K said, glancing at Shen. "The last time you did, it ended quite badly. You wound up on the run from the Triads with a stolen kid in tow."

He followed her gaze and shrugged. "Turned out all right in the end, *neh?*"

ENJEE

11-18-2081
7:58 P.M. Local Time

Grim Fox drove them back to their rented flat. The troll looked like a grown man stuffed into a kid's play car, but EnJee noted he didn't complain once. Sirens wailed in the distance, a sure sign the London bobbies were responding to something upscale. They parked in the small private garage beneath the house.

EnJee walked around to the back of the car and patted the trunk twice. The figure inside thumped and moaned in response. EnJee worked up a smile and kept it on his face as he popped open the trunk. Enzo blinked rapidly, his natural eyes trying to make the dramatic shift from darkness to light. Grim Fox moved in beside EnJee, scooped up Enzo in one arm, and slung the man over his shoulder. He brought him upstairs through the narrow stairwell and dumped Enzo in the room they'd soundproofed for this very purpose.

Shen headed for the kitchen, where she stripped off the plastic rings holding a six pack of beers together. She tossed one to EnJee. She tossed another to Grim Fox when he returned. Each of them found a place to sit in the small living room.

Grim Fox downed his beer quickly, then stood up and went to the kitchen for another. He was smiling from ear to ear and staring at EnJee.

"What?" EnJee said.

"*Nigel*, eh?"

"Bugger off."

EnJee thought for a minute then added, "That thing she say about your tribe true?"

"Ancient history, *omae*."

EnJee went on, "Because you're no samurai, mate. You're better than all of that bollocks. It's right and proper to have a code, but make it your own code, *neh*?"

"Never said I was samurai, *mate*." It was a mockery of EnJee's accent.

"Right." EnJee walked over to the couch and put a hand on each of Grim Fox's arms. He stared at him, adopting a fatherly look. He said, "I want to be clear with you: I have no problems with you believing in something. I don't actually give a frag. What you do is what you do, and that doesn't change who you are to me. It also doesn't change how I act toward you. I'm going to be an arsehole, because that is who I am. We accept each other, mate. That's how it works."

Shen cut in, "Are we really not going to talk about how we get Nero back from the fracking Vory?"

EnJee sighed. Shen had a tightness in her voice that put him on edge. The fact that her ink wasn't showing color made it worse. He didn't often look to her ink as a marker the way Nero did. He knew Shen better than that. He studied it for a time in the early days and even worked with a handful of biotech clinics to shut down the bio-implants. It put them both deep in the red on the nuyen scale. After a time, they'd given up on elective surgeries. Shen learned she could control her body to overcome the biomarkers that triggered the ink response. He knew she was the most dangerous when she was trying to remain in control.

Shen said, "Let's call the Russians and tell them they've got the wrong Moretti. We'll offer them a fair trade. Nero for Enzo. Our guy for theirs."

Grim Fox slouched in the sofa, staring at the ceiling thoughtfully. "Which Vory? The Russian mafia operates in cells. If they hired outside talent to pull the job off here, then they aren't connected to the local cells. Hell, the local Vory might not even know what's going on."

"You're just full of bright tidings, aren't you, mate?"

Shen's tattoos began to glow a dark blue. He knew that color all too well. She was anxious. That was the color that led to bad choices. "Let's just call them and find out. We can negotiate a trade."

Grim Fox said, "What's to say they won't try to shoot us down during the trade?"

EnJee said, "Where's the profit in that? They get what they want, and we get what we want. Easy-peasy."

Shen nodded. "Easy-peasy, I'm in. Let's make the call."

Grim Fox shook his head. "There's another side to this you two aren't seeing. This isn't a corporation we're dealing with—this is the Vory. Profit matters, but respect matters as well."

Shen said, "We aren't the ones who disrespected them. This is all just a case of mistaken identity."

"Whether it is or not depends on how they see it. I don't think it will take too much to convince them we have the authentic product. But we need to be respectful ourselves. We can't expect to call them up, tell them they have the wrong Moretti, and then to wait patiently for us to show up and give them Enzo. We need to be there, package in hand, and then ask for our man in return."

EnJee pointed a thumb over his shoulder at the closed door and said, "Okay then, Grimmie. That means we need to find a way to get this bloke halfway across the world again. It's hard enough to get that kind of passage when you've got a willing passenger. It'll be tougher to take along a bloke like him, kicking and screaming all the way."

Shen said, "There's still the option of grabbing Nero before he gets to Moscow. These runners who took him are probably using a smuggler to get him out of the NEEC."

EnJee said, "That's a dead end. They didn't go overland or VSTOL. I already reached out to the people I know on our drive over, and they talked to who they know. I'm waiting to hear back from a few others, but so far nothing."

Shen interjected, "Abioye?"

EnJee hesitated, then nodded. "He thinks they used another resource—sex traffickers or drug runners. They rent out shipping containers moving on the railways, and store their people inside with a small security escort in case things get out of hand."

Shen's face puckered at that. "If I reach out to the right people, I might still be able to find out which traffickers they used."

He nodded. "But there's a delay. Cargo trains leave for Russia almost daily. We could find ourselves a spot in a day or so if I can connect us to those right people you mentioned."

She perked up. "So there could be a chance they didn't get on a train, and maybe haven't even gotten out of the city yet?"

"You heard Carol K. They're gone."

Shen wasn't phased. "If they departed on a train a day ago, we could intercept the train, pull him out that way."

Grim Fox shook his head and set a hand on her shoulder. "Even if we could track down the train, it would be hard to track down which car. That's your proverbial needle in a haystack. And the haystack's moving at three hundred kilometers per hour."

EnJee let them squabble between themselves. He tapped his commlink, sending feelers out through the Matrix. He put out a request for discreet transport to Moscow. Getting from London to Moscow wasn't as easy as it looked on paper. If he was a SINner, he may have been able to catch a corporate charter or a public flight between the two cities. Even those without SINs or with fake ones had a chance of buzzing through security by greasing the right palms. But they had to drag along an unwilling passenger. The three of them needed to get creative, the way they had when coming in from Africa.

After the first response rolled in, he turned to the pair expecting to share the good news, but one look at Shen stopped him cold. He said, "There's another problem, isn't there?"

The blue in her ink deepened as if she were at war with herself. Frowning, she said, "Nero's not going to let us make this deal."

Grim Fox said, "Of course he will. The guy shot him in the back and dumped in a lake, what's he owe him?"

She wrapped one hand around his cross. "You both know Nero. Those years he spent with the church really messed him up on stuff like this. He's just as likely to demand we rescue Enzo after the exchange as he is to refuse to go along with it in the first place."

They were all silent for a moment, acknowledging the strangeness of their partner. Grim Fox said what everyone was thinking: "Just so we're all clear, we are going to Russia to try and make a face-to-face deal with the Vory to get Nero back. If it turns into an extraction, it means doing it while lugging a prisoner along and without our mage, and likely without any local help we can really trust."

"Well, there's a spot of good tidings in all of this." EnJee said, gesturing to his commlink. "Abioye can get us on a train.

I'll owe the bloke more than one favor now. Your man ought to appreciate that."

"I appreciate it, EnJee," Shen said, as if that closed the matter. In a way, he supposed it did. They had history. She owed him in ways she could never repay, yet he kept reaching for her and the others. They'd been together long enough to call themselves a family, even if they didn't speak the words.

Grim Fox said, "So we're agreed then?"

Each nod cast a silent vote.

NERO

8:30 P.M. Local Time

In the absence of sunlight, the passage of time felt arbitrary. When he first woke up, Nero tried counting as a way to generate a baseline of time. He counted against the steady *clack-clack* noise of the wheels striking the track. All he succeeded in doing was convincing himself that the train was moving very fast. He couldn't figure out how that related to what time it was, where exactly they were going, and how long it would take them to get there. He tried asking his captors, but they weren't much for conversation. Like Nero, they'd done this kind of work before and knew how to handle a client.

They fed him MRE pellets and kept him hydrated. It felt foreign to be the one zip-tied and fed water through a straw. The strangeness wasn't accompanied by any real sense of fear. Nero operated on the other side of what EnJee referred to as the import/export business. The runners wouldn't be paid if Nero didn't survive the transfer.

The runners rested in shifts. One would sleep while the other two kept watch. Nero's own team employed similar practices with high-risk clients. Often Nero employed a watcher spirit to ensure the client didn't attempt to harm themselves. Self-harm was the highest risk in situations such as these, as often the targets of extractions weren't going to a better situation.

Nero clearly was not going to a better situation. He could see it in the faces of each runner gathered in the small space.

The train churned along and the hours dragged by. Once, in what he could forgivably assume was the middle of the night, Nero felt a deep sense of foreboding that radiated up from the ground below him. The air grew cold and still in the dark compartment. The others felt it too, unconsciously huddling closer. The deepening cold felt more like desperation. The glowmoss vial radiated faintly.

Nero said, "That isn't me."

The blond runner reached for her stun baton nonetheless, holding it out toward him as a warning. A minute later, she realized the moss wasn't getting brighter. The color in the fungus looked dull and sick, moving toward black like a photo negative. She lowered her baton and shivered.

That felt like hours ago. Now the train was slowing down and turning. All three runners were on their feet, packing up supplies. The work was largely silent, the familiar routines of a crew playing out like a dance. One of them finally spoke. The pale man with the Euro-accent Nero couldn't place said, "You trust this Johnson to play straight with us?"

The dwarf snorted loudly.

"No," said the blond woman, and didn't elaborate any further.

The dwarf said, "Can't ever really trust a Johnson, *omae*. All we can do is our job, and be ready in case he decides he doesn't want to pay."

All three of them began securing weapons and readying for a fight. It felt like so many other exchanges he'd been on the other side of.

The woman saw him watching and said, "You're thousands of miles from anywhere familiar, chummer. It would be a mistake to try anything now."

He wondered if she was saying it to him, or reminding herself of the situation she was in.

When the train stopped, their entire world lapsed into silence. Wherever he was, it was not in the riotous heart of a sprawl. He heard voices, but they were too far away to understand. The sound of machinery was closer. He guessed it was a gantry crane and decided he was right when he heard a rumble from further down the train.

"Get up." The pale man said, and yanked Nero to his feet. The dwarf watched them both. He twirled the glowmoss vial in one hand while tapping a stun baton against his shoulder with the other.

The man escorted Nero toward the open edge of the cargo car. Without being prodding, Nero jumped down from the train—and into thick snowpack up to his ankles. *I don't have the shoes for this.*

Around him, a skeleton crew of workers unloaded cars packed with crates. Another shipping container was hoisted off the train by the gantry crane and moved along a tall metal scaffold toward a warehouse. The dwarf tapped Nero's knee with the baton and pointed toward an icy sheet of black road a few meters away.

In the darkness, Nero could make out the headlights of three cars parked lengthwise. The people who exited the vehicles had the look of personal security. It wasn't the polished look of a corporate trained detail, but the rough-around-the-edges feel of people trying to play the part. These were mob soldiers.

He put it together, then. The weather, the sense of foreboding as he moved across ley lines and damaged sections of the magical spectrum.

This was Russia.

These men were Vory.

The last man to exit the cars confirmed his theory by presence alone. He wore a fur coat like a caricature of a *bratva* villain. It surprised Nero to see he was an ork. He'd thought the Vory, like the Italian Mafia, decried metahumanity in the upper ranks. Yet this man radiated leadership. He was wide, bordering on overweight. Tusks, black and polished, arched out from his lower lip. He was large even by ork standards, perhaps the size of Grim Fox. His thick brow was marred by splotchy skin, which he tried to cover with a *ushanka* cap.

He grinned furiously and started walking toward them. The blond woman stepped in front of Nero while her two associates moved up to flank him.

The Vory boss spoke in thickly accented English made understandable by his slow cadence and diction. "You are late."

She replied, "We are entirely on time."

"The terms of our agreement were that you were to arrive on the train that I arranged for you, and at the location we specified."

She said, "Your train left too early. We didn't want to end up like the first team. We chose the best time to extract the subject with minimal risk to both he and us."

The wind picked up, blowing loose snow across the road. Nero shivered and tried to huddle in his suit jacket. He eyed the glowmoss, wondering if he could trigger a spell fast enough and large enough to disable the ones closest to him. But where would he run? How far could he get like this?

The Vory boss looked from her to Nero and back again. "Yes, well, your bonus was contingent on a timely delivery."

Her body language gave her away. Nero watched her rock backward slightly, tensing and resetting her feet. She deliberately kept her hands open, palms flat against her sides. She said, "Very well."

If the Vory boss noticed the signs of her annoyance, he didn't care. He offered her a credstick and she accepted it. Then he said, "Were there any complications? Anything we should know?"

She looked back toward Nero and then shoved the glowmoss into her pocket. A curious smile played across her lips, and she replied, "No, nothing whatsoever."

He waved his hands toward the three vehicles and said, "My associates are happy to drive you into the city."

She looked back at Nero again and then toward the car, again considering. "We'll find our own ride, if that's okay with you."

"Very well. Enjoy your evening...and be careful. Moscow has very deep shadows, and not all of them are friendly."

"I'm starting to see that."

His smile was mostly tusk. He said, "It's been a pleasure. I look forward to doing business with you again."

Her curious smile appeared again as she said, "Good luck, Mr. Moretti."

Her crew left Nero's side, and together, they walked back toward the train and disappeared into the darkness.

When they were gone, the Vory man's security walked over the Nero and cut the ties securing his hands. Their boss strode toward him. "Mr. Moretti, I am sorry for the inconvenience wait. It is a pleasure to finally meet you in person. As I said, you should have been here much sooner."

Nero pursed his lips together and nodded. He fixed a smile on his face, like the images in his brother's memory reel. The man did not extend his hand, so Nero did not extend his.

The man said, "I was concerned that you were no longer planning to honor our arrangement. When we observed you meeting with representatives of the Al-Akhirab Aswad Mayid syndicate in Dubai, we began to think you were offering your services to another organization."

"I didn't meet with a syndicate in Dubai. I met with Olive Holdings on another matter entirely." He spoke without thinking, the words coming from his lips hard and pointed. He didn't know if he was defending his brother or himself. He wasn't sure the difference mattered anymore.

"Yes, yes, of course. However, you do understand that we are aware of their affiliations."

Nero's feet were numbing in the snow. He blew on his hands uselessly. All he could think to say was, "I'm freezing."

The Vory boss nodded and escorted him to one of the three cars. Inside, a man wearing an expensive suit grinned at him.

The Vory boss said, "You remember my comrade, Dimitri Molchalin. He insisted on coming along to meet you at the train. All of us are very excited to see what you are able to offer."

Nero recognized the man sitting inside, if only barely. He thought he might be one of the men from the camara feeds EnJee had snatched from the club in Cape Town—the dwarf who had been with Enzo. Nero was terrible with names, but moved his lips silently, linking the name to the face staring back at him.

The car thrummed to life. The heaters powered up and instantly warmed the air. Molchalin's grin never faded as he said, "Tell me, Enzo, are you ready to get started?"

Nero nodded again. He had absolutely no idea what that meant.

ENJEE

11-20-2081
11:30 P.M. Local Time

It didn't take long to confirm how Nero was being moved. EnJee knew a lot of smugglers from the old days, back when he ran with an operation called the Cutters that was sometimes a gang, sometimes an organized crime operation. That had been at the peak of the *Laesa* craze, when the Ghost Cartels were pushing into everyone's market, and business was good.

EnJee dialed up a runner named Blind William who worked the route from London to Moscow. Blind William didn't think Nero would've been moved to Moscow by air. He knew about the night trains, nightly shipments of gray-market goods between the two cities. To hear Blind William tell it, the *Vory v Zakone* kept a handful of train cars in service, moving precious goods in and out of the NEEC. Their business cut into his profits, so he was eager to share what he knew, especially if it meant EnJee would be up for disrupting the service.

"They probably took this same route," Grim Fox said. They were on the night train in a cargo container marked for cold storage. The container was labeled as a *Productos Cultivatos* agricultural shipment, but it belonged to Tamanous. They sat in the thin corridor between stacks of cold storage boxes ranging in size from as small as a hatbox to as large as a coffin. All of them were locked and tabbed with digital temperature readouts.

Abioye called it a working trip. The three of them were responsible for securing their freight from anyone who might want to hijack it along the way. The upside of the arrangement was they could bring as many guns and as much gear as they could carry.

A temperature regulation unit drew power from the engine and kept the space at a perfect 6 degrees Celsius. Grim Fox wondered aloud if the refrigeration was necessary at all, since the temperature outside dipped well below zero. EnJee was forced to point out that temperatures outside a specified range would degrade the tissue to the point where it was unusable and, by default, inedible. Grim Fox didn't ask any more questions after that.

Tamanous genuinely scared EnJee. The truth of it was, killing people was difficult work. Put aside the psychological hurdles necessary to pull the trigger. The Sixth World was so thick with cameras and other forms of mundane and magical surveillance that disappearing a body in a way that didn't leave an evidence trail was tough going. Tamanous didn't have that problem. Their entire business model was centered on getting rid of bodies. What made it worse was the people who ran the organization—and most of whom they served—needed to feast on human organs to get the nutrients they needed to survive.

Shen sat quietly by the door. She kept checking the readout on her commlink and gripping the cross dangling from her neck.

Grim Fox said, "Let's go over what we know. The last contact we had with Nero was this afternoon. If they moved on one of these trains that means they has a head start of up to six hours from the moment we got on this train."

EnJee grimaced. It was a long time to leave their friend in the wind and at the mercy of what they now believed to be a Vory operation. "We have four names. Sacha Drozdov, Timur Kalashnik, and Dimitri Molchalin are the three he met with in Cape Town. They work for a fourth man, Vladimir Smolensky. I scoured the Mosaic for any info on them, and found records of Kalashnik and Drozdov both as former employees of multiple Eastern European banks. I think those two are just accountants. Dimitri Molchalin is still listed as an employee of Metabank, which is run by Evo. I think he's the *sovetnik*—the advisor ultimately responsible for the money matters."

The others listened passively, the way they did when he tried to explain what was really happening on the runs they did. It was part lecture and part exercise in futility, because they never drew the proper conclusions until it was too late to matter.

"Smolensky is the real problem," EnJee continued. "He's a true bruiser. Not clear on his rank in the Vory, but he certainly has a lot of dead bodies connected to his name. I have searchbots trying to dig up more information."

Grim Fox said, "That's all well and good, but we need to find the team who snatched Nero before we try anything else."

"We also need to figure out Smolensky's motivations. We need to learn if it is him or Molchalin making the rules. Then we'll know who to deal with. I still have a feeling this crew of Vory isn't operating with the permission of the organization. It has the feel of a side hustle to me, mates. Couldn't hurt to ask around in the organization about what those two are doing."

Grim Fox looked concerned. "Let's tread softly here. Moscow isn't the NEEC, EnJee. We can't start poking around where we don't belong. We'll raise suspicions. We don't have a bolt hole to run to once things get hot. We don't even have a way out of the city beyond the night train."

"Is that supposed to scare us off, mate?"

Shen cut in, annoyed. "That's supposed to make us play smart. We don't have a sense of how things run there. We don't have time for deep-dive research on who hates who. If we're in it, we're going to be smart about it. You're going to let Grim Fox have final say on how we do this. No going rogue."

EnJee knew from experience that staring her down wasn't going to work. It hadn't worked in a decade. He sighed. For the first time in a long time, he let go, and said, "I suppose that works for me."

"Who do we know on the ground?" Grim Fox asked, suppressing a smile.

"A mate of mine from the Mosaic Data Haven knows this local named Red Anya," said EnJee. "I'm using him to get info from her." The price of that info was access privileges at the Helix. It didn't seem like too high a price on the surface, but he'd need to keep an eye on what the bloke did while he was poking around through their files.

"Ask her for a list of runner bars where out-of-towners can still expect to get a drink."

EnJee said, "How do you know they'll be at a bar?"

"What is it we do after an out-of-town job?"

When the train finally stopped, EnJee slowly became aware of voices and movement outside. Someone banged on the door to their train car. Shen unlimbered her rifle, letting it point toward the ground like a silent warning. Grim Fox unlocked the door and slid it open. He was met with a gust of cold air that made him grimace.

The people outside were dressed in overcoats and the big fur hats Russians called *ushankas*, the wide ears pulled down to guard their faces against the cold. The closest man fiddled with something under the train car. He pulled out a ramp and secured it to the ground. The others filed into the car as if they hadn't even noticed the three runners were there.

None of them spoke English. EnJee switched to German, then to French, to no avail. He gave up and told his crew to pack their things and their prisoner, and headed down the ramp. The glow of Moscow was so distant EnJee could see the stars.

"It's quiet out here." Shen rubbed her gloved hands together. When she blew into them, she made a puff of steam.

Around them, several dozen workers moved goods off the train and toward warehouses the size of a soccer pitch. Nobody seemed to be in charge, but each group of workers functioned without the need for direction.

One of the workers, a dark-haired woman in overalls, tapped EnJee on the shoulder. He pointed to the container he'd just pulled out of their train car and then back to the three of them. She said, "Help."

EnJee shrugged and marched back up the ramp. He grabbed a hatbox-sized container and followed after them. Grim Fox joined him, carrying two larger crates, one under each arm. Shen followed behind, preferring the weight of her rifle to the boxes. She shoved Enzo along in front of her.

Suddenly Shen pulled up short. The same dark-haired worker said something to her in what EnJee assumed was Russian. When Shen didn't respond, she pointed toward the warehouse and said, "Go."

Shen shook her head, refusing to go inside. EnJee followed her gaze toward the entrance to the warehouse.

What waited for them there wasn't anything like Ekon Abioye. It had a sunken face with long hair and black eyes devoid of emotion. Its long legs made it tower even over Grim Fox. It was like a reed swaying in the frozen wind.

EnJee tried German first. He said, "We were promised a vehicle in exchange for our service."

"Once we are sure the cargo was delivered as promised." The ghoul's voice was a feminine rasp. She pointed to where several more ghouls lurked inside, cracking open the containers and studying the contents. EnJee and Grim Fox continued to bring crates inside. Once in a while, a ghoul would look up, studying the two runners longer than needed before turning their head back to the task at hand. Despite his familiarity with the process, EnJee felt his gorge rising.

When the last crate was processed, the workers directed the pair back outside to where the lead ghoul waited. She stood close to Enzo Moretti, who shivered uncontrollably. Shen stood several paces off, unwilling to come closer.

EnJee asked for the car again. The ghoul in charge lingered on Moretti a while, an unasked question playing on her lips. Finally, she shook her head and pointed them to a white Ford Americar that looked older than EnJee. It was better than walking, if barely.

Grim Fox drove. EnJee played co-pilot, overlaying his location data to the troll's PAN to form a makeshift AR heads-up display that guided them away from the trainyard and toward the lights of Moscow proper. The more distance they put between them and the Tamanous ghouls, the more relaxed all of them became. It was nearly a relief when they hit the main circle of the Moscow sprawl and the old Americar synced up with the Gridlink system, falling in beside a handful of other cars on the road.

Red Anya had managed to come up with the name of a runner who matched the description he'd secured from Novak. The runner called herself Turbine Mary, and she ran with two other runners, Hax and Tripper. She also gave them a list of bars still friendly to shadowrunners passing through. Most of the spots were Vory-controlled, and finding one that wasn't proved too difficult to consider.

The team went from bar to bar. When he could, EnJee hacked each node and scanned the interior cameras for their targets. When there weren't cameras inside, Shen went in alone first and checked things out while EnJee and Grim Fox waited in the car.

They found Turbine Mary and her crew in the fourth bar they hit. The name of the place was written in Cyrillic letters. The closest translation EnJee found on his over-the-counter Horizon software was "Whispers."

The team set up their approach the way they had the previous two times. When Shen walked back outside and let them know she'd spotted the trio, Grim Fox went in and took up his position near the back entrance. Shen's role was to get back in the car with the prisoner and provide fire support if needed. Once everyone was in place, EnJee walked inside.

Moscow knew how to do drinking establishments right. The lights were low and the air was cloudy with a haze of smoke that might've been real cigarettes, cigars, or even just fake fumes pumped in for that classic atmosphere. The bar was a thick wooden arc that took up most of the wall furthest from the door. The wall behind the bar showed off dozens of bottles ranging from high-end vodka to the dirty synthahol you got with most well drinks. The regulars crowded the bar, their postures reading like shadowtypes, though they were a mix of the over-the-hill variety, plus young, wet-behind-the-ears toughs and a smattering of beefy people who belonged to one Vory sect or another. There were enough metas taking up space that the only reason Grim Fox stood out was because his Amerind skin and tribal markings made it obvious he wasn't from here.

Mary sat in a booth close enough to the front door to have a clear line of sight, and close enough to the rear to make a play for it if needed. A dwarf sat next to her, and they both sat across from a well-built fellow who had the can't-sit-still mannerisms EnJee associated with bioware muscle augmentations. They didn't seem to expect trouble, but looked ready for it all the same. They watched Grim Fox with a curiosity that bordered on concern. None of the three even noticed EnJee until he pulled up a chair and sat down beside them.

EnJee smiled and said, "Turbine Mary. That's a fine name for a rigger, isn't it?"

Turbine Mary looked up slowly. She used her left hand to pull aside a strand of blond hair that had fallen across her face. Her other hand remained under the table. She said, "I don't know you. In case you're slow, that means you need to stand up and walk away right now."

The dwarf shifted uncomfortably in his seat. EnJee saw the movement for what it was. He and the twitchy one held guns out underneath the table.

EnJee kept his eyes on Turbine Mary and said, "You're a U-CASer. That's how I'm supposed to say it, right? Strange accent. A bit flat off the tongue, don't you think? My mate is from those parts. You see him over there, the smallish one by the bathrooms? He's listening in as well, and he's ready to kill at least one, maybe even all three of you, before you can get to me or get to the exits."

She checked out Grim Fox, who tapped a hand against his temple and winked at her and her crew. Turbine Mary sighed.

"If you do manage to get outside, we've got that covered." EnJee said. He leaned in conspiratorially and whispered, "Snipers."

Turbine Mary said, "You gonna scan what this is all about, or you just here to make threats?"

"Your lot took our guy and we want him back."

"Moretti."

"You're a right quick study, aren't you?"

"We've already turned him over."

"To whom?" He slowed his diction speaking appropriately, calmly. Letting the formality mask his growing anxiety.

"It's a Johnson. We don't work on a name basis."

EnJee said, "You don't lie terribly well."

She grimaced, hesitated, then gave in. "Okay. It's the local Vory," she hissed. "They had an extraction planned for Moretti and it went bad. They brought us in to clean it up."

"Might as well be telling me the ending to Euphoria's first flick. We already know the Vory hired you. People like you and me prefer a bit more data when working under these conditions."

Turbine Mary looked around, the first signs of nervousness dotting her face. "You see where we are, don't you? I plan to get back on one of these trains come morning and get the hell out of this frozen drekhole. Anything more I say to you puts that plan in jeopardy."

EnJee added, "I already have the name. Vladimir Smolensky. I just need a way to contact him."

She shook her head "You don't understand how it works out here. Your man is already gone. He's Vory property now. If they haven't moved him to wherever they plan to keep him, they've at least set up security. Anyone trying to take what's theirs runs the risk of bringing the city down on top of themselves."

Enjee grinned. "Well, that's our problem now, isn't it?"

NERO

11-21-2081
5:30 A.M. Local Time

Moscow did not look like the other cities Nero had spent time in. He'd been here a day, and already the city had the feel of somewhere extremely old, built for a purpose that no longer existed. The streets they drove through were wide in some sections of town, but in others, narrowed off into tight corridors that were little more than choke points leaving Nero to wonder what sort of wars these streets were built in preparation for.

He knew very little about the Vory, but the sociopolitical structure of organizations such as these was familiar to him. He spent time working with the mafia in Italy, largely with the support of his church. Though he'd never say it out loud, he'd recognized the structure of the mafia as a close parallel to that of the Catholic Church, where the heads of a family were the equivalent of archbishops who handed orders and judgement down to those of the family itself. The Vory felt like this as well, though the nature of what he witnessed seemed closer to his own church than a greater organization. The ork, that he'd heard called Vladimir by some, was the bishop who controlled his group of underlings and they, in turn, administered the flock. It did not feel like the ork answered to anyone. If he had bosses, then whatever he was doing with Nero was off the books. In fact, Nero was starting to think Vladimir the Vory ork was trying to start his own organization.

Over the previous evening, Nero had been introduced to a number of people who ranged from town elder to joygirl in appearance. It felt like the big ork was showing him around and showing him off. He had no idea what the Russians wanted with him. He couldn't speak Russian, so what was being said to and about him might have well been gibberish.

When the show tour ended, he was taken to a small mansion far from the heart of the city where he was allowed to sleep for a few hours. They roused him when the last remains of night were streaking away from the sky. He hadn't touched an electronic device since being kidnapped. Nero didn't even know what day it was. He barely had time to think about the others, where they might be—what Shen might be thinking and feeling right now.

Vladimir's soldiers loaded him into another car, and he considered reaching for his magic then. He held back for all the reasons he'd held back before when playing this role as his brother, but beyond that, he was afraid of Moscow itself. He knew the fey were drawn to the place, thought it remained unclear if it was due to the region's strange magical energies or a history unknown to those outside of their fold.

All Nero knew of Russia were her legends. To hear it told by the Matrix, the first ghouls arose out of a 1940s Russian sleep experiment. The Tunguska Carter and the Monument to the Sea King's daughter were places where the ley lines intersected and brought about disturbing magical effects.

Russia remained so steeped in myth and mystery that the only real thing to emerge was fear. As a religious man, Nero understood that some of these myths were rooted in fact while others were outright lies or confusions of the actual magic taking place.

"We need you to begin the process of creating our new shell company as soon as we arrive," Dimitri Molchalin said. The gruff dwarf was seated beside him in the back of the vehicle while two guards rode in front. The ork wasn't with them this morning. Once talk of real work sprang up, he turned the task over to his underling.

Nero hadn't spoken to anyone in hours. His mouth was dry and all he could manage was, "Yes."

He knew they were getting closer to the center of the city because of the number of older buildings mixed in with the new. When they arrived at their destination, Nero was surprised at how ordinary it looked. In this place where architecture reflected power, the place was a simple office building eight stories in height. It was wedged in between a grocery store and what looked to be an apartment building.

The Vory soldiers parked the car on the street and escorted Molchalin and he inside. The four of them rode the elevator up to the top floor, where preparations were being made to establish an office bullpen. Several offices, in various stages of completion, lined the walls surrounding the unfinished bullpen. Workers were bustling about the space, setting up cubicles and laying wiring. It looked like so many of the mid-level office suites he'd done extractions from in the past.

If Molchalin expected Nero to be impressed, it didn't show. He pointed to one of the corner offices. The two Vory men closed in on him and led him toward that office. Nero let it happen. If there would be a time to break and run, it would not be now, when he did not know where or even *when* he was, and worried deeply about what awaited him on the astral plane.

The office door bore his brother's name in English, a sharp contrast to the Cyrillic present elsewhere in the crowded space. Inside the room, the space more resembled a studio apartment than in office. There was a bathroom immediately to the left. He could see through the half-opened door there was a shower as well. A divider split the room into a working area and a sleeping area, featuring a small bed with neatly pressed black sheets. He looked back toward the work area, where there was a desk but no AR rig, nor a Matrix access terminal. Then he noticed the door locked from the outside. *Less office than prison*, he thought.

"This will be your home for the next few weeks, until we feel you have adjusted to this new reality," Molchalin said, the first evidence of a smile edging the sides of his mouth.

Recognition filled him with a shiver. He'd been on the other side of these spaces as well. He'd been the one escorting extractees into their gilded cages as they underwent the corporate onboarding process.

Another man joined them. He was tall and thin. He brandished an obvious cyberarm, but also wore what appeared to be AR glasses. The man offered Nero a distracted wave and then said to Molchalin in English, "My contacts within the Babel Network assure me we can create a new identity for Mr. Moretti within the week."

Molchalin replied, "He will not become another person. He will be no one until he realizes he is one of us."

They spoke as if Nero were not standing there, absorbing this conversation about his future like punches in a street fight. He dimmed visibly with each word, eventually sitting down heavily in the office chair as the two men discussed his future. He found himself reaching for his cross and grasping at the empty space there. He thought about Shen and Grim Fox. He thought about EnJee and wondered how far the hacker would go to save him. How far would EnJee let the others go?

Molchalin said, "Once he can be trusted, we will let him resume his identity. Until then, he will instruct us on how to do what is needed."

This was the fate that once awaited his brother, and it was his own now. Except he didn't know how to setup a business. He recalled Novak's instructions about value and position in investments. He remembered what she said about what she and Enzo did. He remembered how much of this was about confidence, and how they dealt in math, but they really dealt in trust. Then he took a deep breath and said, "What do you think is going on here?"

Molchalin said, "Mr. Moretti, we want you to build us a corporation."

"No."

The two men stared at him in confusion. Then they looked to each other as though the answer to this new riddle could be found there.

"No." Nero frowned and folded his arms. "I'm not operating under these conditions. In fact, I'm not doing a damn thing until I speak to your boss."

Molchalin frowned. "I do not think you understand what you are asking for. Please, do as you are told, and everything else will come to you in time."

"With all due respect, gentlemen, you hired me because of who I am and how I am known to people in the financial markets. You need me. You need my ISDA. All this talk of taking my identity or even changing it is not how I operate. If you want me to do what I do, then we need to establish some ground rules. For that, I need to talk to the big guy first."

Molchalin looked nervous. He wiped at his brow and said, "Vladimir Smolensky is not like you and me. He does not come from our world. He is Chimera, the sole surviving member of his cell. Do you understand what that means?"

Nero did, and alarm bells jangled in his head. Chimera was the name given to a cell of highly trained killers who could get to anyone for the right price. He said, "I don't know or particularly care for any fairy tales you have to share. I'm a businessman. You brought me here because you need me, and I need to talk to the person in charge about these conditions before I do anything."

He folded his arms again like a petulant child, a sign he intended to wait until someone higher up in the organization presented themselves for a conversation. He felt in his bones that this is what Enzo would do. He would sit here, and he would pout or smile because he knew these men needed his cooperation. In the corporate world, deferring to upper management was the way. He could see by their stance and expression that these were not men of violence. There were Vory soldiers nearby that would work violence upon him if asked, but they would then need to answer for his injuries. Ultimately, they would need to explain what he'd asked for and stand in judgement for their response. It was not unlike his time in the church in this way as well, though the church traded violence for repentance.

He waited for one of the men to reach for his commlink. He wondered if they would do so now or wait until later in the day, when their leader was certainly awake. As he waited, he considered what Molchalin had said. Chimera was another Russian myth whispered late at night in the darkest corners of the sprawl. However, this was a myth Nero knew to be real. Chimera had once been the code name for the Federal Security Service's secretive squad of assassins. Over time, those people had fled to the opportunity offered by shadows. They passed their talents down to their sons and daughters. Hits by Chimera assassins were legendary in shadowrunner circles. They were the last people you wanted to cross.

The men's conversation had fallen back into the harsh tonalities of Russian, and Nero had only their expressions to read how things were going. But even that was difficult, as everyone around him seemed to have a perpetual glower on their faces.

There was a commotion outside. Both men turned toward the door. Nero tried to look around them to see what was happening, but he didn't have to wait long. The big ork,

Vladimir Smolensky, walked calmly into the room, flanked by two Vory soldiers. He hadn't seen either man make a call.

Nero stood up in surprise. Vladimir Smolensky held a large-barreled Ruger Super Warhawk pistol in his left hand. He tapped it slowly against his hip. Everyone in Enzo's small office fell silent and turned to stare at the ork. They could sense the impending violence, and shied away from the idea of it and him, as though both belonged to a different world. They belonged to Nero's world, not Enzo's. The collision of the two left him uncertain of how to behave.

Vladimir Smolensky spoke in English when he said, "Dimitri, my old friend. Tell me, was it you or Timur that managed the surveillance of our friend Mr. Moretti?"

Timur spoke up quickly, "I was the—"

Vladimir Smolensky raised the pistol almost faster than Nero could follow. He fired once, the sound echoing like thunder in the small space. When he lowered the gun again, the taller man, Timur, was dead on the ground, the last of his thoughts sprayed against the room's divider.

Nero clutched at his chest for his cross and found nothing. Nevertheless, he reached for his magic, first assensing the space, shifting his vision into the astral spectrum to find the threats he could not see. He returned to his normal spectrum immediately, finding nothing more dangerous than this man whose body looked as cold and mechanical as that of a robot.

"Mr. Molchalin," said Smolensky, "you are fortunate I have decided not to kill all three of you today. Consider that a debt you now owe me. You may begin to show your indebtedness by removing this body with your own hands."

The dwarf nervously cleared his throat. When he could find no words, he merely nodded and grabbed the remains of Timur by the leg and slowly dragged him toward the door.

Nero sensed a potential chance to escape here, but the idea of what this man was rooted him to the ground. He didn't trust that his magic could overwhelm one of the Chimera. Assassins of this caliber trained to resist all manipulations, physical, magical, mental. If he failed now, he stood no chance to defeat the man physically, let alone the other guards in the room. The only way out now was to do as he had done before. He would not think as a shadowrunner. He would think like a corporate operator.

He put up his hands in a show of respect and deference. "I am very sorry. I'm not trying to piss you off, sir, I just wanted to make sure I did exactly what you were asking."

Vladimir Smolensky shook when he laughed. He stepped closer to Nero and the mage shrank back slightly. Smolensky tapped the heavy pistol against his hip and said, "You are an impressive individual. You showed ingenuity. Even I believed you were Enzo Moretti. Well done."

The fear that cut through Nero's chest could've been mistaken for a spasm. He said, "I don't understand what you mean."

"On the other hand, I do not enjoy being made the fool." Smolensky's fist arced toward his face like a scythe. Nero felt a tremendous burst of pain and found himself on the ground, struggling to breathe. His nose was broken. Blood ran down his lips in rivulets.

Smolensky towered over him, grinning down with an expression that did not look the least bit jovial. He said, "However, your efforts were not directed at me, so I feel I can forgive this indiscretion."

Nero felt himself reaching for his magic as Smolensky turned to walk away. As he did so, the ork said, "Clean him up. We will meet his friends soon. Then we decide what to do with all of them."

Nero froze. The pain of the attack must have blurred his senses. He let two of the Vory soldiers stand him up and walk him to the bed that had been prepared for him. He slumped there trying to make sense of what he heard. If true, it meant his friends—his family—were nearby. Had they followed him here?

One of the soldiers forced Nero to sit up. He studied his nose for a moment and then touched it. Fresh pain lanced through Nero's face, and he cried out reflexively. The soldier shook his head. Nero mumbled, "It's fine. Leave it alone."

The soldier did as he asked. He and his companion left the office and locked the door behind them. Nero sucked in a deep breath. He pressed both hands to his nose, placing two fingers on either side to guide the bone and cartilage back into place. He cried out again. The magic of the heal spell moved through his body almost like a reflex, lacing the broken bones back together. He forced himself to stop the spell. He couldn't heal himself here. They didn't know about his magic and that was an advantage he could not waste by showing his abilities. He needed the swelling around his nose and eyes to remain, at least for a little while. Unfortunately, so would the pain.

He breathed deeply and fell back unto the bed. His team was nearby. They planned to strike a deal with this man. Were they going to exchange Enzo for him? He didn't think he could let that happen—not without them knowing exactly who they were dealing with. He didn't know if he could stop them. Nero didn't know where they were.

He reached for his cross reflexively and in that moment, he remembered exactly how to find them. The risk and weirdness of this foreign city terrified him, but it scared him far worse to think what would happen if Shen and the others walked into this situation unprepared.

Nero closed his eyes and felt his true form lift away from his meat body.

ENJEE

11-21-2081
6:35 A.M. Local Time

Afterwards, EnJee said, "You should've let me handle that call, Shen."

They were holed up in the white four-door sedan the Tamanous agent lent them, parked on a side street lined with buildings so far apart alleys sprouted up between each like dark weeds.

Shen opened the passenger door and got out of the car. She ran her fingers through her hair and breathed out harsh clouds of steam. She didn't say anything.

She was the only one who spoke Russian, and that made her the natural choice for making the call.

But Shen was also the closest to Nero, and that made her the wrong choice.

She started toward the alley, getting some space from EnJee and Grim Fox. EnJee let her go.

The call hadn't been a complete bag of shite...at least, not at first.

He spoofed an origination number and used onion routing in case the target attempted to trace them. At the same time, EnJee set up a passive trace routine to locate Smolensky's origin point. It wasn't an exact science and would be useless if he had a hacker on standby managing his calls through a router, but it was all he could do without triggering suspicion.

Shen dialed the number Turbine Mary had given them, and shared the call with the others so they could listen in. He answered on the third ring.

She said, "Mr. Vladimir Smolensky."

"Might I know who you are and who gave you this number?" The man on the other end spoke with an air of confidence and grace that made EnJee want to flick him in the nose.

"You can call me Miyoko. Your associates will know the name. I have Enzo Moretti."

There was silence on the other end of the line for a moment, and then Smolensky said, "*I am not a person who cares for games or riddles.*"

"The man you have is indistinguishable from Enzo Moretti. However, he is not him. The man you have belongs to me."

"*You understand I will require proof of what you are saying.*"

Shen held out the commlink to Enzo. Grim Fox pulled off Enzo's gag. Enzo took a slow breath and then spoke, "Mr. Smolensky?"

"*I am supposed to believe you are Enzo Moretti and the man in my care is not? Why?*"

"Two months ago, we met virtually. It was you, myself, and Sacha Drozdov. It was the first time we met. I told you I wanted to learn your *ofenya*. You told me I was saying it wrong. I remember because I looked it up again afterward."

Again, that long silence. Then he said, "*What is the name I proposed you call our new corporation?*"

"You wanted to call it 'Dacha Matryoshka,' but once I understood what it meant, I suggested it was far too specific and would raise questions."

"*And what is the name that was decided?*"

"Porosha Capital." In following silence, Enzo looked first to Shen, and then EnJee. He had time to say "Hello?" before Smolensky came back on the line.

The Vory man said, "*How is it you came to have my associate?*"

Shen said, "A case of mistaken identity. We were unaware of your relationship with Mr. Moretti at the time we intervened."

"*And now you mean to extort me.*" It sounded less like a question than a statement. In spite of the cold outside, the car was growing hot and uncomfortable. EnJee struggled to hold his tongue. There were things he wanted to say, ways to explain to Smolensky that he didn't have all the leverage here, but he trusted Shen to do her part, even though it pained him to be so imactive.

Shen wiped a wet strand of hair from her face and said, "We are both businesspeople, Mr. Smolensky. We each have what the other wants. I propose an even trade."

"Even trade," he repeated. "After your man has disrespected me with lies and pretending to be who he is not."

She shook her head angrily, even though Smolensky could not see her. "Don't be an idiot. The slight was unintentional, and known only to you and I. As I said, the two men are indistinguishable to those who do not know them."

EnJee slapped his forehead. Shen, realizing what she had just said, added, "Again, this is a frustrating situation. I mean you no disrespect."

The silence on Smolensky's end grew long and hard to bear. Finally, he said, "This number you used to call me, I can use it to call you?"

She looked to EnJee for confirmation before saying, "Yes."

"Stay by your commlink. Soon you will have your answer."

That was when Shen and EnJee had gotten out of the car. He watched as she walked deeper into the alley, preferring to company of the near-dark and her own thoughts. Dawn was peeking over the horizon, spreading pink fingers across the black sky.

EnJee yawned. He hated mornings. He hated being up this late. Above all else, he hated being in a country where he didn't know anyone and didn't have a bolt hole to hide in when things went wrong.

He let Shen fume for a full minute before following her. The alley smelled of sour garbage and decay. He wrinkled his nose and shoved his hands in his pockets. Shen didn't seem to notice. She leaned against a wall that was plastered in a mix of real and AR graffiti. A Noir cigarette hung from her lips. She hadn't lit it.

Shen said, "You think I screwed it up."

EnJee shrugged, "I think you played it your best. I don't much care for this Smolensky bloke. He strikes me as another mob type who feels insulted because he was tricked. That's what worries me."

This corner of the city was mostly quiet. It wouldn't stay that way. Moscow was waking up around them. Already the rats and other creatures of the evening were retreating into their daylight spaces, leaving the pair of runners alone in that thin margin between night and day.

Grim Fox joined them. "Enzo's locked down. He seems as scared of Smolensky as he is of us."

EnJee said, "Bugger that. This is his mess."

Shen lit her cigarette and then used the burning tip to light a second, which she handed to Grim Fox. She took a slow puff and then said, "How long are we supposed to wait?"

Grim Fox puffed on his cigarette and said, "We ought to start putting together a plan of how to find Nero in case this doesn't go our way."

Shen turned to EnJee and said, "Were you able to trace the call?"

EnJee shook his head. "It'll take time to get through his routing. Vory hackers are top shelf. When he calls back, I'll pick up where I left off. I can do it faster running with a hot ASIST."

Shen clutched the cross hanging from her neck. She said, "You think we really have time for all that? Tracking him down and setting up an infiltration, I mean?"

Grim Fox said, "I don't like hitting a location on short notice. Too many things can go wrong."

"How about Nero dying, mate?" EnJee said. "How's that for wrong?"

They waited another thirty minutes before Shen's commlink buzzed again, showing an incoming call from Smolensky. She tapped it, set it to speaker mode and said, "Do we have a deal?"

"*We do.*" Smolensky's voice was calm on the other end. "*I am prepared to share the address of where your associate and I are located.*"

"I prefer somewhere a bit more public. The Bogdana Khmelnitskogo pedestrian bridge." As tourist attractions go, it was one of the few in the city they knew.

"*We might as well exchange parties outside of the Bolshoi Theater,*" he replied.

"Not crowded enough."

"*What was it you said? 'Do not be an idiot?' When you are prepared to properly discuss where to meet, you will call me.*" He ended the call.

Shen said, "Shit."

EnJee cursed under his breath and kicked a can that was unfortunate enough to be near his feet. It rolled deeper into the alley and out of sight. "My scriptbots aren't getting anywhere using a passive trace."

"This isn't all bad," Grim Fox started. "He's negotiating. We can use that."

EnJee said, "He's trying to rag us into meeting entirely on his terms, mate. Ring him back. I'll get his location this time. If he's got Nero with him, we can at least get a look at what we're up against."

Grim Fox shook his head. "We can't call the man back unless we actually have a better suggestion on where to meet. I don't know where that would be."

EnJee clenched his teeth. It was all getting away from him. In another few hours, they'd need to find shelter. They couldn't be hauling around a zip-tied man in in broad daylight in a city they knew nothing about. Worse still, he didn't know who this Smolensky was, or how far through the Vory his reach extended. There could be people out on the streets looking for them right now. He didn't trust Smolensky to play this straight, but he was hyperaware of the fact they were running out of choices.

Grim Fox said what he was thinking: "We knew this would happen before we got on the train. It may be that we have to come around to dealing with this man on his terms."

Shen looked up at him angrily. Then she gasped. EnJee and Grim Fox turned to follow her gaze.

Beside them, Nero was floating a meter off the ground.

NERO

11-21-2081
6:30 A.M. Local Time

The astral world was nothing like the real world. Nero was closer to God here.

He'd heard it described it as a photo negative, a construct of the art world and of a technology largely relegated to a filter effect. The concept made sense. In astral space, the manmade buildings and manufactured landscapes that dominated meatspace appeared only as shapes nearly translucent gray in color. They weren't of the natural world, so their presence here was a shadow-memory of the space they held on the other side. He couldn't make out the details of these things. He couldn't for example, read the number of a building and route his people there.

The traces an individual left in the astral remained like a fire's dying embers, or the smell of something cooked long ago. He followed his own trail downward, back toward the dull structure from which he came. He couldn't tell them where it was, but he could give them a sense of the city around it. He collected what details he could and hurried off. He saw nearby places where mana barriers arced around grayed-out buildings like electric domes. He saw swaths of darkness in the astral like wounds that he knew to avoid. He saw the shapes of landmarks he thought that he could recognize and remember.

Nearby, a creature that was not human nor metahuman turned to look at him, and he moved away quickly. Nero flew high above the city. The earth was far below him, the ground hard and compact as it was in the meat space. Everything else was immaterial. The massive skyscrapers that blotted out the sky in every city were towers of mist here. He flew through buildings with the ease of passing through a cloud.

He felt more than saw something watching him. No, many things watching him. This high in the sky, he sparked like a star, his unmasked aura shining in the astral space around him. He couldn't dawdle here long. This was not his city; it was the domain of others. He could see some of them, dual-natured and observant. He was too far away to make out what they were. Perhaps human or metahuman like himself. Perhaps fey. Perhaps something else entirely.

Things created to give people power over mana were linked to them—so Nero's cross was linked to him. He reached for that link, letting it pull his weightless astral form toward it as the city raced by below him.

At last, he saw them in a space between two gray squares in the shape of buildings. Near the mouth of the alley, he felt himself drawn to a twist of gray mist in the shape of a car. He drew closer and felt the familiar presence of his brother's aura. He almost went to him first, but there was no time. He lowered himself toward the ground near his companions, and then he manifested, bringing his astral self into the physical world. At once he heard and saw them as he would in meatspace, and they saw a version of him.

Shen gasped. He didn't need to see her tattoos; her astral form flared with mingled relief and fear. She moved to hug him but pulled up short, suddenly aware of what he was. "Nero?"

The others turned around to see him. He hung in the air, floating, but heavy with his own emotion and information. He had so much to say, but no idea where to begin.

EnJee's smirk turned into a full-throated laugh, and he said, "Good on you, mate."

Shen started to say something else, but stopped.

He answered anyway, his voice as strong and rich as it was in the physical world. "I'm safe for now. Things got physical when they realized I wasn't Enzo, but they're acting like they need me to make a trade. What will they do about Enzo?"

Shen stepped closer to him, but not close enough to touch. She'd seen him like this before. She'd worked with mages and even a shaman once before him, but that didn't change how strange it was for Nero to be entirely present beside her, yet not there at all.

Grim Fox lacked her deference. He stuck his hand right through Nero's shoulder. Then he said, "Just making sure it's the ghost-you, not real-you."

Nero said, "We have a serious problem."

Grim Fox replied, "We were just discussing that. Smolensky wants to set the meet location."

"Smolensky is Chimera."

EnJee spoke up again. "Well, bollocks. This can't be easy, can it?"

"I have a general sense of where I am, but nothing I can really use to guide you there exactly." He pointed out the landmarks he'd marked on the journey over.

EnJee looked toward the car and then back toward Nero before turning to address Grim Fox. He said, "We may need to pull him out."

Grim Fox said, "Yes, well, that is evident. The real question is, what is our negotiating power? We have Enzo and—"

EnJee placed a hand on Grim Fox's chest, cutting him off. "No. We may need to pull him out on our own. We need to hit them fast, grab our boy, and be on the way to Amsterdam before anyone knows what happened."

"I don't have a plan for that." Grim Fox said.

Nero understood how Grim Fox thought. To the troll, planning was a careful process. You measured out your options until you came up with the one that best fit the situation. This was no quick work. Shadowrunners planned out every step of a run, and considered contingencies in case things did not go well. Since Grim Fox had come aboard, they hadn't rushed into a job half-prepared. There wasn't space for that sort of thinking here, though. There were no contingencies or B-plans available. If things went badly in here in Moscow, there was nowhere they could run.

Nero wasn't sure if he was willing to risk his friends. Maybe he had a half-chance of using his magic to get out on his own. They could meet him somewhere close and escape into the city.

He thought all of this while watching Grim Fox and EnJee bicker over the best way to work out the exchange. But he knew there wouldn't be an exchange, not if he had a say in the matter.

"We cannot leave my brother here," he said.

They stopped arguing.

Nero turned to Shen, who was clasping the cross hanging from her neck. He said, "I watched that man shoot one of his associates because they didn't realize we switched Enzo for myself. He does not tolerate mistakes."

Shen and EnJee shared a look between them, but said nothing. Grim Fox barked, "How can you still be thinking about what's best for Enzo right now? The man left you for dead."

"What he did doesn't change who I am. My faith won't allow me to leave him."

Grim Fox fixed Nero with a stare and said, "Faith and honor I understand, but not at the cost of all of our lives."

"Then leave me. I can try to escape on my own. They don't know what I'm capable of, and it is possible—"

EnJee interrupted, "Here's the part you're not thinking through: what happens after we take Enzo back to his cozy little flat? You think he's going to say, 'thank you' and the two of you pick up like the last dozen years never happened? You think the Vory won't come looking for him again?"

"He'll have the protection of his corporation."

"And that worked out so well for you, right? The way I see it, the Vory is going to get their pound of flesh. We play it my way, and we can get clear with Nero and then tell them where to find their lost pup."

Grim Fox growled, "Is this your play or mine, EnJee?" The sound of his raised voice was loud enough to start dogs barking a block over. Everyone tensed for a moment, suddenly aware of their vulnerability. The sound of barking dogs faded in the renewed silence, but the point was clear to everyone: whatever needed to be done needed to be done soon. Daylight was coming on fast, and as the city came to life, there would be fewer places they could remain hidden.

Grim Fox folded his arms and continued, "If it's your play, then you plan it. You make it go. But if this is my play, then I get to make the call on how it happens. So. My play?"

EnJee scowled, but the scowl morphed into a grimace, and then finally a nod emerged as though exorcised from him.

Grim Fox said, "Okay. I have a way to do this, but it's rough, and I'm going to need more information and major help from you, Nero. For starters, how much lead time do you need to prepare that physical mask spell you used on EnJee and yourself when we grabbed Novak from that clinic in France?"

"It happens instantly as I shift the mana to the subject."

"Back then you were maintaining, what, three or four spells at once?"

"It was five before I became overwhelmed, but not all spells are the same. The focus needed to maintain some is greater than others, and I can maintain them better so long as I have my cross."

Grim Fox looked to Shen and then back to Nero and said, "You'll have it. Now do you think you can make multiple people look like Enzo?"

He nodded. "I'd have to touch each one individually to transfer the effect to them."

"So, then that's what we do. Shen, when you set it up with the Vory, you have to insist on a classic transfer—Nero and his brother each being released at the same time and walking past each other."

Shen nodded, and Grim Fox continued, "Nero, I'm asking a lot of you here. You need to be able to cloak Enzo and yourself with an invisibility spell long enough to confuse the Vory."

"And then what? Once they see us disappear, they'll know something went wrong. I can't guarantee they won't be able to track us, especially since they will have multiple people watching us the moment we disappear."

Shen smiled, picking up the thread. "So we'll need to find a place with a lot of people—enough that you can get lost in the crowd."

Grim Fox's own smile looked sinister. He said, "Not quite. We need to find a crowded place so you can use your physical mask spell make doubles of Enzo, and then get lost in the crowd."

Nero's astral form flared briefly as he said, "I won't put innocent people in harm's way like that."

Shen clasped her hands together gleefully and said, "That's just it, love. You're putting them in the safest situation you can! The Vory *needs* Enzo. They won't shoot anyone who *could* be him."

Grim Fox grinned. EnJee frowned, "Quite a bit riding on our mate doing the thing he couldn't properly do in France."

"I trust him, EnJee." Grim Fox said. Shen nodded as well. In that way, the matter was decided. Grim Fox laid out the specifics and they settled on a location. As he spoke, EnJee relaxed. When Grim Fox was finished explaining, he paused and took another deep breath.

Then he broke into a curious grin and said to Nero, "This time you better win the bet."

ENJEE

11-21-2081
5:59 P.M. Local Time

In a perfect world, the two sides of an asset exchange would meet at a quiet, private location. There would be pleasant conversation—banter, even—and the exchange would occur without the threat of murder dangling above their heads like a cat toy.

But EnJee had never seen a perfect world, even in the trid shows where shadowrunners were the heroes and the corp suits they rescued or transferred were the poor working-class folks who needed the runners to help them escape to a better life.

As day slid back into night, Komsomolskaya Square was filled with those people, rushing to face another moment in their daily lives. Hundreds of them flowed between the three stations that made up Komsomolskaya Square and gave the place its quite ordinary nickname: Three-Station Square. There was next to no police presence. Any real security came from the arcology further up the road. EnJee suspected it was why Smolensky had chosen the location. It was crowded, as they requested. It looked safe. To someone not from around here, it was the perfect place for an exchange.

In the pocket park at the center of the road, a busy expanse of cobblestone led between the statue of a long-forgotten bureaucrat and a large water feature lit up in real space and AR with a virtually rendered dancing bear. Sightseers clapped and giggled at the marvel as it reacted in virtual space to the real water moving in rivulets across the water feature. EnJee marveled at the volume of Intrusion Countermeasures built up around the bear. He guessed more than one hacker had tried to have a spot of fun with the tourist attraction. This would be one end of the exchange, and a possible distraction if it came to that.

EnJee watched it all from the Matrix, his meat body lying flat in the back seat of their borrowed Ford, which was parked alongside a dozen other cars near the entrance to the square's shopping mall. Grim Fox and Enzo Moretti sat quietly in the front seat. Through the lenses of dozens of cameras situated throughout the square, EnJee was able to access an AR rendering of the space. His task was overwatch, which in this instance meant he needed to identify and mark possible Vory agents in the area of operation. He had the easy job. The people wandering idly were the ones to take note of. Moscow wasn't a city of leisure, so those who were leisurely were likely tourists, not the ones he knew to look out for.

Underneath the meat was another layer, hard and knotted and filled with dossers with no room for the niceties of the world. That was his layer. EnJee could recognize its denizens, no matter the city, no matter the language. Multiple Vory men roamed the square, trying to blend in. They were nothing like the tourists who strolled through the area, pausing to capture images of themselves or items of attraction. He could read the intent on their faces. They openly operated on base principles, hindbrain stuff like shows of dominance and purposeful violence.

The people who did well in the shadows were the ones who operated openly and were very clear about consequences. They were the most dangerous types, the ones who spoke little and moved with suddenness when the time called for it. Dimitiri Smolensky was of this world—except, when they called him back to settle on a location, he spoke softly and politely, emulating the behavior he expected. His tone when he spoke to Shen told EnJee what kind of bloke Smolensky was. The rest was just maneuvering.

A shiny corporate Johnson would've seen EnJee's little family's actions over the past few days as part of normal business manipulations. Corpies expected to be screwed, so there was a certain callousness and tolerance they'd built up, like drinking the water anywhere north of Edinburgh.

Now, a bloke like Smolensky, a Vory fellow who came up through the ranks as a part of a feared band of assassins, operated under a very different set of principles. His respect was built on fear. EnJee couldn't only imagine what went through Smolensky's mind when a handful of runners showed up in the dead of night to tell him they've put one over on him. It didn't matter that Shen made it clear it was by no means a slight. You spill soycaf on a man's shirt by accident, the soycaf is still spilled.

The soycaf was on Smolensky's shirt, and no matter how it got there, someone had to pay to clean it up. And everyone that mattered in this man's world needed to take note of that price.

All of that understanding served to confirm to EnJee what they already suspected: Smolensky would let them go, but he was going to make a public show of it before he did. Only the Vory had made one critical mistake. He'd slotted off his own runners enough that Turbine Mary hadn't told him Nero was magically active. From there, Grim Fox's plan began to take shape.

The three stations that gave the square its name were Kazansky Terminal, Leningradsky Terminal, and Yaroslavsky Terminal. The first two were classic pre-awakening Russian architectural pieces. The last was a huge glass building that had been redone following the SURGE. The letters **MOCKBA** flickered through the colors of the Russian flag in the virtual space above the building.

Shen waited just inside that terminal. She'd picked up a hat and overcoat from one of the nearby kiosks to help her blend in. Beneath the coat, she had easy access to a holstered Browning Ultra Power, as well as an Ingram Smartgun XI strapped to a harness at her side.

Beyond the rail terminals and a short walk away from the east end of the square, the streets curved downward and beneath the massive Rostec-Lenin Arcology, Russia's state-owned answer to the Consillium Arcology and, he thought, given its purposeful placement, Japan's Shinjuku Station. If the R-L Arc existed as a sign of what was to come for Moscow, Komsomolskaya Square was a monument to what remained. The Arcology cast its long shadow over Komsomolskaya Square. According to Red Anya, anything inside the arcology was off-limits to the Vory. If things went badly, they'd run there and figure out the rest after.

The daylight warmed the air enough that snow fell in gray sheets over the city. Within the open space of the square, EnJee began making out the targets, tagging them in the virtual space and pushing the recognition tags to his team.

Shen kept moving, playing the part of the tourist as she shifted to adjust to the growing number of Vory soldiers. She moved away from the terminal and made her way toward the center of the square.

EnJee said, "I don't like the look of the weather. It might play to their advantage."

Nobody responded. They were too busy moving to their marks. In his virtual model, he saw Grim Fox open the door and get out of the car. The samurai who wasn't a samurai after all dragged Enzo Moretti out after him, pushing a Cossack cap down on his head so he wouldn't be so easily recognizable. Moretti wore a long coat with a layer of Kevlar body armor underneath. His hands were jammed in his outer pockets. They'd also filled his inside pockets with Nero's cross and other additional items he would need. Grim Fox repeated the warning not to run or do anything they expressly told him not to do. As a reminder of the consequences, the troll opened his own coat, revealing the Defiance T-250 shotgun hiding beneath.

The epicenter of the square was a pocket park that sat in the middle of the road. No less than five lanes of busy traffic flowed on both sides of the park, a fact that complicated their escape options. Smolensky planned to make the exchange there, where he probably felt his men could control the avenues of escape.

There were sixteen Vory men now all outlined in red in the private HUD EnJee fed to his team through their mesh network. Ten were grouping in the pocket park, while a smaller group patrolled near the entrance to Kazansky Terminal. EnJee suspected they'd targeted that terminal because it was equidistant to the other two.

Shen said, "*That's more red than I expected.*"

"We haven't even seen Smolensky yet," said Grim Fox. "I doubt he comes alone."

"I've got him," EnJee said as he watched a nondescript gray van roll up to the edge of the park nearest to the statue. The big ork climbed out wearing an overcoat and a Cossack hat that barely fit over the sides of his massive head. He moved with a cat's grace that suggested some serious cyberware. EnJee tagged him in bright yellow. He tagged the four men that exited beside him in red. Nero was the last to exit the vehicle. He looked like he'd been roughed up.

Grim Fox said, "Remember, we don't know if he plans to shoot Nero, Shen, or me. Once Nero gets to his spot, we all need to move quickly."

Grim Fox and his charge took up position at the opposite end of the park from where Smolnesky disembarked. He acted like a tourist here to see the dancing bear. Shen moved away from the fountain and toward where Smolensky stood near the statue. EnJee noted the extra guards by the terminal were starting to fan out into the pocket park. Likewise, the ten men already in place were moving toward three of the four possible exits, flanking them in groups of three while the tenth man remained as a spotter at the fountain. The final exit to what was quickly becoming a killbox was the one through which Smolensky entered.

He left two guards at that exit. The other two flanked Nero.

The snow was letting up now, promising a bitterly cold evening. EnJee smiled on the inside. Harder to spot an invisible person if it isn't snowing all over them. He could deal with the cold if the change in weather was enough to give them the edge they needed.

Grim Fox said, "Okay. Make the call."

Shen linked them into her comm and dialed the number. Smolensky answered immediately. She said, "*I'm here. I have Enzo nearby.*"

Smolensky's spotter immediately put a hand to his ear and started looking around frantically. Shen didn't try to hide her call. The Vory weren't looking for an elven woman standing alone in the crowd; they were trying to put eyes on Enzo Moretti. They found him quickly, standing a few steps ahead of Grim Fox. The warrior, and by nature all of them, were betting on the hunch Smolensky hadn't brought a sniper and planned to dole out the punishment himself.

"*Shall we do this according to the old ways?*" asked the Vory leader. "*Send both men toward the middle of the walk?*"

Shen replied, "*I wouldn't have it any other way.*"

Grim Fox ushered Enzo forward past the busy fountain and down the stretch of cobblestone leading to the statue and Smolensky. The warrior stopped a few steps later, letting Enzo continue on by himself. On the other end, Nero walked toward Grim Fox. Two Vory men fell in behind him. Unlike Grim Fox, they didn't stop after a few steps. They intended to see this all the way through.

EnJee said, "Get ready, he's close."

Nero walked in a straight line, the Vory soldiers barely a step behind him.

Shen spoke subvocally, her face a stiff smile and her lips barely moving. *"Will this still work with them so close?"*

Grim Fox replied over the channel, *"As long as they aren't touching him."*

The people nearby didn't notice what was happening. To them, there were just a few more people walking toward each other in this populated stretch of park. Enzo kept walking forward. He slowed momentarily, his eyes widening as he saw his brother and the condition he was in. He kept looking as they walked past each other.

Suddenly, Nero veered right and extended his hands toward his brother.

As soon as the two men touched, they blinked out of existence.

NERO

11-21-2081
6:03 P.M. Local Time

Now or never.
  As he passed by his terrified brother, Nero pushed off on his left foot, surging to the right. Soon as he grasped his brother's hands, he completed the spell, weaving the mana into a firm idea that cloaked the two men in invisibility. Together they tumbled to the ground.
  Things happened quickly after that.
  Immediately the two Vory soldiers flanking him drew their pistols and started waving them around, trying to find where he and Enzo went. Nero shifted his focus to the astral plane, where he could make out the form of his brother. He clamped Enzo's mouth with one hand, using the other to feel for Enzo's coat and inside pocket where his cross and other items were stored. He put the cross on quickly, and refocused the mana flowing into the invisibility spell cloaking Enzo so that it was sustained by the energy of his cross. Then he grabbed the earpiece, jammed it in his ear, and popped the AR glasses on his face. There were nearly two dozen men outlined in red. He also saw Shen and Grim Fox outlined in green. Off to his far right, beyond a wall of fast-moving traffic, was a car outlined in green with an AR tag that read *EnJee.*
  "*Nero, are you moving?*" That was Shen's voice. When he switched back to normal vision a few seconds later, all hell had broken loose.
  The first tourist to see guns being waved around didn't even make a sound. She just started running, heels clacking loudly on the pavement. Then a man standing nearby shouted and

started to run as well. In an instant, the calm of the afternoon was shattered. Another woman screamed. The crowd panicked. Nero took advantage of the moment. He dropped the invisibility spell on himself and invoked a mask spell, replacing one illusion for another. When Nero reappeared in the crowd, he now wore EnJee's face.

"There's a handsome bloke. Everyone mark his location," EnJee said, the smile evident in his voice.

The bystanders unfortunate enough to be a part of this action were also part of Grim Fox's plan. Nero stuck out his leg, tripping the person closest to him. He grabbed them by their ankle and pushed the mana through himself, unleashing another spell on the tourist as she scrambled to her feet. When she stood, the physical mask spell had replaced the tourist's face with Enzo's. The Vory men turned in unison and chased after her.

Nero spun and grabbed the ankle of one of the Vory men speeding past him toward Enzo's false double. The Vory soldier stumbled, reflexively reaching out to slow his momentum. Nero released him quickly, and when the man regained his footing, he too wore Enzo's face. A few seconds later, he released the illusion on the bystander and the woman quickly melted into the fleeing crowd. The guards who'd been chasing her stopped, bewildered, and looked around. When they saw their own comrade wearing Enzo's face they started running toward him.

Nero yanked the real Enzo, still invisible, to his feet and started running toward Grim Fox, dragging Enzo along with him. Snow fell against Enzo's huddled form and ruffled the air. Anyone looking hard enough may be able to spot him. Another pedestrian streaked by them, this one a man of roughly the right dimensions, and Nero reached out and grabbed the man, spinning him around. The man flailed, terrified. When Nero released him, he looked like Enzo as well.

Then the first shots rang out.

"They're onto Grimmy, mates. Easiest target!" There was stress in EnJee's voice now. Nero looked to see Grim Fox point a massive pistol at one of the Vory soldiers. He fired twice before diving behind the fountain to avoid a fusillade of return fire. Half the Vory men Nero could see were directing their attention towards Grim Fox. The rest were trying to chase down the nearly half-dozen illusory doubles of Enzo, desperate to grab the man they'd come to capture. People were running in every direction, trying to escape the gunfire. The commotion was large enough that the police would have no choice but to respond, though they would do so at their leisure and likely in force.

Nero made a dash for the fountain, moving against the crowd. He tagged two more fleeing pedestrians with mask spells. He wanted to get to Grim Fox and use his magic to assist in the fight, but his progress was slowed. Enzo kept struggling against his grasp, fighting to escape the chaotic scene.

"*Nero, get clear! Stop moving toward Grim Fox! Smolensky's engaging!*" Shen's voice rang in his earpiece.

When Smolenksy blurred into action, it was nearly faster than Nero could follow. He crossed the space between the statue and the fountain in the time it took Nero to suck in a breath. Grim Fox swiveled toward Smolensky and blasted rounds in his direction, but Smolensky's wire-guided musculature moved too fast to track. The ork fired three shots in return. Grim Fox ducked; the bullets crashed into the thick dermal deposits that covered his broad back. It all happened too fast for Nero to trigger a spell that would help.

Grim Fox crouched low, still visible above the crowd but moving from side to side to keep the remaining crowd between him and Smolensky. The warrior moved with cyberware-aided speed, but even that wasn't fast enough at this range, so he closed the distance and knocked Smolensky's gun aside as it fired.

Smolensky surged forward, ramming Grim Fox so hard that he knocked him over the retaining fence and into oncoming traffic. The troll smashed into the side of a fast-moving car, smashing the windshield and breaking off the side mirror. He rolled off and hit the ground, motionless.

The driver swerved and slammed into another car beside it. A third car struck the two crashed vehicles from behind. People started to get out of their cars, trying to see what happened. Horns began to blare in the distance, rolling from the back of the line of cars to the front like an ocean wave. Smolensky stared down at Grim Fox, teeth bared and reaching for another weapon.

Two more shots careened toward the ork as Shen opened up with her pistol. Smolenksy turned toward her and shouted. A moment later, several Vory soldiers swung their weapons in her direction, trying to track her in the crowd of fleeing and screaming people. It was full-on terror now. People rushed into the streets, mindless of the cars moving on the other side. On the side where the accident occurred, people filled the spaces between the stopped cars. Now people were fleeing to the station and taking cover there, trapped between gunmen on each side.

Grim Fox lumbered to his feet. He staggered, using the nearest car to steady himself. Nero exhaled, letting out a breath he hadn't been aware he was holding. He couldn't stay here trying to help. The longer he did, the longer this fight would go on. He started moving again, changing direction and dragging Enzo along toward the green marker that represented their escape car.

"*Two more taking aim on you, Grimmy,*" came EnJee's voice, calm through the earpiece.

Two shots rang out in succession and Shen said, "*One down, one repositioning to find me.*"

"*Bugger. The big bloke is making a go for you, Shen.*"

Nero looked for her, trying to track the green overlay through the rapidly thinning sea of people, but crowd was too big. Several people slammed into them, thinking the empty space was a path through which they could run. Enzo screamed and the people stumbled, staring confusedly into the empty space but too terrified to stop. As one went by, Nero unleashed another physical mask spell. The victim lashed out an arm defensively, smacking Nero's AR glasses off his face.

Pain from his broken nose lanced through his consciousness. He lost his grip on Enzo and staggered backward, grabbing at his nose. He couldn't see anyone but Grim Fox anymore. When he looked beside him, Nero realized he couldn't see his brother, either.

He shifted his vision to the astral, where his spells glowed like sparklers. A tendril of mana extended from the spell covering his brother to his cross like a tether. He saw Enzo and the others he'd affected. Five in all now. The more spells he cast, the more the fatigue of maintaining them pulled at the threads of his consciousness. It would be so easy to let it all go and drift into a deep sleep...

He shook off the thought and tried to wade toward his brother, pushing past and through people. He was lost in the chaos of it all. Without his AR glasses he didn't know where the car was. He didn't know what else to do but try to get his brother and then get to Shen.

"*More on you, Shen.*" EnJee said over the comm.

Four other Vory men began firing into the crowd in her direction. She ran for the cover of the fountain. Bullets chipped the stone, starting new sprays of water that weren't part of the choreographed water dance.

People were already using the fountain as cover. Several even dove into the water, hoping it would take them out of the action. One, a slim woman with a head of black and blond hair stuck her head up, and Nero watched as her head jerked violently to one side with a spray of red and she slipped back under the water.

With great effort, a focused needle of raw mana shot out from Nero and slammed into Smolensky. The ork stiffened, and then shook as though he felt the force of the magic passing through him. He spun away from his pursuit of Shen, searching the crowd for any sign of this new attacker.

Nero knew it wasn't enough. He'd only managed to slow the Vory leader down.

He tried to muster up the focus for another spell, but the threads of magic he was maintaining felt like chains pulling him in too many different directions. He couldn't bring more mana to bear. He released the mask spell on himself. All he had the strength to do was scream, "*Here!*"

Smolensky shifted in the crowd like a shark sensing blood.

Then Grim Fox hopped the low retaining fence and charged the ork. Shen reached down, unlimbered her Smartgun XI, raised it, and aimed at Smolensky's quickly retreating form. Two bursts drove a half-dozen bullets through the back of his knees. As he stumbled forward, Grim Fox's knee surged upward, catching Smolensky below the chin. The Vory assassin's head twisted unnaturally.

For an instant, the action halted. The last few remaining bystanders still screamed as they fled or hid under whatever cover they could find. The Vory men stopped firing and looked to one another. If this were the trids, they may have dropped their guns or at least fled.

It wasn't.

Shen shot first. She took aim at the nearest Vory, using the brief window of shock and confusion to line up her shot and stitch a burst of SMG fire across the closest two she could find.

Then she dropped down into the rapidly dispersing crowd, moving away from her spot to find another vantage point.

Nero stumbled forward, exhaustion tearing at him. He couldn't breathe. He released another of the mask spells and the number of Enzo clones fell from three to two. Another mask spell failed, and the number dwindled to one. It was all Nero could do to remain upright.

EnJee said, *"Big man is down and his crew is lacking coordination. Staying here any longer is not ideal."*

Nero hardly heard the rest. He shifted his vision back to the astral and staggered toward the base of the statue where Enzo sat, cowering and cloaked by Nero's sole remaining spell. He reached for the cross around his neck, dropping the invisibility spell. He fell to a knee at his brother's side, and then stood again, pulling them both up from the ground.

"Car," he said, as much a question as a demand.

Enzo pointed, and they ran.

EPILOGUE

11-30-2081
9:47 P.M. Local Time

Nero waited more than a week until he went to see Enzo.

He waited until the news of Lewis-Klein Senior Manager Arturo Olgin being murdered in broad daylight had been replaced by talk of the fallout from recent UCAS elections, the late Johnny Spinrad's missing "love child," and other such white noise. He waited until the surveillance Lewis-Klein had left behind decided there was nothing nearby that could be considered an immediate threat to their newly promoted senior manager.

When he finally came to his brother's home, he did so through the astral plane. He and his crew had already left London behind. In the astral realm he traversed the distance between his meat body in Amsterdam and his brother's London home in much less time than a vehicle would have taken.

Enzo was in his room, dutifully preparing his suits for the work week. He wore a T-shirt and shorts. At present he was loading what looked to be a newly purchased travel bag. Enzo Moretti did not see or hear Nero behind him, but some part of him understood he was there and said, "Is that you?"

"*Si.*"

"Speak English now, brother. This is London, after all." Enzo turned toward him. If he was at all surprised by Nero's appearance, he did not show it. The corporate mask was on now. His brother was back to being the unaffected businessman.

Nero said, "Were you questioned about your disappearance?"

"I was, and stuck to the script you gave me. I told them was overwhelmed by the events in Dubai, and decided to spend some time recuperating with a female companion. The sessions were recorded. I'm sure your angry hacker friend was in the system observing my debrief."

After the incident in Komsomolskaya Square, they had returned to the rail yards and taken a train to London, arranged through Aboiye and his Tamanous associates. By the time Enzo Moretti made it back to England, he'd been completely out of touch with his office for several days. Once word got out that he couldn't be reached so soon after his boss's death, Lewis Klein security had started an investigation, which turned up footage of his being escorted out of the building by Turbine Mary.

Nero said, "And now?"

Enzo sighed and turned back to the bed to finish the careful folding of his travel suit. He said, "And now nothing. Our security believes the Dubai kidnapping was directly tied to Arturo. With him dead, they consider the investigation closed."

"Good. Then the matter is finished."

Enzo shook his head. "You murdered a Vory leader. You can't really think they will let that go unpunished."

Nero shook his head in return. "My friends and I are nobody. We are shadows. It serves the Vory no purpose to chase down shadows. You should be more concerned about what they will do to you, *paperetto*."

Enzo set the suit down on top of the bag. "Why did you save me?"

"Do you really believe you have the right to ask me that question?"

"No, but..." he lapsed into silence for a moment and then said, "Why did you come here?"

Nero took a long look around the room, at the bed where he and Shen once slept together, at the walls marked tastefully with pieces of unremarkable art. All of it created the illusion of a life, one that had been won by spilling Nero's own blood—not once, but twice now.

Enzo observed Nero studying the space, watching his eyes spill across the image of Enzo with their parents, his arms around each of them. All three were smiling. Enzo said, "Dad's still alive, you know."

"I know."

"When you died, it broke him, Emiliano. He kept going to work, kept doing all of those things that kept the family running, but the part of him that lived outside of that was broken. We never went to the lake. We hardly spoke."

Nero cocked his head to the side. A look of confusion darkened his face. He thought Enzo may be waiting for forgiveness from *him*. The sadness radiating from Enzo's body spoke of true regret, but for what? For trying to kill him? For failing? Anger began to rise in Nero.

Enzo said, "It was different than when our mother passed. When she died all those years later, he mourned—we both did, but then he was able to move on. He never moved on from you."

And suddenly Nero was that little boy again, nervous and unable to show his emotions. He wanted so badly to shrug and pretend he didn't care. He didn't want Enzo to think he cared.

Enzo went on, "Do you remember how things were once we learned about the magic?"

"You were jealous of me," Nero said. He felt the anger rippling outward through his astral form.

"I hated you. Everything in our lives became about your magic, and you enjoyed all of it. Before that, we were true brothers, true twins. After, you didn't care about us the same way. We were the baggage you were forced to take with you into your new life—"

Nero shouted, "I was *a boy*! I knew *nothing* of the world. I was flattered by the attention, and I did not understand how to behave. That was no reason to try to *kill* me!"

"Mother told me to do it, you understand. She made me choose between you and her. She told me this was how it was meant to be. I was meant to be the one who led the family, and you were meant to be my rival. Did you know your name means that? *Rival.*"

There was a part of Nero that knew the truth of what he spoke, a part of him that had always known. But he still wanted to believe Enzo was evil alone. His mother had been sick for a very long time. He'd tried researching it in the Matrix to find a label he could put to her affliction, and in that manner, exorcise himself of the fear that it was all somehow his fault— that whatever had imbued him with the ability to manipulate mana had at the same time destroyed something within her.

Enzo continued, "Yes. I was angry. Jealous. Some part of me believed that if you were gone, the magic would move to me. I thought because we were twins and you had it, that you had taken all of it. Later, once I was wealthy, I had a ring made at great cost to me. I thought if I wore such a powerful magical object, it would unlock my abilities."

"That is not how magic works," Nero hissed.

Enzo frowned and sat down on the bed. He ran his fingers through his hair and then folded them in his lap. He stared at his hands and said, "Did you take my ring?"

"You are the one who took from me, *paperetto*." Nero started to float backward, wanting to leave. When he did so, Enzo stood up again. He put his hands in his pockets and faced Nero. It was the way businesspeople said goodbye after a meeting or an interview.

Nero stared at his brother, considering his next words carefully. When he was sure, he said, "Our mother was broken, Enzo."

"She was, but she was still our mother."

Nero nodded. He had nothing left that needed to be said.

The old smile returned to Enzo's face. He raised one hand and pointed to the cross that, even in the astral, dangled from Nero's neck. He said, "When did you become so religious?"

"When nothing else in my life made any sense. I think you'll find that part of yourself soon, *paperetto*. It may not be religion that calls you, but it will be something."

Enzo nodded. "So what now?"

"Now you live your life. I cannot control the repercussions of the Vory beyond what we've already done. That is not my responsibility."

Enzo reached out to him the way he did when they were kids. When he touched the space that held Nero's astral form, Enzo's arm passed right through it. He drew his arm back and studied it. "So now I owe you?"

"Debts are a decision. You may decide you owe me and work to repay that debt. You may decide you owe the Vory, and they may decide the same. All of it is one person's choice or another's. I chose to save you because it was the right thing to do. I don't consider it a debt."

Enzo said, "What will you do now?"

"I'll be with my family." Nero turned away from his brother, floating toward the door. He was almost at the exit when his brother spoke again.

"I consider us even."

Nero didn't look back.

When he returned to his body, Shen was waiting for him. She was sitting on the corner of the bed in the one-bedroom doss they often shared. Her eyes were downcast, and she was smoking a Noir. She wore a black dress and she picked at it, noticing imperfections he could not see. Her tattoos betrayed nothing. She fashioned her lips into a smile when he sat up.

He smiled back and then reached for his satchel. There was a commlink inside, and next to it a thin, black credstick, his spoils from the last few jobs. The ring was there as well. Soon he would need to go through the process of linking the magical object to himself.

He reached past the ring and plucked out the credstick, tapped it against his forefinger, thinking. Then he slotted the stick into his commlink. The balance was lower than he liked. He transferred a donation to the church under the name Carla Moretti, and the balance shrank to a third of what it was. It would be even lighter soon. Grim Fox had recovered enough from his injuries that he was ready to go out and celebrate. After what the team had gone through in Russia on his behalf, Nero made it his turn to buy drinks.

Shen said, "EnJee called while you were gone. There's a job."

He nodded. "Vash?"

She nodded back. Things were heating up in the shadows. That was good. He could use the nuyen.

LOOKING FOR MORE SHADOWRUN FICTION, CHUMMER?

WE'LL HOOK YOU UP!

Catalyst Game Labs brings you the very best in *Shadowrun* fiction, available at most ebook retailers, including Amazon, Apple Books, Kobo, Barnes & Noble, and more!

NOVELS

1. *Never Deal with a Dragon* (Secrets of Power #1) by Robert N. Charrette
2. *Choose Your Enemies Carefully* (Secrets of Power #2) by Robert N. Charrette
3. *Find Your Own Truth* (Secrets of Power #3) by Robert N. Charrette
4. *2XS* by Nigel Findley
5. *Changeling* by Chris Kubasik
6. *Never Trust an Elf* by Robert N. Charrette
7. *Shadowplay* by Nigel Findley
8. *Night's Pawn* by Tom Dowd
9. *Striper Assassin* by Nyx Smith
10. *Lone Wolf* by Nigel Findley
11. *Fade to Black* by Nyx Smith
12. *Burning Bright* by Tom Dowd
13. *Who Hunts the Hunter* by Nyx Smith
14. *House of the Sun* by Nigel Findley
15. *Worlds Without End* by Caroline Spector
16. *Just Compensation* by Robert N. Charrette
17. *Preying for Keeps* by Mel Odom
18. *Dead Air* by Jak Koke
19. *The Lucifer Deck* by Lisa Smedman
20. *Steel Rain* by Nyx Smith
21. *Shadowboxer* by Nicholas Pollotta
22. *Stranger Souls* (Dragon Heart Saga #1) by Jak Koke
23. *Headhunters* by Mel Odom
24. *Clockwork Asylum* (Dragon Heart Saga #2) by Jak Koke
25. *Blood Sport* by Lisa Smedman
26. *Beyond the Pale* (Dragon Heart Saga #3) by Jak Koke

27. *Technobabel* by Stephen Kenson
28. *Wolf and Raven* by Michael A. Stackpole
29. *Psychotrope* by Lisa Smedman
30. *The Terminus Experiment* by Jonathan E. Bond and Jak Koke
31. *Run Hard, Die Fast* by Mel Odom
32. *Crossroads* by Stephen Kenson
33. *The Forever Drug* by Lisa Smedman
34. *Ragnarock* by Stephen Kenson
35. *Tails You Lose* by Lisa Smedman
36. *The Burning Time* by Stephen Kenson
37. *Born to Run* (Kellen Colt Trilogy #1) by Stephen Kenson
38. *Poison Agendas* (Kellen Colt Trilogy #2) by Stephen Kenson
39. *Fallen Angels* (Kellen Colt Trilogy #3) by Stephen Kenson
40. *Drops of Corruption* by Jason M. Hardy
41. *Aftershocks* by Jean Rabe & John Helfers
42. *A Fistful of Data* by Stephen Dedman
43. *Fire and Frost* by Kai O'Connal
44. *Hell on Water* by Jason M. Hardy
45. *Dark Resonance* by Phaedra Weldon
46. *Crimson* by Kevin Czarnecki
47. *Shaken: No Job Too Small* by Russell Zimmerman
48. *Borrowed Time* by R.L. King
49. *Deniable Assets* by Mel Odom
50. *Undershadows* by Jason M. Hardy
51. *Shadows Down Under* by Jean Rabe
52. *Makeda Red* by Jennifer Brozek
53. *The Johnson Run* by Kai O'connal
54. *Shadow Dance* by Aaron Rosenberg
55. *Identity: Crisis* by Phaedra Weldon
56. *Stirred* by Russell Zimmerman
57. *Veiled Extraction* by R.L. King
58. *Tourist Trapped* by Bryan CP Steele
59. *For a Few Nuyen More* by Stephen Dedman
60. *On the Rocks* by Russell Zimmerman

ANTHOLOGIES

1. *Spells & Chrome*, edited by John Helfers
2. *World of Shadows*, edited by John Helfers
3. *Drawing Destiny: A Sixth World Tarot Anthology*, edited by John Helfers
4. *Sprawl Stories, Vol. 1*, edited by John Helfers
5. *The Complete Frame Job*, edited by John Helfers

NOVELLAS

1. *Neat* by Russell Zimmerman
2. *The Vladivostok Gauntlet* by Olivier Gagnon
3. *Nothing Personal* by Olivier Gagnon
4. *Another Rainy Night* by Patrick Goodman
5. *Sail Away, Sweet Sister* by Patrick Goodman
6. *The Seattle Gambit* by Olivier Gagnon
7. *DocWagon 19* by Jennifer Brozek
8. *Wolf & Buffalo* by R.L. King
9. *Big Dreams* by R.L. King
10. *Blind Magic* by Dylan Birtolo
11. *The Frame Job, Part 1: Yu* by Dylan Birtolo
12. *The Frame Job, Part 2: Emu* by Brooke Chang
13. *The Frame Job, Part 3: Rude* by Bryan CP Steele
14. *The Frame Job, Part 4: Frostburn* by CZ Wright
15. *The Frame Job, Part 5: Zipfile* by Jason Schmetzer
16. *The Frame Job, Part 6: Retribution* by Jason M. Hardy
17. *Tower of the Scorpion* by Mel Odom
18. *Chaser* by Russell Zimmerman
19. *A Kiss to Die For* by Jennifer Brozek
20. *Crocodile Tears* by Chris A. Jackson
21. *See How She Runs* by Jennifer Brozek
22. *Under Pressure* by Scott Schletz
23. *Kill Penalty* by Clifton Lambert

Made in the USA
Las Vegas, NV
17 January 2022